Mountain Laurel

Center Point
Large Print

Also by Lori Benton and available from Center Point Large Print:

Many Sparrows
The King's Mercy

**This Large Print Book carries the
Seal of Approval of N.A.V.H.**

Mountain Laurel

A KINDRED NOVEL

LORI BENTON

CENTER POINT LARGE PRINT
THORNDIKE, MAINE

This Center Point Large Print edition
is published in the year 2021 by arrangement with
Tyndale House Publishers, Inc.

Scripture quotations are taken from the *Holy Bible*,
King James Version.

Mountain Laurel is a work of fiction. Where real people,
events, establishments, organizations, or locales appear,
they are used fictitiously. All other elements of the novel
are drawn from the author's imagination.

The text of this Large Print edition is unabridged.
In other aspects, this book may vary
from the original edition.
Printed in the United States of America
on permanent paper.
Set in 16-point Times New Roman type.

ISBN: 978-1-64358-836-0

The Library of Congress has cataloged this record
under Library of Congress Control Number: 2020950386

This book is for Wendy Lawton
For never giving up

Mama was the first of Mountain Laurel's slaves to know about the letter. Before Master Hugh posted it away north, he called Mama from her spinning and read that letter to her. You could've knocked me over with duck's down when it happened, but that's how we came to know early on that Master Hugh was asking his half brother, up Boston-way, to send his youngest son back to North Carolina.

Master Hugh's nephew came here once before, but he never paid me no mind that I can recall. He was twelve years old then, the age a boy, whatever color his skin, gets to fancying himself a man. Me, I was half his years and, what was surely worse, a girl. I was nothing to the master's kin. But he was something to me.

Even now I can close my eyes and see him as he was then. Tall for his age. Skinny as a fence rail. Eyes the blue of a jaybird's wing and hair like Mama's spinning flax. It was on account of that flax-pale hair I made my first picture, hunkered under the kitchen lilacs so he wouldn't spy me scratching his likeness on a piece of broken slate.

Rubbing out that drawing lest I get caught with it came hard, but it was only the first. I've made many pictures since then but only one other of him—on a scrap of old paper we was made to strip off the parlor walls, that summer Master Hugh up and married again. It shows his nephew looking off to the side, with that moonbeam hair curling over his brow like the halo of an angel. No one has laid eyes on it but me. Not even Mama.

Every slave keeps to their heart a secret. This one is mine.

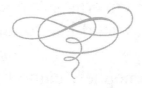

Prologue

Seona had been minding chickens the day Master Hugh's nephew rode away north with his daddy. She was minding chickens the day he rode up again. The tobacco had been suckered and was days from needing cutting. Near-about every morning Miss Lucinda told her to save the washing for later and go with Esther out into those long green rows to pick the worms off the leaves. Some folk let turkeys at their tobacco to eat those worms. Master Hugh didn't keep turkeys, so they made do with chickens—and Seona and Esther and any other hands to spare to catch the worms the chickens missed.

"Eee-ew! Will you look at this nasty thing?"

The crinkly leaf she'd been peering under sprang back as Seona straightened to spot Esther. Some of the plants topped her head; still it took a deal of stooping to be sure the chickens hadn't left any worms down low. They'd hear about it come cutting time if worms ruined the leaves. Master Hugh didn't hold with beating his slaves anymore, but the overseer, Jackson Dawes, was known to strap a back on the sly.

9

Never Seona's, but it was a thing to bear in mind.

She spied the younger girl hunkered among the plants, gaping at a fat green worm. "Quit thinking on it, Esther. Just pick it off and stomp it."

"I can't. It's the king-granddaddy of the lot." Esther's face popped up between the plants. She pushed her skinny self through, mischief in her dark-brown eyes. "What you reckon Miss Rosalyn would do was I to slip that one into her bed?"

Miss Rosalyn Bell, Master Hugh's oldest stepdaughter, thought right high of her clean sheets and fine white skin. Not that Seona's skin was much darker. Or wouldn't be if she spent as much time as Miss Rosalyn did indoors, embroidering linens and arranging her shiny blonde hair.

"Directly after Miss Rosalyn sends that worm on to glory, guess who gonna have to wash those sheets?"

"You?"

"Uh-huh. So put the notion out of your head— and mind those worms."

Esther giggled, then flipped the hem of her petticoat up to fan her face, baring knobby knees. "How much longer we got to do this?"

" 'Til it's done, what do you think?"

Esther rolled her eyes. The girl wasn't used to field work. Miss Lucinda had just that spring judged her old enough, at nine, to lend a hand beyond house and yard. That didn't mean she'd have to put in a full day's work with the men.

Early on Miss Lucinda tried to force that on Seona and her mama, but Master Hugh nipped that notion in the bud. Seona could be spared for days at a time, but her mama already spun flax and wool and wove cloth from it. She made shirts and shifts, petticoats and breeches. Even some for white folk. On top of that her mama tended the ailing and delivered babies for miles about. And she helped Naomi with the cooking. Taken altogether it was enough for one woman to be getting on with, most days.

"House-spoiled is what you are," Seona told Esther, but not meanly. Esther's mama and daddy were dower slaves, come from their old place in Virginia with Miss Lucinda and her daughters. Since Esther had been born to them, she'd been something of a pet to the mistress. Until lately.

It comes hard, that season a child begins to know she's still a slave, no matter how favored.

Sweat trickled down Seona's neck. The stink of ripe tobacco hung thick in the sticky heat. They'd been at the job since breakfast, save to grab a bite of dinner when the sun was high. A couple of the hands were working toward them from the field's far end, but there was a fair piece to go before anyone reached the middle.

Esther scuffed a grimy toe in the dirt, wrinkling

11

her nose as the hen perched on the mound beside Seona pecked a fat worm in half and gulped down the pieces. The hen was a scrawny, speckled creature, unlike most of their plump, shiny-black chickens. It had come as payment for a baby her mama caught two weeks back, on a farm upcreek.

Seona bent to grasp a leaf of the plant under which the hen was feeding. Lightning quick it darted at her, neck stretched low. Seona kicked out and sent that chicken squawking down the row, leaving a cloud of spotted feathers and herself sitting on the ground, fingers pressed over a sting at the base of her thumb.

Esther, gone up the row a ways, rushed back to her side. "You hurt?"

"Just a nip." Seona sucked at the heel of her thumb, bitter with tobacco juice and blood.

"Wicked ol' biddy-hen." Esther slapped a mosquito on her arm, then scratched between the tight plaits of her hair, up under her shade hat.

Seona's braid hung heavy down her back. She wound it up and tucked it under her kerchief, hoping it would stay. Her hair wasn't straight like her mama's crow-black Indian hair, or wiry like Esther's. It was somewhere between—long, springy curls that defied the taming of brush, braid, and head-rag.

She got up off the ground, thinking how Mister Dawes would be making his rounds to see they weren't sitting idle. She bent to the worm-

12

picking. That's when the shouting started up and she straightened again. Shielding her eyes, she spotted Ally, their cook Naomi's son, galumphing through the oaks, calling to her and Esther, waving them in.

Esther put a hand to a skinny hip and hollered, "We ain't near done yet, Ally!"

From a distance Seona saw the grin splitting a gleam in Ally's face. Though a great ox of a man, about her mama's age, inside, Ally was still the age he'd been when a mule kicked him in the head and he didn't wake up for a night and a day. When Seona was small, Ally would wade the creek with her on a Sunday, when they had time to themselves. Other times he'd make a present for her out of something he found—a pretty feather, a shiny rock, or an arrowhead turned up with the plow. Now, when he wasn't working the fields or helping Jubal with the stock, he favored Esther, who'd reached his inside age.

"Maisy want you cleaned up to serve, Esther," Ally hollered back. "Seona needed in the kitchen with our mamas!"

Esther turned to Seona, eyebrows scrunched. "What for? Dinner's done passed."

When they didn't budge, Ally broke into a run again, heading toward them like a charging bull. They stood and waited, too hot to move more than needful. Ally lumbered to a halt, bent over between the tobacco plants, dinner-plate hands splayed on broad knees, gulping breath. "Big supper . . . planned. We gots . . . comp'ny."

"Bound to be someone important," Seona said, "if we're being called in to help."

"Hope it ain't them uppity folk from over Chesterfield," Esther said.

With all her heart Seona said a silent *amen.* Chesterfield was the biggest plantation for miles. Miss Lucinda and her daughters went visiting there more than to any other place. *Like moths to a flame,* she'd heard Naomi grumble. It was something rarer for the flame to come to the moths. But it happened, now and then.

Not today apparently. Ally was wagging his head. "Ain't them. You never guess who it be."

"Who then?" Esther demanded.

"That boy what was here before—Mister Ian. He done said *yes* to Master Hugh's letter and come back, all growed up! Got hisself a roan horse, red as strawberries with cream on the side." Words tumbled out of Ally like rocks rolling downhill. "He come wearin' this coat-o'-many-colors like Joseph from the Bible, with his own manservant on a fine black horse, and another horse loaded down with I-don't-know-what-all. Look like they here to stay."

Esther was bouncing like a worried flea, grinning to match Ally. "Come on, Seona. Let's get shed of these worms!"

The girl grabbed her wrist and pulled. Seona

let herself be tugged along the row, mute as a scarecrow, reeling from this rush of news about horses and colored coats and . . . Master Hugh's nephew.

The boy with the angel-halo hair was back.

PART I
September 1793

What can I offer to set right that which lies between us, save myself, to spend as you deem fit? However dubious an Investment I have thus far shown myself to be, perhaps I may do some Good for Uncle's People—unless North Carolina prove Oil, and I the Water that will not mix.

Nevertheless, my Duty to you, Sir, as Your Most Obedient Servant &c—

Ian Cameron

1

MOUNTAIN LAUREL
A wee bit earlier that day

At the creek that marked the boundary of his uncle's plantation, Ian Cameron paused his horse. The creek's water ran clear, chattering over a pebbled bed, no more than ankle-deep, yet for all his balking to cross it, it might have been the Red Sea.

Ian pressed a hand to the breast of his coat. For eight hundred hot and muggy miles he'd ridden with his uncle's letter tucked there, yet still he hadn't decided whether answering its summons had been an act of desperation. His father's. Or his own.

A black gelding edged up alongside Ian's roan to drink. Its rider swept a hand at the oak wood shading the creek's far bank. "*Kalmia Latifolia.* This is it, then?"

"Aye, Mountain Laurel." Ian shifted in the saddle, eyeing the man, half a year his elder. "Ye've the better head for Latin, Thomas, I'll grant ye. But surely it's unseemly in a slave to flaunt it."

Thomas Ross twisted his mouth in amusement as he gazed down the carriage drive that crossed

19

the creek and curved through the wood, beyond which a house was visible in white slashes. *The big house,* his uncle's slaves had called it, with its two rooms belowstairs and three above. In the eleven years since Ian's last visit to the place, his uncle had remarried, acquiring two stepdaughters in the process. What had seemed a big house indeed for a single man must have proved incommodious with the addition of three females, judging by the new wing jutting from the rear.

"First your uncle inherits it all," Thomas said, his thoughts obviously fixed on the plantation's past as well. "Next you. What's wrong with the place that it goes begging for its heirs?"

Ian shrugged. An older man called Duncan Cameron—no near kin—had settled the place originally. He'd met Ian's uncle, fresh from Scotland, exiled and homeless, down on the Cape Fear River. The elder Cameron had made Ian's uncle his overseer, then left Mountain Laurel to him when he passed—forty years or more ago.

"Uncle Hugh at least *had* a son," Ian said. "He died a long time back. I never met him."

Thomas shot a pointed look at Ian's garb. "I expect your kin's bound to take you for a red savage come calling, rather than *heir presumptive.*"

It was a fair point. Over leather knee breeches—

20

the thigh rent and stitched less artfully than the wound beneath had been—Ian wore a coat cut and collared in European style but pieced of buckskin and lavishly adorned with red, white, and black quillwork and an expanse of ragged fringe. In trade for it, the old Chippewa woman who made the half-breed coat had wheedled from him a twist of tobacco, several prime beaver pelts, and one very fine fox. He felt a mite foolish for wearing it now but had wanted to present himself as truthfully as possible, so there'd be no mistaking what sort of man his uncle was getting. Not the lad he would recall.

Ought he to have done the thing by stages?

And there was Thomas, tricked out in fawn-brown coat, fine linen breeches, and a pair of outlandishly striped stockings—dressed the dandy when he was meant to be a slave.

Which of them would prove the greater consternation to Ian's kin?

"One way to know," he muttered. Girding his will, he touched a heel to the roan's side, where his rifle rode snug in its sling.

Thomas followed on the mount he called Black Huzzah, leading their pack mare, Cricket.

They dismounted in the oak-dappled shade of a stable-yard that appeared much the same as it had eleven years ago, with the stable itself, a long, clapboarded structure, standing quiet in the summer heat. The only creature to mark their arrival, a sorrel in a nearby paddock, whinnied and trotted to the split-rail fence.

Ian turned to the open stable doors to call a greeting and bit it back as a man, trimly bearded and slightly stooped in the shoulder, emerged from the shadows. Even with the stoop, he was of a height with Ian, an inch over six feet, with hair like sugared cinnamon tailed back from a scowling brow. His voice held the clipped snick of a rifle's hammer being cocked, despite the familiar Highland cadence, as he addressed Ian. "I'll ken your name—and your business here."

Ian removed his hat. "It's Ian, sir. Robert's son. Ye sent for me and I've come."

The man's blue eyes snapped from Ian's quilled coat to his face, brows lifting in belated recognition.

"Devil take me if it isna," said Hugh Cameron, his father's elder half brother. He crossed the stable-yard to Ian, who replaced his hat in time to meet his uncle's outstretched hand with his own. The clasp was sure; before Ian saw it coming, his uncle had pulled him into a kinsman's embrace, clapping a hand to his road-dusty back. He pushed Ian away but held him at arm's length, taking in the sight of him with what appeared genuine approval.

"Forgive my brusqueness, laddie," he said. "I kent ye were coming—your da's letter reached us weeks ago—but I didna ken the day. And I must say ye've grown a mite since last I saw ye." His uncle released him, chuckling at that. "Besides, just now I'm a wee bit distracted by goings-on."

Still caught off guard by the warmth of the welcome, Ian gathered his wits to ask, "Did we interrupt ye in some work, Uncle?"

"No, lad, more's the pity. I've a mare ready to drop a foal. Jubal thought she was finally making ready and got her into the double box at the end." He bent his head toward the stable behind him. "But it's proved another false alarm."

Ian minded his uncle's passion for horses. "So ye've taken to breeding?"

"Aye," his uncle said. "A few years now—a couple of colts to show for it. Though I hadn't meant to do so with this mare. I had her from a man in Cross Creek—Fayetteville, it's called now," his uncle explained. "She's docile as a lamb and can pull anything ye hitch her to, but I'd meant her for a saddle horse—for the lasses, aye? We didna ken she was breeding out o' season 'til past midwinter. The mare's blood is of no repute, but the sire's a grandson of Janus."

Ian nodded, assuming *Janus* a name to impress among thoroughbred aficionados. He'd won his horse, Ruaidh—an Indian pony of uncertain origin—gambling with a Frenchman in Canada two years back, and wouldn't trade the compact, unflappable roan for a dozen of his high-strung leggy cousins.

Still, it seemed a fitting name, Janus: Roman god of gateways. Of beginnings. He hoped his da would have thought it a propitious sign.

By all that's holy, lad, dinna throw away another chance to settle. Robert Cameron's parting words weeks ago, delivered with beseeching sobriety, had dogged him south thcsc hundreds of miles to hover in the heat-weighted air of his uncle's stable-yard. *'Tis the last I have to offer ye.*

It was the pack mare letting out an impatient whinny that recalled them to Thomas, who'd stood by unacknowledged, holding the bridles of both their mounts.

"I see ye'd help along the way," Uncle Hugh said. "Did ye engage yon mannie for the journey then?"

"Ah, no," Ian said, casting Thomas a quick glance. "He's mine actually, not hired. Will that be a . . . a problem?"

His uncle's brows flicked high before he answered, "Not at all. But let's get these horses settled, aye?" Turning, his uncle called toward the stable, "Jubal—and, Ally, if ye're there— ye've three new horses here to tend!"

In quick order two of his uncle's slaves exited the stable. The first, a wiry dark-skinned man of middling height, was a stranger to Ian—Jubal, his uncle named him, making introductions. The second man to emerge was several inches taller than either Ian or his uncle and muscled like a blacksmith, though Ian knew he was not.

"Ally," he said, grinning in recognition.

The man halted, peering down at him, eyes soft as a doe's gone wide as he took in Ian's quilled coat. "Yes, sir. You know me, sir?"

"Ye know me too, Ally. Or ye did. I'm Ian Cameron."

Ally's lips pulled wide, showing large white teeth. "I hear you was coming back. But law! I mind you a spindly thing. You done growed up, Mister Ian."

Ian remembered then that, despite his hulking stature, this man of his uncle's had never grown up. Not in mind. There'd been an accident when he was a boy involving . . . what had it been? An ox?

" 'Tis a momentous day," his uncle was telling Ally, who was eyeing Ian's roan and Thomas's black gelding with an eagerness to make their acquaintance. "Go on and help Jubal, and Mister Ian's lad there, get these horses unsaddled. Show them to the boxes we have free. Then go tell your mama in the kitchen we'll need a special supper tonight. She'll ken what to do."

"Yes, sir!" As Ally followed Jubal toward the horses, sunlight breaking through the oaks caught the side of his head, revealing the slight concavity behind his left ear, not quite concealed by a cap of woolly hair.

Mule-kicked, Ian minded.

He took a half step after them, thinking to snatch his rifle from its sling before the others got their hands on his gear, until it struck him to wonder whether toting a rifle into his uncle's house—as if he were entering a British-held fort—would cause offense.

He hesitated, feeling off-footed in this place both remembered and strange.

"*Ciamar a tha thu, a mhac mo bhràthair?*"

Ian started at his uncle's question, taken aback by its perception as well as the language of its phrasing. *How are you, Nephew?*

"*Tha mi . . . gu math—tapadh leat.*" No lie. He was well enough, all things considered. "*Tha mi beò co dhiù,*" he added. *I'm alive, anyway.*

"So ye are," his uncle agreed. "And ye've the *Gaidhlig* still. And is it the faint bells of Aberdeen I'm hearing in your speech? That'll be from your mam."

"And her brother—Callum Lindsay. Ye'll mind I was in Upper Canada with Callum 'til the spring?" Ian eyed his uncle, dappled in the sunlight. How much had the man been apprised of the happenings in the intervening years since their last meeting? He'd have no joy in the telling but best to have it out—in case his da hadn't beaten him to it. "I'm obliged to mention, sir, that it wasn't by my choice I left Boston. When I went west with Callum, I mean, five years back. I don't know whether Da—"

An upraised hand checked him.

"Lad," his uncle said, "who doesna have deeds he'd as soon put behind him? What say we leave the past where it belongs?"

The roan and the black were unsaddled now, the pack mare unloaded. As Jubal, Ally, and Thomas each led a horse away to stable, his uncle added, "That dun mare carried a respectable load. Might ye have brought the tools of your trade along?"

"Aye," Ian said, unsure whether he was more relieved or disconcerted by the change of subject. "It's been a while since I've practiced my cabinetmaking, but I'd hoped, if ye have a shed standing empty, I might set up by way of a shop. Nothing extensive, only there's a bit of work I've promised to do."

The suggestion seemed to please his uncle. "I dinna see why not."

Suddenly overwhelmingly hot, Ian shrugged his way out of the half-breed coat and draped it over his arm. What he wore beneath only reinforced the impression of a man well on his way to *gone native*—fringed hunting shirt, tomahawk and knife thrust through a beaded belt girding his waist. And those worn leather breeches with their stitched rent, still faintly bloodstained.

"Ought I to change, Uncle? I've clothes more befitting . . ." He gestured toward the house, white and commanding beyond a spreading chestnut.

His uncle's gaze had lifted past it, over a scattering of outbuildings to the leafy apple orchard rising toward a hogback ridge. Beyond it rose the higher ridges of the isolated Carraways, rolling westward in thick-wooded waves like a rumpled counterpane.

"The Camerons were first, ye ken."

Ian frowned. "First?"

"To answer the Stuarts' call. I went down from the glen wi' my da and the lads. All but wee Robbie, your da."

"Ye mean the '45?" His uncle spoke of the rising of the Highland clans for Charles Stuart, son of the exiled King James, which had ended in slaughter on a frozen moor—a slaughter that claimed Ian's grandfather and two uncles. Nigh fifty years ago. "What made ye think of that?"

Gazing at the ridge rising beyond his orchard, his uncle didn't seem to hear. "By the spring we'd lost all. Lands, clan, honor. Hope. I was all of twenty at the time. Younger than ye."

Hugh Cameron's voice had gone as hazy as the rising hills. The man himself seemed hazy compared to Ian's memory of him. On closer scrutiny, his complexion was no longer the burnished bronze of a redhead well acquainted with the sun. There was a hint of something sickly in its hue, like copper begun to green.

"*This* land is ours now," he said with sudden fervor. "Cameron land—and none shall take it from us." His uncle's eyes held the blue of distance and a grief as raw as new-dug earth—until behind them a voice spoke.

"Mastah Ian? Where you want all your tools and things to go?"

Thomas had joined them.

Uncle Hugh blinked at the intrusion, then turned to Ian. The distance in his eye diminished. His beard-framed lips softened in something near a smile.

"Here I'm forgetting my manners, Nephew, keeping ye standing in the yard. Your things can bide where they are for now. Come away in—ye and your man." Facing the house, Hugh Cameron firmed his jaw. " 'Tis time ye made the acquaintance of your auntie."

If a woman less inclined to welcome the address of *Auntie* existed, Ian was hard-pressed to imagine her. Straight of carriage, pale of skin, and dark of hair and eye, twenty years younger than his uncle, Lucinda Bell Cameron met them in the parlor prepared to offer tea—judging by the maid stationed at a serving tray. It had been good Scotch whisky his elders partook of in that room years ago. Swift reassessment forced Ian to admit that tea better suited the environs now. The once-masculine sparseness of his uncle's parlor was transformed. Pillowed settles and needlepoint chairs vied for space with delicate tables cluttered with bric-a-brac of the fragile-looking sort.

He halted in the doorway, mindful of road dust and the dirt that caked his boots. His uncle's wife gaped at him for a frozen second; then her gaze swept past him to Thomas, who'd followed them into the house. Her nose, both narrow and long, pinched in disapproval.

"Mr. Cameron, it is not our custom for servants to enter through the front door. Your boy may go around to the kitchen door. In back." She cast a pointed look at Ian's uncle—eliciting support or offering reproof, Ian couldn't be certain.

His uncle smiled. "Aye, Nephew. Naomi will see him settled."

Ian cleared his throat. "Settled where, exactly?"

Lucinda's slanted brows rose. "The servants' quarters, of course."

"Aye," Ian said, hating the need to test the woman's forbearance so soon. "But if it's no inconvenience, I'd prefer Thomas stay near me. In the house."

"Slave quarter be fine," Thomas murmured, loud enough for all to hear.

Mindful of the indignant color staining his aunt's cheeks, Ian caught Thomas by the arm and marched him down the passageway, out of earshot of a whisper. "Ye don't get a say in this. Not in front of them. We'll discuss it later. Meantime keep your mouth shut."

Thomas set his jaw. "I don't need a nursemaid."

Ian tightened his grip. "Look. Ye wanted this. Ye hounded me from Boston 'til ye got your way. Act like ye're meant to." Releasing Thomas, he added in a carrying tone, "Fetch our bags up to the house, all but what the mare carried."

In the front hall his uncle's wife took matters in hand. "Maisy, see Mr. Cameron's boy finds the *back* door."

"Yes'm." The maid sidled out into the hall, headed their way. "Come with me," she said to Thomas, with an echo of her mistress's censure.

Uncle Hugh frowned after the pair retreating down the central passage that ran the house's length, past a wide set of stairs leading to the rooms above, to a narrow back door at the far end. "Ye've not had him long, ye said. A body servant, is he?"

"No, sir," Ian said as he rejoined them. "I don't need a man to dress and shave me."

Too late he heard the criticism implicit in the words, but his uncle's expression showed only faint amusement. "Nor do I, though Mrs. Cameron has done her best to cure me o' the sin."

He cast his wife a wry smile. She failed to return it. "If he is not a body servant, why keep him in the house?"

There was no admitting the truth of the matter. Latching on to the implication his uncle had voiced, Ian managed a tight smile. "Considering he's been in my service but a short while, I think, ma'am, it would be best I keep him close."

His uncle showed him to a bedchamber above the back stairs, and to the storeroom across the passage, where Thomas, with some rearranging of trunks, might spread a bedroll on the floor. "Unless ye'd rather he had a pallet in your room?"

"This will do, Uncle." At least for now it would. Ian turned from the cramped space and asked, "What of your stepdaughters? Are they not at home?"

"Rosalyn and Judith are verra much at home but ye willna see them before supper. No doubt the lasses wish to arrange themselves proper to greet ye—first impressions being a vital thing." His uncle's mouth twitched when Ian raised a brow in acknowledgment of his own failings on that front. "I take ye gladly as ye come, Nephew—quills and all. My wife, now . . . she was once accustomed to a grander living than she presently enjoys, but I dinna expect ye to bow to her airs and fancies should they go against your grain. This is your home now. I mean ye to be at ease in it."

Warmed by the words, Ian lingered in the doorway after his uncle vanished down the narrow back stairs, until he caught the beginnings of a conversation not meant for his ears.

"For heaven's sake, Hugh, is he what you expected? That coat . . . that belt . . . a *tomahawk?*"

Chilled by that cold dash, Ian shut the door and hung the offending garments on a peg behind it, where they were unlikely to incite further indignation.

The room he'd been given belonged to the newer wing. Though smaller than those at the front of the house, it remained untouched by the zealous hand that had had its way belowstairs. The walls were plastered. A braided rug fronted a small fireplace. There was a high-post bed with hangings, a clothespress of rustic make, and a cylinder desk of more elegant design with a drawer that locked; he found the key.

A spindle-backed chair and a washstand completed the furnishings.

It had been weeks since he'd been shut within doors, having camped rather than hire lodging during his journey south from Boston. The room was stifling.

Up went the window beside the desk.

Bathed in a rush of warm but moving air, he stripped off the hunting shirt and flung the garment over a chair, then recalled he'd sent Thomas to fetch the bags and had nothing to change into. While he waited, the sweat drying on his skin, he took in what prospect the window afforded.

Close by stood the kitchen, clapboarded and whitewashed, chimney smoking. Beyond it a wagon track curved between smaller out-buildings. It continued past the apple orchard, skirting a stand of oaks, under which a cluster of tiny cabins sprouted like toadstools. Slave cabins—servants' quarters, as his aunt had called them. To the north of the house, cornfields, interspersed with stretches of broad-leafed tobacco, rolled up to the ridge in the west. Out in those distant rows tiny figures shimmered in the heat. His uncle's field hands at work.

A tap at the door announced the housemaid, Maisy, who entered bearing pitcher and basin. She set them on the washstand, then with a put-upon air, bent to retrieve his saddlebags from the passageway—deposited there by Thomas, presumably. Another mark against him in the maid's opinion, he could tell.

Ian hurried to the door before she could make a second trip and found his long rifle lying in the passage. He brought it into the room to find Maisy casting about as if for anything else left half-done. She frowned at the open window but made no comment.

"I'll have my girl, Esther, air the tick for you, Mister Ian, soon as supper's past," she said. "Speak of supper, Miss Lucinda likes folk to be prompt."

Mindful of his half-dressed state, Ian stowed his rifle behind the door, then gave the woman what he hoped was an engaging grin. "I've the impression Miss Lucinda generally has things arranged to her liking."

His teasing hadn't the intended effect. Wariness sharpened the maid's features before they went a careful blank. "Yes, sir. She do. When the bell ring, come on down to table."

She backed from the room, shutting the door between them.

By the time Ian judged himself presentable as soap and water could render him, enticing smells had thickened on the air belling the window curtains inward. His stomach writhed as he smoothed back his hair and bound it with the least offensive of his ribbons, letting the tail curl over a neckcloth that felt noose-tight in the heat but lent him a semblance of respectability—every scrap of which he'd need if he meant to win over his uncle's patently unimpressed wife.

" 'First impressions being a vital thing,' " he quoted at the quill-free, slicked-down image of himself in the glass above the washbasin.

He donned his only decent coat, a slate-blue specimen he'd brushed nearly clean.

Hearing the scuff of shifted trunks across the passageway, he yanked the door inward and strode into the hall, intending to have a word with Thomas—and instead caught a passing forehead square on the point of his chin. The impact clashed his teeth together, with his tongue clamped between.

"*Uhn!*" he said. So did his inadvertent casualty, a young woman. Her unpinned hair coiled in dark profusion over his coat sleeve as she staggered; he grabbed her to prevent a fall.

"Are ye all right, miss?"

Black lashes swept upward. Large, startled eyes caught the light spilling from his room—green eyes with flecks of amber at their centers. Eyes like the creek he'd just crossed, strewn with mossy pebbles, dazzled with reflected sunlight. He couldn't look away from them.

Gradually it dawned on him he *ought* to look away, that he was practically embracing the girl, to whom he'd yet to be introduced.

He unwound his arms from her and stepped back, leaving her standing in the light from the bedchamber. He knew within two guesses who she must be, though she didn't in the least resemble that cool, rigid lady belowstairs. Her complexion held a deep, sun-drenched luster. Her brow and cheekbones were wide, her nose long and high-bridged but not the least pinched. And that mouth . . . so full and boldly shaped he had the quite improper urge to kiss it.

Bitten though it was, he found his tongue again. "Forgive me. I didn't expect we'd meet 'til supper." Grasping at the vestiges of his early education, he managed a proper bow. "Ian Cameron, your servant—and, happily, your cousin by marriage as well."

The creek-water eyes stared at him unblinking.

"Ye'll be Miss Bell," he continued, thinking her shy as well as lovely. "But is it Rosalyn or . . . ?" What was the other one called? His mind had blanked.

Those vivid eyes rounded, but before his cousin could speak, another voice cut through the moment.

"Seona! Get down to the kitchen and quit pestering Master Hugh's kin." It was Maisy, the housemaid who'd brought the water, scowling up from the stairwell.

Rich color flooded the girl's cheeks, but Ian for the first time noticed something beyond her face. The bodice of her gown was stained, the cuffs at her elbows bedraggled. More so the hem of her petticoat.

"Begging your pardon, Mister Ian," she said, dipping a slight, apologetic curtsy, as if she felt at fault for their collision.

Ian was struck by the low, melodic quality of her voice—and the fact that she wore no shoes. Dirty bare feet flashed as she hurried down the stairs, leaving him tugging at a neckcloth now unbearably tight. What had the housemaid called her? It had sounded like *Shona*.

Not the name of either of his uncle's step-daughters.

A throat cleared behind him. In the doorway to the storeroom, Thomas stood with arms crossed, convulsed in silent mirth.

"How long have ye been standing there?" Ian demanded.

"Long enough."

"Long enough to watch me play the fool. Why didn't ye stop me?"

"Too busy having myself a look." From below came the promised summons of a bell. Thomas drew near, frowning at Ian's throat. "You've a stain—not to worry," he added when Ian swore. Thomas tugged at the neckcloth, refolded it, then stood back to inspect him. "There. Least now you look the part."

"And ye'd best start acting it." Sweat beaded Ian's brow, not all of it due to the heat. Thomas had removed his coat but hadn't washed. Had anyone thought to provide the means? "There's water in the pitcher, yonder in my room. Help yourself. Ye'll find your way to the kitchen, see what they're serving up?"

"Any dog can follow his nose." Thomas raised his chin, sniffed, then met Ian's gaze as no slave would his master's.

"We need to talk, Thomas. About a lot of things."

"You fret like a hen with one chick. Best worry

about yourself." Thomas leaned closer. "For in case you've failed to notice, what they're serving up presently is *you*."

Ian tested his bitten tongue against his teeth. "Aye, well. Pray there's enough to go around."

Brown eyes glinting with a familiar light, Thomas whispered, "*Aonaibh ri chéile.*"

Taken by surprise, Ian laughed. He'd half forgotten the rallying cry the two of them had used as lads bent on mischief in Boston's winding, cobbled streets. The old Gaelic motto of Clan Cameron: *Let us unite.*

2

Seona ducked out the back of the big house and raced down the trellised breezeway, sidestepping Esther emerging from the kitchen with the gravy bowl.

"Seona! Miss Lucinda gonna scold, we keep Mister Ian waiting on his supper."

"You know who's bound to keep him waiting," Seona replied. "It ain't you and me."

Esther batted her lashes like she was ogling herself in a glass, then giggled over the gravy as she hurried off. Seona paused inside the kitchen door, sensing the bustle within before her eyes could adjust to see.

Naomi's bulk passed across the fire's glow. "Get in here, child. Esther can't tote the whole meal herself."

Seona passed behind her mama, who was arranging apple fritters on a plate. Lily's hair was coiled up smooth under her cap, her face agleam in the kitchen's heat. "Ye're flushed as a ripe strawberry, Seona. Where'd ye run off to?"

"Up to our room." Not for the first time Seona wished herself as coppery brown as her mama so her blushes wouldn't show for the world to see. *He'd* thought she was his kin, which meant he must be half-blind now. A pity. He had such pretty eyes. Still blue as a jay's wing.

Since she and Esther got called in from the field, she'd been in motion, helping with the chopping, roasting, boiling, and baking. Finally she'd snatched a space and raced up to the garret to do what she'd itched to do since hearing their company named—have herself a look at that likeness she made of the boy who came to visit, all those years back.

"Ain't nobody meant to be dashing about in this heat." Naomi paused in salting pole beans to blot her streaming face.

"Girl-baby," Lily said, "ye went all the way to the garret and didn't think to put up your hair?"

Only then did she realize. Her braid had come undone! When she collided in the passage with Mister Ian? Or before?

"How many times Lily got to tell you that? Miss Lucinda might call you in to help Maisy serve." Shaking her turbaned head, Naomi snatched a clean apron off a sideboard and thrust it at her. "Put this on, then wash your hands. Can't have prints on the dishes."

Apron donned, Seona dipped her hands in a washbowl while Naomi plunged sturdy fingers into her curls and set to braiding.

His hair had changed, gone a rich, dark gold with only streaks left of the spun-flax shade it used to be. From across the worktable her mama

41

was eyeing her. She hoped Lily couldn't see how her mind was stuck on the sight of Mister Ian grown up tall and wide-shouldered, with his hair tamed down so the only part left curling was the tail. His smile was like she minded, wide above that chin with its tiny dip in the center, like an angel brushed it with a wingtip before his bones had set. Otherwise the rounded face in her drawing had vanished, swallowed up by the lean flesh and strong bones of a man's face.

A final yank to her scalp stung her eyes, but she was too distracted to protest. "Did y'all see him?"

"Had us a glimpse when he come up to the house." Naomi retied her apron strings, then pushed Seona toward the dishes bound for the warming room. "Looking like a wildcat out the woods."

"He's grown into those gangly limbs," Lily added.

"He has," Seona agreed as Esther rushed in, sweating and bothered.

"What's holding you up, Seona?"

"My knees, I reckon." Seona wrapped a towel around a steaming crock, plunked a kiss atop Esther's cap, and hurried out.

On the last trip from the house Seona saw the other new arrival sitting on a bench in the breezeway down at the kitchen end, half-hid by trellis canes heavy with cream-pink roses. She took her time coming along, wanting to get herself a proper view of this new man come with Mister Ian, who obliged by leaning out from behind the roses to get a look at her.

Striped stockings—fine ones that didn't bag—pewter-buckled shoes, and a coat colored like a newborn fawn, fit like it was made for him. He was dandied up more than any serving man she'd seen save the coach drivers at Chesterfield. His skin was middling dark, jaw bony, ears small and set close to a skull nicely shaped. His eyebrows weren't more than a sprinkle of hairs, but his smile was lively and his teeth white and she could tell he thought himself a pleasing sight to behold. He wasn't wrong.

Standing at her approach, still smiling, he said, "Not that I don't find the present view filling in its way, but how's a hungry man meant to get himself a sampling of those vittles I been smelling?"

Seona halted with a hand to her hip. "That man can sit himself back on that bench and wait for what's coming to him. Supper back of the house today is pone and pot likker. Reckon your master feeds you better?"

She was used to puzzlement in the eyes of enslaved or free when they got their first look at her, like what came into Mister Ian's eyes when he realized who she wasn't. This one's eyes were different. They sparkled, as if he knew some private jest—concerning *her*.

"No, ma'am. I'm accustomed to johnnycake— if that's what you mean by *pone*."

She relaxed in the face of his good humor. Judging by his accent, he was a long way from home, wherever that had been. Maybe he'd left a wife or little ones behind. Likely he'd be anxious to find his way into their circle, feel it close round him. If he reckoned his master was come to stay.

"Well then, what are you called?"

"You can call me Thomas. And what do I call you, missy ma'am?"

"Save *ma'am* for your master's kin. I'm plain Seona."

"I take issue with you being *plain* anything." He broadened his smile, making her revise her speculations about a wife. "But what sort of name is Sho-nuh? You got a back name to go with that?"

A *back* name? Of all the cheek. He hadn't known what to make of her after all, fishing about with his *missy* and *ma'am*. This man of Mister Ian's had to be uppity as the day was long. Or none too bright. "It's the name my mama gave me, and no, I don't. Now sit like I told you. By and by I'll bring you out a plate."

He sat quick, like she might scold worse if he didn't. "Yes, *ma'am*—I mean, Seona."

As she swung away, he grabbed the end of her

44

braid. Seona tugged it free but, as she ducked into the kitchen, felt her wayward hair unraveling again.

"Cousin, you've barely eaten enough to satisfy a bird. We thought you'd be ravenous for a decent meal after your journey. Didn't we, Judith?"

Rosalyn Bell didn't glance aside at her younger sister as she spoke. Neither did Ian. He was too busy noting the candle flames mirrored in eyes the exact blue of the cornflowers bedecking the table's chinaware. The elder Miss Bell, who'd captured his attention the moment she glided into the dining room, was the antithesis of the girl he'd collided with abovestairs. Golden-haired and softly rounded, she wore a rose-hued gown cut to reveal an eye-catching expanse of bosom, swelling above a waist nipped in so tight his hands might have spanned it.

"Might we tempt you with an apple fritter? Papa Hugh said you couldn't eat your fill when you visited years ago."

"I'm sure I did my best." Sharing the collective chuckle at his expense, Ian accepted the pastry and took a bite. Rosalyn watched approvingly, a dimple flashing in her cheek. Ian chewed, all but drowning in the blue of her gaze.

"Aye, Judith. Your cousin did arrive bedecked with an Indian tomahawk. Perhaps he'll tell ye how he came by it."

Catching the end of his uncle's prompting remark, Ian realized the other sister had addressed him. Rather plain, just shy of eighteen, Judith Bell might have passed for a girl much younger. She'd taken pains to coil her finer, light-brown hair like her sister's shining curls, but the damp heat permeating the house had wilted them into straggles on her narrow shoulders.

Ian swallowed his mouthful and smiled at her. "I've brought along a few mementos of my years among the Chippewa. Fancy a keek at them after supper, would ye?"

Judith bobbed her head, blushing and beaming. Like her sister, the lass had pretty teeth. She was less plain when she smiled.

"With such unrest among the northern tribes," Uncle Hugh said, snagging Ian's attention, "were ye no' of some trepidation venturing among them?"

Ian cleared his throat. They were dangerously close to what he'd meant to share with the man earlier. Privately. The great scandal of their family that had sent him, barely eighteen at the time, to the wilds of Upper Canada with his mother's younger brother, Callum Lindsey. It was Callum, five years later, who'd carted Ian back to Boston, in danger of losing his leg to wound fever. Ian was hazy now on the timing of those events back in spring, but he minded Callum at his bedside telling him of a second

46

chance to settle in Carolina, to put disgrace behind him.

A grip on his arm, a muttered prayer, and he'd seen no more of the kinsman who for five years had been his refuge. Callum had left him behind. So he'd taken Hugh Cameron up on his offer. Another uncle. Another refuge. Far from a disappointed father.

"I wouldn't have gone alone, sir," Ian told that uncle now. "I had Mam's brother watching out for me. But aye, there's unrest enough in the region with the British refusing to relinquish their forts and so many settlers pushing west. It can be a challenge to run a trapline unmolested. No telling how long that life can last, but I don't regret having lived it for a bit."

"How thrilling, Cousin." Rosalyn tilted her head, sending a cluster of curls swinging against her slender neck. "Though for all its adventure I cannot see how you brought yourself to quit a city like Boston for the society of savages."

The room was stifling. All attention was fixed upon Ian. Feeling a sudden affinity with the gravy-smothered chicken leg congealing on his plate, he replied, "At the time, life on the frontier presented less by way of . . . complications."

"Among the Indians?" Judith blurted. "I wouldn't have supposed so."

Ian silently thanked her for the redirection. "D'ye know of our neighbors to the west, then?"

"I've read Mr. Lawson's *A New Voyage to Carolina*."

"Have ye?" Ian said, surprised into interest.

Rosalyn cut in before he could pursue it further. "Why talk of tiresome books when here sits our cousin, who's actually lived among the red men?"

Ian couldn't help returning her admiring smile. "Aye, Rosalyn, I've stories I could tell." Noting her sister's crestfallen countenance, he added judiciously, "But I'm also a bookbinder's son. *Tiresome* isn't the word I'd use to describe books."

That had both sisters beaming at him.

They talked for a while of Robert Cameron's shop in Boston's North End; then the conversation flowed on to Ian's elder brother, Ned, who worked alongside their father, and whose second son had been born that winter past. But at the first opportunity, Ian turned back to Judith, silent since her sister's mild rebuke.

"I'm familiar with Lawson's survey. I understand many of the tribes he met with are regrettably vanished now. Or exiled from Carolina, like the Tuscaroras."

His uncle's wife had thus far taken small part in the conversation, but now Lucinda Cameron interjected, "I, for one, do not deem the absence of red heathens in our kitchen-yard cause for regret. Do let us not revive the subject."

Judith drew her napkin into her lap. "But, Mama, we do have—"

"Judith."

"I beg your pardon, Aunt," Ian hurried to say. "My years in the wilds have undoubtedly roughened my edges and provided me many a topic of conversation unsuited to the table."

Rosalyn's delighted laughter broke the tension. "I daresay we shall make polishing your rough edges our mission, Cousin. To commence our campaign, might you be willing to escort us to meeting?"

"We wish to show you off to our particular friends, the Pryces, who—" Judith bit off her words, silenced by her sister's quelling stare.

Ian swiped a napkin over his mouth to hide a grin. The lass had apparently committed the unpardonable sin of unveiling their feminine machinations. "Meeting?" he inquired.

"Since leaving Virginia for the back of beyond," Lucinda explained, "my daughters and I have had no proper Anglican service to attend. However, we are lately privileged to have secured the offices of a visiting minister, one Sabbath in the month."

"Which happens to fall Sunday next." Rosalyn leaned toward her sister, adding sotto voce, "We must unearth our Book of Common Prayer, lest our cousin think *us* perfect heathens."

Judith frowned. "But I read from it just this morning. It's—"

49

With a delicate sigh, Rosalyn straightened. "Really, Judith. I was jesting."

"Daughters," Uncle Hugh said, " 'tis all well for ye and your mother, this new meeting and its minister. But Ian willna have been raised Anglican, ye ken."

"True, Uncle. Da went over to the Congregationalists years ago and hasn't looked back. But I've no objection to my cousins' plan." Ian forbore mentioning how long it had been since he'd set foot inside a meetinghouse of any persuasion. He hoped his attendance after such a prodigal stint wouldn't offend the Almighty. His lack of attendance was sure to offend his kin. At least the womenfolk.

"Young Mr. Pryce of Chesterfield Plantation has procured the minister, a Reverend Wilkes," Lucinda was saying. "He's distantly related to the Pryces, also formerly of Virginia."

Was it the subject of religion or Virginia that had sparked his aunt's volubility? Twice she'd uttered the name of the state, imbuing it with loving import. Ian recalled that her first husband, an old acquaintance of his uncle, had been a Tidewater planter in the state.

Rosalyn took a sip from her glass, held it aloft for the maid to fill, and said, "It's a shame Papa Hugh isn't a Quaker."

"Rosalyn, such a thing to say," said her mother. "A Quaker?"

Rosalyn's silvery laughter met her mother's half-amused, half-shocked expression. To Ian she said, "We've little to do with Quakers, of course, save for when we take our corn to mill. Such peculiar folk—I hear they simply sit in silence at their Meetings. But they do swarm like bees in these parts. There must be *three* of their meetinghouses within a day's ride of our door."

"Thomas and I met with a Quaker on our journey," Ian said, again entranced by her lovely smile. "Traveled with him, in fact, as far as Hillsborough."

"Ye came by way of Hillsborough?" Uncle Hugh leaned forward, putting aside his napkin. "I'd assumed ye'd passed through Salem."

"I'd planned to, sir. But Hillsborough was where the Quaker was bound." He was regretting having mentioned the man—another topic better left alone. After all, it was largely the Quaker's fault that Ian hadn't sent Thomas Ross straight back to Boston with his tail between his legs, when he'd last had the chance. He shrugged against the confines of his coat, casting for an explanation that wouldn't reveal too much. "The man requested our company on the road. He was traveling alone, and as I owed him something of a debt by then—"

"Not a *gambling* debt?" Rosalyn asked in feigned astonishment.

"I don't think Quakers gamble," Judith said.

51

Rosalyn threw Ian a wide-eyed appeal. "Am I the only one at this table with a sense of humor?"

"I'm sure your sister's sensibilities do her credit," Ian said. *Even if she doesn't share your wit,* he allowed his eyes to add. "It wasn't to do with gambling, no. Still, it's not the tale to place me in the most flattering of lights, I fear." He paused, hoping Lucinda would again object to their conversation, but the lady remained unhelpfully silent.

"Dinna press your cousin, lass," his uncle admonished. "He may no' wish to speak of it."

"Then he shouldn't have let fall such an intrigue." Rosalyn flashed her dimple. "Do be a gentleman, Cousin, and tell us everything."

Ian's mind spun at the notion. He couldn't tell the half of it. What he did tell, as far as it went, was the truth—that he'd taken a fall in Pennsylvania, landed on his head, and knocked himself senseless, letting them believe it had been from the saddle he'd fallen, not the steep hillside where he'd been attempting to ambush the friend who would not stop trailing him south. He told of waking, bruised and battered, in a camp he'd no memory of pitching.

"Oh, Cousin," Judith said, a pale hand fluttering to her mouth.

"Who was by to aid ye, lad?" his uncle asked.

Ian was touched by their concern, though he hadn't meant to elicit it. "Thomas was . . . near to hand by then," he said with only the slightest hesitation, the irony of that statement his alone to savor. He wondered briefly if Thomas had found his own supper. Perhaps in company of the green-eyed girl?

"But where does the Quaker come into the tale?" Rosalyn prompted.

"He was there in camp, too, when I woke—sipping coffee from *my* cup," he added, hoping to lighten the account. A stranger clad in sober gray, a chance-met traveler who'd come upon Thomas attempting to revive Ian after his fall, Benjamin Eden had introduced himself as a schoolmaster from Easton Town, on his way to join his cousin's Meeting in Hillsborough. "After inquiring most solicitously after my injuries and noting the condition I was in—*commotio cerebri*, he called it—the man offered to physic me, him being well-read in texts of a medical nature. I resigned myself to his ministrations but might have done without his telling us of the fever epidemic in Philadelphia, which I'd unwittingly avoided, having skirted the city."

Attempting to shake Thomas off his trail, he didn't add.

In the silence that followed, he heard the clock ticking on the mantel through the open parlor doors. All sounds of eating had ceased. His aunt's glass had halted midway to her lips.

"Epidemic?" she echoed in a voice stripped of

53

its firmness. "Coastal cities such as Philadelphia are plagued with fevers every season. Was it merely the summer ague?"

"No, ma'am. The Quaker said yellow fever. He was quite descriptive of its presentation— gleaned from travelers he'd met on the road, fleeing to the countryside. Languor and nausea, vomiting, delirium, yellowing of the skin, livid spots on the body akin to the bites of . . ."

Ian fell silent, noting that though his cousins still hung upon his every word, it wasn't with fascination or sympathy. Rather with expressions of dawning horror.

Lucinda Cameron's complexion had blanched to the shade of chalk powder. The glass in her hand seemed to tremble. "You traveled in company with a man exposed to *yellow fever?*"

"No," Ian hastened to say. "As I said, the man never—"

His reply was cut short as the glass slipped from his aunt's lifted hand, spilling its contents in a thin cascade before shattering on the hardwood floor.

3

"Of course I didn't tell them everything," Ian said, tamping down his exasperation—and the level of his voice; though he'd bid his uncle an awkward good night after the girls had helped their mother to her room abovestairs, only a short passage and a door separated the newer wing of the house from the rooms in which the women slept. He'd come up the back stairs to find Thomas in his cupboard of a room, tiny window propped, a breeze stirring the warmth of the house's upper story. "I'd have left out the yellow fever had I known mention of it was enough to cause a swoon."

His uncle had insisted he wasn't to blame for his aunt's indisposition. Ian couldn't have known yellow fever had claimed the lives of Lucinda Cameron's first husband and two young sons, or that Judith, who had survived it, shared her mother's mortal terror of the disease.

Chagrined regardless, Ian loosened the confines of his neckcloth and sat on a nearby trunk, disregarding its layer of dust. "Ye should've heard me skating around every subject that arose, with the ice cracking under me all the while. There's not a chapter in the narrative of my life fit for civilized conversation."

He winced, regretting his choice of words. Thomas, who'd unearthed a low stool to sit on, glanced at a slim brown volume, corners rubbed and pages well-thumbed, that peeked from his satchel below the window: *The Interesting Narrative of the Life of Olaudah Equiano.*

Ian could justly impugn the author of that narrative with inspiring Thomas to risk life and liberty by following him to North Carolina, attempting to overtake him and join the journey south. Thomas had revealed the book after the Quaker, Benjamin Eden, had examined Ian's head wound—a wound he'd taken in a last attempt to elude the pursuit.

More gravely injured than he'd let on to his kin, Ian had been muddled enough to think he could get up on his horse and continue his journey, leaving Thomas and the meddling Quaker behind. He'd gotten as far as the picketed horses before Thomas caught him and thrust the book under his nose.

"One of my da's?" Ian had asked, though he'd no need. Even with a battered skull he'd have recognized his father's work. Or Ned's. The volume was bound by neither Cameron. Then he'd taken in the title. "*Olaudah Equiano.* What sort of name is that?"

"African," Thomas had said with pride. "He was stolen from his tribe, made a slave. He bought his freedom and wrote of his enslavement. Listen." Turning to a marked passage, Thomas read,

" 'Indeed, on the most trifling occasions, they were loaded with chains; and often instruments of torture were added. The iron muzzle, thumb-screws—' "

"Thomas," Ian cut in. "My uncle doesn't commit savageries against his slaves. I've been there, aye? I've seen them."

"As a boy. You probably didn't notice."

"I'd have noticed iron muzzles!" He'd been twelve that spring he visited Mountain Laurel, giddy with the adventure of traveling nigh the length of their new-won nation with his da, smug in thinking for once he'd been chosen over Ned. It was years before he understood Robert Cameron hadn't asked him along purely for the pleasure of his company. "It's no concern of yours. Nor is my business."

Thomas squared his jaw. "A slave goes where his master goes, so your business is mine."

"Ye're not my slave!"

"I could be." Thomas's eyes had burned with a dark fire. "I mean to see if what Equiano writes of those Southern plantations is true. See with my own eyes. Your kin need never know who I am."

Ian glared now at the narrative tucked into the satchel below the window. As though he minded that fraught conversation as well, Thomas started to reach for it, then caught Ian's glower and refrained.

"Spot any iron muzzles lying about the kitchen?" Ian asked.

Sweating in the warmth of the house, Thomas regarded him. "Do you still not understand why I had to do this?"

Ian snorted as he rose, pausing in the doorway. "I barely understand what I'm doing here."

"That I don't doubt. But thanks to Benjamin I'm certain of playing my part."

Within hours of making their acquaintance, the Quaker had called out Thomas on his playacting. Instead of siding with Ian to convince Thomas of his foolishness, the man had offered to tutor him in the Art and Mystery of Acting the Slave— should they agree to his company on the road to Carolina.

It had been two against one, and that one with his wits knocked agley. He'd stalked off alone, seeking solitude to cobble together an argument with force enough to turn one stubborn, brown-hided cooper back north to the free life he should be leading. He'd burdens enough to bear on that journey without adding Thomas Ross to the load.

In the end he hadn't found it in him to resist the force of such conviction, no matter how reckless, and in quiet despair he'd wondered—was wondering still—if he was fated to be forever eddied along on the tide of other men's zeal.

"D'ye need anything before I seek my bed?" he

asked, discomfited by sight of the narrow bedroll on the dusty floor.

The question elicited a clucking noise. Before Ian could bristle at the mother hen reference, Thomas grinned. "I'm fine, Mastah Ian. Go on to bed. And sweet dreams on that feather tick they've given you."

"Aye," Ian said gruffly. "Thanks."

His dreams, however, proved anything but sweet. In them he was a lad running down the cobbled streets of Boston's North End, shoving through the door beneath the shingle that read *Messrs. Cameron & Ross, Binders & Sellers of Fine Books.* He flew past Thomas's father—the Ross of *Cameron & Ross*—and ducked the counter flap to race past the great trimming press, past stacks of pasteboard and dye trays, while above his head marbled endpapers festooned air thick with the smell of binder's glue . . .

At the rear of the shop a man bends over the sewing frame, hair clubbed, shirtsleeves turned high.

"Da! Da!"

His father rounds on him. "Have I no' told ye, Ian? Dinna go haring through the shop like ye've a band of wild Indians after ye." Da turns his back. "There now. D'ye see?" The sharp is gone from his voice; Ned is at the sewing frame. "Ye loop the threads through the folds, then bind them to the cords . . . so."

"Aye, Da," says dutiful Ned—insufferably smug Ned—while Ian backs away. He misjudges his footing and bumps a bench bearing an open tray of marbling dye, sloshing the contents onto the floor.

"IAN!"

He came awake, wincing at the echo of his da's bellow. Reaching instinctively for his rifle, he felt empty bed linen, not smooth hardwood or cold gunmetal; the rifle wasn't beside him where it had rested each night for most of the past five years. He'd left it propped beside the door, he remembered, as the shadowed contours of the room in his uncle's house replaced the dream of his da's shop. But the bellowing went on.

His heart thundered as he listened. The shouts were muffled. The banging that next erupted wasn't, nor the woman's voice that arose outside his room: "Lily—get you down here this instant!"

Ian clawed his way off the feather tick and sprang for the door.

Lucinda Cameron, swathed in a wrapper and candlelight, stood at the top of the back stairwell, where a door was thrown open to reveal another stair, twisting narrowly up to what must be a garret. Belowstairs that other voice called, the words still unintelligible. His uncle's voice.

The door across the passage cracked open. Thomas peered out but had the sense to remain concealed as stair treads creaked and a slender figure in pale homespun descended from above, clutching a wooden box. Ian had a glimpse of coppery skin and a long black braid before Lucinda thrust the woman toward the stairs and the voice below, still raised in agitation.

"I feared his coming would bring this on," his aunt snapped. "Quickly now. Calm him!"

Before she vanished down the stairwell, the woman from the garret glanced up, raising to Ian a familiar face—dark eyes above wide cheekbones, a graceful jaw.

Seconds later, the shouts from below grew abruptly comprehensible: "Lily! Ye'll ken where he is. Aidan! Where have they taken him?"

"Aunt? What's amiss?" Ian hadn't seen his uncle's wife since she'd left the table.

"We have it well in hand, Mr. Cameron." Lucinda's face pinched in disapproval as she regarded him. He'd emerged wearing the shirt he'd slept in and nothing more. It covered him to midthigh, but the open neck had slid to his shoulders.

"I was startled out of sleep," he began, but she was already halfway down the stairs, no more attention to spare him.

The shouting had abated. The woman from the garret, or something from her box, was having the desired effect.

Thomas opened his door wider. "Your uncle?"

"Aye, but I've no idea what's wrong." The

name his uncle had been shouting. *Aidan*. Had that been his cousin's name? "I'll see what's to be known come morning. Speaking of which—have ye a notion of the time?"

More footsteps made them turn. The door in the passage to the front of the house had burst open. Through it came Rosalyn, golden hair streaming. "It's three o' the clock—oh, Cousin!" she wailed and threw herself into Ian's arms.

Permitting a lass into one's room in the dead of night was an act of pure folly, especially when one was barely clothed and the lass in only her shift. Rosalyn clung to him, carried away on a tide of weeping, forcing him to speak into her hair. "Miss Bell—Rosalyn—what's amiss belowstairs?"

"It's Papa Hugh. He's had these spells of late. Mama said . . . But I'm not to speak of it!"

Gently he shushed her, as over her shoulder he watched the door, heart going at a gallop. Thomas had disappeared into his storeroom and shut fast the door. Had Ian any sense, he'd toss his fair cousin back into the passage and do likewise. But his arms were full of her now and . . . her waist *was* tiny enough to span with his hands.

"Rosalyn." Her name came out a croak. "Who was my uncle calling? It sounded like—"

"His son! His *dead* son."

He'd thought so. But why should his arrival

make his uncle think his son, Aidan, was alive? Surely that's what his aunt had been implying. "That woman from the garret—it was Lily?"

Rosalyn pulled away slightly, and he stifled the unthinking urge to draw her close again.

"It must have been. Mama wouldn't call for *Seona*."

He felt a jolt at the name. "Seona? I met her earlier. I thought . . ." He knew no delicate way to phrase it. "Is she some kin to ye?"

"Kin?" Rosalyn's lip curled. "She's Lily's girl, born right here at Mountain Laurel— *before* Mama married Papa Hugh." Saying her stepfather's name recalled her distress. She gave a little sob and clung to him again.

Ian sought furiously to think. "I'm sure it'll be all right. Ye said yourself this has happened before, aye? Should ye not return to your room?"

Preferably before her mother came back up the stairs.

"Oh." It was a breathless sound, as though she'd just noticed the rumpled bed, or the fact they stood beside it, barely clad. And embracing. She extricated herself from his arms, leaving his shirt damp, his flesh burning. A strand of her hair snagged in the stubble of his beard. She reached to free it, then caressed his face and stood on tiptoe to brush her lips against the corner of his mouth.

Startled by the gesture, Ian grasped her hand

and might have pulled her to him, save that in place of her moonlit face he suddenly saw another.

"Rosalyn. *Go.*" His voice croaked.

For a frozen second she stared, then stepped back from him.

"Yes—of course. I'm better now." At the door she paused, a swirl of shift and flowing hair. "I'm glad you're here, Cousin."

His heart was thundering again. When she was gone, he sank onto the tick and waited for its pounding to settle. That other face still swam before his eyes, more vivid than he'd seen it in years. The mouth that smiled and hid its secrets. The eyes that lingered, holding his too long.

Five years, and still they rose up to haunt him—and complicate his life.

He might never forgive Thomas for throwing that history in his face as he'd done on their journey. The Quaker, Benjamin Eden, had sat by the fire in their camp while off in the shadows by the picketed horses, Thomas had done his utmost to convince Ian his quest to pose as a slave was reasonable.

"What of your coopering?" Ian had protested, the first objection that sprang to mind. But Thomas had anticipated that.

"Your uncle grows tobacco. He'll need hogsheads."

"Ye walked away from a position in a thriving

port like Boston on the chance a backcountry planter won't already have a cooper?"

"Like you walked away from your apprenticeship to spend the past five years trapping furs?"

"I didn't walk away."

"True, Ian. You skulked."

Ian would have thought Thomas would back down, given the warning that must have flashed in his gaze. He hadn't.

"You ever mean to tell me what happened to end it so badly? I never set foot in Cambridge, never saw your master—or his wife. Half his age, they say. And there you were a lad in their home, growing up in front of her eyes. Occurred to me she might've been the one to start it . . ."

But Thomas couldn't have imagined the whole of it. No one could have.

With a jerk of his head Ian dispelled both memories and ghosts. He got up and shut the door.

Morning birdsong wove through his senses, muddling dreams of Boston with memories of turmoil in the night. It took a moment to realize he hadn't dreamt his uncle calling out. Or his cousin coming out of the dark. Into his arms.

He scrubbed a hand down his face and groaned.

Even after he dressed and shaved, the rest of the household seemed asleep. Belowstairs all was quiet, his uncle's door firmly shut. After a moment's indecision, he stepped out the back door.

Sunlight splashed the east-facing ridge beyond the orchard with a liquid light that flowed downslope, oozing toward him up the track bordering the fields, pooling in pockets down by the stable. In the shelter of the house the kitchen-yard lay in shadow. Linking house and kitchen was a latticed breezeway, built over a flagstone walk and entwined with pale-pink roses. The smell of bacon frying competed with their scent as he passed beneath, minding how, as a visiting lad, he'd slipped into the kitchen between mealtimes in hope of wheedling a morsel from the cook, Naomi. Most often he'd been successful.

The breezeway ended a pace or two short of the kitchen door, standing wide to the morning's cool. Ian paused to pluck a rose, its petals dew-beaded, then stepped into the open. Over the high garden pales to his left he glimpsed a figure slipping from sight among the pole beans.

The girl from the upstairs passage. Had she seen him first?

"Think this time he gonna stay?"

The question, a child's, had issued from the kitchen.

"We must bide and see what the Almighty wills," replied a voice Ian recognized: that of Malcolm, his uncle's oldest slave. Creaky

66

as a rusted hinge now, it had lost none of its improbable Scots burr, acquired as a boy when he was purchased by Mountain Laurel's original homesteader; Duncan Cameron had taught the handful of slaves he'd bought to settle Mountain Laurel—sixty, seventy years past—to speak Gaelic so he needn't suffer English spoken in his presence. Ian recalled his da and those left of the original slaves nattering on in the tongue when they visited years ago. The Gaelic had flown too fast to follow; strange hearing it come from those dark-skinned faces. Was Malcolm now the last of them?

"Why didn't he stay on before?" asked the same childish voice.

"His daddy didna wish it."

"He don't got to do what his daddy say no more?"

"Or his daddy changed his mind," said the old man.

"I heard the misses carrying on how *he so handsome*. Think he'll marry one of 'em?"

There was a snort from a third party, a woman. "If Miss Lucinda have her way, he will—never mind all that swooning at table."

"Why he want to come back here for anyway?" the child asked.

Ian stepped up to the threshold. "That's one question easily answered. Naomi's cooking lured me back."

It was dim inside the kitchen. At first all he could see was the gleam of firelight on copper and the sway of braided onions above his head. Faces emerged from shadow, in varying shades of brown, blank as the crocks lining the pantry shelves. The white-bearded man seated on a corner stool recovered first. Stiffly he stood, straight-limbed but stooped over a hand-whittled stick.

Ian strode inside, stopping at the long worktable to grip the man's arm. Startled at the feel of shrunken flesh, he gentled his touch. "Malcolm."

Dark eyes peered up at him, appraising from deep-netted wrinkles in a sun-spotted face. "I kent ye'd make a tallish man, Mister Ian, but ye've outstripped my expectations. I'm thinkin' ye didna pine overmuch for Naomi's vittles. Someone's been feeding ye."

Still plump in middle age, still turbaned in faded calico, Naomi had her hands wrist-deep in biscuit dough. "You wouldn't be hungry now, would you, Mister Ian?" As if on cue, Ian's belly rumbled. The sound drew a giggle from behind the cook's ample hips. "Esther, get out here and give Mister Ian proper greetin'."

The child obeyed. Thin-faced and bright-eyed, she put him in mind of another new face he'd seen since his arrival. "Ye'll be Maisy's lass, aye?"

The girl grinned. "Uh-huh. And Jubal be my

daddy. He tends Master Hugh's horses. Yours too, I reckon."

"You first say, *Yes, sir,* when Mister Ian ask a question," Naomi cut in when the girl drew breath.

Esther bobbed her knees. "Yes, sir."

Ian extended the rose to her. Esther took it, wide-eyed. She thrust it at Naomi as if it were a live coal and scampered out the door.

A pop of grease drew Ian's attention to the kitchen's fourth occupant, who set a platter of bacon on the table and covered it with a cloth.

"Mister Ian," Lily said with a faint lilt that minded him of his kin. "Welcome back to Mountain Laurel." No trace of the previous night's upset was visible in her countenance. Not even time, it seemed, had ruffled the smoothness of her skin. She appeared unchanged. "Have some bacon to tide ye over."

"There's plenty for the table." Naomi beckoned Malcolm. "Daddy, pone's cool to eat."

The old man settled on a stool before a plate bearing a slab of corn bread drizzled with molasses. Ian realized the wheaten-flour biscuits Naomi was arranging in a pan, and likely everything else, were destined for the house table. "Thank ye for yesterday's fine supper. We arrived unannounced and put ye to a deal of trouble."

In the beat of silence that followed his words,

Ian felt a twinge of unease and wondered if *this* unannounced visit wasn't an intrusion. Then Naomi said, "We heard you didn't have much appetite."

"I mean to rectify that presently." He lifted the cloth and took a slice of bacon, biting off a mouthful before he noticed Malcolm bowed over his plate.

"Bethankit, Lord Jesus," the old man prayed, "for health and strength, for this food to keep us in both. Bethankit for bringin' Mister Ian and his lad, Thomas, safe to journey's end, and for Thy loving-kindness to us all. Amen."

"Amen," Naomi and Lily echoed, looking up from their work.

Ian swallowed, but the bacon felt lodged in his throat. When no one else spoke, he ventured, "There were a couple of lads when I was here before. Maybe they're field hands now? The older one, he'd a funny scar on his forehead, shaped like a fishing hook."

This time the silence stretched. And stretched.

"You meaning Ruby's boys, Sammy and Eli." Naomi busied herself cracking eggs into a bowl. "It was Sammy had the scar, but they gone from here, Mister Ian. Sold some years back."

The words fell like stones into a dry well. When at last they hit bottom, Ian asked, "And their mother, Ruby?"

No one returned his gaze or gave him answer.

Ruby was dead, he guessed, or sold away like her sons.

He backed toward the door. "I'll leave ye to breakfast. It's good to see ye again."

Ian stepped into the morning sunlight in time to hear Lucinda's voice lifted in complaint. Seconds later the window of his room banged shut. Maisy's face peered down at him. He hesitated, then giving way to impulse, slipped through the gate into the garden.

He found Seona still among the pole beans, crouched between the shaded rows, pinching off the pods and dropping them into a shallow basket. The faded-blue kerchief she wore barely restrained the dark mass of ringlets tumbling to her waist.

"Seona?"

She shot to her feet, snatching up the basket, spilling a green cascade over the side.

Ian hurried forward along the row, ducking the leafy canopy where the runners overgrew their stakes. "Let me help."

She knelt again. "No, Mister Ian. You'll get yourself dirty."

He laughed at that but squatted back on his heels while she gathered up the beans. "I didn't mean to give ye a fright. I didn't want to go back inside yet."

Clutching the basket to her hip, securely this time, she stood. So did he, inclining his head to keep it out of the arching vines. Her eyes flashed up at him, bright even in that sheltered light, the brows above them a graceful sweep. *Lily's girl, born right here at Mountain Laurel.* He judged she'd have been maybe six years old when he visited with his da. He minded a small girl, vaguely. Maybe Thomas was right and there was much he hadn't noticed.

"About yesterday, in the passage . . . if I caused ye trouble, I'm sorry."

A ladybug swooped between them and landed on her hand, red as a spot of blood. She flicked her wrist to shoo it away. "You didn't cause no trouble, Mister Ian."

"Good," he said, though he wasn't certain she spoke truthfully. He swallowed the lingering taste of bacon. "I hadn't met my cousins. Not that they're truly my cousins—but ye know that, aye?"

She seemed about to speak but once again was robbed of the chance.

"Seona! Where are you?"

Seona flinched. "That's Miss Rosalyn. Begging your pardon, Mister Ian."

He pressed back against the vines so she could pass, then watched her disappear around the end of the row.

"There you are," Rosalyn said. "Leave that basket. I need your help inside."

Seona replied but Ian didn't catch her words.

He lingered among the vines, picking a handful of beans. Emerging from the row, he dropped them into Seona's abandoned basket, then glanced up at the house. Another face withdrew from an upstairs window, this one pale. Judith, he thought.

He'd started off wrong-footed with the lot of them, kin and slave. Deciding to make a thorough job of it, he stooped for the basket, shot a grin at the fluttering curtains, and ducked back into the bean rows.

4

Ian rolled his aching neck, then stared at the stack of ledgers on his uncle's desk. Each chronicled a year of Mountain Laurel's affairs: weather, planting dates, crop conditions, harvest yields; the health of livestock, family, and slaves. Lily, he'd learned, was a midwife, her services sought by folk of the surrounding hills. Noted also were visits to the Quakers' gristmill and a lumber mill at Chesterfield Plantation; journeys to Salisbury, Fayetteville, Salem; visits from his uncle's solicitor; debts accrued and, less and less punctually, accounts paid. Mountain Laurel operated on a prospective yearly income from crops, with purchases made in expectation of that income. But for several years now the value of the main cash crop, tobacco, had failed to keep pace with expenditures.

His uncle had made no mention of the farm's mounting debt when he invited Ian into his room, following a morning spent helping with the tobacco harvest, now into its second day. He'd merely plunked the ledgers onto the fall front of his desk, expressed his wish to give Ian "a sense of the place, aye?" and taken himself off to the stable in hopes that his new mare was finally ready to drop her late-season foal.

Ian had dutifully skimmed the most recent columns penned in his uncle's scrawling hand, then, in growing concern, gone back further into the records, to the time of Hugh Cameron's second marriage.

Forced to sell her Tidewater plantation in payment of her late husband's debts, Lucinda Bell had retained two slaves—Maisy and Jubal—a modest carriage with its team, and an impressive array of household furnishings. Even in his uncle's room the trappings of former wealth were evident. Fine hangings on the high-post bed, a richly patterned carpet spanning the pinewood floor, the Hepplewhite desk at which Ian sat with its triple finials and glass-paneled bookcase—all gave the illusion of increased income. But the trimmings of affluence, and her daughters, were all that remained of Lucinda's life in Virginia.

There were a lot of books. Ian opened the case above the desk to visually caress the wealth—volumes of Shakespeare, Defoe, Swift, Johnson, Locke, Boswell, Smollett, and Fielding. A collection of poems by that young Scots Lowlander, Burns. Most were leather-bound, some worked in gilt. A familiar spine caught his eye, a book of Norse legends he'd read as a lad.

Ian tugged it free. Inside was an inscription in his da's hand: *1767. Inverness. My first Bound Book. "Hugin and Munin fly each day the wide earth over. I fear for Hugin lest he fare not back—yet I watch the more for Munin." As we fly the earth over, Brother . . . Think and Remember.*

Twin to one his parents owned, the book bore early evidence of Robert Cameron's distinctive tooled style, though the line inscribed about Hugin and Munin—that mythical pair of ravens the Norse god Odin sent out to roam the earth each morning—was an interesting glimpse into his da's mind. Robert Cameron rarely spoke of the past, or the father and much older half brothers he'd lost during the failed Jacobite Rising, when the Highland clans fell at Culloden. Including Hugh, imprisoned and exiled to what was then the colonies.

Think and Remember. Ian brought the book to his nose, smelled the aging leather, and for an instant was back in his da's shop in Boston.

He returned the book and leaned back against the chair's scrolled uprights. His uncle's room was warming as midday approached and despite the open window smelled of pipe tobacco. He'd been smelling tobacco—in the air, on his person, in his sleep—for the past two days.

His uncle had joined them at the breakfast table after that first tumultuous night, a haggardness about his eyes the only indication anything untoward had occurred. Ian had wanted to speak of it, but the presence of his aunt and cousins—particularly Rosalyn with her wide blue eyes—had curtailed the urge to venture the topic.

76

After breakfast his uncle, anxious for his new foal to drop, had lingered for a quarter hour at the stable before joining Ian and Thomas to ride to the fields, where the tobacco harvest had begun.

His uncle's overseer had met them as they'd reined their horses into the shade of a bordering chestnut. Jackson Dawes bunked in a cabin nearer the slave quarters than the house, Ian had been told, and aside from his duties as overseer mainly kept to himself.

"Pryce's hands doing their share?" Uncle Hugh inquired.

Despite the wobbly beginnings of a paunch at his belt, Dawes was an imposing figure in his middle years, square-jawed and barrel-chested. "Fair enough," he allowed, seemingly taciturn by nature as well as solitary.

"Some of these men aren't yours?" Ian surveyed the figures at work among the rows. Mountain Laurel managed with its own field hands most of the year, his uncle had explained. But at harvest more were hired on from Chesterfield, the only neighboring plantation with a workforce to spare. "Which are?"

From the back of his sorrel gelding, his uncle named them. Aside from Naomi's son, Ally— easily identifiable by his size—there were Will and Pete, both around twenty years of age, and Munro, a decade older. Others who could be spared had pitched in. Lily and Seona, and the girl, Esther, were among the rows. Jubal would have been, his uncle said, if not for needing to watch over the broodmare.

"Could use another set of hands," Dawes said, addressing Ian. "Your boy work the ground?"

"He's a cooper by trade."

"A cooper?" Hugh Cameron appraised Thomas with new interest. "Ye didna tell me that."

"I meant to, Uncle," Ian began but, seeing Thomas dismount, followed suit, guessing his intention. "Ye don't know the first thing about harvesting tobacco."

Thomas had already begun turning up his shirtsleeves, as Dawes sized up his thick shoulders and sturdy back. "I'll learn, Mastah Ian."

Ian had lowered his voice. "If I ride off and leave, ye won't be treated special."

Thomas flashed a grin. "Should I be?"

Ian had rolled his eyes. Resignedly he'd shrugged off his coat, announcing his intention to pitch in as well—to his uncle's approval.

Tobacco was harvested with a long-bladed knife, slit up the stalk and laid in the sun. Once wilted, the stalks were piled in a cart and driven to the curing barn, a capacious ventilated structure, where the leaves were hung by slender rods high in the rafters to cure.

"I avow it's needful to study our means of living, Cousin," Rosalyn had remarked at the end of that first day, wrinkling her nose at the pungent scent that clung to him despite having washed and changed his clothes. "But why wallow in the business?"

From what Ian had observed, his aunt and cousins did precious little of the sort. Despite her reduced circumstances, Lucinda Bell Cameron still conducted herself like the mistress of a seaboard plantation, a charade his uncle maintained by the long-suffering of his creditors, as the ledgers on his desk plainly attested.

But he'd had enough of his uncle's finances for one sitting; it occurred to him to wonder what was happening with that foal.

Pushing back from the desk, Ian stretched until his joints cracked, then headed through the house, meaning to join his uncle. At the parlor door he halted, spying Seona within. She was early back from the fields, though still at work, as the ash piggin at her feet attested. Neatly capped and aproned, she was cleaning out the hearth. Or she had been. At present she was simply staring at the mantel . . . no, at the painting above it. Several such oils hung throughout the house. This one Ian minded from his boyhood visit. What had been a splash of color in the room then was all but lost amidst the clutter of the present decor.

Not lost on the girl staring at it, though, her back to him. Ian held his breath, afraid to break the spell she seemed to have fallen under.

The back door opened, startling them both. Ian made to draw away, but Seona didn't turn. She snatched up the piggin and hastened out through the room's other exit, into the dining room. As she vanished from sight, Ian stepped into the parlor through the passage doorway. He heard the housemaid's voice, then the back door shut.

Silence descended belowstairs, though he heard his cousins' voices from their room above, and knew his aunt was just across the passage in the smaller sitting room, where the women liked to sew. The parlor still contained the spell of Seona's captivation. He let himself be drawn, coming to stand in her place.

She'd have seen the painting countless times—a rendering of a stream running through a hollow, the birches on its mossy banks decked in autumn's yellow-gold. Deeper in, partly obscured by the trees, a waterfall gleamed, spilling over tall rocks draped in scarlet creeper.

He stepped closer, peering at a lower corner where the artist had signed the work: *M. M. Cameron 1762*. Not Duncan. Not his uncle. His uncle's first wife?

"Mister Ian?"

He whirled to find Seona had come upon him as silently as he'd done her, catching him gaping at the painting. With no means of covering his startlement, he gave her a self-deprecating smile.

"I thought ye'd gone out," he said, warmth stealing into his face.

"No, sir." She dipped a slight curtsy, as if to hide the puzzlement taken hold of her features. "Maisy says Master Hugh wants you at the stable on account of that mare looks to be dropping her foal at last."

He couldn't suppress his broadening grin. "I was on my way there, actually." He paused, catching in her gaze an echo of his own eagerness. "D'ye want to come with me?"

Those creek-water eyes flared. "I can't, Mister Ian. I got chores to finish, then best get back out to the fields." She glanced at the stairs behind her, then lowered her voice. "But Maisy say don't tell the misses. Master Hugh don't want a crowd pressing in. Just you."

Though neither as hot nor as muggy as it had been the day of his arrival, the sky was clear, the sun high and blazing. Stepping into the stable, Ian was enveloped by the nose-tickle of hay and manure before his eyes adjusted. Shadows resolved into the structure's spacious center aisle bordered left and right by box stalls, their posts hung with tack.

He minded his uncle saying the mare was stabled at the far end, but he'd walked into a pungent wall of horse sweat and ammonia before he reached the spacious box where his uncle stood peering over the gate, stripped to his shirtsleeves and sweating freely. Not only from the day's warmth, to judge by the tension radiating from him.

None of the neighboring stalls were presently occupied. The stable doors at that end were closed fast, as was the outer door of the box, creating a dim, womb-like atmosphere. The only source of light was a pierced-tin lantern hung from a nearby beam. It shed a fractured glow over heaving bay flanks and revealed Jubal, his uncle's stableman, crouched with an arm elbow-deep inside the mare.

"Ally will be sore he missed this when he comes in from the fields tonight," Uncle Hugh said.

Fresh from his uncle's troubling ledgers, Ian felt the compulsion to head out to those fields directly after the birth, to work alongside Ally and the others until sundown.

"Is it well?" he asked, low-voiced, frowning at Jubal still rooting around for the unborn foal.

His uncle was about to reply when Jubal spoke, the strain of effort in his voice. "Got that hoof straight. Hold on . . . there now. Here the nose where it ought to be. Two front hooves coming first."

"Aye," Uncle Hugh said on a breath that carried patent relief, as Jubal withdrew his arm and rose to wash in a bucket set outside the stall. "Aye,

I think so. We'll leave her to it. See how things progress."

Things progressed swiftly, as it happened. While his uncle spoke, Jubal had stood from the wash bucket and cast his gaze over the laboring mare.

"Here she go," he said.

Forgetting conversation, Ian and his uncle turned back to the box to see the foal's emerging hooves, encased still in its birth sac, followed by a muzzle as the membrane tore. Another contraction brought forth its shoulders. Ian gripped the box gate until the foal was out at last in a sprawl of slender legs, dark and seal-wet in the lantern light. The mare raised her head to view the creature she'd expelled and nickered, as if in surprise.

Sensing the man beside him at once drained of tension and wound tight with joy, Ian softly laughed. "Congratulations, Uncle. Though I'm jiggered if I can tell from here whether ye've a filly or a colt."

At a nod from Uncle Hugh, Jubal slipped back into the stall and ran fingers over the foal's nostrils. The creature sneezed, sending a spray of mucus over the man. "Be a filly, Master Hugh. A fine one."

"A worthy scion of Janus, I dare hope. As will be the foals I get from her one day."

"Juturna," Ian murmured, realizing he'd

spoken the name aloud when he sensed his uncle regarding him. "In the Roman mythos," he explained, "Juturna was the consort of Janus."

He'd mythic figures on the brain, apparently, after reading his da's inscription in the Norse book.

Uncle Hugh was nodding, thoughtful. "Aye. That'll do."

Understanding took a beat to sink in. "I didn't mean to presume to name her, Uncle. Wouldn't my cousins wish to do so?"

"No, lad. There'll be others for them to name, God willing. 'Tis no coincidence, this one arriving out of season, practically on your heels. Juturna she'll be called." His uncle studied him in the lantern's dim light. "Ye'll be book-learned, then? Latin and Greek, if my memory of Robert's letters serve."

"Aye, sir. I can manage some of both. The man who held my indenture had a proper library to hand. I put it to use."

"Ye'll have seen what passes for my own library?" his uncle asked. "Ye're welcome to borrow any book that catches your fancy."

"Thank ye, Uncle," Ian managed. Talk of his indenture had cast a shadow; while by day Ian had been taught the cabinetmaker's art in Wilburt Pringle's Cambridge shop, by night those books that lined the man's parlor shelves had been a consuming passion, though the master cabinetmaker whom he'd served hadn't shared his literary interests. Pringle's wife had.

And *that* put Ian in mind of a further detail about Janus. The pagan deity was a two-faced god, looking to the future, aye, but also to the past. A god of endings, as well as beginnings.

Jubal went to fix a bran mash for the mare, but Uncle Hugh lingered. They'd been leaning on the box gate, observing the filly's first attempt to stand. The gangly creature had pitched and buckled three, four times, before its tiny hooves bore up its weight. Now Ian caught the man eyeing him again, his smile over the filly's success fading into thoughtful furrows, as though he sensed Ian's troubled thoughts.

"So," his uncle said. "Ye've had a keek at the ledgers?"

Ian straightened. "Aye, sir. We should talk about them."

"And we will." His uncle reached for his coat, draped over an empty stall, his voice recapturing some of its earlier glow as he added, "But not just now, with a new filly to toast. Let's go share a wee dram—and tell the lasses about our Juturna."

Our Juturna. He followed his uncle from the stable, thinking that the man seemed certain this arrangement would work, that Ian's mere presence at Mountain Laurel had sealed it. He hadn't wanted to speak of Ian's past transgressions, as though they could be brushed aside and left behind. But Ian was still the man he was. The man those transgressions had made him.

He might presume to name his uncle's filly, but he dared not presume to own his uncle's heart— or respect. Not yet.

He nearly missed them as he and his uncle strode beneath the chestnut at the yard's edge, crossing the lawn to the veranda; movement caught from the corner of his eye drew his attention to the two slender figures darting from the washhouse across the lane to the stable— Seona and the wee lass, Esther.

Maisy's daughter ducked inside the stable doors, but Seona hesitated long enough to slide a glance their way—and caught Ian looking straight at her.

Before his uncle, mounting the veranda steps ahead of him, could notice, Ian gave the lass what he hoped she'd read across the distance as a conspiratorial grin. Then he turned his back, pretending he hadn't caught her in an act of flagrant deceit.

5

Head hung over the box gate, Master Hugh's sorrel was nuzzling the last of the turnip tops from Seona's hand when she heard them ride in, back from their Sunday meeting. Mister Ian spoke to Jubal in the stable-yard, where he left his roan horse. She waited, expecting to hear the mistress getting down from the carriage, but the next to speak was Thomas.

"No reason I cannot help. They're my master's horses."

"But my stable to keep." Jubal's dismissive words fell like slaps. " 'Sides, wouldn't want you sullying them fancy trappings."

Hurrying from the stable, Seona spotted Thomas heading for the house, stiff-backed and discouraged in his stride. She called to him before she saw the figure climbing the front porch steps—Mister Ian. They both swung round at her call.

Thomas's set features softened. "Where you bound, Seona?"

"The kitchen."

Thomas fell in beside her. Mister Ian still stood on the steps, watching them—just like he'd seen her that day the filly was born. Did he think she'd lied to him that day? Truly she hadn't meant to go to the stable, but that Esther . . . she could pester a body into doing what she never meant to do just to gain a little peace.

Mister Ian hadn't told on her, far as she knew. Hadn't even questioned her about it. She wondered at that but just now thought it best she give Thomas her attention. "You get near enough the meetinghouse to catch anything the new preacher man said?"

"Nothing worth hearing," Thomas muttered.

" 'Slaves, obey your masters,' or the like?"

"Uh-huh."

Thomas said no more, but she knew it wasn't preaching words that had him glum. "Don't pay Jubal no mind. He's jealous over his place, is all."

"I don't aim to take his place," Thomas said as they passed under the big chestnut. "Long as I'm here, I aim to do my part. That's all."

"Long as you're here? You leaving anytime soon?"

"Just a manner of speaking."

His answer came quick enough, but she wondered . . . had Mister Ian decided not to stay after all and Thomas knew it? She was surprised to find she hoped that wasn't so.

"Give it time," she said, watching him close. "You'll find your place here."

Thomas paused at the kitchen breezeway, smiling at last, though her words held more hope than truth. Staying on at Mountain Laurel or going back to Boston aside, Mister Ian could up and sell Thomas tomorrow if he took a notion. Their lives hadn't been torn apart that way in many a year. Not since Ruby and her boys. Still the possibility always lurked. Like a spider in a corner beyond the reach of a broom.

"For now," she added, giving her voice starch as she eyed his brushed coat and striped hose, "change out of that frippery afore you dirty it and come whining to me to get it clean. I've laundry enough without you making extra."

Thomas's eyes sparkled. "Yes, ma'am," he said and swept his hat off to her.

Never mind his coat was worn and his buckled shoes scuffed—he made such a dandified picture, standing on the back stoop grinning, she went laughing down the breezeway thinking how maybe she'd like to draw him in those clothes.

She *did* hope they stayed. It was nice having cause to laugh.

His uncle was napping, Maisy informed Ian. "We having a nice supper this evening for Miss Judith's birthday, but I laid out some pickin's in the warming room. Miss Lucinda done stayed for tea with the Pryces?"

"Aye, they all did." Ian had evaded the invitation to take tea with the widow Pryce and her daughter at the conclusion of the church meeting by accepting one for the following Sunday, when the presently absent Gideon Pryce—the son and master—would be at Chesterfield to receive him.

Grabbing a biscuit from the sideboard, he headed for the stair. The heat hit him halfway up, a suffocating shroud. He propped open the window in his room, closed again in his absence.

Halfway through a change of clothes he heard the door across the passage open.

When he crossed to the storeroom, Thomas was sitting on the low stool, stripped to the waist, back glistening as he hunched over the trunk he used for a table, writing in what appeared to be a journal. Ian had seen the little book before, during those last days of their journey. Had the Quaker given it to him?

He leaned in the doorway, sweating in his thinnest shirt. "Ye're welcome to use my desk."

Thomas dipped the quill. "This suits me."

"Fine. But ye'd do well to keep the door shut while ye're at it. Ye're probably safe at present, but I doubt my kin would much regard the notion ye can read and write." He got no answer to that and frowned at Thomas's hunched back. "Thought you meant to see to the horses."

"Jubal has it in hand."

"What's wrong? Aren't my uncle's slaves welcoming ye to their bosoms?"

Thomas swiveled on the stool, scowling, but

his brows rose as he took in Ian's appearance. "You've left off the tomahawk. That intentional?"

Ian grinned. "Didn't want to alarm the housemaid." Along with a plain linen shirt, he'd donned the buckskin breeches, beaded belt, and hunting knife. "We've a few hours to ourselves before supper. We could traipse the wood. Explore some. It'd be cooler than inside."

Thomas gestured at the journal. "I mean to write for a spell."

"Suit yourself—but don't think ye've dodged my question. Ye've been in a sulk since we left the meetinghouse."

So had Ian, for that matter. As they'd approached the small frame meetinghouse that morning, on the edge of Chesterfield land, something in him had hoped for . . . what exactly, he still couldn't say. A sense of welcome? Acceptance? From whom? Had the congregants known his past or the state of his soul, they'd have quick enough tossed him out on his ear. At least no lightning bolts had fallen for his brazenness at being in their midst.

"I'm fine, Ian," Thomas said. "I've been told I'll find my place here in time."

"Did Seona tell ye so?" He'd seen them talking, coming up from the stable, but regretted mentioning the girl when what might have been a smile twitched Thomas's mouth. "At least she's taken a liking to ye."

"Seems so," Thomas agreed. There was no doubt about the smile now.

Eastbound clouds, white against dazzling blue, raced shadows across the ridge flanking his uncle's land. The sight fed Ian's soul, as did the moment's quiet, alone on the front veranda. While solitude suited his mood, idleness didn't. His hands wanted occupation. He flexed them, turning that revelation over like a fine piece of wood. He lacked a lathe, but he had his miter box, handsaws, planes, augers, chisels—and, admittedly, a rusty set of skills.

Only one remedy for that, and he'd promised Catriona, after all. He called her to mind, poised at the foot of his sickbed back in spring, furious as no one but a stripling of a sister could be that he'd run off to the wilds and stayed gone *five whole years,* only to slink back threatening to die of wound fever. But he might yet make it up to her.

'Tis a table desk you'll make for me, Ian. And I'll have none of that common fan embellishment on it. I want a desk with morning glories. *With as many morning glories as it will aesthetically sustain.*

An artist born, Catriona, one who knew her mind.

Ian's thoughts swirled now, designs blossoming from imaginary wood grain as his gaze wandered over the yard sloping down to the stables, where, deep in oak shade, Jubal sat oiling tack. Leaving the veranda, he strode across the drive and down the yard into the pungent scents of hay and manure, heavy on the warm air.

Jubal stood at his approach, cloth in hand. "Mister Ian, you be taking the roan back out?"

The man had likely just finished grooming Ruaidh after the ride back from meeting. "I may do. I'll see to him if so."

At the sound of his voice, Ruaidh's whinny pierced the air. Ian reached the box midway along the aisle and with gruff affection took the horse's questing head between his hands. A ride would be good, he decided, but before he could heft his saddle from a nearby bench, a high-pitched squeal rent the air.

Abandoning the saddle, Ian moved to the far doorway, open today to the rear stable-yard, and halted at the spectacle unfolding there.

Skirts kilted, bare feet flying, Seona and Esther were attempting to catch a shoat. Shaking with mirth, old Malcolm leaned against the farrowing pen, where a sow and the rest of her half-grown litter milled and grunted encouragement to the escapee.

"Esther—he's coming at you!"

"I see it!" Esther made a grab for the shoat, skinny arms closing round its hindquarters. "Be still you—ow!"

The shoat kicked free and bolted, aiming for

Seona, whose skirt chose the moment she lunged to come tumbling round her ankles. She tripped, landing in a heap. Dodging her, the shoat reached the pen and snuffled along its length in search of entry.

Malcolm bent to slap his knee. "That be one pertinacious wee pig, is all I can say!"

"Is that all?" Seona brushed her skirts down and stood, hair curling round her shoulders like a wind-driven cloud. She fixed Malcolm with a gimlet glare. "What use is a man if all he does is hang back spouting fancy words when his womenfolk need a hand?"

Impervious to this blaze of indignation, Malcolm shook his head. "No' a bit o' use, lassie!"

Esther hadn't taken her eyes off the rooting shoat. "Hush now! It ain't looking." She darted for it, but the pig was too quick. With a refractory grunt it dashed for the stable.

Though convulsed with silent laughter, Ian was ready. He burst from the shadows and swooped low as the shoat made to scoot past. Embracing the squealing pig like a barrel, he staggered into the yard, rolled, and fetched up on his back with the animal kicking at the sky. Its protests split the air, which had otherwise gone still. Ian pinned the struggling creature to his chest and peered between its ears at two wide-eyed faces, one dark, one honey-gold.

"That," he said, breathing hard, "is how ye catch a pig."

Malcolm wiped at tearing eyes. "Mister Ian, ye've saved the Reynolds' bacon. I dinna think these lasses would have shown it a scrap of mercy had they got their hands on it again."

Ian hoisted the animal in his arms and stood, surveying the pen. "This isn't one of ours?"

"Not no more it ain't." Indignation unlocked Esther's tongue. "It's the piglet Mister Reynold, over yon—" she waved in the direction of the wood beyond the house—"bought off Master Hugh. But *it* ain't cottoned to the notion."

" 'Tis the third time we've seen it back," Malcolm said.

"Huh-uh." Esther pushed out her bottom lip. "It's the *fourth*."

"Seems ye've an intractable case on your hands," Ian said and saw the corner of Seona's mouth curl.

"More fancy words from menfolk," she murmured.

"An incurable lot," Ian agreed. "Though hopefully I've atoned to some degree for the general uselessness of men." Clutching the shoat to his chest, he made them an old-fashioned leg.

Esther giggled, while color bloomed in Seona's cheeks.

"They're neighbors, then, the Reynolds?"

"Yes, sir," Seona said. "Mama looks in on Miss Cecily regular."

A page from his uncle's ledgers came to mind—a John Reynold owned a bordering tract of land, a parcel Hugh Cameron had sold off two years back—an instant before the shoat landed a kick to his ribs, and he winced.

"Esther, dinna stand gawping," Malcolm said. "Go tell Ally he's to take the pig back to Mister John."

"I've yet to meet the man," Ian said. "I'd be pleased to have occasion to do so—should someone care to show me the way." He flicked a glance at Seona, with a small surge of anticipation, but Esther was too quick.

"I'll show you, Mister Ian." The child shot toward the house before anyone could object, calling back, "Let me tell my mama where I'm bound."

"She's meant to be on her way to the kitchen." Seona brushed at her skirts, stirring up a musky sweetness from the folds. Lavender.

"Clever miss." Not bothering to hide his regret, Ian hoisted the pig under one arm and strode after the girl.

Mister Ian's hair had been tailed back Sunday-smart when he came lunging from the stable fit to scare her to death. Now it was tangled loose on his shoulders. Dirt streaked the back of his shirt. Though come morning she'd be the one scrubbing it clean, Seona reckoned it worth a kettle of laundry to see a white man do what he'd just done.

He wore a belt sewn with tiny colored beads and hung with a wicked-long knife. Indian stuff, she reckoned, as she watched him striding toward the house after Esther. Even with a kicking pig tucked under one arm, Mister Ian moved like a painter-cat, all golden and smooth.

Like a wildcat out the woods. Naomi had called that right.

A crumpled blue ribbon lay on the ground where he'd tackled the pig. Bending, she slipped it into her skirt pocket, glancing at Malcolm, who was staring toward the house too.

"Mister Ian doesna seem overworrit for his dignity," he observed.

"There's some would call that refreshing, for white folk." Seona gave her petticoat a final smack with the flat of her hand. "I best see how Mama and Naomi are getting on."

"Aye, ye do that. And give Mister Ian his hair ribbon back when next ye see him."

Seona marched off to the kitchen, not letting Malcolm see her burning face. Lily and Naomi were up to their elbows in baking when she came in. "Didn't y'all hear the ruckus in the yard?"

"We heard." Naomi added a handful of flour to something in a bowl, then clasped it to her bosom and set to stirring. "No time to stand gaping at that fool pig."

Lily folded a mound of dough and gave it a punch. "Who caught it this time?"

"You'll never guess—Mister Ian! He's toting it back, with Esther showing the way."

"That child." Naomi whacked her spoon against the bowl like it was a bare backside. "When I was a bitty thing, weren't no running off from this kitchen at the drop of a hat, never mind it be Sunday. As for Mister Ian—" she set the bowl down with a thunk—"reckon he could have found his way."

Seona's hand dipped into her pocket and found the ribbon, cool and silky. "You should've seen him, Naomi, rolling in the dirt and coming up with that pig in his arms, grinning like he'd hung the moon."

Lily was watching her. "It's not wise, going round Mister Ian with your hair unbound. I've told ye, girl-baby."

Sighing, Seona pulled her hand from her pocket and set to work on her rebellious hair, fingering it into a plait, yanking at hopeless snarls. Maisy could put Esther's hair in braids and it would stay put for days. Why couldn't hers have come out that way?

"Mama, what does *intractable* mean?"

"Where'd ye hear such a word?"

Her fingers flew, working down to the ends of

98

her hair. She thought of tying it off with the blue ribbon, then thought better. "Mister Ian said it of the Reynolds' pig."

"Can't mean nothing nice, then," Naomi said.

"What y'all making for the supper?"

"Green beans, beef and carrot pie, and later on a sugar cake."

Seona eyed a basket on the bench by the door, getting herself an idea. "Miss Judith fancies blueberries."

"She do," Naomi agreed. "But if she wanted blueberries on her birthday, she should've been born last month."

"There might be some left. Can't hurt to look."

"You done the weeding and picked the beans. No more you need do 'til supper. But your mama and me could *find* work for you to do, if you that bored." Naomi shot a meaningful glance at a row of carrots waiting to be chopped.

"Picking berries ain't work." Figuring a quick escape had worked for Esther, Seona snatched up the basket and ducked out the door.

6

"I've about had my fill of ye," Ian declared through gritted teeth. "Fractious, prickly wee . . ." Words failed him—decent ones at least.

He'd left Esther at the trail's fork with the child's assurance he'd find the Reynolds' cabin at the end of the right-hand branch. Near as he could figure, he'd trudged the instructed half mile farther, following the footpath—an erratic track no doubt blazed by inebriated deer—over, around, and all but under the wooded ridge. What had he to show for his good deed? A welter of bruises from thrashing hooves and a patience badly frayed.

Good deed. The thought reminded him unpleasantly of Benjamin Eden and another conversation with the Quaker—the one Thomas didn't know he'd overheard.

After argument had failed to dissuade Thomas from following him another mile south—and before the Quaker had seen through the slave charade—Ian had stalked off to be alone for a space, returning at dusk through a drizzling rain to find the camp shifted to a pine thicket for shelter. Ian had passed soft-footed under cover of the falling rain into the range of Eden's voice.

"I would speak a concern to thee, friend."

A pot lid had clanked; the smell of cooking beans had set Ian's mouth to watering. Keeping to shadows, he'd crept round the baggage for a better view.

Beneath the shelter of needled boughs, the Quaker had set up a campstool. A journal lay open on his knees. Firelight glinted off an inkwell nestled in pine straw at his feet, but the hand holding the quill had stilled. "Thee needn't go with this man. A house, and people disposed to aid thee, lies eastward on the Susquehanna. Or hast thee a wife or child in bondage, to hold thee to Ian Cameron?"

Squatting at the fire, Thomas stirred the beans. "Neither. Reckon Mastah Ian will look after me in Carolina. Won't let no meanness trouble me."

Eden leaned forward, intent. "Do not believe it, friend. I have observed the effects of slaveholding upon even a man deemed God-fearing. That narrative I see in thy possession says it best."

" 'But is not the slave trade entirely at war with the heart of man?' " Thomas quoted, as no slave ought to be able to do. " 'And surely that which is begun by breaking down the barriers of virtue involves in its continuance destruction to every principle . . .' "

Eden eyed him, startled but thoughtful. "Would thee say Ian Cameron is a God-fearing man?"

Silence fell, troubled by the rain's patter, the fire's snap, the sound of tree frogs in the wood.

101

Thomas said, "Don't know as it be my call to say who, or what, he fear."

"Surely 'tis thy concern," the Quaker pressed. "The acquiring of chattel wealth is a slow corruption to the soul. It will be to *his* soul. I entreat thee to consider my offer."

Thomas hadn't, of course—stubborn fool. Ian had made his presence known. Shortly after, Benjamin Eden had called Thomas's bluff.

Trudging through the trees with a pig thrashing in his arms, Ian shook off the memory—and promptly snagged his shirt shouldering through a clump of elderberry overhanging the path. Vexed and sweating, he tore free, broke through the tangle, and halted. Swelling warm on the air was the most tantalizing aroma he'd encountered outside the range of Naomi's kitchen.

Following his nose, he soon emerged from the thinning trees.

The Reynold cabin was a tidy affair, situated in a clearing skirted on three sides by woods, on the fourth by a cornfield planted up to the dooryard. Beyond the cabin rose a barn that dwarfed the dwelling. In the barn's shadow was a man, kneeling in the dirt by a fenced pen, hands slack, head bowed.

The man's head jerked up when the shoat loosed a squeal. He stood and came into the sunlight, black-haired and summer-bronzed, an expression of wonder on his mild features as he hurried to intercept Ian.

"Might I have the name of the man come bearing the most immediate answer to prayer I've ever received?" he called, not long out of London by his speech. "Or is it an angel I address, sent to restore our winter's bacon?"

Before Ian could reply to either query, a second voice spoke. "*Certainement, chéri.* An angel he is. With that hair, what else?"

Ian tossed a tangle of *that hair* from his eyes as a woman emerged from the cabin. Like the man she was dark-haired, though her features were fine, her skin porcelain-fair, her belly vastly swollen with child. The shoat gave *his* belly another kick. Wincing through his teeth, Ian said, "I doubt an angel would have employed the language I've had cause to utter since taking up acquaintance with your . . . *pig.*"

The man's smile broadened. "I daresay the creature would try a saint's patience."

"I'm hardly that. Ian Cameron, nephew to your neighbor at Mountain Laurel, and I'd shake your hand if relieved of this burden."

"At once, then."

The transfer was made, squeals and flailing notwithstanding. Ian passed a grimed shirtsleeve across his brow. "Ye've my gratitude, sir."

The man hoisted the heavy shoat for a better grip. "John Reynold. And the gratitude is mine.

We were discussing which to undertake first, chasing down this rogue or repairing its pen, when I looked up to see you striding from the wood, pig returned, predicament solved."

"We?" Ian glanced beyond the man toward the barn for sign of a third party—a son, perhaps, or servant.

"The Almighty and I." Ian snapped his gaze back to find John Reynold smiling, in earnest. "But look you—the matter of a handshake lies between us."

Ian's mouth twitched. "My hands are at liberty."

"Whereas mine . . . as you see." Humor glinted in Reynold's brown eyes. "What say you? How do we proceed?"

"*Bouffon.*" Reynold's wife shook her head. "Put the little scoundrel in the cabin, *s'il te plaît.* I will distract it with sweet rolls while you repair its abode."

"Madam," Ian said, "I'll not presume the offer of sweet rolls for scoundrels extends to me, but if I may be so bold—I'd have walked twice the distance with yon wee hellion kicking me every step for a whiff of whatever that is ye're baking."

The woman beamed. "*Merci vraiment.* For your trouble you shall have better than a whiff."

Reynold thrust the shoat into the cabin and shut the door. "Ian Cameron, may I present my wife, Marguerite Cécile Louise Reynold."

Reynold's very pregnant wife was dressed in

homespun, besmeared with flour, yet there was an air about her that made Ian want to doff his hat—had he worn one. He bowed as she dipped an awkward curtsy.

"I am happy to make your acquaintance, Mr. Cameron," she said. "You will not start for home without your promised reward?"

Ian drew an exaggerated sniff. "Wouldn't dream of it, ma'am."

"*Bien.* But you must call me Cecily, as I am named since leaving France." Exultant grunts issued from the cabin; alarm widened Cecily Reynold's eyes. "I for the present must leave you to John. *Merci.*"

As his wife wedged herself through the opened door, unleashing a barrage of French upon the shoat, John Reynold turned to Ian. "If you'll permit me the comparison, I feel rather like Job."

Scrambling through his dusty recollection of Old Testament Scripture, Ian frowned. "I don't recall Job's wife baking sweet rolls to comfort him in his trials."

"Verily. It was the book's last chapter I had in mind. 'So the Lord blessed the latter end of Job more than his beginning.' "

Ian shot him a wry glance. "Ye've a pig raising a ruckus in your cabin and the dubious honor of my company."

"And should you have both time and

inclination," Reynold said, "I'd ask you to honor me with the latter whilst I attend to the former."

"I'll lend ye more than company, if another pair of hands can serve."

Reynold gave Ian's shoulder an amiable thump, then regarded the knife at his belt. "You've showed yourself a proper hand at catching pigs. How do you whittling pegs?"

"Oh," Ian replied as nonchalantly as he could, "I'm told I've some skill with wood."

They sat in the porch shade, soiled, sweating, replete with the satisfaction of a finished task— and sweet rolls that tasted even better than they'd smelled. John Reynold licked a crumb from his finger. "Normally I'd refrain from such work on the Sabbath, but necessity is unmindful of the day it visits."

"Necessity? Is that what ye're calling yon pig?" Ian bent a nod toward the fugitive, reinstated in its pen.

"Perhaps I shall!" Reynold's laughter was full. "Thankfully we've a God as rich in common sense as He is humor. It was our Lord, after all, who said, 'Which of you shall have an ass or an ox fallen into a pit, and will not straightway pull him out on the sabbath day?' Though I note He makes no mention of pigs."

Laughing in his turn, Ian studied the man. Reynold made no attempt to hide his religion, and yet . . . "Did I miss ye and your wife at service this morn?"

"If you mean at Pryce's meeting, we weren't in attendance. The Reverend Wilkes and I hold a certain strongly opposing view which has rendered me unwelcome amongst his congregants." Reynold reached for a gourd hung from a water barrel by the door, dipped it full, and took a swallow. "I'd live in peace with my neighbors, as our Lord bids, but I cannot sit quiet in a pew whilst bondage is condoned—even championed—from the pulpit."

Ian eyed the man but saw no evidence of censure directed at him—the nephew of a slave-owning planter. "One might venture to say ye've fetched up at the wrong end of the country, given such sensibilities."

"One might. But the Lord knows what He's about. Here He planted us, and here we'll sink our roots." Reynold offered the gourd. More to Ian's present interest was bread. One sweet roll remained between them. His neighbor read his straying glance but made no move to thwart him.

Ian shooed a questing fly, hesitated, then tore the roll in half. Reynold took his portion with a solemn nod, acknowledging the sacrifice.

Ian leaned against the cabin wall, stretched his legs until the toes of his boots caught a sliver of sunlight at the porch's edge, and surveyed the homestead. They might be largely at rest on this Sabbath day, but the orderliness of the place testified to the Reynolds' industry during the other six. The man had related his story while they'd worked. At twenty-six, after his father's death, Reynold had sailed for the newly independent United States with funds from the sale of the family's London tailor shop. He met Cecily aboard ship, fleeing the turbulent revolution in France. They were wed in Wilmington. Months later, having traveled deep into the Piedmont, Reynold purchased fifty acres from Hugh Cameron, built a cabin, cleared a hill, and planted it in Indian corn.

Ian, in turn, had told of his years spent fur-trapping in Canada—for which efforts he'd far less to show.

"We've our own Sabbath meeting here," Reynold said now. "A family from over the ridge—the Allens—and a fellow by name of Charles Spencer. It's a small attendance, unless you count Charlie's hounds." Reynold gestured westward, beyond the cornstalks, to the rising hills. "I expect him anytime. He's wont to come early, to claim his spot in the hay."

"Ye hold your meeting in the barn?"

"We do. And you're welcome to join us."

"It's kindly offered," Ian replied, "but I should start back. There's a supper later that would be imprudent of me to miss." He stood to take his leave but asked, "Has my uncle ever come here—to worship with ye?"

"I've invited your kin. They've never come."

Ian couldn't imagine his aunt and cousins abandoning the society of Chesterfield for straw in their hair and manure on their shoes.

"Tell me something, Ian." Reynold's chin lifted askance, as though he were trying to catch a distant sound. "By your speech I judge you Scotland-born, though I'm guessing you've lived most of your life this side of the Atlantic, with the past few years, by your own accounting, on the frontier. Why have you come to Carolina?"

The question, and the man's uncanny accuracy, startled. Ian caught his gaze, which was guileless as the day was warm. "Och, awa' wi' ye," he said, easing into the broad speech of his mother's kin. "Ye kent who and what I was when I came oot o' the wood totin' yer bacon. Own it, man."

Reynold rubbed the back of his neck, then broke into his easy smile. "There's little news doesn't find its way to the mill before long. But I didn't learn of you by hearsay. Your uncle told me, after he wrote to you, late last winter."

"Then ye know why I'm here." Ian's grin faded under Reynold's scrutiny.

"I know why your uncle sent for you," his neighbor corrected easily. "Not why you've come."

7

Ian cupped his hands in the creek's flow to bathe his sweating face. He'd spent longer than intended with the Reynolds. He liked the Englishman, despite the fact their last exchange troubled him like a pebble lodged in his boot.

I know why your uncle sent for you. Not why you've come.

"For my sins," Ian had quipped, then mumbled something about a broken apprenticeship, familial disappointment, his uncle Callum refusing to take him back to Canada. "It was best I left Boston and I'd nowhere else to go." He'd shrugged as though speaking of it didn't cause his chest to ache. "I mean to—hope to—settle to a life that will atone, I suppose."

Reynold had regarded him, head tilted in that odd, listening way. "Without vision the people perish," he'd said, leaving Ian baffled as to his meaning. He hadn't asked, hadn't wanted to pitch camp on the discomfiting topic.

Removing his neckcloth, Ian used it to douse himself head to shoulders, letting the creek water trickle beneath his open shirt, then shook his dripping hair back from his face. He'd lost his ribbon. No knowing where. The bitty things were as shifty in his keeping as the Reynolds' shoat.

Squinting through the boughs overhead, he judged he'd still time to make himself presentable before showing his face at table. He was a dozen yards farther along the path when he heard the voice, distant but clear.

"Och, will ye hark to her now."

Hand falling to his knife, he scanned the stone-pocked ridge rising on his left, then downslope through the wood on his right. No matter his uncle owned this land, much of it was virgin forest. Cover enough for bear or panther—or man—to pass unseen. Not necessarily unheard.

"Come here to me, love."

Certain the voice had issued from a point upstream, where the creek tumbled from the higher ridge, Ian stepped off the trail. The land rose under him, rocky, rooty, brush-tangled, but intermittent comments from above drew him on.

"Will ye no' gang wi' me, lass?"

"Aye, she'll go," Ian muttered. "Ye both shall, once I ferret ye out."

He ascended by handholds the last few yards, grasping a woody laurel shrub to haul himself over a final rise.

Before him the creek cut into the hillside for the distance of a stone's throw, before the ridge's higher slopes folded in to form a hollow where birch trees clustered, knee-deep in ferns and mossy stones. Sunlight lanced their mottled trunks. Through them he glimpsed lichen-speckled stone outcroppings mounting the slope beyond, creating a sort of curved wall over which the stream spilled in a narrow, glassy waterfall, twice a man's height.

The setting was unexpected, yet he'd the oddest sense of having seen the place before.

Then he caught what he'd come seeking: a flash of faded-blue cloth, deep within the grove, near the base of the waterfall. He marked a path through the ferns, plotting his approach.

A harsh *kruk* rent the stillness. Then a woman's voice spoke.

"Hush, now. Let me finish."

He stalked the unsuspecting pair, guided by the patch of blue. It broadened into the curve of a shoulder. The woman's, surely. He still saw no sign of the first speaker. The man. Pierced by suspicion, Ian paused and scanned his back trail, then the hollow to left and right.

Nothing. Only the woman. Had the man climbed farther up the ridge?

He pressed forward. The shoulder he'd spied dipped to a slender waist, brushed by dark tumbled ringlets. *Seona.*

She sat on a rock, back turned nearly full to him. At her bare feet spread a pool that deepened over a stony basin, into which the waterfall emptied. A basket, nestled in the grass beside her, held what appeared to be a scattering of half-withered blueberries. They weren't on her mind at present, however. Grasping the last tree separating them, Ian leaned out.

Across her lap lay a yellowed scrap of paper, over which her hand moved in short, purposeful strokes. He shifted for a better view; beneath his boot a stick snapped.

Seona sprang up, whirling to face him as something large and black—a raven—launched from behind the rock, startling him back a pace as it took wing.

He recovered almost instantly from surprise. Seona had already thrust the paper behind her back, but knowledge of it blazed from her eyes.

He stepped from the birches, coming to stand before her. "What are ye doing?"

Her eyes darted sidelong, as though she, too, contemplated flight. Then, resignedly, she brought forth what was hidden and held it out to him. The paper was damp where she'd clenched it with fingers smudged a telltale black, but there was no writing on it. Not even letters. Ringing the paper's ragged border were charcoal sketches of the raven's head, with a full-bodied likeness of the bird in the center, rendered down to the delineation of its feathers and a sparkle of life in the dark-beaded eye.

Ian felt his heart rush a beat as admiration—appreciation, astonishment even—flooded him. Mere accuracy couldn't have quickened his artistic sensibilities the way these drawings were doing. There was life on the page, an expression of joy that robbed him of speech. Seona was staring at her feet. A tendril of her hair lifted on the breeze and pressed against her cheek.

"These are good," he said at last. "Good as most book illustrations I've seen. Better than some."

Her head jerked up. He watched her face as the meaning of his words took hold. For an instant she seemed startled, pleased even. Then her eyes flicked up at him, wary.

"It ain't writing."

He almost smiled at that. "No, it isn't." And he'd never heard that drawing was forbidden to slaves. Was that the point she was making? Or was it forbidden, and she hoped he wouldn't know that?

He considered the sketches again, drinking in the grace of line and proportion. "And clearly this isn't the first ye've attempted this."

She hesitated, a flinch of her brows the only indication the question rattled her. Forbidden or not, she didn't like that he'd caught her at it.

"I been making pictures since . . . since I was little."

He could believe it. Her skill spoke of untold hours' work. Where had she found those hours? He glanced at the basket and its meager gleaning of berries and suppressed another smile. "Does anyone ken what it is ye can do? Has anyone seen?" When she shook her head, eyes veiled by downswept lashes, he asked, "Not even Lily?"

"No one knows, Mister Ian." She pulled her lower lip between her teeth. "Except you."

So she had kept it secret, for whatever reason. It struck him that, unless she was lying to him, she'd never heard her drawing praised. Moreover, whatever satisfaction she'd derived from the pursuit would have been tainted by dread of this very thing. Discovery. It hadn't stopped her doing it.

He'd had that heart's affair with woodworking, once upon a time. Seeing it here, in this unlikely manifestation, he yearned for it again.

"It's true, Seona. These are very good." He saw no response to his praise now. "Is this a thing ye oughtn't to be doing?"

Her brows drew together. Fear strained her features. "I . . . I reckon Miss Lucinda wouldn't like it."

He wondered what his aunt's reaction would be if she knew. Putting a stop to it, no doubt. Exacting some sort of punishment besides?

"Mister Ian, what you meaning to do?"

The fragile sense of connection with her dissolved as he realized *he*—her master's kin— *was* meant to do something. He drew breath, not knowing what he intended to say until the words left his mouth. "I'll keep your secret, Seona."

Silence followed, screaming with mistrust. "Why?"

"Why?" he echoed, even as the possible implication seared through his mind—as it must have been racing through hers. He grew conscious of her hair loose in the breeze, the curve of her waist, the dark-lashed eyes that stunned with their vivid green. He couldn't prevent the surge of heat in his face and sounded more defensive than he'd meant to when he said, "Because I won't be the one to quench a gift such as yours, nor see ye punished for creating something beautiful."

Her eyes flared in surprise. She frowned but took the paper he held out to her.

"Have ye others? Other pictures? Where d'ye keep them?"

It was clear on her face the instant she resigned herself and her secret to his keeping. "Above your head when you sleep at night."

"The garret?"

"Yes, sir."

Wind shifted the white boughs above them. Sunlight streamed over her, striking sparks down the length of her hair. Not a true black, as he'd thought, it glinted bronze where the sun touched it. She lifted her eyes and stared at the base of his throat. He was standing close to her, towering like a reeking bear, hair dripping down the open neck of his shirt, clothing streaked with sweat and barn filth. He stepped back.

It was then he felt the prickle at the base of his

skull. He tensed, certain of being watched.

The man. He'd gone clean out of mind. But though he scanned the place, there was no one. Only the raven, perched in a lone birch tree across the pool, into which it had flown when he'd startled it. He swung to face Seona again. "Was it the raven ye were speaking to?"

She'd been staring at him but slid her eyes away. "Yes, sir."

A moment before, when he'd praised her drawing, her expression had been as transparent as he'd ever seen on a slave's face. Now she was closed to him, her features a mask, and he felt as he had those first weeks with his uncle Callum among the Chippewa, stumbling over a bafflingly nuanced language, striving for subtlety and missing the mark by a mile. To blazes with subtlety, then.

"Seona, who was speaking to *ye*? Where has he gone?"

"Nowhere, Mister Ian."

"Are ye lying to me again?"

"Again?" Understanding rippled over her features and she rushed on to say, "I didn't lie that day, about the filly. Esther talked me into sneaking to the stable—after I saw you in the parlor."

That he could believe. Maisy's daughter had a quick tongue and apparently knew how to use it to get her way. Still, he was all but certain

117

Seona was lying now. The voice he'd heard had belonged to a Scot or someone who spoke as one. Malcolm? The notion of the old man out in the wood wooing a lass young enough to be his great-granddaughter was absurd.

"Who are ye protecting? Another of my uncle's slaves?"

He'd made no threatening move, yet she stepped back, pointing across the pool. "Mister Ian—he's right there. You heard that old raven talking. Here—" She thrust the drawing at him and raised her arm.

Ian ducked as the raven launched toward them, swept past his face, and settled with a flapping of wings on Seona's outstretched forearm. It balanced there a moment, then hopped down to a moss-dappled stone to eye them.

Ian lowered himself onto the rock she'd vacated, just a wee bit rattled. "It's a tame raven?"

Seona crouched in front of the bird, fingers clamped over her sleeve where the raven had perched. "Not so tame as it was. Master Hugh's son had it from a chick."

"My cousin, ye mean?" The rock beneath him, the leaf-filtered light, the drawing in his hand—all felt insubstantial, as though in stepping into the birch hollow, he'd fallen into a dream. Or a painting of a dream . . . that was where he'd seen this place. The painting in the parlor. "Seona,

118

it must be fifteen years since Aidan Cameron died."

"Longer back than that. Afore I was born."

"How old are ye?" he asked, suddenly curious.

"Ten years and eight."

She was of an age with Judith. That took him aback. Judith seemed barely out of girlhood, whereas Seona . . . no need to be told her childhood, such as it had been, had ended long ago.

"He taught the raven to speak, did Aidan?"

"I don't know as he set out to teach him," Seona said, gazing at the bird. "More like Munin picked up speech on his own, being nigh Mister Aidan all the time. So Mama tells it."

He frowned. "What did ye call it—the raven?"

"Munin. From a book, Mama said."

Ian minded his da's inscription in the book of Norse legends above his uncle's desk, clear as if he read the words afresh. " 'I fear for Hugin lest he fare not back,' " he quoted. " 'Yet I watch the more for Munin.' "

Seona's eyes widened. "You know those words?"

"My da sent that book to Uncle Hugh. We've a copy in Boston." He paused, staring at the raven. "Thought and memory . . ." Seeing her puzzlement, he explained, "The ravens in the story that line's from, that's what their names mean. *Hugin* is thought. *Munin* is memory. Each dawn

119

the Norse god, Odin, sent the pair to fly over the world, acting his spies. They'd return and perch on his shoulder to whisper the secrets of men."

She smiled at that, a light in her eyes. "Mama once said be careful what you tell a raven. They don't keep secrets."

A breeze stirred, brushing the curls from her face. The sun had deepened her skin to a light-cinnamon hue across the bridge of her nose. Along the delicate turn of her collarbones. The hollow between.

Such thoughts fled when a third voice said, "I fear for Hugin."

Ian stared at the raven, the flesh of his scalp crawling. The enunciation of the words, their tonal quality, was uncannily human, but the bird hadn't spoken with any voice he recognized. If ravens were mimics—and apparently they were—was the voice that had drawn him to the hollow that of his long-dead cousin?

Or the raven's memory of it.

"Mister Aidan was fond of animals," Seona was saying. "Mama says there was a doe he had from a fawn. It would eat from his hand like a hound. It went back wild after—" She broke off as a cloud darted over the sun, throwing the hollow into shadow. She stood, on her face a dawning comprehension that matched Ian's own.

"Judith's supper," he said.

Seona snatched up the basket at their feet.

120

From the pocket of her petticoat she tugged a cap. Something else slipped out. A length of blue ribbon that fluttered to the ground.

"I found that in the stable-yard." She bent for it and thrust it at him. "Mister Ian, I got to get back. Naomi's gonna skin me."

"That'll never do." Ian pocketed the ribbon. The raven was still there, eyeing him from its stony perch. Quelling the absurd urge to bid it farewell, he led the way back through the birches, reaching to help Seona over the first steep drop. He grasped her arm to steady her but released her when she winced. Crimson splotched the edge of her sleeve.

Ignoring her protests, he pushed it up to bare her forearm. Small wounds marred her skin where the raven's talons had gripped. "Ye'll have Lily look at these?"

"There ain't time."

"I'll take the blame if supper's late. Let Lily clean them, first thing."

The drawing had fallen. It had lodged in the branches of a laurel. He untangled it and on impulse asked, "Would ye mind if I kept this?"

Furrows formed between her brows. "What you meaning to do with it?"

"Treasure it." He rolled the scrap of paper with care and gave her what he hoped was a reassuring smile. "It isn't every day a man discovers such a wonder in the wood."

8

Seona snapped a cucumber off its stem and dropped it into her basket, then paused to listen. There was some big doings, out behind the garden. Mister Ian, Master Hugh, and Thomas had gone inside the old cooper shed that had been shut up since Malcolm's rheumatics got so bad. She'd watched through a crack in the garden pales as they unbolted the door and filed inside. For a spell not a sound had come. Then a racket of nail-banging commenced. She'd picked every cucumber she could spot fit for pickling before Master Hugh and Mister Ian stepped back out into the sunlight.

" 'Tis generous of ye, Uncle," Mister Ian said.

"This is your home now, lad. Ye've a right to make use of it. Malcolm can give your man a hand getting started."

What Mister Ian said to that last mystifying statement got buried under the scuff of their boots on the gravel path as they passed out of hearing.

Seona sat back on her heels, biting her lip in thought. Though she'd kept out of Mister Ian's sight as much as possible since he caught her in the hollow, knowing he held her secret—and her drawing—was like a fly buzzing round her brain, worrying her to distraction. What was he up to now?

Naomi was alone in the kitchen, kneading bread dough for the house table, when Seona came in with the cucumbers. "Put them on the table. Now I need grape leaves and dill."

"All right." Seona spied the leftovers from breakfast. "You got plans for this bite of pone?"

"Have it if you hungry," Naomi said.

"Thought I'd carry it to Thomas afore I get on with the wash—and fetch those leaves and dill."

"You figure he didn't get breakfast enough with the rest of us?" Naomi's chuckle filled the kitchen. "Go on. Might get you some news ahead of Esther for once. Maisy got her busy in the house."

Armed with the corn pone wrapped in a towel and a jar of buttermilk from the morning's churning, Seona stood on the threshold of the cooper shed. The smell of cut wood sparked memories of the years Malcolm had spent his days shaving oak staves for the hogsheads Master Hugh's tobacco went to market in. Another set of doors took up the shop's far end, which faced the work-yard shared by the washhouse. They stood open. By the light pouring through, she saw the shed wasn't long for being one big space. The end where she stood was being portioned off by pine planks raised to a half wall.

She stepped inside and set her offering on an upturned barrel. "Brought you this," she said, loud enough to carry over the hammering.

Up popped Thomas from behind the half wall. He spied her, set down his hammer, and came out brushing his hands. "My stomach must be gnawing louder than my hammering." He unwrapped the pone, downed it in two bites, drained the buttermilk, and came up smirking through a milky mustache ringed with crumbs.

Seona thrust the towel at him. "I never seen a man make more mess with his vittles. Wipe your face." While he did, she eyed the shed with its dusty tool racks, shaving horses, and jointers pushed against the wall. "What they got you doing in this old shed? Mister Ian putting you to some proper work at last?"

"That's the short of it." Thomas dropped the towel on the barrel, scattering crumbs.

"And the long? What is it you do?"

"Coopering, girl. From time I was twelve."

She wondered what a trained cooper could have done to get himself sold off to Mister Ian. Sassed the wrong boss man, most like.

She made a circuit of the shed, running fingers over dusty hammers, saws, and drawknives. She turned a half-finished stave over in her hands, then brushed off the gritty film it left in the folds of her petticoat.

"We ain't had a regular cooper since Malcolm got where he couldn't carry on."

Thomas was watching her. "Why didn't your master buy another to do the work?"

"He bought two. One ran off after a week. The Jackdaw never found him. Another was so pitiful lazy, Master Hugh turned round and sold him again."

She came back to the barrel. Thomas had those scanty brows pushed high. "Jackdaw? That what you call Jackson Dawes—when he ain't by to hear?"

She shrugged. "It's a kind of crow. From England or someplace. Mama told me."

"I know what it is. Jackdaw ain't the nicest bird, I hear. But clever like a crow. Steals pretty things it takes a fancy to. I wonder how your mama knows that."

She wondered that herself but only shrugged again. "What's this wall going up for?"

"Master Ian. He'll be working up front there."

"What sort of work?"

"He didn't tell you he's a cabinetmaker?"

She stiffened. "Why should Mister Ian tell me anything?"

Thomas's smirk returned. "You never know with him. He don't always do what's expected and does plenty that isn't. I could tell you stories."

Her quick glance betrayed her interest, so she asked, "What stories?"

"For starters, he left his indenture with a cabinetmaker afore he was meant to. Got his journeyman papers signed anyway but something

125

about it fell out wrong. Master Ian came home claiming he'd no more heart for cabinetmaking. Caused a mighty rift."

"With who?"

"His daddy mainly but his mama was nowise pleased either."

"How do you know all this?"

Thomas's mouth flattened. "I rode by his side for four hundred miles. We talked." Seeming to mind he was meant to be working, he stooped for a board, settled it into place, and drove a nail through it.

"Reckon Mister Ian got his heart back," she said. "For cabinetmaking, I mean."

"Or he's already bored with farming."

What with the hammering, Seona wasn't sure she'd caught those muttered words.

"Heard them mention a sawmill hereabouts."

Having heard *that* just fine, Seona felt her stomach curl into a ball. "Over to Chesterfield."

"That's right. Said this Gideon Pryce brings fine lumber up from Fayetteville. But Master Ian took a shine to that seasoned maple there." Thomas nodded toward a dusty pile of lumber resting on wall racks. "Promised his sister back in Boston he'd make her a table desk." The grin he flashed was impudence itself. "You heard enough yet about Master Ian to make bringing me that johnnycake worth your while?"

"More'n I bargained for." Annoyed at being found out, she took up the jar and towel.

"Bide a moment now." Thomas put aside the hammer and closed the space between them in two strides. "I got questions too."

She gripped the jar tighter. "What questions?"

"To start with, how's a girl white as you come to be a slave to Master Ian's kin?"

The question shocked her speechless. At last she sputtered, "I—I ain't *white*."

Thomas grabbed her wrist and turned it over, fingers dark against her skin. "Near as can be and *not* be, then. Master Ian took you for his cousin, first time he laid eyes on you."

"How do you know that?"

"I was standing right there. Neither of you had attention to spare, though." Still holding her wrist, with the other hand he took up a spiral of hair worked loose from her kerchief. "This hair now. Tells me some great-granddaddy of yours likely made the Middle Passage—same as mine. But you got Indian in you, too."

Seona jerked her head, wincing as her hair pulled free of his grasp. "You know who my mama is. But *her* mama—"

"It's who your daddy is got me wondering," Thomas interrupted. "Can't imagine it's the Jackdaw, though I don't guess Lily would've had much say in the matter."

She'd had the thought before, sick-making

127

though it was. Jackson Dawes had never made claim on her, and he never bothered her mama, but he'd been there working for Master Hugh longer than she'd been drawing breath.

"But I don't see aught of Jackson Dawes in you," Thomas went on. "I *could* see your daddy being Hugh Cameron, which would make you the one should be mistress here and ol' Mastah Ian could just take himself back—"

She wrenched out of his grasp so hard the jar fell and shattered.

"Now look!" She crouched to scoop the milky pottery shards into the towel.

"It's my fault, Seona. Let me clear it up."

She ignored his offer. "You gonna tell Miss Lucinda why her dairy's a jar short?"

Humor darted in Thomas's eyes when she stood, like all there was between them was a broken jar. "Put one from the kitchen in its place."

"Never you mind what I do about it. I got work waiting on me."

"I expect you do."

His composure needled her, but she clamped her lips shut and fled the shop, letting him have the last word.

No breeze stirred the misty hollows or scattered dew from the ferns edging the path to the Reynolds'. Birdsong filled the upper reaches of the hardwoods, but down below all was still . . .

128

until a familiar flash of blue through the trees ahead caught Ian's eye.

Hoisting his rifle, he lengthened his stride. When at last she heard his approach along the path, she whirled to face him. He slowed as he neared, watching her expression shift from alarm to wariness.

"I've startled ye again," he said, smiling in apology. "Ye're bound for the Reynolds' too?"

"Yes, sir." She turned to continue, treading the path a step ahead. "Mama was to visit Miss Cecily this morn. Then she got called to mend that rose gown Miss Rosalyn means to wear to Chesterfield."

He watched the end of her braid, an explosion of curls swinging just above her waist. "John Reynold's stony field be thanked, I've evaded another encounter with the denizens of Chesterfield. D'ye think I'll be forgiven?"

Seona's gaze stayed fixed on the path ahead. "I reckon, Mister Ian."

Truth, his cousins and aunt were more than a bit put out with him. He'd refused to alter his plans to help John Reynold harvest stones from his cleared acres when the women changed their Chesterfield visit from Sunday to Saturday, after learning Gideon Pryce would again be away on business—to Hillsborough this time—the following morn.

"Have ye been to Chesterfield?" he asked,

thinking like as not she'd little to do with the wealthiest of their neighbors, who from all accounts lived like lords of the eastern seaboard in their grand Piedmont abode.

"Yes, sir," she said. "A few times."

Surprised, he asked, "And do the Pryces call at Mountain Laurel?"

"Not often."

The path widened. He moved up beside her. In the cool morning light her profile seemed stronger, her mother's blood evident in her prominent cheekbones and raven-wing brows. He wondered if she'd returned to the hollow in the past week, or if it was a place she only went on Sundays, the only day his uncle's slaves had mostly to themselves. He hoped he hadn't scared her off the place. The few times their paths had crossed since that encounter, he'd barely gotten a word out before she was lowering her eyes and scurrying off to perform some urgent task.

Avoiding him?

"I've not seen much of ye, these past days."

"No, sir." Her shoulders rose in a shrug. Or was it a flinch?

"I realize there's been trouble of late at the house. Everyone adjusting to how things are now." Just yesterday there'd been a blowup over Thomas, who'd left the house through the front door, right under the noses of Ian's cousins. Ian hadn't decided if it had been a moment of absentmindedness on Thomas's part or flagrant flaunting of his aunt's wishes. "No blame if ye've taken to lying low 'til the dust settles."

The forest around them was waking by degrees as they walked. Chittering squirrels joined the birds. A small breeze came down the ridge, pushing the mist off with it, whispering in the tops of the hardwoods, ruffling Seona's kerchief.

"House business ain't my trouble, Mister Ian."

"Am I your trouble?" He'd asked it under his breath, but loud enough.

Seona quickened her pace. Pretending not to have heard? He slowed his step to study her. She had been avoiding him. She was doing it now.

"I never meant to be," he said, too soft for her to hear.

Save for the finches darting among the garden sunflowers, the Reynolds' yard was still. The shoat, resigned to captivity, lay on its side in its refurbished sty, a pale blotch in the barn's shadow. The animal kicked a hoof but otherwise ignored their arrival. Not so the cow. It bawled from its pen in obvious distress, its bag distended. On its heels another cry came, so thin and muffled Ian thought he'd imagined it.

The next was louder.

Seona halted when he did, shooting him a look that froze him with dread. "Mama says it'll be a boy," she blurted, then sprinted toward the cabin.

They found Cecily Reynold at the foot of the bedstead, a sheet pooled round her on the plank floor. Ian hung back as Seona rushed to her side. A spindle wound with scarlet had fallen from the table, the thread snarled across the cabin like a trail of blood. He set his rifle down and bent to gather it up. He was still winding thread when Seona rose and came to him.

"Mister John went early to the field. Miss Cecily was to tell you to meet him there."

He tried not to gape at Cecily, at her belly stretching taut the thin fabric of her shift. "D'ye want me to go for him? Or for Lily?"

Seona reached for a chair back and gripped it hard. "Mister Ian, I don't think there's time for either. First babies generally come slow, but this one's in a hurry."

On the cabin floor Cecily groaned.

Ian felt the blood leave his face. The panic in Seona's eyes mirrored his own. He took a hard grip on his nerves and said, "Aye. Tell me what to do."

Relief rippled over her features. "Can you get her onto the birthing stool?"

He slipped off his canteen, then found the chair she meant tucked beside a clothespress. He'd seen the like before, high-backed with sturdy arms, the seat cut away to a crescent. He set it where Seona directed, between the hearth and the bed, then bent to John's wife. Her hair was plastered to her brow, dark as seaweed.

"Cecily, I'm going to lift ye." She was surprisingly heavy, the child a hard bulge against his ribs. A turn, a step, and he eased her down on the birthing stool. She gripped the arms of the chair and cried out.

In the short time that had taken, Seona had stoked the fire under the kettle and was already scrubbing with lye soap. "Wash up, Mister Ian, if you aim to help me."

Lathered to his wrists, he asked, low-voiced, "Ye've done this before, aye?"

"With Mama." Her face was stiff with fear, but when she turned to Cecily, she'd composed herself and radiated nothing but confidence. Whether it was the slave's trick again, donning a mask that hid all true feeling, he couldn't tell, but he'd an instant to be glad she hadn't hidden her fear from him.

For the next hour he did his best to slide gracefully into as complete a reversal of roles as he'd experienced. Seona gave the orders. He obeyed. Between the fetching of clean cloths, warm water, boiled twine, or the vial of oil Lily had left for this moment, his eyes followed Seona, who performed the mysteries of a midwife with an air of capable calm, ministering reassurance to their neighbor—in the process to him—from the instant she took charge until the wrenching, jubilant moment the Reynolds' firstborn issued, red-faced and squalling, into her waiting hands.

. . .

Ian sat on the split-log bench outside the Reynolds' cabin door, sweat still drying at his temples. He'd done a bit of barn work, milked the long-suffering cow. The covered pail rested at his feet, while inside, the women's voices softly rose and fell. He let his head droop, feeling wrung, though he knew he hadn't done the true work. That had been Cecily. And Seona.

"Ian?"

He jerked his head up to see John Reynold standing at the edge of the cornfield. "John!" Ian sprang to his feet, stricken that he'd nearly dozed off. He'd only meant to rest a moment before fetching John from the distant field.

The man flashed a puzzled smile, black hair shining in the sunlight. "I put in two hours' work waiting on you, and here I find you idling outside my cabin?"

The urge to laugh filled Ian's chest. "I wouldn't exactly call it *idling*."

"Mister John?" Seona had stepped into the doorway beside him, holding a damp rag, her face still radiant with joy. "You want to come inside and meet your son?"

A matching joy warmed Ian's chest as a newborn's mewling cry broke the morning quiet and John came toward them, running.

9

By the time Seona returned with news of the birthing, the morning's cool had vanished. Sweat prickled under her head-rag as she swept the parlor grate and longed for summer's end. Her absence had vexed Miss Lucinda, who'd snapped off a list of extra house chores to fill her day since Lily would need to spend the next few at the Reynolds' tending Miss Cecily and the baby, and Maisy was to go to Chesterfield.

Better Maisy than Seona. Thought of visiting Chesterfield was enough to make her run for the hollow—even if Mister Ian knew she went there.

He was back now too, since John Reynold had given up stone-grubbing for the day. She heard his voice from Master Hugh's room down the passage but didn't pause her work to make out what he was saying. Miss Judith was perched on the settle with a book, waiting for her sister to get over fussing with her hair so they could go.

Seona dumped the ash sweepings in the piggin and set to polishing the tongs, thoughts turning to Miss Cecily's baby with his tiny fingers and toes that she'd been first on this earth to count. Trouble was, Mister Ian had got himself wound round every thought of that baby, tight as thread on a bobbin.

She'd never bossed a white man like she'd bossed him around that little cabin.

"Were you afraid?"

The question shattered her thoughts. The tongs clanked as she set them back in their stand. "Beg pardon, Miss Judith?"

The book lay open on Miss Judith's lap. Her clear brown eyes were fixed on Seona. "I've never seen a baby's borning. It's a blessing Cousin Ian was there to help you. But . . . what was it like?"

It was terrifying. It was nerve-rattling. It was joyous. Where did she even begin?

"It was a miracle."

Mister Ian's voice went through her like a blade. He'd come to stand in the parlor doorway, wearing finer clothes than those he'd worn for field work, buckled shoes instead of boots.

"One day ye'll know what it's like," he said, coming into the room. "Better than anyone could explain it to ye. Or I hope ye will."

Miss Judith's cheeks went bright as beets. Seona hid a smile. None of them heard Miss Rosalyn descend the stairs in her dainty shoes until she said, "What do you hope, Cousin? That we'll have a pleasant visit to Chesterfield?"

Seona set to work polishing the andirons, watching the rest of them sidelong.

Miss Rosalyn came into the parlor, giving off a scent like a dousing of syrup as she took Mister

136

Ian's hand in hers. "It would add immeasurably to our pleasure if you'd stop feigning busyness and join us in paying our neighbors a call."

Ian's smile seemed a mite stiff. "I just welcomed the newest of them into the world, aye?"

"Goose!" Miss Rosalyn hit playfully at his arm. "I don't mean the Reynolds. Come with us to Chesterfield—for some proper society."

Miss Judith added her plea. "Would you, Cousin? Since Mr. Reynold won't be working his field today after all?"

Before Mister Ian could utter a word, Miss Lucinda swept into the parlor. "I did hear you speak of wanting to see Pryce's mill, Mr. Cameron."

Mister Ian appeared for an instant like a deer strayed into a hunter's camp. Then he fixed another smile on his face. "Since ye put it so persuasively, I'll just go saddle my horse."

Delighted exclamations ushered him from the room. Seona lowered her eyes but felt a prickle between her shoulders.

"We must take a girl along, Mama," Miss Rosalyn said. "Phyllida says it's still done so in Virginia, when one goes calling."

"I've said we'll take Maisy."

Drawing a breath of relief, Seona set the andirons back in place. Nothing left but to tote out the ashes. She stood.

"Stay," Miss Rosalyn told her. "Mama, let's take Seona instead."

Miss Judith shut her book. "I don't think she wants—"

Miss Rosalyn shot her a silencing glare, then smiled at Seona. "You'd like to see Chesterfield again, wouldn't you? It would be a treat, after that messy business you had to attend this morning."

Seona clenched the piggin's handle. Her mouth felt stuffed with rags. "If Miss Lucinda says."

"*I* say," Miss Rosalyn snapped. "Go put on something decent and be quick about it."

Miss Lucinda sighed, then gestured at the ash piggin. "Leave that for Maisy. Go wash your face. You look as though you've rolled in the hearth."

The snare was sprung too fast for sidestepping. "Yes, ma'am." Seona dropped a wobbly curtsy, setting down the piggin so hard it nearly overturned. She hurried past Miss Rosalyn, who smiled, pleased as a cat whisker-deep in cream.

Sunlight spilled over the stacked mahogany, setting the top planks ablaze. They were warm to the touch, as though the red heartwood pulsed beneath Ian's fingertips. While the vertical blade at the mill's far end gnashed its way through some lesser wood, while gears creaked and water splashed and the sawyer barked orders at the slaves guiding the carriage, Ian filled his lungs with wood-scent and gave himself over to longing.

"From a West Indies shipment, transported upriver a month past." Dressed in a coat tapered smartly away at midchest, Gideon Pryce stood in the center of those gathered in the lumber room, a walled annex far enough removed from the mill's main floor to be heard without shouting. "Beautiful, is it not, Mr. Cameron?"

Ian forbore dissembling. "Aye, it is. And ye'd charge me my firstborn for it, no doubt."

Hugh Cameron snorted, but Pryce smiled complacently. The man was near thirty, dark-haired, with eyes the murky green of pond water. Beneath their placid surfaces, shadows teemed.

"I may be persuaded to part with this hoard without so great a sacrifice on your part."

Ian raised a brow. "What have ye in mind?"

"A ship's captain of my acquaintance is soon to put into Wilmington with another Indies cargo. He's willing to see it brought upriver as far as Fayetteville, contingent upon my finding a market for the wood. I'd meant to do so in Hillsborough in the coming week, but my sister tells me you're a cabinetmaker, that you mean to practice the trade at Mountain Laurel."

The implied question hung in the wood-dusted air. "I am," Ian said, and though plans beyond the desk for Catriona remained as unformed as the mahogany his fingers longed to stroke again, he added, "and I do."

"And I," said Pryce, smoothing the ruffled neckcloth at his throat, "am a man in need of another cooper's skill."

Ian turned toward Thomas, hovering at the doorway. His uncle had suggested they bring him along to choose wood for the hogsheads he'd be making for Mountain Laurel's tobacco crop, there being no time for seasoning their own—but they hadn't yet mentioned the need to Pryce, nor the fact that Thomas was a cooper.

"News flows like water in these hills, Nephew," his uncle said. "And generally has its confluence here at the mill."

"If I may offer a caution." Pryce leaned close, giving off a whiff of pipe tobacco and a musky lavender cologne. "Do heed your words in the presence of our womenfolk. They've a means of communication I've yet to uncover—trained pigeons, I daresay. What one hears at breakfast, the others know by luncheon. But leaving aside such feminine mysteries . . . It is true, then—your boy's a cooper?"

"He is," Ian said, attempting to mask his wariness.

"I was obliged to rid myself of my best some months back. Skilled as he was, he wouldn't stay put. Doubt I ever took the lash to a back as often as I did that buck, but I never hit upon a measure

140

that would curb his running. Sold the fool south to the rice fields."

A shudder vibrated through the boards beneath Ian's feet as the log on the carriage came apart. The noise of the blade momentarily hushed.

"Point of the matter is," Pryce continued, "I'm left with a curing crop that will need prizing. I was set to inquire toward Hillsborough for hogsheads to make up what we cannot supply when I heard Mountain Laurel had gained a cooper along with a kinsman. I've the workspace, the tools, and of course . . ." He gestured to the stacks of oak overflowing the lumber room.

"If ye wish him to take on the work, Nephew, it could be done at Mountain Laurel," Uncle Hugh suggested. "We've everything there but the wood."

Tiredness shadowed his uncle's eyes. Though surprised he'd decided to join the family outing, Ian was glad of his presence. "Aye, that might be best. Malcolm's there to give Thomas a hand."

"Begging your pardon, Mastah Ian, but Malcolm ain't got hands to spare from the work he already do." Everyone turned toward Thomas, who raised a shrug. "Why move the lumber when it's easier to move me?"

"A fair point, if brazenly made," Pryce said, turning a frown on Thomas. "Are you minded to stay put and do as you're bid, boy?"

Ian hoped he was the only one who noted the brief flash of rancor before Thomas stood straight, his face a careful blank. "Yes, sir."

Alarm bells ringing, Ian moved to intervene. "Thomas—"

Pryce lifted a hand. "Do hear me out before you decide, Mr. Cameron. I see you are loath to lose his labor, but might you consider trading just a week of your boy's exclusive time for . . . half the mahogany here?"

Despite his every intent to decline, Ian allowed himself to envision what he'd do with the wood, until Pryce once again addressed Thomas. "I have observed a skilled cooper turn out eight barrels in a day. What say you to that?"

Thomas grinned. "This one turns out nine, sir— on a good day."

"Excellent," Pryce said. "Well, Mr. Cameron? If you can spare him, shall I have the keeping of your boy for a week?"

They'd dropped their horses back from Pryce and his uncle as they rode up the lane to Chesterfield House. Ian reined in close, brushing knees with Thomas. Wood-lust had overcome him long enough for his better sense to crumble; he'd made the deal, but around that cooling passion now unease was trickling in. "Does my uncle treat his slaves better than ye looked for? Ye need to see how Pryce's fare?"

Thomas's hat brim shaded his eyes, but Ian knew that tightening of lip.

"It's what I came here for."

Ian jerked his head toward Pryce's back. "Just do the work and don't provoke him, aye? If ye end up striped like a tabby cat, I'll be tempted to do the man harm."

Judging by all he'd witnessed at the mill, Pryce was respected by his neighbors. He was cordial, gracious, his manners refined. Yet something about the man troubled Ian, beyond the admittance of brutal punishment of recalcitrant slaves. Perhaps it was those eyes, so strangely flat. Like those of the sharks he'd seen as a boy, landed by fishermen on the wharves of Boston, Pryce's eyes had borne no relation to his smiling mouth.

After Thomas was shown to the cooperage and left to get settled, they found the women taking tea on a wide veranda reached through a series of high-ceilinged rooms. The veranda was deep in shade, though sunlight drenched an ornamental garden beyond.

"Here they are, Mama." Rosalyn rose, advancing toward Pryce with a hand extended, over which he bowed. She favored him with a smile, then freed her hand and took Ian by the arm. "Cousin, do give your opinion. Miss Josephine has told us of a marvel some fellow in Georgia has contrived, meant to be the salvation of us all. It's to do with cotton."

She led him to chairs arranged near a table bearing an elaborate tea service. Ian made his greeting to his hostesses, the widow Josephine Pryce and her daughter, Phyllida, dark-haired like her brother, before taking the seat Rosalyn all but pushed him into. Pryce took the chair next to Uncle Hugh. A slave began serving.

Seona stepped from behind his aunt's chair to assist. Ian's glance flicked to her while she arranged a plate with a slice of cake, then moved around the circle to offer it to his uncle. Her shoulders were rigid as she turned, revealing the seated figure of Gideon Pryce, eyeing her, nostrils flared like a hound catching scent.

"Faith, Mr. Cameron. We craved your opinion, but I vow you've not attended to a word Mama has said."

Phyllida Pryce's teasing rebuke recaptured Ian's attention.

"Does the warmth of the day cause you languor, Mr. Cameron?" Josephine Pryce inquired, her own face shining in the humidity despite a layer of powder. "You'll be unaccustomed to our Southern climes, I daresay."

"A fair observation, ma'am. Forgive my inattention." Forcing a smile, Ian accepted a cup of tea from Pryce's maid.

Lucinda revived the faltering conversation. "Josephine has been informing us of this so-called cotton engine."

"*Gin,* Mama," Rosalyn cut in. "It's called a gin."

"Yes, darling. But now Mr. Pryce is here, perhaps he'll oblige us with a thorough explanation?"

"Ye dinna propose leaving off wi' tobacco?" Uncle Hugh asked, turning to their host.

"That," Pryce said, "is precisely what I propose. You may remember my cousin Edward Stoddard?"

"Aye," Uncle Hugh said. "The merchant."

"Back in spring he visited a Georgia plantation, home of Caty Green, widow of the late war general," Pryce continued. "During his stay a young man employed as tutor for the family's children—Whitney, he's called—unveiled his model of a cotton gin to a group of planters. It caused a sensation."

While Pryce spoke, Seona offered Ian a slice of cake. A tremor shook the chinaware as he took it from her hand. He let his fingers cover hers, holding her with a questioning look. She shook her head almost imperceptibly and moved away.

"Stoddard rendered a version of the gin on paper before returning north," Pryce was saying. "I've a copy of the plans. I'll show it to you— once we've finished entertaining the ladies."

Pryce had paused to stare at Ian, who returned it, asking, "How does the device improve upon the current system?"

The man gave a condescending laugh. "The problem with cotton *is* the current system, as any Southern planter knows. The difficulty lies in separating the seeds from the fibers, a vexing process. Presently it takes a pair of hands a day to clean a pound of cotton. Using Whitney's contrivance, those same hands could manage fifty pounds."

Lucinda leaned forward in her chair. "How is that possible?"

"Because, Mrs. Cameron, this engine has *teeth*. It devours the cotton and spits out the seeds." Pryce paused for the expected murmurs of appreciative laughter, then went on to explain the device in less picturesque detail.

"Sounds as if anyone wi' a bit of carpentry skill could reproduce a working model," Uncle Hugh said with guarded interest. "Does Whitney hold a patent for the device?"

With everyone served, Seona had returned to his aunt's chair, yet her unease ran like a current across the veranda floor. Pryce flicked another glance at her.

Ian felt the skin of his face grow taut.

"There was talk of securing a patent," Pryce admitted. "But if the gin proves as revolutionary as it appears on paper, a patent won't stop its common usage. Those overly concerned with such particulars are bound to do themselves a disservice."

"He who dithers is lost?" Rosalyn interjected.

"Or she," Pryce replied, one brow pointedly raised.

A tinge of pink crept into her cheeks. "Cousin Ian would construct the finest cotton gin in the Old North State, should he set himself to do so."

"Your confidence is flattering," Ian said. "But ye've yet to see me craft so much as a dovetail joint."

Rosalyn took his hand in hers and proceeded to trace his callused palm with a fingertip. The intimacy of the touch sent a jolt through him. His hand closed on hers—to halt rather than hold.

Rosalyn raised her eyes and fixed not him, but Pryce, in her blue gaze. "I can tell."

Ian pulled his hand away. He set his plate on the table, cake untouched.

"Transitioning to cotton," Uncle Hugh said, seemingly oblivious to his stepdaughter's coquetry, "would demand a considerable labor force and an outlay in capital."

Pryce shifted his attention smoothly. "True. I'll be in the market for field hands come winter."

Rosalyn sat back with a tiny huff. "Winter? I could wish for a breath of it now. I've left my fan in the carriage. Do fetch it, Seona."

"Yes, ma'am." Seona curtsied and hurried off the long veranda.

Ian watched her go, until Rosalyn placed a hand on his arm.

"It's bound to be cooler under those maples yonder. I see a breeze ruffling them now. Shall we take a turn through the garden, Cousin, while we wait for Seona?"

"Let's join them," Phyllida said, beckoning to Judith. "Mama?"

Josephine Pryce waved a lazy hand, declaring herself more inclined toward a nap than a stroll. Phyllida's brother, still discussing the merits of cotton with Ian's aunt and uncle, paid them no heed.

The ornamental garden wasn't large, but the hedges were tall enough to interrupt the view of the veranda. Ian and his escort made a turn around its inner perimeter, the girls chattering about the widow at whose plantation the cotton gin had had its genesis.

"A friend in Virginia, whose parents are particular companions of the Washingtons," Phyllida said, "wrote that Caty Greene stood up with the president at assembly and danced *three hours straight,* without so much as a pause for punch."

Through the hedges Ian glimpsed his uncle on the veranda, filling his pipe. Lucinda and Josephine Pryce had moved off to examine a piece of stitching in a standing frame, while the housemaid tidied the table. Though she'd had ample time to complete her errand, there was no sign of Seona. Nor of Gideon Pryce.

"This won't do, Mr. Cameron. You've let us prattle on since we left the veranda, which is hardly fair."

Ian blinked down into Phyllida's shining eyes as the girl clasped his arm.

"We've been discussing a ball, Cousin," Rosalyn said, taking possessive grip of his other arm. "But Judith and I have failed to learn whether or not you favor dancing."

"Surely you dance, Mr. Cameron?" Phyllida inquired.

Judith, bereft of an arm to cling to, waited hopefully.

"Poorly, I fear." When next he caught a glimpse, the tableau on the veranda was unchanged. "I've no objections to a ball, though I may safely say dancing three thirsty hours straight is a feat I'm not likely to match."

"You *were* attending to our conversation," said Phyllida. "How sly you are, Mr. Cameron!"

Not sly enough by half.

"Begging your pardon, ladies. I should see how Thomas is getting on."

Ignoring their protests, he detached himself and struck out in the direction Seona had taken, toward the side of the house connected to the summer kitchen. When he turned a corner to be confronted by a cluster of framed buildings, he halted. The few slaves he saw ducked quickly out of sight. He was on the verge of shouting for

149

Seona when the shrubbery at the corner of the nearest building shivered, though the breeze had died.

"Mister Gideon, please. Miss Rosalyn—"

"Can wait."

Ian rounded the structure to find Seona backed into a gap in the hedge, pinned against the clapboards by the hips and hands of Gideon Pryce, who was bending his face to hers. She twisted away and saw him. "Mister Ian!"

Pryce pushed away from her. Seona stumbled through the hedge, putting Ian between herself and Pryce, who emerged from the shrubbery with slow deliberation, tugging at rumpled clothing.

His cousin's fan lay on the ground. Ian retrieved it and held it out to Seona. "Go." She went, leaving him glaring at Pryce. "What the devil d'ye think ye're doing?"

Pryce lifted a careless shoulder. "You can hardly blame me, tempting a piece as she is."

Ian's hands convulsed. He imagined the crunch of the man's teeth against his knuckles, felt them break loose from their moorings, felt the wet spurt of blood.

Though he held himself rigid, whatever Pryce saw in his face made him step back, but he covered the retreat with a calculating smirk. "Fancy yourself a knight to her rescue? An admirable sentiment, though hardly appropriate."

"I doubt my uncle would approve of such

interference with his property, which makes it very appropriate, I should think."

"Whether or not he approves, I expect he's allowed it a time or two."

"Allowed?" Ian echoed, before he understood. Seona herself was living proof.

Awareness of their surroundings penetrated his rage. The cluster of buildings appeared unnaturally deserted, until he caught sight of a tiny child wobbling in the doorway of a nearby cabin. The round little body was sugar-brown, head crowned with a mop of loose black curls. A darker hand reached from the cabin's depths and drew the child from sight.

Ian fixed Chesterfield's master with a level stare. "Do as ye will with your own slaves, Pryce. Don't trifle with my uncle's again."

Pryce's mouth smiled pleasantly. "Marking your territory?"

"Ye might say."

"Well then. As it seems we've boundaries to settle between us, might I ask . . . does your fair cousin, Miss Bell, lie within your newly marked precincts?"

"Rosalyn? How d'ye mean?"

"I'm referring to her display earlier." Pryce batted his fingers as if in a caress. "You'll admit, having witnessed the lady take such liberties upon your person, a man might presume he'd been displaced in her affections."

"I hold no claim on her affections . . . as yet."
Sheer perverseness made him add that last.
"And have *ye* some understanding of which I'm
unaware? Ye'll admit I've more than a passing
interest in the matter—as her kinsman."

"There's no formal understanding between us."
The *as yet* went unspoken, but Ian heard it plain.
Pryce gestured toward the house. "I'm certain
our absence has been remarked upon. Shall we
rejoin your uncle and the women?"

Ian stood his ground, forcing Pryce to turn his
back and lead the way.

"I wondered where the pair of ye'd gone, and
why ye were so grim-faced when ye returned."
Wrapped in a banyan, seated at his desk, Hugh
Cameron swore—scathingly. "Though he's never
been so bold as to outright suggest it, Pryce has
hinted the debt I owe him would be canceled
should I give him Seona."

Ian perched on a bench at the foot of his uncle's
bed, rigid as the polished hickory supporting
him. He'd waited until they returned to Mountain
Laurel, and supper past, to inform his uncle of
the encounter with Pryce and Seona. "He'll not
have another chance to trifle with her behind
your back, sir. But what's this about owing the
man?" Ian gestured at the ledgers on his uncle's
desk. "I never saw—"

It was at that point his aunt intruded, cotton

on her mind; she'd been present when Pryce unrolled the plans for the gin. It took her several effusive seconds, however, to register their tight-lipped faces and demand explanation for such dour countenances.

"That won't do at all," she said in alarm, when informed of Pryce's attempted violation of Seona. "I'll not have white babies among the servants. Why not give her to Will? The buck has asked for her often enough."

Ian had risen at her entry. "Has he, Aunt?"

"Will has a woman," his uncle said. "At Chesterfield."

"And whose are the babies he gets on her?" Lucinda's mouth pinched over the words. "Put him to Seona and they'll be ours."

Ian started to protest but his uncle was swifter. "Lucinda, all I mean to say concerning Seona is this: she willna attend ye to Chesterfield again. If ye wish a servant along when ye visit, take Maisy. As for cotton, I dinna mean to risk our livelihood on such a venture 'til I've thought the matter through—and ken Ian's mind on it."

"Indeed?" Lucinda scorched him with a glance before she turned on her heel and left them.

Uncle Hugh deflated at her going, sinking into his chair. "Ye asked me about the debt owing Pryce," he said, as if his wife hadn't interrupted. "He's acted my factor, informally, these past three years. His connections to markets reach a deal farther than mine. But more than that, the man's made me a cash loan, of which I've no' paid back a shilling. Ye won't find record of it in the ledgers," he added. "Lucinda doesna ken."

Ian absorbed the information but, unwilling to be sidetracked, asked, "Did ye mean it, about Seona?"

"I'll keep the lass from Pryce's reach, but I'll no' take up the matter against him since no lasting harm was done. Can ye abide wi' that?"

Could Seona?

"As long as nothing of the like happens again," Ian said.

Beyond the slatted blinds darkness had fallen to the chirp of crickets, audible through the glass. Uncle Hugh appeared in dire need of his bed.

"Ye guarded my back today, Nephew."

"I cannot say it was my pleasure, but I'm glad I was there to prevent . . ." What was it his uncle had called it? "Lasting harm."

His uncle studied him in silence before asking, "Ye'll be staying on, then?"

The question caught Ian unprepared. There was an instant when panic fluttered beneath his breastbone, another when he might have acted upon it and offered some refusal—ended it all then and there. He steadied himself and it passed.

"I'd thought ye'd wish to be certain before ye committed to *me*."

Likely it was the wavering candlelight, but

for an instant Ian thought he saw a glint of desperation in his uncle's weary eyes. "Lad, dinna be daft. I'm certain. I only need ken that ye are."

Seona stepped from the warming room, candle in hand, as Ian shut the door to his uncle's room. He met her at the back stair. "On your way to sleep?"

She stood on the bottom step, eye-to-eye with him. The candle, set in a cracked clay dish, threw shadows on her tired face. "Yes, sir. I'm done for the day."

Done in was nearer the truth. He glanced back along the passage to the lamp-glow from the parlor: Maisy putting the house to rights. He kept his voice low. "Are ye all right?"

"I'm fine, Mister Ian."

"Has Gideon Pryce bothered ye before today?" He caught the tiniest flinch of her features before she shook her head. He took the candle from her, lifting it to better read her face. "D'ye tell me true?"

Her lips pressed tight; then she said, "I don't want no trouble."

"There won't be trouble."

She raised her eyes, their expression almost pitying as she sighed. "One other time he got me cornered, put his hands on me. Like today."

The saucer's edge cut into his palm. "When?"

"Back in summer. Out in the washhouse one

155

day he was visiting. He's never done no worse than what you saw."

He thought of her pinned, face twisted with revulsion, fear. The candle wavered in his hand, spilling hot wax down his wrist. She snatched it from him an instant before the flame doused. "Your hand—"

"It's fine." The pain was quick to pass. "Go on to bed now."

She started to obey but paused on the turning of the stair when he said her name.

"Had I known how it was with Pryce, I'd have prevented your going today. Ye never need go there again. I've settled that with my uncle. But should Pryce come here and trouble ye at all . . . find me."

The candle flame danced in the fanning of her breath. "Then what?"

Ian felt the wax on his flesh crack as his hand curled tight. "I've skinned wolves before, aye? I'll skin another before I let one harm ye."

PART II

September–October 1793

What did you see when we were here together? Did you speak of it? Or did you ride away North again with the Knowledge shut up in your Soul, and me never knowing? Until now.

10

The table desk had taken form beneath his hands, dovetailed corners tight-fitted, moldings and edges smoothed. A swipe of the rag removed the sanded residue from the slanted top. Ian tossed the cloth aside. Eyes closed, he shut out the smell of shavings and glue, everything but the silken wood over which his fingertips now glided. His right hand paused, described a circle, and again. *Just there.* A spot that needed another sanding.

He'd long denied himself the gratification of shaping seasoned hardwood into a thing of beauty—not since he left the Pringles and their troubled home. But he'd held on to the memories of countless hours in Wilburt Pringle's shop and all the master cabinetmaker had taught him. They'd flooded back since he'd commenced crafting the desk, most of them good memories of like-minded souls engaged in fulfilling work.

Only in one regard had he set his heels in opposition to the status quo of Pringle's shop. Had he built this desk under Pringle's guidance, the man would have insisted he stain it with lampblack, Spanish brown, or some other darkening agent. To Ian's mind, if the wood was quality, then a piece needed no finish save an application of beeswax and turpentine rubbed into the grain and buffed to a mellow sheen. He'd debated the issue with Pringle a dozen times, those final months of his apprenticeship. As for his sister's desk, the seasoned maple would age like wine, deepening through subtle tones of amber until it darkened to honeyed brown.

But he was getting ahead of himself. The true challenge still lay before him: the design for the drawer face that would make this piece uniquely Catriona's.

"Morning glories," he murmured, as though his sister hovered at his elbow. "I've not forgotten."

He opened his eyes to see Seona in the doorway, clutching a tray covered with checked linen. It was a mild day, with a teasing presage of autumn in the air. Below her kerchief the dark cloud of her hair moved like a live thing on the breeze.

"You missed dinner, Mister Ian." She set the tray on a bench inside the door and lifted the cloth from a bowl heaped with dinner leavings. The long-ignored gnawing in his middle made itself audibly known.

"Just in time," he said, wiping his hands down his leather apron. He transferred the bowl and a cup of the season's first pressed cider to the workbench. Seona stepped back as though to leave. "Would ye bide while I eat? I'll make quick work of it."

"Thomas said he'd leave his shavings for kindling. I could gather those."

160

Had she come there before now to visit Thomas? Briefly he watched her move toward the rear of the shop, where Thomas had left off carving barrel staves the day they went to Chesterfield, then began an assault on the dinner she'd brought him. While he ate, he flipped through his battered copy of Chippendale's directory, perusing it for patterns that might suggest the morning glories his sister desired, something to serve as a basis for the half-formed design he had in mind. He didn't want a spray of blossoms in the center of the outer drawer—too like the commonplace fan embellishments Catriona had spurned.

Something less regimented was in order. An entwining pattern perhaps, suggestive of the climbing-vine quality of her favorite flowers?

He could with reasonable competence carve such a design from a well-sketched pattern, but the vision was beyond his rusty skill to reproduce on paper, and he'd no intention of ruining good maple attempting to transfer the image straight from his head to the wood.

He dabbed a crumb from the bowl and wiped his mouth with the cloth, turning pages.

"You finished, Mister Ian?"

Seona had fetched up at his side, apron bundled around the gathered shavings. She stole a glance at the desk. He pretended to misunderstand her question. "I've work yet to do before it can be called finished. It's meant for my younger sister and she's a demanding patron."

Seeming unaware of his scrutiny, she made a study of the desk's lines. He wondered if she liked it, and if so, would she tell him?

"What's your sister called?" she asked.

"Her given name's Catriona. She prefers to be called Cat, though Mam makes every attempt to forbid it." That drew a hint of a smile. Encouraged, he went on, "She'll outgrow the notion and be properly Catriona before long. Though I allow we've spoilt her, being the youngest and only girl. A table desk she's wanting and here I am setting about it, five years and more out of practice." He hoped she might remark upon the desk at last, but her mind was fixed on its intended recipient.

"Does your sister look like you?"

He thought about that, then with the back of a knuckle tapped his chin with its slight cleft. "We all inherited the Cameron chin—me, Catriona, our brother, Ned. But Catriona's hair is like my da's. Darker, almost red. Not as red as Uncle Hugh's used to be." He raised the desk lid and stepped back. The interior was empty save for the long, shallow drawers lining the back. "For her brushes, pencils, bits of chalk," he explained. "Catriona's an artist. Like ye."

A shadow in the door-yard made Seona start. Only a passing cloud dimming the brightness of the day. "We'd hear anyone coming," he said.

She relaxed enough to finger one of the brass handles laid out on the bench. "Did you make these?"

"I bought them years ago, thinking this would be my life's work. Da kept them for me, while I was in Canada." He pulled the outer drawer until it was halfway open. "Look here. D'ye notice aught unusual?"

"The wood's a different kind? On the inside, I mean."

Not the answer he'd looked for, but he nodded. "Aye. It's common practice to use an inferior wood for the parts that won't be seen. And since I'm revealing the mysteries of my trade, have another keek at that drawer."

Seona peered within, then stepped back to study the case's exterior. "The drawers inside are shallow to make room for other stuff to go in, but this one on the outside . . ." She opened the outer drawer further. "It goes underneath the bottom of the main part inside, but it don't look as deep as it could be. Why's that?"

"Reach in and see."

Still clutching the bulging apron with one hand, she reached inside the drawer and felt along its floor, then its sides.

"Run your fingers along the back," he suggested.

"Oh . . . there's a latch. It's tiny."

"Pull it toward ye."

There was a click. She yanked her hand back as though it had been a snake's rattle, then with a grin she bit down on to suppress, felt inside again. "The back panel's fallen down. There's a space tucked behind. That's clever, Mister Ian."

He felt a surge of pleasure. "I've never made a secret compartment before, but Catriona was insistent. Took a little time to devise it."

"Compartment," Seona repeated, as though trying out the word. She tilted a look at him. "What would your sister be wanting to hide?"

He blinked at her. "I never thought to wonder. But that's what she wants. A secret compartment. And morning glories."

"Morning glories . . . you mean some kind of fancy work to pretty it up?"

"Carved across the drawer front—here." He made a bracket with his hands to show her the area, then set the pattern book between them and began turning the pages. Slowly.

She leaned close, pointing to a page of stylized roses. "Like these?"

"More like a flowering vine, I'm thinking. I haven't any drawings of the sort I need, though."

A strand of her hair lay dark against the linen of her sleeve. Without thinking he lifted it, seeing in its coil an echo of the design trapped in his head. She stilled at his touch, while he stared with dawning speculation. "Seona . . . I can manage the carving but was never much of a hand at sketching. Would ye care to give it a try?"

"Draw something for your sister's desk?" Astonishment took hold of her features, and something else he'd almost have called eagerness, before it was snuffed like a candle's guttered flame. "I best not, Mister Ian."

She reached for the bowl, preparing to go. He put a hand on her arm. "No one else knows what ye do. We'd be careful, aye?"

"I don't know. . . ." She bit her lower lip, indecision palpable. He waited, uncertain which way she would swing. At last she said, barely above a whisper, "What would I draw with?"

He held back the grin straining to break free. "Ye've never held a quill, I take it? No? What about a lead?"

"No, sir. Just bits of charcoal." He could see the pulse at the base of her throat, hammering to match his own. "But if you got one to lend me . . . reckon I could learn."

Little Robin Reynold's head lay warm in the bend of Seona's arm, under the dogwood where they'd spread a coverlet to sit.

Miss Cecily leaned in close. "You see, Seona? He is looking at you."

Seona doubted four days was old enough to be seeing her face clearly. Her mama would know, but since Miss Cecily and her baby were thriving,

Lily had been called back to work at home. It was Seona who'd come to collect the birthing fee Miss Lucinda named—one of Miss Cecily's fine laying hens—and snatch herself a visit.

It was balm to sit in the dogwood shade with a breeze cooling her neck, putting off thought of the endless work waiting back down the footpath. Laundry in the washhouse, apples to press, summer's last garden gleanings to put up for the winter. What was waiting in Mister Ian's shop . . . She couldn't have put that out of mind had she wanted to.

After dinner had been served and cleaned up, she'd slipped in to find him looking over the sketches of morning glory vines she'd added to his book of drawings over the past two days— and known right off he liked how she'd put that lead-stick to work.

"Especially this one," he'd said, pointing to her own favorite. "There's good movement in this one."

That had puzzled her. "Mister Ian, it ain't moving. How could it?"

He'd laughed softly, then bent near and traced the drawing with a fingertip. "See how ye've drawn the main vine to coil left to right, yet the flowers and this smaller tendril at the end turn the eye back over the design? That's what I mean. It keeps your *eye* moving."

Such a notion hadn't entered her head when

she arranged the bit of vine cut from the garden pales. All she'd done was poke at it until how it lay pleased her, not thinking why. The way Mister Ian talked about her drawing was like showing her a door in the big house to a room she never knew was there. Turned out it was more than just her fancy, why certain of her drawings pleased her more than others. *Principles of design,* he called it.

With her head so crowded with *principles,* she'd near forgot she was meant to go fetch the hen from Miss Cecily. When she'd said as much, Mister Ian had asked did she mind his company on the way since he wanted to go see Mister John.

Only thing she minded were the questions piling up in her head, budging up against all those *principles.* Things to ask Mister Ian—about drawing, about his sister the artist, about the desk he was building, about his life before he came to them—would tumble through her thoughts when she was weeding the garden or boiling wash or doing a dozen other things. But whenever he was nigh, the two of them shut up in the shop, she couldn't squeeze a one past her lips. She'd sit on a low stool behind him, skirt hiding the bit of vine laid out on the floor. If anyone came seeking Mister Ian—or her—she'd tuck what she was doing out of sight and pretend to be gathering wood shavings. He let some fall for her to gather, just in case.

She didn't dare speak of it to a soul at home.

No matter what Mister Ian said, she couldn't shake the fear someone would put a stop to it, or worse, if she got caught. Yet there was such joy in what she was doing it made her want to dance and shout. And *tell* someone.

"*Comment ça va?*"

It was the question Miss Cecily always started with when she got a notion to teach Seona some French words. She scrambled for the ones she already knew. "*Ça va . . . bien.*"

She laid the baby on the coverlet in the dappled shade, feeling Miss Cecily eyeing her.

"You are different today, Seona. *Dis-moi, je t'en prie?*"

Would she tell her? "I don't know if I can."

Miss Cecily's head tilted. "Is it the language over which you stumble? Then never mind the French. Just tell me."

Seona glanced toward the cornfield, where Mister Ian and John Reynold had gone to check the crop. Turning back, she caught the hope on Miss Cecily's face. Before she lost the tiny scrap of courage to do so, she blurted, "Mister Ian's letting me draw for him. I'm helping him with a desk he's making. I been drawing the likeness of things since I was a girl. But no one else knows."

Miss Cecily's slender dark brows soared high. "Seona, *alors*. That is . . . *magnifique.*"

Magnificent. It was that. And mighty frightening.

"But you have done this drawing in secret,

you say?" Miss Cecily asked. "How then did Ian come to know this of you?"

Seona touched the baby's cheek. His eyelids minded her of flower petals, so fine-veined. She minded how blue Mister Ian's eyes had looked when he praised her drawings, the warm-wood smell of his hair when he bent near.

"I never meant him to know," she said. "He found me out."

The Reynolds' corn stood tall, tasseled ears thrusting through brown blades. John peeled back a husk to reveal the kernels.

"Soon?" Ian asked, peering at the ear.

"Very. This hot summer dried the ears early. The green corn ripened early too." As they headed for the cabin, John tossed a grin over his shoulder, pressing through the stalks in his wake. "Ever been to a corn-shucking?"

"I'm a town lad, John. My father raises books." And the people of Callum Lindsay's settlement had had different traditions.

"Town lad, eh?" John quirked a brow at the tomahawk adorning Ian's belt. "You should come, then. It's a deal of work, but quite the frolic, too. Singing, dancing—"

"Sweet rolls?"

"Absolutely."

"I'll be there," Ian promised. "So, is it to be tobacco in the new field, or Indian corn?"

John paused, letting him catch up. "There's some swear tobacco's what a man must seed if his farm's to profit him. But I'm convinced it's too hard on the soil."

"Aye. So I've gathered. I'll be clearing some of my uncle's higher acreage for new planting come spring."

"Your uncle has acres to spare—for now. Eventually he'll run out of suitable land to clear."

"And fast, if my aunt has any say. She speaks of naught but cotton since she heard of that contraption Pryce is building."

"I've seen the plans for the gin. Intriguing, I'll admit."

"Will ye go to cotton, then?"

John fingered a corn leaf, eyes lit with an inner spark. "I'll tell you what I'd do if the Almighty were to drop a bounty from heaven straight into my outstretched arms—had I means to keep us fed for a while without a cash crop, in other words. I'd grow trees."

Ian snorted. "Ye've still trees covering most of your land."

John waved a hand to the wooded ridges surrounding his cornfield. "But who can say it won't soon be fences, not forest, that mark our lots? I've Robin to consider. I want him to know this land as I've known it, and his sons after him. Not a treeless desert with soil too lean to sustain them. I'm their steward, see? I must take the long view."

Before Ian could reply, Cecily's charming laughter rang out. Drawn to the sound like a homing pigeon, John hurried to the end of the row. Ian followed. They emerged from the corn to see Seona and Cecily beneath the dogwood that shaded the cabin-yard, wee Robin between them on a coverlet.

"What new astonishment has my son performed?" John inquired, ducking beneath a low-hanging bough to kneel beside his beaming wife.

"He smiled, *chéri*. Was it not a smile, Seona?"

Ian ducked the bough and straightened. Though the tips of his boots were mere inches from her, Seona kept her head bent, her eyes fixed on the baby.

"I reckon, Miss Cecily."

The bairn gave a prodigious yawn. His parental audience made fitting sounds of admiration.

Ian grinned at their besotted fascination, until he saw what else lay on the blanket. A tiny drawing on a scrap of paper, scarcely more than a few lines and shadings: the curve of a cradled head, the stub of a nose, eyes half-lidded in utter contentment. Seona clutched the string-wrapped lead Ian had lent her. He hadn't known she'd brought it out of the shop.

John spotted the half-finished portrait. "What's this?"

"Seona's been doing some drawing for me," he explained hastily. "At my request. Chisel and plane I can master, but I'm no great hand at sketching. I wanted something special for Catriona—my sister."

Thoughts bombarded in the silence that followed. Had Cecily somehow guessed Seona's secret and pressed this demonstration upon her, or had Seona confessed it? A half-guilty glance, dappled green as the light through the dogwood boughs, gave him answer.

"Have ye time to finish it?" he asked her, keeping his voice matter-of-fact.

"Oh, please," Cecily begged. When Seona nodded, she lifted her baby into her arms. "Was his head turned so?"

"Near enough," Seona said, a richer color blooming in her cheeks.

Despite her obvious discomfort having an audience near, Ian lingered to watch. At first Seona's strokes were tentative, but gradually the lines of her body eased and her hand responded with surer movements. A breeze rustled the dogwood boughs. Something less tangible stirred below, invisible threads spinning out between Seona and the bairn.

"Ian," John said, voice too soft to break the spell. "There's a book I meant to show you. I'll fetch it from the cabin."

Ian nodded, only half-hearing. Seona's cap

lay crumpled behind her on the blanket. Her hair was gathered to the side in a hasty knot, the ends spiraling loose over her shoulder. The tips of the curls glinted that surprising bronze in the patch of sunlight that fell across the neck of her bodice, very like Catriona's, if darker. A furrow deepened between her brows as she worked, eyes flicking from the bairn to the emerging portrait. As he watched, she caught her lower lip between her teeth. The expression was so reminiscent of his sister at work at her easel that only reluctance to disturb her suppressed a chuckle.

The breeze scattered coins of sunlight over the coverlet. A strand of hair swept across Seona's cheek. Rather than pause to finger it behind an ear, she nudged it away with a toss of her chin, again as he'd seen Catriona do a hundred times.

He stared at that chin, dipping and tilting as she worked—a chin that bore a slight but definite cleft. A mirror of his sister's chin. Of his father's. And his own.

He forgot for a moment to breathe.

Blood will tell, he'd heard it said. So, it seemed, would bone.

Or was he imagining things? His thumb found the familiar indentation in his chin, traced the telling contour beneath the flesh. For the first time he wondered whether, beneath his beard, his uncle bore this feature that marked Ian and his siblings with the stamp of their Cameron blood.

He was stabbed by an image of Lily, remote in her dignity and grace. But reserve alone was no barrier to a white man's lust—and surely Seona's father had been white. What white man had been closer to Lily her lifelong than his uncle?

Born right here at Mountain Laurel, Rosalyn had said of Seona. *Before Mama married Papa Hugh . . .* But mightn't it have been anyone, all those years ago? A visitor. A neighbor. A predatory sort, someone of Gideon Pryce's ilk.

In a rush of denial Ian closed his eyes, in darkness dissecting Seona's face, feature by feature. The creek-water eyes set deep beneath arched lids, the wide cheekbones with their prominent cast . . . those weren't his blood. As for the rest—a trick of the shadows. When he opened his eyes again, he'd see his uncle's slave. Lily's daughter. Nothing else.

But that wasn't all he saw.

"Ian! I have it here. Come into the sunlight, will you?"

At John's hail he turned—and cracked his forehead on the dogwood's low bough. Leaves shaken loose from the jostled branch drifted across the coverlet. One landed on the hand now hovering over the portrait.

"Mister Ian, you all right?" Seona asked.

"Aye—fine." Forehead smarting, half-blinded by revelation, he ducked the limb and crossed the yard. He took the book John held out, a weight of pasteboard and cracked calfskin.

"*Sylva, or a Discourse of Forest-Trees, and the Propagation of Timber in His Majesty's Dominions*," John said, reading the title aloud. "Penned by a Fellow of the Royal Society. I had it from my father when he passed."

Having taken in but one word in three, Ian said, "Ye want to plant trees?"

"That's what I've been telling you. But not pine for naval stores as they do down on the Cape Fear. Hardwoods for cabinetmakers and carpenters, craftsmen like yourself." John took the volume from Ian's unresisting hands and rifled the musty pages, pausing to expound on certain texts.

Cousin . . . cousin. It was the only word Ian could hear. It sounded a drumbeat in his head. He nearly jumped out of his skin when Seona spoke behind him.

"I best be getting back, Mister Ian. There's a heap of wash waiting. You staying on?" She was holding a chicken. The cap was back on her head.

"No," he said. "I'll go with ye."

The brush of her petticoat against the ferns, the snap of a twig beneath her foot, the occasional *cruck* of the chicken she carried, rose like gunshots above the surrounding forest sounds, so heightened was Ian's awareness of Seona behind

175

him on the path. At the point where the stream's course bent—to follow it would lead upslope to the birch hollow—he halted and turned.

Seona walked into his chest. His arms went out to steady her, and briefly he pressed his cheek against her cap, feeling through the linen the warmth of her, the firmness of bone. That telling bone.

She struggled against him. "Mister Ian—turn me loose!"

He released her, to find it wasn't him she fought but the half-smothered chicken. The flapping bird found its way into his grasp and he wrestled it into submission against his side.

"Are ye hurt?"

She brushed a bit of feather-down from the tip of her nose. "Miss Cecily's chickens ain't of a mind to peck. Not like those laying hens we keep. They're downright wicked, those birds. I could show you the scars."

Show me, he wanted to say. Her gaze passed over his face, settling on his brow, as if she'd read the thought. What did she see? Did she know? Had she known all along?

"You're gonna have a bruise, Mister Ian."

"Bruise?" He touched his brow, felt the tender swelling there. "That limb . . . aye." He didn't care about his face. He wanted to take her hand and climb to the hollow. Climb as high as they could and look out over his uncle's land and breathe the air. Maybe then his thoughts would come clear.

She hadn't the time. The wash awaited.

"Do they know not to speak of it?"

He'd changed course without warning again, but this time she followed him nimbly. "Miss Cecily promised not to tell. I know she won't."

"She'll warn John?"

Seona nodded.

"Did ye tell Cecily about the hollow?"

"No, sir. That secret's still my own."

"Ours." He wanted to touch her, but the memory of her cornered by Gideon Pryce came vividly to mind, inhibiting the impulse. The chicken gave a squawk. He eased his grip on the bird and blurted the first thing that came to mind. "The bairn—did he really smile?"

That made *her* smile. "No, but he did get the sweetest look just then. I think he's happy to be in the world."

"Who wouldn't be, landing in the laps of those two?"

One child's mother a freewoman. Less than a mile away, another child's mother a slave. Fate dealt out like cards. Winning hand, losing hand. Happiness a happenstance of birth.

"Let me take that bird, Mister Ian. It ain't fitting, you toting it home."

What wasn't fitting was the life she'd been forced to lead.

"I'd like ye to come to the shop," he said as he handed over the chicken. "I know ye've the wash waiting now, but whenever ye've the time, even after we finish the desk, ye could come, keep drawing in my book. Would ye like that?"

Her pleased expression made him glad he'd followed his impulse. "I would. If we're careful."

"Aye," he said. "We will be." But he was thinking that if he handled things right, they might not need to be.

11

He'd never heard it said his kin possessed the second sight, yet Ian swore his uncle had sensed the confrontation coming. Shortly before he returned from the Reynolds', determined to present Hugh Cameron with his revelation of Seona's parentage and challenge her enslavement, Ian's uncle shut himself up in his room. And would admit no entry—at least from him.

"It is no cause for fretting," his aunt said briskly when Uncle Hugh failed to appear at supper. "Your uncle has overspent himself since your arrival. He needs rest."

"Fixing to have hisself another ailing spell," Maisy muttered, emerging from his uncle's room next morning with an untouched breakfast tray. "He done had a dose of his medicine, Mister Ian. Won't do no good to trouble him."

"Medicine? What sort?"

"That black draft," Maisy said, screwing up a sour face.

Laudanum.

Forced to bide his time, Ian rode to the fields, lending his labor where needed, approving or amending whatever decisions Dawes had made in his uncle's absence. In every other available moment that day and the next he worked on his sister's desk. And simmered.

"Mister Ian?"

He'd hoped a fervent application of beeswax to the finished desk would distract him from his bottled frustration. All it had accomplished was working up a sweat. Now he turned to Seona, seated on the low stool, pattern book open on her lap, taking advantage of a few stolen moments to draw, as he'd invited her to do.

She held up the lead, point worn flat.

"Let me shave that for ye." He tossed aside the buffing rag. She handed him the lead. He took up a knife and began shaving the point. "My uncle . . . he's had spells like this before, aye?"

"A few times. Last was late up in the winter, afore he sent that letter to your daddy."

Was that what had prompted his uncle to send for him again, after so many years?

"How long did it last?" He was staring, but he couldn't help it. Though Seona's resemblance to his sister came and went like sunlight through scattered clouds, the stamp of her Cameron blood was clear. Now he'd the eyes to see it.

"A week or so. He ain't been himself since, though Mama thought lately he was doing better. Master Hugh sets high store by Mama's dosing."

He'd seen Lily tend the slaves, dressing a burn or minor gash, and to judge by Seona's

180

competence, she was a skilled midwife. "Who taught Lily the midwifery and the rest?"

The question seemed to surprise her. "The old mistress, Master Hugh's first wife. Taught Mama spinning and weaving too. From a girl."

He noted the sudden color blooming in her cheeks. "Should I not have asked that?"

She shook her head. "It's fine, you asking. I forget you ain't been here but a few weeks. Sometimes it feels like you was always here."

Warmed by the unexpected admission, he handed her the sharpened lead and asked, "Who was Lily's mother? A Cherokee woman?"

Seona took the lead but didn't go back to drawing. "Reckon the answer to that is yes and no."

"Yes *and* no?"

She smiled briefly, then stared through the open door at the green wall of trees beyond as she told him, "Militia soldiers had Mama's mama in tow when they passed through on the road yonder, back when there was trouble with the Cherokees and men went overmountain to settle 'em down."

"During the French War," he said. "Was she a prisoner?"

"Yes, sir. Reckon so, by then."

By then. "And my uncle's wife took her in?"

"What I hear tell, the old mistress would've taken in most any needy soul if Master Hugh had let her. Like Mister Aidan with his critters. The soldiers—they'd stopped here for water or a rest, or some such—said they mistook my grandma Sadie for a white woman when they seen her in the Indian camp. It was a dawn raid, not much light. Thought they was saving a captive when they snatched her up. Come full light and space to study her proper, they seen she was near as much African as white and who knew what else, maybe Indian too. They took her for a runaway then. All but gave her to Master Hugh's wife—to be shed of her afore her baby came, we reckon. A few days later she birthed Mama and died of it."

Ian frowned, absorbing the astonishing tale. "Ye said her name was Sadie?"

"That's what Naomi made of it."

"Made of it? Didn't she tell them who she was, where she came from?"

"She never spoke at all 'cept in the Indian tongue. What she called herself sounded a bit like *Sadie,* so that's what we've always known her by."

Seona fingered the end of her braid, absently coiling the strands round and round. The skin across her knuckles was chapped, but the hands themselves were well-shaped, slender and long.

"Did my uncle's wife take Lily to raise?"

"Yes, but not right off. Naomi had Ally to suck, so she put Mama alongside him. She was weaned afore the old mistress took her into the house."

"And named her?"

"No, sir. Her mama that died named her. It was the last my grandma Sadie spoke, when she knew she'd had a baby girl. They reckoned it was meant for a name."

"But Lily is an English name."

"*Lily*'s what it got made into. What my grandma said afore she died was *Tsigalili*."

"Tsigalili? D'ye ken what it means?"

She shook her head. "Guess no one but my grandma knew. And the Cherokees. Ain't none of them around these parts to ask."

Ian leaned his forearms on the workbench, thinking of Mountain Laurel's dead. A hapless runaway with no past and no sure name. A cousin and an aunt, both prone to shelter strays. Even Ruby and the boys he'd known as a lad—Sammy, Eli. Not dead perhaps, but memory of them haunted. "Seona . . . d'ye know how old Aidan Cameron was when *his* mam died?"

A pucker formed between her brows. "I don't think Mister Aidan was grown. She was breeding again and the baby come early. Mama was still a girl. Didn't know what all to do when things went so wrong, and there weren't no doctor near enough then to call in time, though Master Hugh rode out to find one. Mama's a heap more skilled now," she hurried to add. "From practice."

As if shaking off the shadow their talk had cast, Seona stood with the pattern book clasped close and ran a fingertip over the desk's carving. The trailing vines, buffed to a silken sheen, terminated at either end in a trumpeting spray of blossoms.

"Reckon your sister will be pleased with this we done?"

"I think so," he said, smiling briefly at *we*. "No notion when I'll see it into her keeping though."

"Thomas said you promised to make this afore you left Boston to come here."

She'd reminded him: Thomas's tenure at Chesterfield was to end that evening. Ian was meant to take the wagon out to fetch him. And the mahogany his labor had bought. He thought he'd time for one more story. "Aye. A deathbed promise, no less."

Seona tilted her head at him. "Mister Ian, how could you have been on your deathbed making promises yet be standing here talking to me now? I know you ain't a ghost."

It was the boldest thing she'd said to him, just this side of sauce. He liked it.

"I'd a wound that festered. It's a long story but suffice it to say Callum Lindsey—another uncle of mine—brought me back to Boston on account of it, fearing I'd die in the wilds and Mam would hold *him* to account." He suppressed the darker memories of those days. His battle with fever. His mam's battle with the Boston physicians who'd have taken his leg to save him. The measures she'd taken to save life *and* limb. "I mind Cat clinging to my bedpost, blue eyes snapping in the

184

candlelight, telling me she had her heart set on a table desk and no one could craft it proper save her coof of a brother, so I'd best heal up and get on with it. All the while Mam's trying to pull her away to let me rest."

Seona bit her bottom lip but couldn't quell her grin. "Oh my."

"That wasn't what I said at the time," he told her. "I promised her the desk—to be rid of her. She meant to hold me to it, she said, as Mam dragged her from the room, so I dared not die and break my word."

"What did you say then?" Seona asked, clutching the pattern book.

"That I wouldn't dream of dying with such a burden on my conscience."

Seona was smiling unabashedly now. "I like your sister, Mister Ian."

"That's mighty charitable of you, Seona," said a voice intruding into the conversation. "Seeing as you've never set eyes on the girl."

Startled, they turned as Thomas strode into the shop, passing them to open the rear doors to a blaze of sunlight. Ian stared after him. "I meant to drive the wagon over to fetch ye and the lumber. Did Pryce write ye a pass?"

"Didn't need one," Thomas said. "By your leave, I'll go tote in that fine mahogany we traded a week of my sweat for."

"Did ye carry it here on your head?" Ian called,

then swiveled round as his uncle entered the shop, two visitors close on his heels. The first was a stranger, a man of middle years clad in a coat of fashionable broadcloth. The second was Gideon Pryce.

Haggard and gray-faced after two days in his room, Uncle Hugh halted at sight of Seona, causing the stranger to jostle him from behind. Pryce sidestepped the pair, catching sight of Seona in the shuffle. Ian shifted to stand between. Their gazes clashed across an outwardly civil greeting, before Uncle Hugh introduced the third man as Pryce's cousin, the merchant, Edward Stoddard.

Ian wiped his hands, apologizing for the turpentine, but Stoddard's handshake was unhesitating. "Nothing amiss with the stain of honest work," he said in the same Tidewater accent as Pryce's.

"I've heard of ye, sir. Your name was mentioned at Chesterfield."

"I showed the Camerons the plans for the cotton gin," Pryce explained.

Stoddard's enthusiasm was immediate. "Amazing contrivance! And you've only viewed the plans. When you've seen the machine itself, then you'll have seen a thing, gentlemen. Mark my words, Whitney's gin will bring change for the betterment to Southern planters. To the country as a whole."

Pryce had moved several paces to the side. Ian

shifted again, countering his attempt to gain an unobstructed view of Seona.

"We fought a war to govern ourselves," Stoddard was saying, "but it's native-grown cloth will prove our country's economic independence. It would not astonish me were half the Piedmont producing short-staple cotton five years hence."

Pryce's flat green eyes invited challenge. "I forecast a profit in far less time—for any willing to invest in the necessary labor force."

Ian wasn't about to be drawn into debate over purchasing slaves, not with his mind bent on reducing the number of his uncle's by one. And keeping that one forever beyond Chesterfield's reach. An objective presently demanding a disproportionate amount of his attention. Stoddard snatched at what little was to spare, indicating the desk.

"While we're on the subject of productivity, might I take a look?"

"By all means." Ian stepped back to allow Stoddard access. His heel came down on something soft. A bare foot. It was snatched back with a muffled gasp. Slipping a hand behind his back, he brushed Seona's fingers, taking them in a swift apologetic squeeze—and jerked at the sensation that shot up his arm when she squeezed back.

Uncle Hugh frowned his way, questioning, as

Stoddard lifted the slanted desktop to examine the inner drawers.

"This is meant for an artist, is it not?" the man asked.

"Aye, sir. My sister, in fact."

"Hugh tells me you were apprenticed to a cabinetmaker in Boston."

"Cambridge, actually. Though 'til now I hadn't practiced the trade since my apprenticeship ended."

"If I may observe, you haven't lost the knack."

Pryce started to circle the workbench, as if to join the examination. Ian took a step to head him off, but two things happened to avert the need.

Rosalyn entered through the nearer doorway, exclaiming, "Gideon Pryce! You aren't fixing to take your leave without a word to me and Mama?"

Then through the doors opposite, Thomas reappeared, a stack of lumber balanced across one shoulder. "Where you want these, Mastah Ian?"

Pryce's hesitation was minuscule, before he transferred his attention to Rosalyn. "I wouldn't dream of such neglect. We've but a small matter of business to conclude here."

Thomas awaited instruction. "Mastah Ian?"

"Put them on the benches 'til I've made space." Ian turned back to Pryce, loath to take his eyes off the man, to find Rosalyn seemingly likewise afflicted.

"Oh, tosh! Here's my cousin's wood delivered

188

and his boy returned. What is to conclude? Come sit with Mama and me and explain why Phyllida hasn't come to call."

With an indulgent smile, Pryce tucked her hand through the crook of his arm. "Will you join us, Ed? No doubt an eyewitness account of your meeting with Whitney would delight one and all."

Stoddard was still nose-deep in the desk, pulling out drawers and examining dovetailed joints. "I'll be along presently—if the lady doesn't object."

Far from objecting, Rosalyn shot Ian a probing glance, then towed Pryce out the door. As their heels crunched the gravel path, Stoddard stepped back from the desk, a hand to his chin.

"D'ye find aught to puzzle ye, Edward?" Uncle Hugh spoke mildly enough, but the look he cast Ian was still sharp with question. And, oddly, warning.

"Puzzle, no. Intrigue, yes." Stoddard noticed the pattern book, lying where Seona had left it. "Might I?" he inquired of Ian.

There was no polite way to refuse. At Ian's nod, Stoddard turned the pages, examining each intently, until he came to the morning glory sketches. Uncle Hugh came forward to view the page. His eyes narrowed.

"Are these designs of your making, Mr. Cameron?" Stoddard inquired.

189

"Most are in general use in New England." Ian moved sideways so Seona could escape the shop, now Pryce no longer barred the door.

She remained rooted, frozen as a mouse among cats.

Stoddard tapped a finger next to a morning glory sketch. "I've had occasion to view such pattern books from Savannah to Philadelphia, yet I've never encountered designs like these."

"I daresay ye haven't. My sister was particular about the design. They're of her making." Ian faced his uncle straight on as he lied and saw that look of warning change to relief.

Stoddard was headed south on the morrow but announced his intention of passing through Salisbury, a town west of the Yadkin River, on his return north.

"I understand this desk is bespoke, but if you can oblige me by having them in Salisbury by early October, I'd be pleased to acquire as many similar pieces as you can craft in that time—be it two or ten. Fix your price. I'll call before I take my leave to settle the arrangement, should it prove agreeable."

Ian's pride of craftsmanship was quick to rouse at the prodding. "Very agreeable. I'll draw up a contract and have it ready, sir."

Uncle Hugh, silent during the negotiation, now addressed Seona. "Do ye show our guest to the parlor, lass. Then be off to mind whatever ye're meant to be about." To Stoddard he added, "We'll be along presently. I've a word or two to say to my nephew first."

"Yes, sir," Seona said.

Ian didn't take his eyes off his uncle, who, as Seona's and their guest's footsteps receded on the path, opened the pattern book. Ian could almost hear the gears of his mind grinding above the rustle of turning pages.

"Which of them are hers?"

"The morning glories," Ian replied. "How long have ye known?"

His uncle shut the book. "I've kent for years."

Ian felt the heat gathering under his breastbone. "And ye let her go on with it in secret when ye might have acknowledged her?"

"As ye've done?" Uncle Hugh spread a hand over the pattern book, fingers splayed as if to contain what lay between its bindings. "What did ye think to gain by teaching her . . . this?"

"I didn't teach her. I haven't her skill. Catriona does. And Da. A family trait, ye could say."

Uncle Hugh's face, already pasty from whatever had ailed him the past days, went gray as plaster. "What d'ye mean by that?"

"Tell me, Uncle," Ian said. "How have ye lived with another man's offspring under your roof, taking advantage of your connections and property, while ye let your daughter wear their rags and eat their scraps?"

A brittle silence followed, torn through by a throat's clearing at the shop's other end.

"Thought I'd work while the light lasts. You decide where you want this wood, Mastah Ian?"

Ian cut a glare across the partition wall as Thomas dropped another length of mahogany onto the first. Thomas straightened, waiting. Streaming sunlight cast him in unmoving silhouette.

"Not now, Thomas!"

Thomas drew his next words out with slow deliberation. "Yes, suh. I'll just close up shop and leave you be."

The light dimmed as the far doors shut.

The change in Ian's uncle was more subtle. A stoop of shoulders. A sag of face. But it conspired to make Hugh Cameron appear all of his sixty-odd years and more.

"When I wrote your da earlier in the year," he said, "I kent I'd waited overlong. I ought to have pressed Robert harder when ye were a lad, when ye came here and 'twas clear ye had some liking for the place. Or was I wrong about that?"

"Ye weren't wrong," Ian said. "What has that to do with Seona?"

"Aye, good, then," his uncle continued as if he hadn't heard the question. "I wanted ye here then, and I want ye now. But understand the one thing: I'd rather ye take yourself back north, or wherever ye will, if all ye mean to do is tear down around me what remains of the life I've built."

Lips clamped upon the final word, his uncle turned to leave. In the doorway he paused, clutching the frame. "Mind ye give that thought, Nephew. Maybe ye'll see what 'tis to do with Seona."

12

As Pryce's wagon disappeared down the carriage drive, Ian sought out Seona. She wasn't in the washhouse. Or the kitchen. Or the shop. Ducking out again, he spied her coming through the orchard, a basket heaped with apples on her hip, Thomas at her side.

Ian headed for them. The sky had clouded in the hour past. A thickening scud of gray hid the sun. A breeze pressed Seona's petticoat against her thighs as he halted under the laden boughs. Thomas took the basket from her, eyeing Ian with the same censure he'd had from his uncle. At a nod from Seona he trudged off toward the kitchen.

"They've gone," Ian said. "Are ye all right?"

A raindrop spattered cold on the back of his hand. Seona blinked as a drop hit the curve of her cheekbone. It ran down like a tear. "Mister Ian, I got wash to get in afore it's soaked."

He wanted to say more, offer reassurance, but couldn't find a single word that would do.

"Go on," he said and watched her race off through the trees. Pelted by raindrops, he headed back to the shop, knowing the conversation with his uncle wasn't finished, composing how he'd come at the subject of Seona yet again. When he stepped within, Rosalyn stood at the workbench, head bowed, pale gown ethereal in the dim light.

Brought up short, he demanded, "What are ye doing?"

Her head came up. A hand fluttered mothlike to her throat. "Cousin. You gave me a start, creeping in soft as an Indian."

"I'd hardly creep into my own shop."

She widened her eyes. "Bristly as a porcupine still, I see. You positively brooded over tea."

The hour in the parlor with his kin and their guests had been a seething feat of endurance. He rounded the workbench, pasting on a counterfeit smile. "Better?"

Rosalyn stared, then gave a spiraling little laugh. "Tolerably so. Come now, Cousin. Is it the turn of weather, or has Gideon's visit put you out of temper? You don't care for him, do you?"

"Nor should ye."

She appeared taken aback. "Whyever not?"

"Have ye taken a stroll through his slave quarters? The man cannot keep his breeches fastened."

His cousin flushed at the bald statement—with anger or embarrassment, Ian couldn't have said. "Of course I haven't. Nor ever shall."

"Aye, well. What d'ye want, Rosalyn?"

She smoothed her hands over the pattern book, open on the bench. "Mr. Stoddard had such praise for your work over tea, I decided to come see what the fuss was about. If I might ask, where did you come by these designs?" She traced a fingertip across one of Seona's drawings. "I've never seen the like. Are they all the rage in Boston?"

He stiffened. "The book was given me by my Cambridge master."

"These are his designs?" she asked, still touching the morning glories.

"Some of them."

"The vines and flowers?" she persisted.

"My sister drew those."

Rosalyn's mouth firmed before she managed another smile. "I must write to your sister and tell her what a lovely grace she has for ornamentation." She closed the book. "By the by, Cousin, I happened to look out the window before Gideon's arrival. I saw Seona slipping in here. I've seen her come and go before today. I'd thought she'd taken a fancy to your Thomas. Then Thomas went to Chesterfield, and still she came."

He shrugged. "Naomi sent her with a meal a time or two, when I was too busy to come to table. And speaking of busy, I must ask ye to excuse me. I need to get that mahogany sorted."

There was a glitter in her eyes he didn't like, but she kept her voice measured. "How silly of me to intrude. I suppose, having gone off to live with savages, you'd prefer the company of Papa Hugh's slaves to that of his stepdaughters."

This was getting out of hand. "Rosalyn—"

"Say what you will of Gideon," she continued, dropping all pretense of indifference. "He's gentleman enough to show a lady preference. He even attends to Judith, for heaven's sake!"

"I meant no insult."

"Of course you did, but never mind. I've plenty to occupy me elsewhere." She swept out, leaving behind a ringing silence.

Blast the girl. He *had* meant to nettle her into leaving, before she worked out too much of the truth. As for that . . .

He closed the shop and headed for the house, meaning to find his uncle and have that truth from him.

Drops ticked at the window in Mister Ian's room. Seona's hands shook as she opened the clothespress and tucked away his clean shirt, snatched off the line before it took a soaking. She ought to have closed the press and left his room then, but the things he kept hid away were a fascination. That red wool shirt with its neck stitched round in flowers. She'd never seen him wear it. Did those Indians he lived with up north fancy gaudy clothes, or was it something Mister Ian fancied for himself? Sometimes it seemed he'd come from a lot farther off than Boston.

"Maybe the moon," she said, then peeped over the bed. It was quiet in the passage.

Her eyes snagged on the half-breed coat hung

behind the door, and the belt with the tomahawk. First time she came into his room to put up laundry, she'd touched those things, pressed her face to them. They smelled of smoke and horses. And something else she couldn't name. Some bit of the northern wilds still clinging to them, maybe.

As she moved to close the press, a roll of yellowed paper tumbled out, tied with the blue ribbon she'd last seen in the hollow. Heart banging, she slipped off the ribbon and spread out her picture. He'd put it up careful, but the ravens were smudged now.

A breeze kicked up, pushing raindrops through the open window. She couldn't sit there sorting her thoughts like so much laundry. She blew to scatter the charcoal dust so she could stash the drawing back in the press and finish her chore.

The creak of a floorboard was all the warning she got that she'd been caught.

"I knew it!" Miss Rosalyn rounded the bed and snatched the picture from her hands. "Those morning glory drawings are yours!"

Seona shot to her feet. "Mister Ian's sister . . ." Her voice, dry as dust, failed her.

Miss Rosalyn narrowed her eyes. "You're lying to me." She tossed the raven picture onto the bed, shedding fine black grains on the counterpane. She grabbed Seona's wrist and hauled her from the room.

"I got laundry—"

"Never mind that." Miss Rosalyn towed her down the passage to the room she and Miss Judith shared, where she gestured at the plastered walls. "All this white is tiresome. I won't bear it another day. Phyllida Pryce's room has fancy borders around the door and windows. I want you to ornament my room with those same designs you drew for Cousin Ian. That's *all*. No need for such dissembling."

"You want me to draw . . . on the walls?" Seona must have looked as thunderstruck as she felt.

Miss Rosalyn narrowed her eyes again. "Did I not speak plainly?" She snatched a pencil off Miss Judith's writing table and thrust it into Seona's hand. "Use this to start with. I'll ask Papa Hugh about getting some paint."

"I . . . I can't." If she did, all hope of her secret being kept was gone.

But it was gone already.

Miss Rosalyn's mouth drew in small. "I can be on your side in this. I can speak up for you. You choose." She pointed at the doorframe. "Morning glories. Exactly as you drew them in Cousin Ian's book. Make a border all around. Like they're climbing the wall. I'll be back to check on you."

She went out, leaving Seona as stunned as if she'd taken a switch to her back. Miss Rosalyn . . . on *her* side? Her knees banged and she sat down, staring at the pencil rolling across the floorboards.

• • •

She got herself in hand and did as she was told. She drew morning glory vines twining up the side of the door, standing on the bed stool when it got too high to reach. Miss Rosalyn came back once, grunted her approval, and went out again.

Here Seona had thought pigs would fly afore she did a thing that pleased that girl. But the pencil nearly snapped in her hand when Miss Lucinda's bottle-green skirt lashed by the open door. Catching sight of her, the mistress swished to a halt.

"What are you doing?"

"Drawing pictures, ma'am. Like Miss Rosalyn bid me do."

Miss Lucinda jabbed a finger at the floor. "Get down."

In her haste to obey Seona sent the stool crashing. She set it to rights and faced Miss Lucinda, who was staring at the wall, knuckles planted on her hips.

"Rosalyn told you to do this? Why?"

"She wants her walls to look like Miss Phyllida's. I'm to do the drawing now and she'll ask Master Hugh about paint." The pencil had grown slick in her grasp. Seona went on talking, heart tripping like the sudden burst of rain against the window. "Pokeberry juice would work if no paint's to hand. Makes a nice dark pink. Be right pretty . . ."

Miss Lucinda whipped around to face her. "How are you able to do this?"

Too late for lying. Seona drew a shaky breath. "I drew patterns for Mister Ian. For his work."

"Did *he* teach you to draw?"

"No, ma'am."

"Who then? That Frenchwoman?"

"No, ma'am. I taught myself to make a likeness. Long back afore you came here, I . . . I found an old slate and scratched on it with a rock." Cold slipped down her back, hearing those words out of her mouth.

"Is that all you've used? A rock and slate?"

"No, ma'am. I've used other things."

The mistress glanced at the pencil in Seona's hand. "My daughters' belongings?"

"No, ma'am. I never took nothing wasn't thrown out as rubbish."

"Really?" Miss Lucinda's eyes were stones. "You've managed to astonish me, Seona."

She could number on one hand the times Lucinda Cameron had called her by her given name. Not one of those times had ended well.

"It occurs to me to wonder what I'd find if I went up to the garret right now." Satisfaction drew Miss Lucinda's features tight. "Let's do that together, shall we?"

His uncle's pipe had gone out. Uncle Hugh knocked the dottle into the grate, then crossed to his desk and took out a tobacco tin. The smell of the leaf filled the room, pungent, cloying. Ian would have thought the man unruffled but for the trembling of his hands.

Seated on the dressing bench at the foot of his uncle's bed, Ian rubbed a hand down his face. "How have ye borne it, Uncle, watching Seona grow up a slave? Why haven't ye freed her—if not for Lily's sake, then for the sake of your own blood? Our blood."

Uncle Hugh eyed him as though he'd lost his head. "D'ye think it that simple? That I pen the words and the lass is free? Aye, I suppose ye do."

Ian was momentarily silenced. He hadn't thought past his outrage for Seona's sake to the particulars of the process. "Tell me, then. What's to be done?"

His uncle sighed as he sat. "First a man must petition the General Assembly, giving cause for any slave he'd see manumitted. *Meritorious service*, it's called. Should the assembly deem such service worthy of freedom and grant the request, a freed slave is obliged to leave the state within months of manumission—or risk reenslavement." He shook his head at Ian's frown. "Aye, Nephew. Where would Seona go? She might pass for white, but what manner of living would she have with no man to protect her or provide?"

Ian read the grim possibilities in his uncle's

202

strained face. "I'd let nothing of the kind befall her."

"Easy to say. But 'tis never so simple as what ye will or no'."

"It can be. Let me take her north, see her settled in Boston with Da and Mam. I'll come back to ye then—and remain here."

Uncle Hugh closed his eyes. "No."

"Why? Because ye'd not be parted from your last surviving child even if it means she stays a slave?"

"Dinna put words into my mouth, Ian. I never claimed the lass was mine."

He thought his uncle meant to say more, but voices had risen beyond the door, checking them both.

"Mama . . . cannot this wait until Seona's finished?"

"I've made my decision. I'll have them out of this house *today*."

13

Seona sat on a trunk beside her rolled pallet, absorbing yet another shock. "How long have you known, Mama?"

Lily's hands stilled on the bundle she was tying up. "Since the day we moved into this garret."

The day Master Hugh returned from Virginia, bringing his new family with their carriage and slaves and hired wagons heaped with house plunder.

"I took up your pallet to see had ye dusted these old boards afore putting it down, and there they were, your beautiful drawings."

They didn't seem beautiful to Seona now the mistress had put them both from the house.

"Take your things to the cabin next to Naomi's," Miss Lucinda had ordered, standing over Seona's pallet flung aside to reveal scattered scraps of paper bearing likenesses of ravens, deer, foxes—all manner of wild things from the woods—and faces done from memory. She'd spied Mister Ian's boyhood likeness staring up at her and put her foot down on it a second before Miss Lucinda's eyes swept over the mess. "You and your mother will sleep there now—where you have always belonged." She'd curled her lip at Ally's face, grinning up at her from the floor. "As for this rubbish—burn it!"

As the rain drummed overhead, Lily sat beside her on the trunk and rubbed her back like she was still small enough to comfort so. "I've been so proud, girl-baby. Peeking at your drawings over the years, seeing them getting better and better." Her mama was quiet for a space, then in a different tone asked, "How long has Mister Ian known?"

"Since the day he caught the Reynolds' pig." Head aching, heavy with the garret's heat, she told how Mister Ian learned her secret, then got the notion for her to help with his cabinetmaking. "It's all Munin's fault, I reckon."

"That old raven." Lily gave her hand a squeeze. "Well, we've trouble enough for one day. Best get our things shifted."

They heard the voices as they reached the foot of the garret stairs, several talking over each other, down below in the passage. All of them angry. Seona froze, but Lily put a hand to her shoulder. "Never fear what man can do, girl-baby. The Lord's watching over our lot."

Seona tried to believe it, but each step down the back stairs was harder to take for dread, like she was Daniel going down into that den of hungry lions. Mister Ian's voice was the first to come free of the snarl: "What she's done was at my bidding. It's no cause for casting them from their place."

"Their place is where I say it is!" Miss Lucinda snapped.

"My *room,* Mama," Miss Rosalyn cut in. "Let Seona finish what she started."

In the passage outside Master Hugh's room the mistress and her daughters confronted Mister Ian like hounds with a possum treed. When Seona stepped off the last stair, bundle clutched to her chest, Mister Ian put his back to Miss Lucinda and came to her, face tight with anger, hair rumpled like he'd scrubbed his fingers through it, forgetting it was tailed.

"Ye and Lily take your things back upstairs," he told her, but when she started to obey, her mama put a firm hand on her shoulder.

"Mister Ian, no. Let this happen."

"For once, Lily, we are in agreement." Miss Lucinda thrust between them and Mister Ian, forcing Seona and Lily practically into the warming room. She yanked open the back door. A breeze swept into the house, moist with rain and a flood of watery light. "My decision stands, whether or not *you* agree, Mr. Cameron."

Seona reached for Lily. Her mama was no longer beside her. Probably ducked into the warming room when the mistress pushed them aside. She didn't steal a glance to see.

"I gave her permission to draw," Mister Ian said, still arguing against the inevitable. "If that was wrong, then it was my wrong. Not hers."

"I don't want her punished—not yet." Miss Rosalyn seemed cross at everyone. Miss Judith, clearly distressed, raised a hand to her sister's sleeve but Miss Rosalyn jerked away. "She's meant to finish my room!"

"Neither of you appear to understand," Miss Lucinda said, "that the girl has admitted to years of lying. No doubt thievery as well. Putting her from this house is the least she deserves. It's within my rights to have her whipped."

"If I hear ye speak again of whipping, madam, ye will regret it."

Seona shrank back at the hard set of Mister Ian's jaw, his harder words. She clutched at the warming room doorway, almost wishing she'd never picked up that slate, never spied on a blue-eyed boy with hair pale as moonlight.

"Put the notion of whipping out of your head, Lucinda—as I told ye once long ago." Every eye turned to see Master Hugh standing in the doorway of his room. "Seona's drawing is no news to me."

"You knew?" The mistress sounded strangled.

"I've kent it since Seona was a wee lass—I saw her at it, though she didna ken I was watching." He looked her way, in his eyes a mingling of warmth and sorrow that wrenched her heart somehow more than his startling confession. " 'Twas my choice to let her alone to draw as she wished. Your coming here didna alter that."

"It would seem," Miss Lucinda said with shaking fury, "that my coming here altered very little whatsoever."

For an instant Seona felt a stab of pity for the mistress. But she hadn't room in her spinning head to hold such a thing. Master Hugh had known her secret all this time too.

He didn't acknowledge his wife's bitter words. "As Ian has explained, there's no need for casting Seona and Lily from this house."

"Let me be the judge of *need*." In the weighted silence that followed her words, Miss Lucinda thrust out her chin. "You don't want them removed because you don't wish to suffer the inconvenience of having Lily so far from your bed."

"Mama." Miss Judith took a timid step forward and touched her mother's arm. "I'm sure that isn't true. Lily can care for Papa Hugh no matter where she sleeps."

The mistress drew back her hand and slapped her daughter's face. Miss Judith sat down hard in the middle of the passage, petticoats a-billow, hand over her cheek. For a second no one moved. No one spoke. Miss Lucinda raising a hand to one of her girls had stolen the air from all their lungs—even the one who'd done the slapping.

Then Mister Ian made a noise like a growl. He pushed past Miss Lucinda and bent to help Miss Judith to her feet. "Are ye all right, lass?"

Miss Judith's stunned face crumpled. She clung to his shirtfront, forcing him to hold her while she sniffled and sobbed.

"This is utterly ridiculous!" Miss Rosalyn glared at her sister in Mister Ian's arms.

Miss Lucinda's face had gone stark white. "Oh, Judith. Do get control of yourself!"

But at her mama's words Miss Judith sobbed louder.

Master Hugh stood braced against the doorframe of his room, watching his kinfolk quarrel. Then his face lifted, going ashen. Or was it just the light? Seona tried to tell as he stared past them all, through the open back door, a distance in his eyes like he was trying to spot something away up on the ridge. The skin across his brow broke out in beads of sweat despite the breeze trickling in.

Movement drew Seona's attention to a figure down the passage. *Mama.* She'd gone around through the parlor. But why . . . ?

Her gaze jerked back to Master Hugh. Every other eye was fixed on Miss Judith clinging to Mister Ian. None but Seona—and the figure hurrying down the passage—saw when Master Hugh slumped against the doorframe. The rest went on weeping and quarreling.

Then, save for the rain's patter, there was silence for an everlasting second before their voices broke around Seona like glass splintering.

"Uncle Hugh!"

"Papa!"

And she knew they'd turned in time to see what she'd seen—Master Hugh, eyes blank and knees buckling, sliding down the door molding, coming to rest in the circle of Lily's arms.

The little basket where she kept her treasures—pretty pebbles, a few arrowheads, a redbird's feather Ally once gave her—sat nestled atop the faded quilt in her arms as Seona stood for the last time at the top of the garret stair. The heat trapped under the roof pressed in as she stared at the place her and her mama's pallets had lain. Dust lay over the house-clutter heaped about, but those two spots were bare. Sight of them saddened her, like the passing of someone she'd taken for granted.

She drew breath to say a prayer for Master Hugh.

"Seona?" Mister Ian peered up at her, shoulders filling the tight stairwell. She hadn't seen him since he hauled Master Hugh up from her mama's arms and half carried him to his bed. "Is there aught I can bring down for ye?"

"No, Mister Ian. This is the last of it." She descended the stair. When he reached to steady her, she was tempted to do like Miss Judith and cling to him. Such liberty wasn't hers to take. "How is he?"

"My aunt has him smothered under quilts with

a fire laid and him sweating away, white as the sheets. And naught I can say to dissuade the woman." Mister Ian's mouth twisted like he'd tasted something bitter. "She's keen of a sudden to have your mother by."

He reached for her armload, into which she'd tucked her drawings. If ever she aimed to speak of it, now was the time. "Mister Ian . . . I'm meant to burn all my pictures."

He pulled her into his room. The toting basket sat on the floor where she'd left it hours ago when Miss Rosalyn hauled her off.

"Take care of that if ye must," he said, seeing her eye the laundry, still needing put up. "Come back to me after, aye?"

He was sitting on the edge of the bedtick when she returned. Across the counterpane he'd spread her drawings—including the one of him. "Rosalyn was in the shop earlier, looking at the patterns. I knew she had her suspicions, but she didn't say *why* she was so keen on those morning glory designs. Has ye drawing on her walls, does she?"

"She wants her room to look like Miss Phyllida's." Amazing she could sound so calm with his likeness lying in plain sight.

He reached for it and held it between his hands. "Ye did this from memory?"

"Yes, sir. After you'd gone back north." As she spoke, the room brightened. Sunlight streamed through the window behind Mister Ian, yellowing the scraps of paper littering the bed. His eyes should have been in shadow. Instead they caught some odd bend of light in the room and blazed up bright.

"There'll be no burning. I'll keep them for ye." He handled her drawings with care, rolling them inside the raven picture. He tied the ribbon and set them aside. "I wanted ye to see what more ye could do. I knew what could come of it but told myself I'd stand between, that I wouldn't let it touch ye. I'm sorry."

"Turns out Master Hugh knew all along. Mama, too." Before he could say something more, she spoke up first. "Mister Ian, can I ask you something?"

"Aye, of course."

"Did you mean it a kindness, that day in the hollow you said you'd let me go on drawing and wouldn't tell?"

Slanting light struck his cheekbone and the line of his nose, making plain the strain of that day and his remorse.

"I did."

"Then you did what you meant to do, letting me draw for you." There was a burning in her eyes. She wanted to say this right. It mattered. She blinked hard and hurried her words. "I'm glad you let me help because I never in my life seen anything so fine as what you made of that desk for your sister."

The blue of his eyes warmed, spilling over her like the light. "The praise of the praiseworthy," he said. "I'm honored."

The praise of the praiseworthy. Distracted by those lovely words, Seona missed her footing on the bottom stair and stumbled. She hung on to the bedding, but the little basket flew off the pile, hit the wall, and burst open. Pebbles and arrowheads went rattling across the floor. She was after them at once, but Miss Lucinda got there first, drawn from Master Hugh's room by the clatter.

"Reckless girl! Is there no end to the turmoil you will inflict upon this household?" She snatched up the basket and came at Seona, then winced, swished aside her petticoat, and picked up the pebble she'd trodden upon. She stared at it in her hand.

"Seems we've had a squirrel nesting over our heads." Miss Rosalyn had emerged from Master Hugh's room, behind her mother.

Ignoring her, Miss Lucinda stepped closer, Seona's basket in one hand, pebble in the other. "Where did you get this?"

"I gave that old basket to Seona, years ago." Miss Judith had come to the door too. A faint handprint still showed pink on one cheek. "You patched it up, I see." Miss Judith blinked at Seona, smiling though her eyes were pained.

"Thank you for clarifying, Judith." The mistress spoke with exaggerated patience. "Ladies, go

213

back to your stepfather and shut the door. I'll help Seona gather her things."

Her daughters shared a puzzled look behind her back but did as she said, leaving Seona alone in the passage with their mother.

"I'll tidy this, ma'am, and—"

Miss Lucinda tossed the basket aside and grabbed her arm. "I wasn't speaking of that ratty old basket." She held out her hand, showing the pebble. It was one of the prettier ones, a knobby yellow thing, shiny, big as a hazelnut. "Where did you get *this?*"

"Likely from Ally. He'd give me pebbles like that when I was little."

"Naomi's half-wit found this? Where?"

"I don't know exactly. He turned up some in the fields. Found some in the creek. He didn't usually tell me where."

Miss Lucinda's eyes felt like they were boring into her. She turned her loose. "Clean up this mess. Keep the basket if you wish."

Seona started scooping up the pebbles nearest to hand, as Miss Lucinda's fist slipped into the side seam of her skirt, like she was reaching for the pocket tied beneath.

When his knock went unanswered, Ian opened the door across the passage from his room wide enough to see Thomas, candlelit, hunched before the trunk he used for a desk, writing in his journal. "Have ye aught becoming to say of me in your wee book?"

Thomas didn't turn. "I shouldn't wager on it."

"I haven't coin enough to make it worthwhile—yet." Leaving the door open in hopes of drawing a breeze through the half-open window, Ian sat on a crate pushed against the wall. He set the covered plate he carried beside him. "Look, Thomas. I didn't mean to snap at ye before, in the shop. It was wrong of me."

The sun had set on that tumultuous day. The light outside was purpling toward twilight, but the candle shed a warm glow on Thomas's sweating brow.

"Reckon that depends on your point of view."

"What d'ye mean?" Ian scowled. "Put down that quill and face me to talk."

With meticulous care, Thomas set the pen in its stand and swiveled on the stool. "You do recall my being your slave is a ruse?"

Ian pressed the heels of his hands against his eyes, then blew out a sigh. "Let me start this again. In the shop, with my uncle, I was preoccupied with an issue that had naught to do with ye—as I'm sure ye've heard though ye wisely kept clear of it. Still I addressed ye in a manner ye didn't deserve. For that I ask your pardon."

Thomas eyed him a moment more, then inclined his head. "Granted."

"As for recalling our ruse," Ian continued,

dropping his voice. "What d'ye take me for?"

"Since you ask—"

"It was rhetorical, aye? Besides, it's down to your own muleheadedness ye're here. I see no remedy save I escort ye back to Boston, which I cannot do with my uncle taken to his bed."

"What is it ailing him?" Thomas asked.

"My aunt's pestering to send for a physician but my uncle won't allow it," Ian said. "Says he knows well enough it's his heart. Takes to fluttering and skipping—paining him sharp if he pushes too hard, leaving him weak for days. I take it this time it's worse, though."

Thomas nodded. "Don't add worry about me to your troubles. I'm content to stay for now."

"Are ye? Content, I mean. Ye worked for a man and I was paid for it."

With that scene in the shop still a bruise between them, it occurred to Ian the accusation leveled at him moments ago might have some substance—a realization as uncomfortable as the heat. Treating Thomas as a slave without making him feel like one was a line too blighted obscure to walk cleanly.

Swallowing frustration, he said, "That mahogany by rights is yours."

Thomas nodded, a fleeting satisfaction curving his lips. Then he waved a hand. "Make those desks for Stoddard. I got what I wanted from the arrangement." Before Ian could inquire further into that, Thomas shot a glance at the covered plate. "Peace offering?"

"Supper." Ian drew back the linen from a mound of biscuits, roasted chicken, and boiled sweet potatoes, still faintly steaming.

Their stomachs rumbled in unison. Ian dragged another trunk from its place. He set the plate between them, then reached around the doorway, bringing in two pewter cups and a cider jug. They ate in companionable silence until Ian ventured, "So. Chesterfield. How was it?"

Thomas popped the last of a potato into his mouth and shrugged. "I made hogsheads, sunup to sundown. Took my meals on a bench outside the kitchen. Pryce came by every other day or so to ogle my work. Seemed pleased enough."

"Did ye have time to yourself—aside from meals and sleeping?"

"An hour or two at night. Besides two other cooper's apprentices, I had a boy helping me. Josiah. His mama works in the kitchen." Thomas's mouth softened briefly but firmed again as he said, "Pryce hinted he'd be agreeable to having me train Jo for the coopering—to my master's further benefit, of course."

"Pryce wants ye back? He never said so to me."

Belowstairs a door closed. Voices drifted up. Lucinda and Rosalyn. Ian waited until their conversation receded toward the front of the house, amused to see Thomas's shoulders relaxing with his own. Through the window a breeze wafted. Ian loosened his neckcloth.

"Listen," he said. "I don't think it wise to form attachments at Chesterfield. This lad—"

"Speaking of attachments," Thomas interrupted, "Seona told me what's been going on between you two. She wouldn't say how you found her out."

She hadn't mentioned the birch hollow. Ian was glad of it. "I offered her the chance to draw. She took it. I meant to please her."

"Please her? She's a slave, *Mastah* Ian."

"I know what she is."

Thomas began a retort but broke it off, turning toward the doorway.

"Cousin?" a diffident voice cut in. Judith stood with a lighted taper in a saucer. "I fear we neglected supper." She smiled a little ruefully at sight of the plate on the trunk, scattered with crumbs and chicken bones. "I see you've managed to fend for yourself."

"Aye, we have." He searched her face. "Are ye better now?"

She lifted a hand to her cheek. "Mama was distraught. I don't hold it against her." She seemed to mean it.

"I mind ye tried to speak up for Seona and Lily. Thank ye for that."

Judith's cheeks stained pink. "You were being kind. I could see that. I'll say good night, Cousin . . . and Thomas," she added.

As the glow of her candle faded, he noticed Thomas watching him with speculation. "It's more than your uncle having taken to his bed, why you won't go back to Boston."

"Her?" Ian waved a dismissive hand at the spot Judith had vacated.

"I didn't mean your *cousin*."

Ian stood, mistrusting the emphasis Thomas placed on that word. "What, then?"

"You want to redeem yourself in your daddy's eyes. But I knew that wouldn't be enough to hold you here. Not when you saw how it is."

"Ye don't know my mind—not as well as ye think. Part of me wants nothing more than to saddle Ruaidh, leave this place, and never look back."

Surprise flickered in Thomas's eyes. "What hinders you?"

The light was gone now, save for the candle's. Ian took up the plate and jug.

"I've Stoddard's contract to draw up," he said but paused at the door. It galled him to admit Thomas—and that meddlesome Quaker—had been right. How could he in clean conscience entangle himself in this life of slaveholding? Yet how could he walk away?

He was caught in it now, the issue taken on flesh and blood. His own.

"I cannot, is all," he said and crossed the passage to his room.

14

They were still up to their knees in corn. Across the mound left between them, Ian caught Seona's glance as she flung a shucked ear into a nearby bucket. Ignoring the burn of blisters, he redoubled his efforts. *Grip, rip, and jerk. Rip and jerk. Snap and toss.* He was getting the hang of it; Seona was husking only three ears now to his one.

The race had begun at dusk, when John Reynold divided the mountain of corn gleaned from his field with a row of marking sticks, then split his work force—Ian, Thomas, most of the Cameron slaves, Charlie Spencer, and a neighboring family, the Allens—into two teams. Ian and Thomas, neither having husked an ear of corn before, were banished to opposing sides. While the smallest Allen children frolicked with Spencer's motley pack of hounds, they'd set to work in a spirit of genial competition. A bonfire burned outside the barn. A cider barrel stood ready for a dip of the gourd.

Halfway through the work, with the fire sparking against a star-strewn sky, Naomi, Cecily Reynold, and Rebecca Allen had abandoned them to see to the feast to follow the husking.

They were down to the bottom of the mound now. Discarded husks lay in drifts. Naomi and Rebecca Allen trooped from the lantern-lit barn, waving off cries of help from Esther, husking corn with furious zeal at Ian's side.

Seona tossed away another ear and paused to tug up the shawl she wore against the chill. It was a length of wool, predominantly green, crossed with faded bands of blue with a rusty cord running through the center. An old plaid, worn, but fine of weave.

"D'ye know what this is?" Ian had asked as they walked the forest path to the Reynolds' with his uncle's slaves.

"This old shawl? Mama says it came from the old mistress."

"It's an arisaid. A thing a Highland woman would wear." He'd wondered, had his uncle's first wife been a Scot? The woman had died round about the time Ian's da crossed the Atlantic and settled in Boston. Not until then had Robert Cameron begun a regular correspondence with the half brother he hadn't seen for nigh thirty years. By the time Ian was old enough to be aware of distant kin he'd never met, his aunt was so long dead she'd sparked no curiosity.

Now, in the firelight, he was mindful only of what the garment's color did for Seona's eyes, until a nudge from Esther recalled him to his task. *Grip, rip, and jerk. Rip and jerk. Snap . . .*

He tossed the ear into the nearest bucket, narrowly missing little Ruthie Allen, whose task it was, along with her brother, to drag the buckets to the crib, empty them, and bring them back ready to fill again.

As Ian reached for another ear, Thomas, perched on the log beside Seona, brushed shoulders with her, speaking too low for Ian to hear. She flung away an ear, laughter in her eyes.

Grip, rip, jerk . . . snap. Ian flung the ear, making Ruthie Allen dodge and squeal as if it were a game. It should have been, but Ian's mood darkened as Thomas's laughter rose above the hum of conversation. Annoyed, he turned away. Down the double line of huskers, he saw a dark face shining in the firelight, as unsmiling as his own: Will, his uncle's field hand, shucking corn with his eyes fixed on Seona.

Teeth grinding like millstones, Ian turned his attention to the corn piled at his feet, fumbled the ear he'd half-husked and grabbed for it blindly, catching it before it fell.

"By jingo, lookit there! I'd have sworn there weren't a red ear in this batch."

Charlie Spencer's exclamation brought Ian upright. He stared blankly at the scruffy little man, then beyond him as conversation fell away. Necks craned. Fingers pointed. Beside him on the log, Esther bounced with excitement. "Who you gonna kiss, Mister Ian?"

On her other side, Jubal shushed her. "Don't you be asking Mister Ian such a thing."

"But he got to kiss *some*body."

Ian frowned. "I do?"

"Look at him." Spencer pushed a derelict hat back on his balding head. "Ain't got a clue what we're on about."

From the other end of the dwindling mound of corn, John Reynold explained. "You've found a red ear, Ian. Tradition grants you your pick of present female company to kiss in exchange for it—should she let you."

"The *unmarried* women," Zeb Allen clarified, catching sight of his own wife, heavily pregnant with their sixth offspring, coming back from the cabin with Cecily Reynold.

Ian stared at the half-husked ear in his hands. The exposed kernels were a mottled red, as was his face—or so it felt when he looked straight into the drowning green of Seona's eyes.

Helpful shouts arose:

"Pass it along if you can't decide!"

"There's some here won't dither!"

It sounded a good course. He thrust the ear at Spencer, who raised his hands to ward him off. "I'm a bachelor confirmed. Ain't about to go messing with that."

Ian turned in desperation to John, to find his neighbor enjoying his discomfort. "Sorry, my friend. I don't need a red ear to get a kiss." So saying, he swept Cecily into his arms.

"Take care," Zeb Allen warned, "or there'll be another mouth to feed next harvest."

Spencer slapped his knee. "Reckon you should know, Zeb."

Rebecca Allen rolled her eyes at her husband's waggled brows.

Laughter died, leaving everyone staring. Heat washed to the roots of Ian's hair. The rush of blood brought inspiration. Ruthie Allen stood by the bucket, elfin face splashed orange with firelight. Sweeping off his hat, Ian dropped a knee to the ground. "Would ye honor me with a kiss, Miss Ruthie, in exchange for this bonny red ear?"

Ruthie sidled up to him, took the speckled ear, and presented her cheek for the kiss. And got it, with all the relief-born gallantry Ian could muster. The child put a hand to her face, then crooked a finger. He leaned close to hear her whisper, "Your face scratches like Papa's."

Ian gave her blonde braid a tug.

"If you're of a mind to court my Ruthie, Mr. Cameron," Zeb Allen called out, "come round to my cabin and announce your suit . . . in another ten years' time!"

Whoops of laughter accompanied Ruthie's giggles as she skipped away with her prize. Ian clapped his hat on his head and grinned at her father. "I may, sir—if Spencer doesn't mend his ways and beat me to your door."

John raised a warning hand. "Take care, Ian. Don't scare Charlie into lighting for home before the rest of this corn makes it into the crib."

Ian joined in the laughter, grateful the attention had shifted. Sensing they were unobserved, he risked a look at Seona. Before their eyes could meet, she averted her face, from which a dusky tide was ebbing.

Mister Charlie had saved back a jug of his apple brandy. The men sat at table, laughing over tales of a hound Mister Charlie once had that would tree a coon, then climb the tree after it. " 'Twas over in the Tennessee—afore I'd had me enough of frontier living and come back across those high blue mountains."

Talk turned to Mister Charlie's years spent fur-trapping overmountain, during the time the western part of North Carolina tried to break free and call itself the State of Franklin.

Their voices washed over Seona as she sat with the hearth warming her back, Miss Cecily beside her rocking the baby's cradle with her foot. Seona reckoned everyone but Lily thought she'd gone back with them through the wood, toting the corn that was their pay for the night's work. She was weary enough she ought to have gone, snatched what sleep was left to be had. But such days as this came rare. There'd been a frolic in the barn after the feasting. Zeb Allen had plied his fiddle. She must have danced a turn with every man there. Save the one who found the red ear, who glanced at her now with those jay-wing eyes, making her wish this night might never end.

Then Mister Charlie said a thing that perked her ears. "Reynold tells me you spent some years trappin' too, up north among the Chippewa."

"Five years, aye." Mister Ian turned back to his brandy. "I've an uncle who's a fur trader. He came to Boston to visit my mam, took me back west with him. I was nigh eighteen, green as summer apples, and Uncle Callum not inclined to coddle me."

The air of the cabin rippled as the men settled in for a new tale. Mister Charlie lit a pipe. Soon the rafters filled with smoke. All Seona's being was fixed on Mister Ian as he spoke of his first weeks in the northern wilds, living in a mixed settlement of Indians, Frenchmen, and a few other Scots who spent their winters trapping furs.

Mister Ian had a pleasing voice, pitched deeper than one would expect. He'd taken off his coat and draped it over his chair. Watching the play of his muscles when he leaned forward and the shirt tightened across his shoulders, she tried to picture his life before coming to Mountain Laurel, tried to peer through the cracks between his words as he told of a sugar camp, where the Chippewa people moved in early springtime to tap the maple trees for sap to boil into sweetening.

John Reynold poured himself some cider. "I

don't think you've ever mentioned why you returned to Boston."

"Get your heart broke by a red lassie?" asked Mister Charlie, always ready to poke fun at anything hinting of romance.

Mister Ian tilted his head, firelight washing gold over his hair. "No, Charlie. It was a red laddie that did for me."

Mister Charlie choked on a draw of his pipe. "I'm jiggered," he said between fits of coughing. "Broke your heart, did he?"

Mister Ian laughed. "Never got near my heart. But he took a slice out of my leg." His fingers passed over the stitched-up rent in his leather breeches, which Seona had seen before and wondered about. "That's a tale for another time, though."

Mister Ian looked ready to put his head on the table and sleep where he sat. If this was their own cabin, Seona thought, she'd get up and go to him, untie his hair and spread it out between her fingers to see it loose in the firelight, brown as barley underneath, paling to a dozen shades of wheaten gold, bleached almost flaxen at the tips . . .

Mister Ian chose that moment to turn her way. "Seona, it's late . . . or is it early?"

"Early, by my reckoning," Mister John said, stifling a yawn.

The chair scraped back as Mister Ian stood, a little unsteady. "Late or early, it's time we left ye good people to your rest." He crossed to her and held out a hand.

As if from far away, Seona saw her fingers curl around his, and when he lifted her to stand, it felt like she was floating free, held to earth by his touch alone.

Ian took a pine-knot torch to light their way. Despite blistered hands and aching back, he was in good spirits—and full of them. The harvest moon shone bright, filtering cold through the trees. When they reached the stream that ran alongside the path, he picked his way to it and tossed the unneeded torch into the flow.

Seona came toward him in the moonlight, eyes dark pools. He'd lost track of the times he'd caught himself looking toward the hearth, where firelight glossed her skin and struck sparks in her thicket of hair. It had come loose from its braid, a warmer mantle than the arisaid knotted at her breast. He made her a leg, doffing his hat and bowing deep.

Seona stopped on the path. "What do you call yourself doing, Mister Ian?"

"What I'd have done while Zeb fiddled—were I less a coward. May I have the honor of this dance?"

"I don't hear no music."

He tilted his head, pretending to listen. "Don't ye?"

She laughed, and it was a lovely sound.

"I like it when ye do that. Ye've a laugh like the creek's singing. It suits your eyes."

"My eyes?"

"Like water over rocks, all mossy green and brown. Creek-water eyes . . . creek-water laugh."

She surveyed him with hands on hips. "I'm thinking you had a mite too much of Mister Charlie's apple brandy."

"Maybe so," he admitted.

"May bees don't fly in autumn, Mister Ian. You're drunk."

His gaiety sputtered and died, doused as surely as the torch. "Don't call me that."

Her face lifted to him. "Don't call you drunk?"

"Don't call me Mister Ian."

"What else am I to call you?"

"Just . . . *Ian*."

"You know I can't."

He took a step closer, heart beating fast. "Not in front of anyone else . . . but it's only us here. Say my name. Just the once."

"Now?"

"Aye, now." His hand found her arm. He pulled her close enough to feel her breath brush his throat when she spoke.

"Ian—"

He kissed her while his name still hung between them. The night had chilled her lips, but they warmed under his, tasting of cider.

A jolt of desire made him step back, aware suddenly of what he was doing. The forest tilted under his feet like a pitching ship. He swayed, then steadied himself.

"Why'd you do that?"

She sounded stunned. Angry? He didn't think so. But he'd managed to rattle himself.

"Because . . ." Because he was drunk and making a fool of himself. Because he'd wanted to kiss her since their collision in the upstairs passage but had firmly squelched such thoughts—or thought he had—knowing he'd no business wanting to kiss one of his uncle's slaves.

Only now he knew she was more than that. He'd tried to get the truth from his uncle, but did Seona know the truth?

"Because surely ye know whose daughter ye are?" he blurted, which had nothing to do with what she'd asked but accomplished what he'd hoped it would. Distracted them from that kiss.

Her face in the moonlight appeared carved of stone. "Lily's daughter."

"I mean your father."

"Slaves that look like me don't ask after their daddies." True or not, they were words meant to thrust him away. He wasn't budging.

"Lily's never told ye?"

"No."

That surprised him. "Did ye never wonder?"

She didn't answer that and he felt ten times an idiot. Who in her place wouldn't wonder?

"Did Master Hugh tell you something about me?" She asked it with more wariness than curiosity, but she'd asked.

"He didn't deny it."

"That ain't the same as claiming me."

"Ye're right. It isn't." She was shaking when he touched her again, lifting her chin. "So I'm claiming ye."

She jerked her head back. "You meaning to ask Master Hugh to sell me to you?"

"That's not what I'm saying. I meant only to call ye what ye are to me—my kin. I could no more own ye than I could my sister." He didn't know what he'd expected from her—certainly not the recoil of panic in her voice.

"Don't be talking to me like this, Mister Ian."

"*Ian.* Seona, I know ye're afraid—"

"Afraid? Mister Ian, you scare the ever-living sense out of me."

That jarred him. "Then why have ye come to the shop and drawn for me? I thought . . ." What *had* he thought? That they were friends? That she trusted him?

"I wanted to," she said, then whispered, "For *me.* I still do. But half the time I don't know how to be with you. I ain't your sister."

"My cousin."

She shook her head hard, like a deer shedding flies. "No, sir. Your slave."

That, ye'll never be, he thought to say, but a burst of liquid birdsong checked him. The moon was setting below the ridge, yet when he sought Seona's face again, he could see her clearly. The graying of the dark shot panic through him.

"We better get back."

Seona took his proffered hand despite an instant's hesitation, and sobered with the need for haste, he led her through the waking forest at a run.

15

Seona barely made it to her bed before she heard Lily waking. She lay unmoving, the scratch of her blanket against her cheek, thoughts turning tumbles in her head. Mister Ian . . . Master Hugh . . . Mama.

Back when her mama kept the house and garden both, Seona had worked at her side, but whenever her small hands weren't needed, she'd go up to the garret, if it wasn't too hot or too cold, and draw for a spell, until someone called her down to help again. Then they got their new mistress and everything changed. Seona was put in her *proper place,* which meant out of the house except to work or sleep. But now and then she'd sneak inside.

She minded one time when she'd been dead tired of pulling garden weeds and wondered could she make an escape. Her mama had been a few rows over in the pole beans. No one else had been by to see her slip off . . .

She made it through the garden pales, down the rose trellis path to the back door of the house. Tipping on bare toes like a cat, she crept inside, hoping to find Miss Judith up in her room, nose in a book.

How that girl liked her books! Sometimes she'd read aloud and spin Seona's head full of story pictures so vivid they begged her to take up the bits of charcoal and paper she'd hid under her pallet and set them down afore they faded.

She tread the back stairs to the new wing of the house and scampered down the passage toward the old front rooms, stopping when she got to Miss Lucinda's door. Peeking round the molding, she saw the mistress at her dressing table, dabbing a finger into a pot and smearing something over her brows, making them stand out dark. Seona had never heard tell of such doings. Her mama's eyebrows were smooth and black as crows' wings with no help from a pot.

It struck her funny. She clapped a hand over her mouth.

Her hand clamped tighter as Miss Rosalyn's voice issued from the room: "It's dull as porridge here, Mama. Can't we go back to Virginia?"

Miss Lucinda said, "Whining does not become a lady, Rosalyn. Your sister doesn't complain of dullness."

Miss Rosalyn huffed. "Judith's too boring to notice whether or not she's bored."

Seona scooted past the doorway,

glimpsing Miss Rosalyn sitting on her mama's bed, gazing out the window, looking cross and forlorn. She made it safe to Miss Judith's room—sure enough the girl was reading—and whispered what she'd just seen. Forgetting the book, they crept downstairs, made sure Maisy wasn't by to catch them, and blacked each other's eyebrows with soot from the parlor hearth. They never heard Miss Rosalyn, drawn by their giggles, until she was hollering for her mama to come see what they'd done.

Next thing Seona knew, Miss Lucinda was sweeping in with those false-black brows drawn tight, taking in what they'd done to their faces. "Judith Anne Bell! I warned you to leave this girl be. Is she teaching you to mock me?"

Miss Judith went white-faced, save for the patches above her eyes—like fuzzy black caterpillars perched on her forehead. Seona glanced up at Miss Lucinda, glowering down at her. Cold bloomed in her chest.

"I'll teach you not to scorn your betters. Rosalyn, fetch my strap."

All the while Seona was hauled out to the yard and her skirt yanked up to bare her bottom, Miss Judith begged her mama to please, please stop. But Miss Lucinda pinned Seona's skinny wrists hard enough to make the bones grind and wouldn't turn her loose. When the strap fell, she yelped and tried to tuck her knees, but her feet slid from under her in the rain-slick grass. She sprawled there, seeing nothing but her tangled hair, braced for another sting . . . that didn't come.

Seona twisted to look. Her mama had hold of Miss Lucinda's arm, locked in silent battle over that strap. Miss Lucinda gave her mama a shove that sent her staggering. The strap found Seona again, but only once before her mama fell across her, knocking her flat. After that Miss Lucinda didn't seem to care who got beat. The taste of grass was sour in Seona's mouth, mingled with the salt of tears. Every jerk of her mama's body shuddered through her. She heard herself whimpering, but nothing from her mama, just the thunder of a heartbeat against her back.

Then hooves clattered on the drive. Master Hugh's voice broke like thunder. "Lucinda!"

A cry rose that wasn't from her mama. Seona peeked through their tangled limbs. Master Hugh had hold of his wife, dragging her away to the house.

Last thing Seona minded before a pair of brown arms gathered her up was the sight of that strap abandoned on the crushed grass, Miss Judith in a heap beside it, soot smeared down her face and pink mouth wailing, "I'm sorry," over and over like nothing in the world could make her stop.

Naomi got Seona and her mama up off the ground. As they passed round back of the house, they heard Master Hugh hollering that he didn't care what Miss Lucinda's first husband did with his slaves, she was never—ever—to put strap to them again. There came a crash of glass breaking, but the sound didn't drown out Miss Lucinda's shattered cry: "What *is* she to you?"

A door slammed. Silence fell over house and yard, bottomless and still. They all dropped into it and Seona thought they'd go on dropping forever, with nobody daring to break the fall.

Seona dipped into the clay pot and rubbed the salve between her fingers, then took up Malcolm's knobby hand and commenced kneading, gentle to start. As his swollen joints eased, she dug deeper, while he sipped the birch-leaf tea her mama had steeped. Breakfast was frying on the hearth, but the kitchen hadn't lost its chill. Cooking would warm things up until they'd have the door propped. But not yet. Early morning, snug in the kitchen, was Seona's favorite part of the day—even when she was so bruised-eyed tired she'd had to drag herself from the cabin to get there. Though the Reynolds' shucking had been days ago, she hadn't caught up on her sleep.

Malcolm hunched over the table, eyes shut, the skin of his face all crinkles and sags. His shoulders hadn't stooped so bad after last year's harvest. He winced and opened his eyes. She'd hit a painful spot.

"Sorry," she said, reaching again for the pot, stifling a yawn.

"There's no helpin' some hurt in the healing."

"Mama does a better job of it."

"Ye've her touch, *a leannan*."

Sweetheart. Malcolm didn't talk Gaelic much these days. Seona liked it when he did. He was the last of Mountain Laurel's slaves who could. Naomi was the only other slave who'd been there when the old master, Duncan Cameron, was still living, but he'd died when she was still a girl. She'd long since forgot whatever she'd known of that tongue.

"You fixing to take Master Hugh his tea?"

At Naomi's question Seona noticed her mama wiping her hands on a cloth. "Best I get it to him," Lily answered. "He's turned restless, threatening to be up afore he ought."

"You add a little something to change his mind?"

Lily smiled. "Just chamomile."

There came a soft rap on the kitchen door. Mister Ian stuck his head in, giving them all good morning. Outside a cloudy dawn was starting to gray. He spied Seona at the table. "I'm for an early start in the shop. Join me when ye've a moment?"

Seona felt all eyes on her. Mister Ian wanted her to come draw. Or was that what he wanted everyone to think? It was no secret now, but other things were. Maybe he meant to talk more about Master Hugh and her mama. Or was it another kiss he had in mind?

That night on the footpath had turned her world on its head. But a white man had asked something of her. Whatever else had changed, she knew what was expected. "Yes, sir. Can I finish here?"

"Of course." He gave a nod and pulled the door shut on the silence.

The table was as scarred and worn as Malcolm's hand. Seona didn't lift her eyes from it. The fire crackled. Ham for the house table sizzled. No one spoke. Lily went into the herb room behind the loft ladder. Seona heard her leave through the back way, taking Master Hugh his tea.

"Ye're doin' a fine job," Malcolm said, picking up the thread of their talk, Seona thought, until he added, "Ye do fine work for Mister Ian, too."

Naomi clattered a pan. "Weren't for Mister Ian,

'spect we'd still be wondering what you did on a Sunday whenever you run off to the woods. Picking berries for Miss Judith, huh?"

When Seona said nothing to that, Naomi asked, "You have a nice visit with Miss Cecily, after the shucking?"

Seona studied on working salve into the base of Malcolm's thumb. "Mister Ian told Mama he'd see me home. I didn't expect he'd stay so late."

"You and Mister Ian spending a heap of time together, seem like."

"Somebody's got to take him dinner when he's too busy—"

"Child, you think no one here got eyes in their head?"

"Meaning?"

"Meaning you letting Mister Ian make a pet of you, and folks is noticing." Naomi bent to turn the ham. "Mister Ian weren't raised knowing how to be with our kind. He don't know how to keep separate—but you do."

"Our kind," Seona said, tasting the bitter in her voice.

Malcolm's big-jointed fingers closed over hers. "Heed Naomi, lass. And take heed to yourself. Mister Ian's looked on ye kindly, but he may no' always be here."

Gripped by mild alarm, she blurted, "Has he talked of leaving?"

"No' to me. But what Mister Ian sets himself to

do and what the Lord has in mind might no' b one and the same. But if he leaves, ye think Miss Lucinda will go on favorin' ye as he's done?"

They all knew the answer to that. "Master Hugh knew about my drawing and let it go on."

"There's no promise Master Hugh will long be here to shield ye, either." Malcolm's white brows puckered as he searched her face. "Is that how it is, then? Are ye hopin' Mister Ian will come to care for ye so he'll keep ye and your mama safe?"

Seona pulled her hand away before Malcolm could feel it shaking. She'd no doubt what the mistress would do to her and Lily if Master Hugh were gone. She'd have her revenge—for whatever wrong she thought Lily had done her. *And on me for being born?*

"You heard me tell him I'd go to the shop."

Naomi swung a kettle of porridge from the fire. "Do like you said. Just don't be giving Miss Lucinda reason to cast eyes your way on account of Mister Ian. She got her plans for him, and sure as I'm bound for glory, they don't include you." She ladled the porridge and plunked down two bowls. "Now tuck in, you two, and let's get this day commenced."

Despite the interruptions of the corn harvest and his uncle's infirmity, Ian was confident of having Stoddard's bespoke work—not ten desks, but more than two—done on schedule. Barring an

inability to keep his mind on the work. Tracing the outline of tail joints to the matching pin board clamped to the bench was proving no match for the distraction of Seona, seated behind him with pattern book and lead. Chance hadn't afforded opportunity to exchange a word with her since their own corn harvest; he'd tried to create the occasion, intruding upon her in the kitchen before the sun was up, all but ordering her to the shop.

She'd been too long in coming. Thomas had preceded her and was at work on the cooperage side of the shop. It was maddening. The partition wall might shield Seona from sight, but it wouldn't shield their conversation.

Ian inscribed the last joint marking and reached for the saw. Behind him, the scratch of lead abruptly ceased. His hand wavered. Was she as impatient to speak as he? Or did she dread it?

He'd forgotten which tool he'd reached for. *Hang it all.* He turned and went down on one knee beside her. "Let's see what ye've done."

Seona turned the pattern book on her lap. Chary of wasting paper, she'd confined her work to a single page: practice sketches of scuppernong vines and three completed designs. Two were simple, like the one she'd drawn for Catriona's desk. The third was more ambitious, a corner design that made elaborate use of the vine's tendency to curl.

"Bent on challenging my carving skills, I see.

242

But what's this?" He turned the book to the door's light, better to see a small sketch in the page's bottom corner. A pair of mice, bright-eyed and bewhiskered, one dressed in frilled gown and bonnet, the other in workaday clothes. Surprised and charmed, he said, " 'The Town Mouse and the Country Mouse'?"

"You know that story?" Seona's mouth lifted at the corners, bringing to mind what he'd tried to forget: that reckless moonlit kiss.

A moment passed before he found his voice. "Aye. I read *Aesop's Fables* as a lad."

"Miss Judith read them to me."

"Judith?" There was no concealing his astonishment. "Does she read to ye still?"

"Miss Lucinda put a stop to that, long time back." Seona rose and set the pattern book aside.

The case for the fourth desk he meant for Edward Stoddard's order sat atop the bench, dovetailed corners tight as any he'd ever produced. Seona ran a finger along the interlocking seam. "That night at the Reynolds', you said what made you come back from the wilds was an Indian?"

His heart gave a thump. He'd thought she'd been about to speak of . . . but she wouldn't. Not with Thomas listening. "Said that, did I?"

She pitched her voice low, capturing his faint Scots lilt. " 'It was a red laddie that did for me.' That's what you said."

Thomas's laughter filled the shop. He'd moved

to a jointer plane to finish the beveling work on a set of staves. "If it's a story you want, that's a good one. Don't let him put you off."

Ian stood and shot a look at his alleged slave, who shrugged and went on with his work.

"Aye, I'll tell ye then," he said, gladdened when Seona smiled. "It was late last winter it happened. The rice and the dried stuffs were near gone in the settlement and no fresh provisions to be had from Detroit for a month or more, so Uncle Callum and I went hunting. For meat. Not furs." They'd traveled eastward but game was scarce. They'd crossed into hunting grounds disputed with the Seneca and fell to tracking a small herd of elk. But the Seneca had empty bellies, too. Five warriors from the east converged on them, claiming the same herd. There'd been heated words, a scuffle; a warrior armed with musket and bayonet had slashed open Ian's thigh. "More by accident than design, I think now. I overreacted—wrenched the weapon from him and clubbed him with it. Then I was hit from behind."

Next thing he'd known, the Seneca had cleared out and Callum was kneeling over him, cursing him roundly as he stanched the flow of blood into the snow.

"He bound me up," Ian continued. "But the wound was deep. He rigged a travois and pulled me with it, then had me into a canoe. After a day my wound festered. I thought he was taking me back to the settlement but was too muddled with fever for a time to know. We'd reached the Carrying Place between Wood Creek and the Mohawk River before I realized we were heading east through New York."

Twice during the hellish journey the gash to his leg had half-healed, only to break open again with a foul seepage. And fever. The third time, in Boston, was the worst.

"But heal it did, in the end. As ye see." He slapped a hand against his thigh, where his breeches hid the ugly scar.

"He's making light of it," Thomas said. "The saw-blades wanted his leg off and would've had it, too, if not for his mama. She the one saved his leg, though for all his carrying on you'd think she'd half killed him doing it."

Seona's brows pulled together. "You weren't with Mister Ian in Boston, were you?"

Ian bit back the caution that leapt to his lips.

The silence was brief before Thomas answered, "Think I ain't heard this tale before?" Then he gathered up staves, trusses, and windlass and went out to the yard.

With so many distractions, Ian had done nothing toward seeing Thomas safely back north. Harvest was past, but there was still the tobacco in the curing barn, in need of hogsheads to bring it to market. Hogsheads Thomas was making now . . .

It was becoming far too easy to let Thomas stay.

"Why didn't you go back west with your uncle, after your leg healed?" Seona's question yanked Ian from his thoughts.

"I wanted to," he replied. "But it was weeks before I could sit a horse again. Besides . . . when I left Boston the first time, I wasn't on the best of terms with my da." A laughable understatement. "Callum wanted me to stay and settle what was between us. I expect he thought by time my leg healed, I'd have found a way." He hadn't, though by then he'd wanted to. "Uncle Hugh's letter arrived when I was barely on my feet, and it was decided I should come here instead."

Seona returned her attention to the half-constructed desk. "I'm glad you didn't lose your leg, Mister Ian, or die of that wound."

Ian's mouth tugged sideways. She didn't regret his existence. That was something, after his behavior on the path that night. He glanced through the open doors to see Thomas in the yard, fitting a ring of staves into a trussing hoop. Malcolm was lending a hand. Still he lowered his voice. "I asked ye to call me *Ian*."

She reached for the pattern book, as if needing something besides him on which to focus. "I know."

"Did ye think I wouldn't remember?" He hadn't been *that* drunk.

Her grip on the book tightened. "How can you know about me when Master Hugh won't say it's so? Has he?"

"No. But your face speaks to the truth of it."

She lifted a hand to her chin, then seeing him watching, snatched it away. But the gesture was telling. Ian was conscious of noises beyond the shop, senses stretched to catch any intrusion—a step on the gravel path, an approaching voice. Thomas's mallet banged out a reassuring rhythm.

"I aim to see ye freed. Like ye deserve."

Her brows drew tight. "Deserve? On account I look whiter than Mama? Or Thomas?"

He'd said he couldn't own her, but there was Thomas, making him seem the hypocrite. He wished he could explain. "Seona, the color of your skin isn't at issue. Your blood is. As for Lily, ye think I *like* seeing those ye love in bondage?"

What if he managed to wrest one slave's freedom from his uncle—and the General Assembly? He might find a place for Seona in Boston. Maybe even Lily. But the lot of them? Neither he nor his parents had the means to shoulder a responsibility of that magnitude. Not that his uncle would countenance it. If he was to do anything about freeing slaves, apart from Seona, it would have to be over the long term. He'd have to stay at Mountain Laurel, live the life of a planter, bide his time . . .

Maisy's voice reached them from the yard,

but he didn't catch her words. Thomas ceased his racket and called a reply. "Come on through, Maisy. You'll find her in the shop yonder."

Before either Ian or Seona could stir, Maisy was there, silhouetted against the sunlight, hands on hips. "I got beds to make, Seona, but I don't see no linens drying on that line."

"Mister Ian?" A second voice, hesitant and deep, came from behind them. Filling the door to Ian's side of the shop, Ally snatched his battered straw hat from his head and crumpled it in his hands. "They sitting round the curing barn waiting to be told what they meant to do."

"They *who,* Ally?"

"Will, Pete, Munro. They's sitting idle."

Ian pressed his fingers to his temples. "I expect they're meant to be doing whatever Dawes told them to do."

"That's just it." Ally twisted his hat. "We ain't seen Mister Dawes."

Behind him Maisy said, "Seona, the bedclothes ain't gonna wash themselves."

Ian lowered his hand as Ally's words sank in. "Ye've not seen Dawes today? At all?"

Ally wagged his head. "No, sir. Didn't want to bother Master Hugh, him feeling poorly, but what you reckon he'd want us doing?"

Heaving a sigh, Ian turned to Seona, to find she'd already slipped away.

16

Ian opened the door of Dawes's cabin and recoiled. Gulping a clean breath, he flung the door wide. Crumpled clothing, bits of rubbish, and a considerable quantity of fired jugs littered the table and a narrow bed frame, but Dawes wasn't lying sprawled among the disorder. Ian picked his way to the hearth and squatted there: no hint of warmth from the grate met his outstretched hand.

"Dawes does his job well enough sober," his uncle had informed him, spending worrisome breath after taking to his bed in relaying such warnings and instruction. "But the man bears watching to keep him so."

Ian stood, resentment mounting. He hadn't time for this. He'd desks to build. And heaven help him, slaves to sort. The latter proved a sullen group, lounging outside the tobacco barn, disinclined to be helpful when Ian asked what they were meant to be about.

"Don't know, Mister Ian." It was Will put himself forward as spokesman, mouth curved with insolence thinly veiled. "Nobody tell us."

Ian reached for patience, wishing himself anywhere else. The role of slave driver fit him like an ill-made coat. How did a man grow to abide it? Perhaps he found the wherewithal at the bottom of a jug.

"Right, then. The barn roof. There's the corner letting in rain, aye?"

No evidence of recent patching met his scrutiny. He set Pete to splitting shingles and, after an exchange with Ally, put him and Will to braking the flax harvest, stored in the weaving shed since the summer. Munro went to the orchard to glean the last of the apples. Ian set off for the house, in powerful need of someone on whom to vent his spleen. As chance had it, his aunt was crossing the front hall toward the stairs when he came through the back door.

"Madam," he called, striding down the passage, regarding neither his soiled boots nor the level of his voice. "Might I inquire after the whereabouts of your husband's so-called overseer?"

Lucinda halted, one hand on the banister. "Should I know of Mr. Dawes's whereabouts?" Her expression had worked itself into affronted bafflement, yet her grip on the banister was white-knuckled. "The man isn't accountable to me."

"Apparently Dawes holds himself accountable to naught but a whisky jug. Would it interest ye to learn the field hands sat idle half the morn for lack of supervision?"

"If you're telling me the hands are lazy, Mr. Cameron, that is no news to me. I daresay you'll find they require far stiffer measures than your Yankee-born sensibilities would seem to allow."

"If anyone needs a whip to drive him, madam—" Ian broke off at the sound of his uncle's door opening. It wasn't Uncle Hugh who stepped into the passage, but Lily. Though she'd every right to visit his uncle's room at present, the sight of her stirred the suspicion he'd lately entertained, suspicion mirrored in his aunt's brittle glare; Uncle Hugh—surprisingly on his feet—had joined Lily in the passage, speaking in an undertone. Lily nodded and made for the back door.

Lucinda raised her voice. "Hugh, should you be out of bed?"

Ian's uncle drew himself up, face gray with strain. "I should be many things, Lucinda. For the present, since I'm no' permitted peace, it would seem I'm to be arbitrator. Dinna question Ian on matters of running the farm. However stiff the measures he sees fit to mete out to our hands—or to Dawes—I trust he's able to discern the matter, though the lad's no more Yankee-born than I."

Lucinda absorbed the rebuke in frosty silence.

A rustle and murmur close to hand drew Ian's glance upward to see Judith and Rosalyn peeping over the banister, just as Maisy appeared in the parlor doorway.

"Beg pardon, ma'am. I seen through the window that Mister Dawes is back. Thought you'd want to know."

"Send him word to come to me," Uncle Hugh said from down the passage.

Lucinda and Ian both started to protest, but Maisy said, "I seen too . . . Mister Gideon Pryce and Miss Phyllida have ridden into the stable-yard."

Excited squeals erupted abovestairs; his cousins' craning heads disappeared.

Lucinda brightened. "Send to the kitchen for tea," she ordered Maisy. "Tell Naomi to use the chinaware."

Ian made for the back door as well, pausing only to tell his uncle, "I'll deal with Dawes, now he's back." And a sight more readily than he'd have done five minutes ago. If he'd little wish to reprove an inebriated overseer, he'd less to be corralled into the parlor with Gideon Pryce.

Despite Ian's hopes of evasion, he found Pryce loitering in the empty shop when he returned from dealing with Dawes.

"Mr. Cameron, you're a hard man to track down."

"I'm obliged to wear a number of hats these days." Ian flung his own onto the bench by the door and reached for his discarded leather apron, ill-tempered after enduring the overseer's vague excuse of sleeping off a drunk behind the tavern, miles away near the new county courthouse. "Which can I don for ye?"

It was then Pryce let fall news of the decision

made while Ian was off sorting Dawes. "I spoke to your uncle about the thermal springs in the mountains west of Morristown. As you'll be traveling nearly half the distance to deliver your . . . trade," he said with a nod at the current desk on the workbench, "I put it forward as an opportunity for your uncle to avail himself of the springs' renowned benefits. Mrs. Cameron embraced the notion with enthusiasm."

Ian soon learned Pryce had understated matters on that score. According to his aunt, they had been advised of a miracle cure, "sure to bring bloom to the cheek, tone to the languid pulse, and vigor to the wasted frame." Ian's acquaintance with the plan had come too late for intervention, even if upon reflection he'd have taken that course. Who could say the springs wouldn't do his uncle good? He might even have begun to anticipate the lengthened trip, were it not for Rosalyn.

She made her request at supper—his uncle joining them for the first time since his collapse—after Pryce's visit. "Papa Hugh, might I be permitted to accompany you and Cousin Ian to Salisbury?"

In the seconds of stunned silence that prevailed over the table, Ian assured himself there was no cause for concern. His uncle would forestall such foolishness. But he'd forgotten how the girl could charm—when she set her mind to do so. While he watched, perplexed by her persistence, Rosalyn weathered her stepfather's resistance with talk of shops and change of scenery and the everlasting boredom of the farm.

Sensing his wavering, Ian cut in, "We've no intention of lingering in Salisbury. We'll stay at most one night—hardly time for ye to stroll the shops."

Confronted with this dire prediction, Rosalyn didn't blink. "That will be sufficient to satisfy my expectations."

"But who will escort ye? I've business to attend, as ye know."

Surely his business wouldn't occupy him more than a few hours, she contended, and didn't he also have purchases to make? "If I must, I will content myself with visiting the shops you patronize."

"It would mean accompanying us to the mountains as well." Ian drew an easier breath, certain this would settle the issue. "Or did ye expect us to bring ye home first?"

"Why, Cousin, it would positively thrill me to see *real* mountains, for I never have, save our hills and ridges." Having swatted away his protests like so many buzzing flies, Rosalyn appealed to her stepfather. "It's been *a hundred years* since I went anywhere other than to meeting or Chesterfield."

That won a teasing smile. "Ye wear those years well, Daughter."

"It would be a good experience for her, Hugh,"

Lucinda said, surprisingly in favor of the notion. "Why not permit it?"

"For one thing," Ian said, "we've no idea what amenities these springs may boast. I'm prepared to camp rough on the riverbank."

"Camp?" Lucinda raised her brows. "It seems you weren't favored with Gideon's full account of the place. The springs were purchased by a gentleman with every intention of catering to invalids who come to take the waters."

Ian alone seemed conscious of his uncle's quiet wincing at *invalids*.

"Gideon assures us there's an inn on the property now," his aunt added. "It's quite respectable."

Judith had sat silent throughout the conversation, Ian noted. His uncle must have made the same observation. "Ye're gey quiet on the subject, Judith. Have ye no fancy to see the mountains?"

Judith briefly raised her eyes to Ian, then said, "No, Papa Hugh. I shall do very well here at home and . . . await your happy return."

Would that her sister showed such sense. Ian made a last attempt to drum a bit of it into her pretty head. "Rosalyn, ye'll not be coddled. Lily's to come along to help care for my uncle. Not to serve *ye*."

"I shall do very well without a maid," Rosalyn asserted. "I could even be of assistance. Papa Hugh, don't you agree? Cousin Ian has his business to attend. It would be to everyone's benefit for Lily *and* me to tend you while he's occupied. I'm certain she can tell me what is needed."

"All right," his uncle said, caving in at last. "Aye, ye may come along—if ye're truly minded to do as ye say and be a help and no' a hindrance. And pack only the one trunk, for we've all Ian's desks to convey."

Over the following days Rosalyn made good on her promise, shadowing Lily, asking after the proper dose of laudanum or the nature of the herbs in her stepfather's teas. Were they calming? Did they induce vigor? Bring on sleep?

Ian took to avoiding his uncle's room. Continuing to protest Rosalyn's presence on the journey, no matter how begrudged, had begun to feel mean-spirited. What couldn't be changed must be endured, a feat more easily accomplished when Seona was near.

The trees high on the ridge were beginning to blush scarlet, but inside Ian's shop it felt like spring. While Seona filled his pattern book, he filled the air with wood-scent and memories, letting fall a stream of boyhood recollections— his earliest of Scotland, which he strained to recall for her; Boston and the hardships of the British blockade, the hungry time when his father was caught outside the city with the militia; British retreat and different ships at anchor; the playing of militia-soldier in the cobbled streets; sled parties, fishing boats, ocean brine and seashells—as he flowed in on the tide of his past, feeling his way into her soul.

They didn't speak of kinship, her future, or his uncle, who sat by the fire in his room, summoning strength for the journey. He simply poured out his history, spilling memories with abandon, until the day the final beeswax coat was rubbed to a silken sheen, the desks were wrapped and stowed in the wagon, the canvas raised, and his uncle made comfortable in the sheltered bed. Rosalyn and her one trunk were ensconced therein, protected from dust and sun.

While he hitched Ruaidh to the wagon's bed, Ian found his gaze winging across the stable-yard where Seona stood with Lily, heads bent in earnest talk. Watching them, he felt a pang so wrenching he almost went to Seona himself. Then Lily broke away and hurried to him. He handed her up onto the board. Climbing up beside her, he took the reins and chirruped to the horses.

He'd a final glimpse of Seona standing alone, staring after them, arms wrapped in solitary embrace. Then the wagon creaked into motion down the drive.

Seona sat at the worktable, shoulders aching after hefting wash all day. The bread dough Naomi readied for morning filled the kitchen with its yeasty smell. Malcolm's cane chair was drawn near the fire where he sat, chin low on his chest. Ally had gone to help Jubal put the stock to bed. She thought about going to see the filly, Juturna, but laid her head on her arms instead. . . .

"Ye'll have never seen the sea?"

She shook her head and told him no, while from the stool she watched him saw through a length of poplar. His forearms were sun-browned, sprinkled with bleached hairs that curved round his wrist. His hand on the saw was long-fingered, lean and graceful in its shape.

"Tell me about it, the sea."

Through the chinks in his words she saw a boy racing barefoot over wet sand and splashing his feet in something like their creek, only colder, darker, and no end to it. Then the boy stopped and hunkered down, and she tried to draw the thing he'd bent to pick up off the sea bank, a thing he called a sand-dollar . . .

"What's ailing you this evening?"

Seona raised her head to see Naomi looking up from her kneading. *Missing Ian.* It was in her mind so fast she almost let it slip. "Missing Mama."

She didn't want the talk she sensed coming and got to her feet. Too late.

"Might as well say it. Your mama ain't the only one you miss." Naomi gave the dough a punch. "Mister Ian wanting you by him all the time, it seem."

Malcolm hadn't lifted his chin off his chest, but she knew he wasn't sleeping.

"Most times Thomas is with us." It was all Seona could think of to say. They were seeing more of Thomas these days. The mistress wouldn't have him in the big house with Ian and Master Hugh gone. The day they left, he'd shifted his things down to the cabins. She'd given him hers and her mama's and taken her pallet next door to Naomi and Malcolm's, rather than cleaning out the rickety one that stood empty save for cobwebs, dirt, and spiders.

Naomi ignored her mention of Thomas. "We know Mister Ian been filling your head with stories of his kin up north, like you got some pressing need to know all that. I'm telling you now because I done worked this row with—" The fire shot a hiss of sparks across the hearth bricks. Naomi turned to stamp them out. "You mark me, no good's gonna come of it."

Seona caught the snag in her words. *I done worked this row with your mama,* her mind filled in behind Naomi's back. And all this time she'd no more than half believed it. Mama and Master Hugh . . .

"Am I no good?"

Malcolm's head was up now, heavy-lidded eyes sorrowful and concerned, but it was Naomi who answered. "Ain't nobody in this kitchen ever thought such a thing of you. Was you and

259

your mama our own blood, we couldn't love you more'n we do."

Seona was glad at her words but wasn't sure Naomi had taken her meaning. Or maybe she had. Maybe they all had and she was the simple one, netted like a bird in a bush, caught between Ian and Master Hugh and her mama and everyone on both sides of the warming room with their closed faces and their shove-away words and their secrets.

A chill crept under the door from the dark outside, curling around her feet.

"That isna what Naomi meant," Malcolm said. "Your mama carries a mountain of grief along with her love for ye. Naomi wants to see ye spared that. So do we all."

Pain pressed sharp against her breastbone. "Spared the love or the grief?"

Naomi plunked the bread dough into a bowl and covered it to rise. "The two goes hand in hand for the likes of us, but you don't got to make it worse than it has to be. There's no future in you pining after a white man."

They stood outside the stable with their heads bent close, drawn off from the wagon where Mister Ian waited. "This work ye've been doing for him," Lily said, " 'tis done now. I've kept quiet, but now I'm speaking up. After we come back, don't be going no more to Mister Ian's shop."

Seona felt rebellion surging down to her toes,

but the fear at the back of her mama's eyes unnerved her.

"Girl-baby, can't ye see what's happening? Keep on like ye've been and time'll come when ye could ask that man anything and he won't be able to tell ye no."

She wanted to ask was that such a bad thing, having that kind of power over a white man. The very idea seemed thrilling, but hardly possible. "Mama, don't talk foolish—"

"Foolish? Wake up to what ye're doing." Lily gripped her shoulder. "They're waiting on me. God keep ye, girl-baby." Lily kissed her and went. Seona watched Ian's strong hands lift her mama onto the wagon, wishing it was her he was pulling up beside him.

Pining after a white man. Naomi's words to her now rocked her back on her heels. "Wasn't my daddy a white man?"

"You know as much if you look in a glass. That's all you need know."

"How you figure that's all I need know? Ian—Mister Ian—you want to know what *he* thinks? He says—"

"Seona." Malcolm's tone silenced her. "When Mister Ian's back with us, do what ye can to put off his attentions. That's all anyone's askin'."

What about what she was asking?

Her head was down, her eyes on the flagstones. A crack split the stone just inside the door. How long

261

had it been there, and why hadn't she ever noticed?

"Can't you see it's for the best?" Naomi asked.

"It's a hard-shelled creature, a lobster. Ye take it from the sea and boil it, then crack it open and eat the meat inside—fresh with butter and salt." He smacked his lips like a hound waiting on its supper.

Seona shook her head, trying not to laugh. "I can't picture it."

"It's like a crawdad, aye? Only bigger and bloody red when boiled."

He took the pattern book off her lap and the lead from her hand; her breath caught when their fingers brushed and she minded that kiss, every blinding second of it. They'd never mentioned it again. He'd never tried to kiss her again. Did he want to, or wish he'd never?

When he turned the book round again, her face was hot with the thoughts she'd been having, until she saw what he'd put on the page and laughed. The odd-jointed thing bore no likeness to any crawdad she ever saw. He laughed too, eyes merry as the boy's she minded from long ago.

"Ye see why I need ye so much? I cannot draw to save myself."

Don't look a white man in the eye—*she'd been told that since she could mind. But she'd forgotten how to look away from his. Not with his smile washing her like sunlight, and his words swirling in her head.*

I need ye so much.

PART III

October–November 1793

I stand upon a Riverbank, not knowing should I wade in, taking her with me, or step back from this perilous Shore and find another way. What would ye do?

17

They crossed the Yadkin River by ferry, no small undertaking with horses and wagon. While Ian's uncle and cousin remained under canvas, Lily stood on deck with him, near the cross-tied team. She seemed fascinated with the rocking, creaking, watery procedure—a tad chary as well, bracing herself as the rope-guided craft lurched free of its moorings and settled beneath their weight.

"My da and I made this crossing years back without a dunking," Ian assured her as the ferryman strode the deck, poling toward the opposite bank. "And it's a sturdier craft by far than was provided then. Have ye never crossed a river before?"

"No, Mister Ian. I've never been more than a day's ride from Mountain Laurel, 'til now."

Behind them Rosalyn said, "Neither have I but twice since Papa Hugh brought us from Virginia. We cannot all be as footloose as you, Cousin."

Ian turned to see her clambering from the wagon's interior. Between the ferry's rocking and her hampering petticoat, she lost her balance and nearly tumbled to the deck. He hastened across the battens and ropes to reach her. "Did I not ask ye to remain within?"

"Papa Hugh wished to see the river." Rosalyn gestured to the opening in the wagon's canvas, through which his uncle peered. "I was attempting to help him."

"If 'tis a bother, lad," his uncle said, "I'll stay put. I dinna mean to unsettle the horses."

"No, sir. Ruaidh doesn't blink at a crossing and the team's steady enough. Let me help ye."

Rosalyn arched a brow at his inequitable solicitude but held her peace and scooted aside to give her stepfather room to maneuver.

Disembarked from the wagon, Uncle Hugh stood at the ferry's raised gangplank, in full force of the river's breeze but out of the way of the ferryman, a burly fellow who touched his hat before turning to pole down the ferry's length. When Rosalyn's straw bonnet hove into view beside him, Ian watched the river and the wooded patchwork of the approaching bank.

"It's brisk on the water," she said.

"Ye might have brought out a shawl."

Rosalyn stared ahead, mouth a curve of unhappiness. Color flushed her cheeks and moisture spiked her lashes. The wind might account for either. Still Ian took her chilled hand and tucked it into the crook of his arm. She appeared so taken aback by the kind gesture his conscience smote him. "Ye must think me utterly out of humor."

She raised her eyes, so blue as to dazzle.

266

"Whereas I must seem an outrageous nuisance. I'm quite sensible of it," she said when he made to protest. "But I shall make you think better of me."

Ian caught the glance of the passing ferryman—one that conveyed the man's blatant admiration of his cousin and amicable envy. It caught Ian off guard. Had he grown inured to Rosalyn's beauty in so short a time? He'd thought her one of the most alluring lasses he'd ever laid eyes on that first night at Mountain Laurel, across the candlelit supper table—and in the night, when she'd sought his comfort in her shift. More than her exquisite features and abundant gold hair, there was the tiny waist, the rounded hips, one of which was just now pressed against his thigh.

Another face filled his mind, eclipsing her fair comeliness. A face framed in riotous dark curls . . . He edged away from Rosalyn just enough they no longer touched so intimately.

They were past midchannel, marked by a wooded islet already tinted with autumn hues. Uncle Hugh was gripping the ferry's side, watching the approaching bank. Suddenly he faced them, expression lit with such pleasure the marks of years and illness seemed to melt away.

"D'ye mind it, lad, first time we made this crossing? Ye were in such a fizz, scampering aboot, I thought ye'd gi' yourself a dunking midstream."

Only the river's lap against the ferry's tarred planking broke the silence.

Rosalyn stared.

Lily's face was a careful blank.

There was a queer sort of twisting in Ian's belly. "'Twas Da and me made this crossing when I was a lad, on our way to see ye. I never made it with ye, Uncle. Did I?"

He knew he hadn't.

The pale blue of his uncle's eyes cleared, but the light went out of them. "Aye . . . Ian. Of course ye didna."

Business with Edward Stoddard was conducted in the Salisbury inn where they'd taken lodging. Paid for his labors and satisfied with the transaction—Stoddard had requested six more desks, to be completed over the winter—Ian found his uncle asleep in one of two rooms they'd hired abovestairs. Lily sat at the window, mending in her lap, but rose to meet him at the door. "He may sleep for the night, but if he wakes, I'm hoping he'll take a bite of supper."

Ian glanced to where Lily's simples box lay open on a table by the bed, filled with packets and paper twists. The door of the adjoining room where, he presumed, Rosalyn rested from the journey thus far, was closed. "I've business in town. Best I see to it. We'll make an early start tomorrow."

Quickly he made his way to the taproom. He'd met the rail-thin tap-keeper, called Sprouse, over drinks with Stoddard. The man watched Ian make his way past a straggle of men gathered round a game of draughts.

"Your uncle find the room to his liking?" the man inquired.

Ian nodded. "He will when he wakes long enough to take note. Meantime, might ye know a place to purchase a quire of paper? And, er . . ." What did one call them? "Women's fancies?"

"Ribbons and the like?" The barman eyed Ian from beneath beetling brows as he nodded, face warming. "And paper? They intended for the same lady?"

"Aye. The lady's an artist."

Sprouse named a merchant likely to carry the paper, another for the fancies. His glance strayed toward the door. "Would the artist be *your* young lady?"

"In a manner of speaking. She's my—"

"Cousin?"

He turned to find Rosalyn in the taproom doorway, dressed in an embroidered velvet jacket that fit her figure snugly over a tight-waisted gown. The knot of men at the gaming board unraveled, craning for a view. A low whistle from the group propelled Ian across the room. He took Rosalyn by the arm and marched her out the front door.

Once outside, she pulled from his grasp. "Was that necessary? We did agree to do our shopping together."

She had him there.

"We did," he allowed with what spirit he could muster. While he could explain away the paper he intended to purchase for Seona, how was he to make his other purchase without arousing Rosalyn's curiosity?

Perhaps a timely distraction would present itself. He offered her his arm. "Shall we, then?"

Her smile rivaled the westering sun as she slid her arm through his. "Lead on, Cousin. I shall tamely follow."

Aside from a table, two chairs, and a clothespress, a single narrow bedstead furnished the room at the Warm Springs Inn Ian shared with his uncle. When he retired for their last night, Uncle Hugh was asleep in it, worn from the past several days spent soaking in the mineral springs tucked into their mountain retreat, or in conversation in the inn's taproom with the proprietor, Neilson, a fellow Scotsman. And his wife and numerous children. And other guests taking the waters. And the locals who came and went at all hours.

Ian had never considered himself a loner—his childhood companions had been Thomas, Ned, and the lads he'd attended school with; after that, his fellow apprentices and the master joiner,

Pringle; after *that,* he'd had Uncle Callum and those of his settlement, Chippewa, French, and Scots—but while he thought the springs were aiding his uncle's recovery, the noisy bustle of the place was wearing on *his* nerves. He longed for solitude. And silence. But his bone-deep weariness this night had more particularly to do with Rosalyn and her unrelenting attentions.

They hadn't ceased after Salisbury, where he'd barely managed to make the clandestine purchase he'd intended without rousing her suspicion. Since reaching the inn, whenever Lily was occupied with his uncle, it had fallen to Ian to keep Rosalyn from languishing with boredom and discontent. Understandable, perhaps; their accommodations had proved more rustic than his aunt had glowingly predicted. Rosalyn had lamented the plainness of the food provided, despite its abundance, but table fare wasn't the only aspect of the inn on the banks of the French Broad River to have occasioned her disappointment. The rooms were tiny and minimally apportioned. The maids were slatternly. And not a soul in the vicinity matched her notion of fitting society. Only Ian's constant attention would do—as companion or guardian, he was never quite sure. Perhaps the lass was afraid, though she'd denied it the one time he'd asked.

Suspecting she was doing her utmost to

comport herself as charmingly as possible in a situation she very much regretted having entered, he'd schooled himself to rigid patience and hadn't reminded her—more than once—that it had been at her own insistence she was there at all. Most men, to judge by the envious looks he'd received from guests and backwoods locals alike, would have relished his lovely cousin's attentions, but Rosalyn had exhausted him with seemingly endless conversation during strolls along the river or by the hour in the taproom or at the springs while they waited and waited for the steaming, stinking water to work its restorative magic on his uncle.

Today had been the worst. Despite three river walks over the course of the day, Rosalyn had clung to him like a chatty leech through supper and beyond. He'd finally shed her moments ago, in the passage between their rooms. Now all he wanted was sleep. In the morning, to his relief, they would be starting for Mountain Laurel.

The room was more than sufficiently warmed by the fire in the hearth, but he dared not open the window to the chill mountain night. Undressed to his shirt, he stretched out on a quilt beside his uncle's cot. In the grate a log shifted. Sparks spurted and died, wafting ash toward his face. He blinked in drowsy reaction, vision blurring.

He might be more than fatigued. He felt unwell. Seona's face swam in his mind, for the hundredth time since leaving her. From the moment they crested a slope west of Salisbury to see the mountains rising before them, wave upon blue wave, he'd wished her there in Rosalyn's place. She'd have wanted to draw them . . .

Putting out a hand from the quilt, he fumbled for his knapsack beneath the cot and the small, wrapped parcel within. Before he could draw back his hand, the irresistible tide of sleep had pulled him under.

He dreamt of a woman in his arms, at first no more than the taste of lips, the brush of tumbled hair. Then he knew her—*Seona*. He pulled her to him, groaning . . . and woke thinking for a bewildering instant he was back in his room at Mountain Laurel and the touch was real. The woman real. The weight of her in his arms *real*.

"Ian . . ."

That was real. He sat up, limbs tangled in a woman's shift, a woman's clinging hair. Not raven, but golden. He reached for a stick of firewood and flung it onto the hearth, raising a swirl of sparks, then took his cousin by the shoulders.

"What . . . ?" His tongue felt thick, his brain thicker. "What the devil are ye playing at?"

Shock had reduced his voice to a slurred hiss. Rosalyn made no effort to lower hers. "Playing? I don't—you're hurting me!"

Fire caught the stick he'd thrown on the grate, casting her in amber. A flash of unblushing truth darkened her eyes and he recoiled, the old shame rolling over him like a foul oil. Memories surfaced, of his cousin seeking comfort in the night once before. Of her persistent need of him on this trip. Now . . . this?

"Is *this* why ye begged to come along? Ye meant to *seduce* me?"

"No. It's only, Lily said we're leaving for home in the morning and . . ." Rosalyn glanced down, for an instant appearing vulnerable, almost ashamed. Then something hard took hold of her face. "I don't have to explain myself to you."

He blinked at her, disbelieving his ears. "I'd say it's the least ye owe me."

"What about what you owe me?"

His spinning head could make no sense of that. "What d'ye mean?"

"For days now you've made me think you would welcome this—paying me such attentions."

Either she was out of her mind, or he was. "Rosalyn, I was being *polite*."

She winced at that. "You were toying with me. You knew what I hoped. I've waited and waited for you to propose. Given you every opportunity. But you haven't!"

He winced as well, but only at the level of her voice, which was growing shrill. He hadn't had a clue what she'd intended. *Marriage?* Was that why she campaigned so hard to join them on this sojourn?

"I've been running from ye every waking moment since we started this journey," he said. "Or wishing I could. How could ye think I'd ever propose to marry ye?"

"How dare—"

He clapped a hand across her mouth. She struggled but he held her still, listening. How was it possible his uncle hadn't stirred, all the noise they were making?

"Keep your voice down or—"

She bit him. With a muffled growl he thrust her away. She caught herself with a hand, then waved the other carelessly at the bed. "Papa Hugh won't wake. I gave him an extra dose of laudanum. A deal more than I gave you."

Ian stared, the words burrowing into his brain like worms. Lily was the one who dosed his uncle. Did Rosalyn mean she'd given him twice the laudanum he needed?

A deal more than I gave you. She'd dosed *him.* When?

With effort he summoned memory of the last few hours. After supper she'd asked him to fetch her shawl, left behind in the dining room—just after he'd settled with a last whisky, which he'd left her minding in the parlor. Had that been her plan? Charm him into a marriage proposal. If charm didn't work, seduce him. And if *that* didn't work . . . compromise him into it, apparently.

"Get out," he tried to say. What issued was more snarl than speech.

In a blur of white she was on her feet. Before she reached the door, it opened inward. Lily entered with a lighted candle. With a furious sob Rosalyn shoved past her. By then Ian was at his uncle's side.

"Uncle? Wake up!" He shook the still form in the bed. His efforts drew a groan; then his uncle's mouth fell slack.

Lily's voice penetrated the panicked beat of his blood. "Mister Ian, tell me what's wrong."

"She dosed him a second time . . . *and* me. Laudanum." Dizziness swayed him, an effect of the black draft—which he ought to have recognized sooner, as much of the hateful stuff as his mam had made him swallow back in spring. "She didn't give me enough to matter. But *him*—will he be all right?"

Lily brought the candle nearer his uncle's face, fingers to his wrist, ear poised above his parted lips. His uncle's eyes rolled behind purple lids. "If she gave him again what I gave—just some to help him sleep. She's seen me give it enough times to know."

Ian made a disgusted noise. "He'll dream."

"He does." Lily glanced up, studying him not as a slave, but a healer. "I'll watch, Mister Ian, if ye need to sleep this off."

The opiate coursing through his blood dragged

at him like a tide. He fought it. "I'm all right. I'll stay by him. Go back to my cousin. Make her tell ye how much she gave him—to the drop." He didn't trust himself to do that deed without wringing her pretty neck. "If it proves more than ye thought, come back to me."

He wanted to believe he'd dreamt the episode. That Rosalyn, for all the conniving her beauty apparently concealed, wouldn't risk her reputation and prospects—not to mention his uncle's well-being—to drug him, seduce him, and . . . what? Had she expected his uncle to wake come morning, find them together, and promptly insist on a publishing of banns?

Fool lass, to think a little opiate was enough to have her way with him. That would take greater finesse than she possessed, the patience of a seduction spanning years, a web spun so gently he was bound long before he even noticed the strands.

Sickened, Ian sat beside the bed and bowed his head into his hands, shutting out the spill of firelight over his uncle's form. The chair edge bit into his thighs. He pressed harder, wanting pain. Wanting penance. He deserved every bit of insult Rosalyn had dealt him. Was it even the lass he should be blaming, or had his aunt been the instigator? Lucinda had been keen for Rosalyn to accompany them on the journey. But why would they have conceived the thing at all? Better to have approached the matter in the cold light of day. He'd have received that with far more grace. Refused it in the end but . . . Or did they know that?

A sobering chill shot through his veins as he recalled that first morning at Mountain Laurel, words overheard outside the kitchen—about him and his uncle's stepdaughters. *Think he'll marry one of 'em?* Esther had asked, and Naomi had said, *If Miss Lucinda have her way, he will. . . .* He'd dismissed it then as backyard gossip. But even if it was true, his aunt and cousin wouldn't have gone to these lengths to see such a marriage secured unless they had reason to suspect another had stolen his heart . . .

His uncle's body jerked beneath the quilts. With no more warning Hugh Cameron sat bolt upright, tumbling the quilts, and cried out with a violence that raised the hair across Ian's scalp. "Aidan!"

18

"Aidan . . . lad. They told me ye were *dead*." His uncle's flesh was iron, unbending, his eyes wide and fixed on Ian with a longing not meant for him, a recognition misplaced.

"No, Uncle. It's . . ." He'd started to object but on impulse changed his mind, giving in to his uncle's delusion. "Aye . . . Da. I'm here now. Please, will ye rest easy?"

There was a knock, a muffled query. The door opened and the proprietor, Neilson, banyan hastily wrapped, thrust a Betty lamp into the room. "Mr. Cameron?" he said, accent thickened with the grogginess of one yanked rudely from sleep. "What's agley then? The hollerin' had us leapin' oot o' our beds."

Ian started to pull away, but his uncle gripped his wrist. "Stay, Aidan. Dinna go so quick."

Aware of Lily crowding into the doorway behind the proprietor, Ian said, "I'm sorry, sir. My uncle's dream-fuddled, is all."

" 'Twill be the black draft," Neilson said, accepting the explanation in stride. "And here's your lass come tae gi' ye a hand." He made way for Lily. "Need ye aught from me and mine then?"

"No, sir. Again, I'm sorry to disturb ye."

"Och, lad," came Neilson's weary reply. "'Twould nay be the first time a wee stramash has come ower in these rooms, and nay the last. Guid night tae ye—morning, rather, for I think it all but is."

Lily shut the door on his departing back and turned, shift flowing pale round her shins. Candlelight glossed her high cheekbones and coppery skin.

His uncle's features lit at sight of her. "Look ye, Lily. 'Tis Aidan—come back to us." He stretched a hand from the bed, the other still clutching Ian. "Come here to me, lass. I've a thing needs saying to the both of ye."

Lily stepped back, stumbled, and nearly dropped the candle, crying out as hot wax spattered her hand. "It's too late for this, Master Hugh. Too late!"

She wrenched open the door and fled.

His uncle's head fell back on the pillow, face a mirror of Ian's bewilderment, a vague disquiet in his eyes. Until they slid back to Ian and warmed. "D'ye mind the wee deer, Aidan? The one ye made a pet?"

Seona had told him of a deer . . . "She used to feed from our hands," he said, snatching at the scrap of memory.

"Only from yours, lad. 'Twas ye had that touch with the creature." Uncle Hugh's grip tightened as a spasm of pain, of mind or body Ian couldn't

280

tell, bowed his mouth. "I could wish ye'd come back to me sooner. I did a terrible thing . . . thinking ye dead."

Ian shook his head. "What . . . what did ye do?"

" 'Tis no' your fault, see? I dinna blame ye. But what I did . . . 'tis unspeakable."

Did his uncle mean his second marriage, perhaps made in hope of producing another son? But his uncle's union with Lucinda couldn't be called *unspeakable*. Unless deep down he saw it as a betrayal of Lily and Seona.

The man's stricken eyes searched his. "Dinna stare so at me, lad. I kent 'twas wrong to do it, that ye'd despise me for it. Ye were always after me to free them."

Them. Whatever this was tormenting his uncle, it couldn't have to do with Seona. Aidan Cameron had died before she was born. "Who, Unc—Da? Is it to do with Lily?"

Uncle Hugh grimaced. Then, almost dreamily, his mouth relaxed.

"Ye mind how your mother found the wee raven chick, and ye took it to tend? What did ye call it? 'Twas after that bit of old verse . . ."

His uncle's mind had veered away from Lily. Or flinched away. His eyelids drooped, concealing the sinking flame behind them. The grip on Ian's wrist relaxed. Half-lost in the dream now himself, he pulled his hand away and turned to the window, where the first rose of dawn outlined the mountains.

"*I* mind it," he said. "He called it Munin." *Memory.*

The clang and bump of the awakening inn went on beyond the door, but they were left undisturbed in their room. Ian sat by his uncle's bed. Lily— come back to them dressed and composed not a quarter hour later—occupied a chair at its foot, her braid glinting blue-black in the dawn light chinking through the curtains, a shawl draping her shoulders. She hadn't mentioned Rosalyn. Ian hadn't inquired. There were questions more pressing.

"What happened to my cousin, Aidan? How did he die?"

Lily's head had drooped, but when he spoke, she jerked it up, awareness in her red-rimmed eyes. She hadn't been asleep.

"Tell me what my uncle did because of him— the thing that haunts him, that makes him look at me and see the son he lost."

Lily drew breath and let it out in a silent heave. "No one kens the whole of it, Mister Ian. Or if so, she's gone now beyond the telling."

"Who's gone?" His uncle's first wife, he thought, but that wasn't who Lily meant.

"Ye maybe won't mind Ruby," she said. "But ye do her boys."

In the kitchen that first morning, that awkward ending to the conversation when he'd asked about Sammy and Eli. "Naomi mentioned Ruby when I asked after those two. The brothers, one with the scar on his brow like a hook."

"Sammy, the older one." In the hearth a log shifted, spilling ash from the grate. Lily didn't seem to notice. "Their daddy, Esau, was one of Master Hugh's field hands. Ruby was a pretty gal, her boys wee things I tended back then, while she worked. One day we heard a shot away off in the fields. Thought it was a hunter—maybe even Aidan. He'd gone out with his musket. Then Mister Dawes came in, Esau trussed in the back of a cart, Ruby stumbling behind weeping—" Her voice caught. "And Aidan, shot by his own musket, laid out dead. Esau's doing, Mister Dawes said."

Ian glanced at his uncle, fathoms deep and undisturbed by their voices, features still as a figure on a tomb. The bones beneath his grayish skin seemed nearer the surface than they had, as though in the night the flesh between had melted away. He was far less certain than he'd been upon lying down to sleep that this trip had been of any lasting benefit.

"Do ye truly want to hear this, Mister Ian?" Lily asked.

"I think I must."

Lily sighed in acquiescence. "I didn't stay by to see what happened next. I was in no state— we were all distraught. Naomi told me later how

283

Master Hugh and Mister Dawes strung Esau from that big chestnut by the house. Mister Dawes went to round up witnesses so the whipping would be done legal. But Master Hugh was taken wild with grief. We never were sure he kent what he was doing 'til it was too late."

"What did he do?" Ian asked, though by now he hardly needed to be told.

"Before Mister Dawes came back, Master Hugh took up the whip and started in on Esau. He hadn't struck more than a handful of times before Esau stopped hollering and went limp. He was dead."

"By a few lashes?"

"Shock, we reckoned. Made his heart give out."

A door slammed somewhere out in the passage. It jarred Ian to recall a world disconnected from the grief and regret that seeped from his uncle, a hemorrhage saturating all it touched. But Ian suspected there was more, something darker that had twisted inside his uncle, a bitterness that had trailed him down the years. "Aidan was shot, ye said? How did Esau get hold of . . . ? What was it? A musket?"

Sorrow shadowed Lily's eyes. "They say Aidan was out hunting. He come upon Ruby in the fields, tried to . . ."

Ian waited, then realized what she didn't want to say. "He tried to *violate* her?"

She nodded, pulling her shawl higher. "Esau

284

seen it and come running. That's what brought Mister Dawes, seeing Esau leave off his work. But Esau got there quicker and lit into Aidan, got hold of his musket and shot him. I think it broke Master Hugh's mind as well as his heart, seeing his son murdered, hearing what he'd done to Ruby. Killing Esau made it worse. For days he wasn't right in the head. He never saw Aidan put in the earth. Sometimes I think that's why he forgets Aidan's gone. He had a stone put up after a time, but he never saw his son go beneath it."

Ian straightened, back and neck protesting, tired mind sorting through all he'd heard. Lily had raised more questions than she'd answered. He could feel them piling in a jam behind his skull.

Family . . . kin. His mind kept coming back to that.

"I'm told my uncle's wife—his first—cared for ye, that ye were like a daughter to her."

Lily's brows rose like wings. "Did Seona tell ye so? I reckon I was, for a while."

"And my cousin—was he like a brother?"

She fixed her eyes on the crumpled bed linen. "No."

"But, Lily, my uncle said something before, thinking me Aidan. 'Ye were always after me to free them.' Did my cousin want to give ye your freedom?"

"Not just me. He didn't want to own slaves at

285

all. He and Master Hugh argued something fierce over it."

She yawned and covered her mouth. Not before he caught the yawn and gave it back tenfold. He bent forward in the chair and rested on the feather tick, head pillowed on his arms. Sleep reached for him, but something in Lily's account wouldn't square. Why would Aidan Cameron have pressed his father to free their slaves, then turn around and abuse one in such a brutal manner? He would rest a moment, then ask . . .

When he woke, Lily was no longer in the room.

Groaning at the throbbing of his head, Ian pushed up and rubbed his face, feeling the quilt wrinkles indented in his stubbled cheek. He blinked at the head of the bed. His uncle's eyes were haggard, but open.

"Uncle?" It came out a croak.

"Ye look terrible, Nephew. Did ye no' sleep well?"

Ian barked a laugh. "I did not." He thought his uncle jesting, but closer scrutiny revealed no memory of the night's turmoil in his questioning gaze.

"Feel up to helping me dress?" his uncle asked.

"In a bit. Just now we're going to speak of Seona."

Uncle Hugh raised a wary brow. "What of Seona? Though I'm sure I can guess."

Ian helped his uncle sit up, then took his seat beside the bed. "There's no more room for guessing between us, sir. I'll be as plain as I know how. Unless ye grant Seona her freedom, I will bid ye farewell the hour we return to Mountain Laurel and ye can do what ye will with your land and everything on it. I'll have no part in it."

He was bluffing, of course. He could never simply walk away now. But he kept that knowledge hidden far down in his soul as his uncle received his ultimatum unflinching. To Ian's surprise he said, "I'll petition the General Assembly for her freedom because I choose to, not because ye press me to it. And on two conditions of my own."

Ian's heart began to pound. It wasn't the answer he'd expected. Not without a fight. But he kept his voice level as he asked, "Why? Why now, I mean, if not because I press ye to it?"

His uncle's mouth twisted. "Lad, we both ken I'll not live to make old bones. I never for a moment believed this—" he gestured at the room and beyond, to the river with its healing springs—"would be my cure."

"Then why trouble to come all this way?"

"I wanted to see the mountains again. That's all." His uncle's eyes, momentarily wistful, hardened against the pity that must have shown on Ian's face. "So then. Let's have this settled between us."

Ian swallowed, nodding once. "Ye spoke of conditions. Name them."

Uncle Hugh straightened against the pillows

at his back. "Granted I do this thing ye ask, how d'ye expect Seona to survive? I ken ye thought to send her to Robert. I'm nowise convinced my brother will blithely take her into his home, though I ken he took in that soldier after the war, even let the man work in his establishment."

"That soldier saved Da's life in battle, at Freeman's Farm," Ian said of Oliver Ross, Thomas's father, who'd died before Ian returned from the frontier. "Da taught him his trade and made him partner. Not from gratitude alone. From friendship."

"I take it the man never made claim of kinship on Robert?"

"No. But he was like an uncle to *me*." And Thomas closer than his own brother. Once upon a time.

Uncle Hugh's flinch was barely discernible. "All I'm asking is that ye write to Robert, put the question to him. If he'll take the lass, see her kept decent, educated, and in time a place—or a good match—for her found . . . that's the first condition."

Ian knew the next already by the weight settling in his chest. "The second is that I remain at Mountain Laurel." Trade his soul for Seona's freedom.

For a moment he thought he would be sick.

"Ye understand, then," said his uncle, watching him.

"Aye." He'd freed Seona—or as good as—

and in so doing shackled himself. His uncle believed he stood at death's door, but until the day he crossed that threshold, months from now, or years, Hugh Cameron would be master of Mountain Laurel. But after, as his uncle's heir, Ian might do as he saw fit with the place and its people. Could he bear the waiting?

He hated this, measuring his endurance against the span of a man's life. Had such thoughts come into Aidan's mind, all those years ago when he'd argued in vain for the freedom of his father's slaves?

But Seona would be free. Free to make at least a few choices for herself. Free in distant Boston, if his da would help him.

"We'll see this put in writing," Uncle Hugh said, breaking into his troubled thoughts. There was ink and quill in the room for the purpose. Ian had paper aplenty in his own possession. "And we've witnesses beyond that door."

"Aye, we do." Ian's hand shook. He made a fist of it.

His uncle sighed. "Set it down then. I'll read it when ye've done."

"Ye maybe notice, I'm no' insisting ye marry one of the lasses as part of this arrangement, though Lucinda would no doubt bid me do so." Uncle Hugh eyed him from the chair opposite, having risen and wrapped himself in a banyan while Ian wrote. "But I have noticed ye spending a deal of time with Rosalyn these past days."

Pausing to dip the quill, Ian raised a brow at that. "It could hardly be avoided, but I doubt she'd have me now."

"What did ye do, lad? Fend her off a tad too rough?"

The quill jerked in Ian's hand as heat smote his face. He didn't mean to let on about that intrusion into his bed. No reason to widen the ring of shame—his own or Rosalyn's. None of it mattered now. "I may have said a thing or two I oughtn't have," he admitted.

Uncle Hugh snorted. "She'll be after vexing a man, lovely as she is. Tell her ye didna mean a word of it. Buy her a bauble on the journey home—maybe that paint she's wanted for her room, can such be found along the way. She'll sweeten up in time."

Ian made a noise of assent and concentrated on his penmanship, willing the blood from his face before his uncle noticed.

Neilson was called to witness as they set their signatures to words promising a petition of the General Assembly for Seona's freedom, provided one Robert Cameron of Boston, Massachusetts, agreed to take her under his covering. And, in the event of that agreement, Ian's vow to remain at Mountain Laurel. Heir apparent. As long as his uncle lived.

19

She was sick to death of entrails, of rendered fat and bacon slabs and hog bristles. And with finding Ally blubbering behind the kitchen when he was meant to be helping with the butchering.

"I can't, Seona," he'd moan, snuffling tears behind fingers thick as sausage links. "Them helpless little things . . ."

No sense reminding him *them helpless little things* were full-growed, beechnut-fed hogs that might've turned on her and Naomi and done their own butchering without the men by with their clubs. Every year Ally fretted himself over killing the hogs. "Just get busy with something. Don't let the Jackdaw catch you idle."

Truth, though, they hadn't seen the overseer for days. Naomi had directed them through the last of the scalding, scraping, cleaning, salting, and stuffing.

Sunday had finally come around. With the smokehouse full to bursting, Naomi had given Seona leave to lie abed, but it wasn't sleep she most craved. While Jubal drove Miss Lucinda and Miss Judith to their church meeting, Seona went to Ian's shop, took the paper and lead he'd set by for her, then struck out through the orchard to where the ridge began its climb.

She settled with her back to a tulip poplar. A few leaves had already drifted down. She twirled one by its stem, wishing for paints to put its yellow to paper. She'd never seen an artist's paints. Did Ian's sister have some? How many colors? How did it work, getting them onto paper or a canvas like the ones that hung in the big house?

Letting the leaf fall, she took the lead from her pocket and set to drawing the view before her, long rows of apple trees sloping down to the house, rising white at the other end.

She heard the crackle in the brush before she saw them, a doe and two big fawns come down the ridge, headed for the orchard to browse on windfall apples. With the paper against her knees, she drew quick, like she'd learned to do with Munin, and managed a likeness before they moved off into the trees.

"Thank you kindly," she said and nearly jumped out of her skin when a voice answered.

"Aye . . . bethankit."

Spying the raven perched in a bough above, her heartbeat slowed. "You always find me when I'm drawing, vain thing."

Munin glided down to the ground and set to preening his wing feathers. Biting back a laugh, Seona obliged the bird, thinking on how she'd felt when Ian praised her drawings in the hollow—like something had broke open inside her and poured out light. Tiny at first, like a candle's flame. Then he'd taken what she'd done and used it to make those desks, and the light blazed up a bonfire. How could she leave off thinking of him? Every way she turned, he was there in her head. Maybe when he came back from the mountains, she wouldn't spend all her waking time trying to capture every word and look of him. Maybe she'd stop seeing him in her sleep. . . .

What with the butchering and helping in the kitchen in Lily's place, it seemed she couldn't sit still long and stay wakeful, even to draw. Drowsy now, she lay aside lead and paper, leaned back against the tree, and closed her eyes.

A rustling worked its way into her doze. The deer heading back up the ridge, or Munin scratching in the leaves. The rustle grew nearer. And stopped.

"Lookit here what I done found." The voice drifted through her sleep-fog. Munin's, she thought, though it struck her as wrong . . .

"Not now," she murmured.

Something hard prodded her thigh. Seona started awake, her hand coming down on the toe of a boot. Above her loomed the Jackdaw. A scratch scored his jowly cheek like a red thread snagged in the stubble of his beard. His clothes were filthy, the smell of him ripe.

"A man might take a notion you was waiting here apurpose. Waiting on him to come along."

His slow, stripping appraisal raked a claw of fear up her spine. She was on her feet quick. It was rare these days she got so close to the overseer. He was big. Tall as Ian but barrel-built where Ian was lean. She shrank down, tried to make herself small, eyes on his boots.

"I didn't know you was coming along, Mister Dawes."

"But here I am. And your white knight's gone and left you lonely, ain't he?" The boots edged closer. They were caked with clay and pine needles. "You know what I'm talking about."

He spat a stream of tobacco juice into the leaves at her feet.

"I best get back to work." She didn't glance at the drawing left under the tree, but as she made to step past him, the Jackdaw's big hand closed over her arm. Seona caught a fresh whiff of his reek before his other hand knotted in her hair, forcing her face up. She yelped.

He shushed her with his mouth.

His breath was a foulness. She struggled to get free and when she couldn't, she bit. His bellow hollowed out her lungs before he shoved her away. Her head hit the poplar's trunk in a burst of white stars. She was on the ground, bits of leaf stuck to her cheek. Blood and tobacco chaw were in her mouth. She got to her knees, gagging, while Mister Dawes stood over her, wiping his lips.

"Tarnation, girl! Was just having some fun with you. Thought you fancied a white man. Like your mama done."

She tried to crawl away. He got hold of her from behind, hoisted her off the ground like she weighed nothing. She kicked, but her bare heels made no impact on his booted shins. His voice rasped in her ear. "Think all he wants is pretty pictures? I could show you what he wants."

The Jackdaw pulled her tight against him, an arm crushing her ribs. She writhed to get a breath.

"That's it, wildcat. You got the idea."

Her stomach heaved and she prayed to be sick on him. Before that happened, she felt his body jerk. Then she was back on the ground, gasping like a landed fish.

"Mister Dawes."

Seona raised her head. Thomas was standing at the orchard's edge. Behind him like a fence row stood the field hands, Will, Pete, and Munro, feet planted wide, arms crossed. It might've seemed funny had she not been so relieved.

The Jackdaw didn't think it funny either. "What you boys doing?" His voice was a snarl, yet Seona heard the fear in it.

Ignoring him, Thomas took a step toward her. "Can you stand?"

The Jackdaw whipped a pistol from the back of his waistband. Its hammer snicking into cocked sounded loud as a shot. "Not one step closer, any one of you boys."

Thomas didn't flinch. "Seona, how bad's he hurt you? Can you stand?"

He didn't need to ask a third time. She lurched to her feet and ran into the orchard like a rabbit for its hole.

Had she been thinking straight, she'd have gone to earth in Naomi's cabin, not the one Thomas was using now. But there was water in the cracked pitcher. With shaking hands she splashed her face, filling her mouth and spitting out the taste of Jackson Dawes.

Her breath made a ragged whimper as she sat on the edge of Lily's bed. She heard feet scuff the dirt, saw breeches and bare brown shins. Jerked when Thomas touched her. He pushed the hair from her forehead.

"You got a pumpknot coming up."

"Threw me up against a tree," she got out, then clapped a hand over her mouth.

"Was he drunk?"

They'd all thought Mister Dawes off on one of his drinking spells, taking his time about it with Master Hugh and Ian away. But she hadn't smelled a hint of spirits on him.

A shadow in the doorway made her jump. Will stepped in, winded from running. "Jackdaw got some things out his cabin. Now he gone back up the ridge."

Thomas stared. "Back up the ridge? Why?"

"Hanged if I know. But we gonna be in a heap of trouble over this."

"Look what he's done to her. You think Cameron would keep him on if he owned to it?"

"What's he gonna hold over us to make sure we don't talk?"

Seona groaned. Their fussing was making her sicker. She made it to the basin before she retched.

"She needs tending," Will said. "Come on, Seona. I'll take you to Naomi."

Thomas didn't try to touch her again but said, "Will's right. Besides, Master Ian told me to look after you."

Will crowded forward, jaw set. "I said I'd take her."

Seona wiped her mouth. "I know where the kitchen is. I'll take myself."

She set out, pretending not to notice the footsteps on her heels. One set. She got as far as the chicken coop before Esther caught sight of her and came running out. "Seona—look at the knot on your head! And *blood*. Who done that to you?"

"She fell in the woods," a voice said behind her. Thomas.

"I hit a tree," Seona added, sounding almost normal.

Esther hopped around for a better view. "Hit it with your head?"

"That's right." A scream wanted to tear its way out of her.

Thomas cleared his throat. "You left the coop open, pester-bug."

Esther glowered at the name, then whirled to see the slatted door of the henhouse swinging, the meanest hen slipping out.

Seona didn't stay to watch her dart after it.

She sprinkled dried geranium in a saucer, then poured in a cupful of water. While it steeped, she found the cloths for washing wounds. Thomas, who'd followed her into the herb shed, caught her shaking hand. "Let me do it. You can't see your own head."

"How'd you find me?" They kept their voices low. Nothing but a door stood between them and the kitchen, where Naomi was working. Seona would have to go in and help soon but needed time to gather all her pieces.

"I followed you," Thomas said, not a bit shamefaced to admit it. "Saw Dawes come down the ridge. Only took a moment to round up the hands."

She flinched as he pressed the cloth to her brow, feeling sullied by what happened. No amount of water was going to help that stain. Tears swelled behind her eyes until the hurt of holding them back was too much. Thomas put the cloth down and took her in his arms. She cried silent into his shirt, yearning to be where Ian was, to sink into one of those warm springs, let the water come over her head.

Gradually she realized Thomas was talking.

". . . woman over at Chesterfield, a kitchen girl. And her boy. They'll go with me when the time comes."

She took her head off his shoulder, wiping her nose. "Go? What are you saying?"

Thomas dropped his voice even lower. "I'm saying it doesn't have to be this way. Not for you. I aim to go back north before winter. Can't promise to take many with me this time, but you and your mama should come."

Had that tree knocked her wits loose, or was Thomas saying he meant to turn runaway and carry off two Chesterfield slaves? And he was inviting her into it?

"I heard your mistress talking to the mousy daughter, that Miss Judith," he said. "She means to put you with Will, to make new little slaves for her. Figures it's only a matter of time before she brings Master Hugh around to it. Or she'll wait 'til he's gone."

Seona's throat clenched too tight to speak.

"You know in the end she'll get her way . . . unless you come north with me. Find a place no one knows you and pass for white. You could do it, if that's what you want. Or maybe you could stay with me. Whatever."

Leave Mountain Laurel? Pass for white? She gaped at Thomas, hardly knowing what to say first to this crazy talk. "How you meaning to get safe away?"

Thomas stared back, weighing his words. "There's a man promised to help me. A white man we met coming south. A Quaker."

"How you meaning to find a Quaker?"

Thomas narrowed his eyes at her, then shook his head. "Reckon that's all I'll say, for now."

Too much already, Seona was thinking. "Does Mister Ian know what you're planning?"

Thomas's mouth twisted. "Wouldn't that put a hitch in things, if he did?" Which was him telling her plain to keep her mouth shut. "Just think on it, Seona. *Freedom.*"

Thomas was waiting, wanting her to say she'd do this fool thing, when Naomi opened the door to the kitchen and saw her face.

Seona fled the kitchen after supper was cleared. She'd the slaves' washing, which had to be done on her own time, and was hanging out the last of it by lantern when she pushed aside a shift to find a man standing on the other side. She leapt back and nearly fell over the toting basket. "Will! You trying to scare me dead? What you doing up by the house this time of night?"

Will glared in the lantern's glow. "Come to ask you somethin'."

Seona snatched up basket and lantern and made for the washhouse to put them up. Will waited outside, then fell in with her as she started for the cabins.

"Ask me what?"

"Why would Mister Ian want you looked after?"

She stopped in her tracks. "What's it to you if he's mindful of my well-being?"

"Well-being?" Will stared, then shook his head. "You know better. White men be like chilluns—find themselves a pretty toy to play with and leave it in the dirt when they done. They don't care about no *well-being*."

Her face went hot, though the rest of her was chilled. "You don't know—"

"Where you think *you* come from, girl? Or why your mama never give to Ally or Munro for a broomstick match? Master Hugh long since done with her, but he won't share, neither."

It was the nearest anyone had ever come to admitting Master Hugh was her daddy. Except for Ian. "Ian—Mister Ian ain't like that."

She'd caught herself too late.

"Don't got you calling him *mister* no more, do he? You got some notion he *in love* with you?" He made the words sound dirty.

"Of course not. He's just . . ." She wasn't sure

what she'd meant to say, but Will wasn't listening anyway.

"You know that woman they let me be with, away at Chesterfield? She done had two chilluns since—both of 'em near white as you."

Seona had never seen the woman Master Hugh and Gideon Pryce let Will visit twice a month, but Will's skin was dark as blackberries. Pity came over her. She reached for his hand.

His fingers closed on hers, eager and warm. "I asked Master Hugh for you, but he won't pay me heed. You ask him, girl. He do what you want."

"You got a wife."

"That woman ain't *mine*. Ain't you listening?"

She tried to pull away, but Will's fingers latched tighter. "Maybe it ain't Mister Ian you want. I seen you with Thomas aplenty."

Head throbbing, Seona shut her eyes. "I'm too tired for this, Will."

"Then wake up, girl! What is it you want? You got to figure what that is and how you gonna take it. Ain't nobody gonna give it to you. Those that would ain't got it to give, and those that got it gonna keep it to spite you."

She broke free and fled to Naomi's cabin, Will's words beating in her aching head.

20

The air inside the shop prickled with the scent of fresh wood shavings, but there was no sign of Thomas when Ian entered. More pressing to his mind was Seona's whereabouts.

As if his thoughts had summoned her, he turned at the scuff of footsteps to see her framed in the doorway. Little more than a fortnight had passed since their parting, yet it might have been a year for the jolt he felt at seeing her. For the first time since waking to Rosalyn, he remembered the dream he'd had at the inn—and who the dream-woman in his arms, hair tumbled loose and lips softly yielding, had been.

The memory broke upon him with such force it threatened to knock him off his feet. Seona came into the shop, took his arm, and gently pushed him onto the stool. He went down unresisting, the hard surface taking his weight.

"You all right?" Her creek-water eyes were fixed on him. She'd a kerchief pulled low on her forehead, hair loose down her back. A long, dark coil of it fell over her shoulder. He took it, looped it round his finger.

Holding her tethered. Grinning like an idiot. "I brought ye something," he said and felt it to his soul when her eyes smiled into his.

"What is it?"

He let go her hair to rise and fish it from his knapsack, wrapped in a handkerchief. He held it out to her, resting on his palm. "Unwrap it and see."

Her fingertips brushed his skin as she did, sending shivers up his arm. She peeled back the final fold, stared at the polished horn comb, then took her hands away.

"I can't have that," she said.

"Aye, ye can. Unless it doesn't please ye?"

"It's beautiful. But I can't. I can't even have it in my cabin. What if Miss Lucinda takes a notion to go poking round?"

He frowned. "Why would she?"

"She's done it. Turned out the cabins when something went missing. She'll say I stole it."

He started to tell her she'd nothing left to fear from his aunt, but memory of his name scrawled below a contract, witnessed and legal, that would send her away from Mountain Laurel stole his voice. Send her away, when all he wanted to do in that moment was hold her close.

Seeming to weaken in the face of his silence, Seona reached for the comb. This time she took it from his hand, holding it closer to examine the carving. "Morning glories," she said with a catch that might have been a laugh. "Where did you find it?"

"A shop in Salisbury. I saw it and knew . . . it was meant for ye."

She raised her eyes to him. "No one's ever taken such thought over me."

"It's long past time they did." He brushed the edge of her kerchief, drawn down nearly to her brows. "Will ye let me?"

Her eyes searched his, regret-filled. "You know I can never wear it."

"Not yet," he said with a confidence he couldn't bring himself to explain. "But just for a moment? So I can see." He pushed back the kerchief as he spoke, smoothing the hair at her temple, and saw a bruise, a half-healed scrape.

He fumbled the comb, which clattered on the wood-dusted floor. "Seona. What happened?"

"Nothing."

She bent for the comb, sending her kerchief tumbling, but he grasped her arm. "Plainly it was something."

"I fell—in the woods. I'd gone to draw. Thomas was by."

"Was he?"

Her glance flicked up at his sharpened tone. "You asked him to look after me?"

"I did. I hated to leave ye. I wanted ye with me a dozen times."

"You did?"

"A hundred times." Still gripping her, he bent to kiss her brow, her cheek, then hesitantly, her lips. She might have been made of wood for all she responded.

He drew back, a hollowness where his heart had seconds ago beat strong. "That's it, then? Ye feel nothing for me?"

She clamped her lips tight, but a sound escaped her. A groan. He held her inches from him.

"If ye want me to leave ye alone, I will. But say it, Seona. Say what ye feel. Not what ye think I want to hear."

She raised a hand to his face. Trembling fingertips moved over his lips; then she laid her cheek against his breastbone. "What have my feelings got to do with anything?"

"Everything," he said, before her head reared up, silencing him. He heard it too: footsteps on the path beyond the door.

They sprang apart. Before he could prevent her, she fled the shop.

Seconds later Thomas stood in the doorway, frowning after Seona, then at Ian. "Guess I'm not the first to welcome you home, Mastah Ian."

He brushed past Ian, then halted to bend down. With a face as blank as any born slave's, he placed Seona's kerchief and the comb atop the workbench, then moved to his side of the shop.

"Pryce paid a call while you were away. He begs another week of my labor."

Ian was about to protest any further arrangement with Pryce, until it struck him what having Thomas away from Mountain Laurel for a spell could mean. One less pair of eyes . . .

"Is it something ye want to do?"

"It is." Appearing startled at his swift capitulation, Thomas jerked his chin toward the bench by the door. "He left the contract."

Ian tucked kerchief and comb into a coat pocket on his way to the door. "I'll sign it. Let me speak to my uncle, see how we're set for hogsheads here. Maybe in a week ye can go."

Ignoring Thomas's sardonic, "Yessir, Mastah Ian," he started for the weaving shed, from which issued a rhythmic thud—Lily, home scarce an hour and back at work—but hesitated. If Seona had fled to her mother, he couldn't speak to her. If she hadn't, no point in asking.

He halted outside the empty washhouse. Above him arched a bowl of cloudless blue. The slopes beyond the orchard flamed gold and scarlet, patched with the green of pine and laurel.

The orchard. She'd sought refuge there the day Stoddard visited, the day of his uncle's collapse.

He found her there again, alone this time with a basket at her hip, searching for windfall apples—or giving the appearance of it.

She saw him coming and started walking fast. Away from him.

"Seona, wait!"

He caught her easily. She dropped the basket,

scattering half-rotted fruit in a tumble of sweet decay. She didn't fight his grip on her arm. "Miss Lucinda means to give me to Will. Reckon on account he's asked for me and—"

He gave her a brief shake. "No other man will have ye, Seona. Ye're *mine*."

Her head jerked back as if he'd struck her. He dropped his hands from her, knowing he'd said it in the worst possible way.

"Listen to me. It won't happen—whatever my aunt's scheming. I've seen to it." Aye, he'd seen to it. With every moment it struck deeper: he'd bargained away any future he might have had with her, for her freedom.

She stared past him, empty-eyed. "I ain't worth what it takes to feed and clothe me. I don't do nothing Maisy or Esther can't do as well. If I start breeding, they can get their worth of me. But I can't be having white babies."

Something dark swelled in Ian's chest, jagged and sharp. "No one," he said, forcing words past the barrier, "is going to do that to ye. Not while I live and breathe."

"If it comes down to making babies or being sold," she said, as if she hadn't heard, "I choose the babies. You been kind to me but Mama's right. It's got to stop now."

Did Lily want him to leave her daughter alone? She'd said nothing of the sort to him, not in all those days they'd journeyed together. Even if

308

she had, he wasn't certain he could heed such a warning now.

He lifted his hands to cradle Seona's face. "Hear what I'm saying to ye. *It won't happen.*"

He drew her to him, held her, murmured her name, until the sharp thing in his chest began to blunt. Leaves dropped scarlet from the trees around them, swirling like his thoughts. He stepped back, holding her at arm's length, his heart beating heavy with a desperate idea. "My aunt won't breed ye like stock nor sell ye away. Not if I marry ye first."

She didn't shake her head so much as sway it, side to side. That he'd stunned her was no surprise. He felt poleaxed himself. But he was also more certain of this than he'd ever been of anything in his life.

"I want ye, Seona." He held out his hand, but she didn't take it.

"I saw Master Hugh going into the house," she said. "Looking no better for all your pains getting him to those springs. Bide a while. I'll be yours for the taking."

His heart plummeted with the weight of stones. "Ye say a thing like that to me? D'ye think that's all I want—this?" He pulled her to him and kissed her. He wasn't quick about it or very gentle, and they broke apart like combatants, breathing hard.

Her eyes were snapping now. "What else is it you see in me you want so bad?"

309

"Everything," he said. "Your courage, your kindness, your strength, the beauty of your soul . . . *everything,* Seona. I want the work of your hands and the work of your heart to be for me—for *us.* I want to blister my hands and brown my face in the sun to give ye everything ye've gone without. I want your love . . . and I want your children. Our children."

"Ian . . ." She shut her eyes as if the picture he painted with his words was unbearable. "I can't marry a white man. Or any man. Not legal. There ain't a way."

There wasn't, true, while she was enslaved. And in North Carolina. Both circumstances were going to change, but he couldn't bear to tell her that. Not now.

"Look at me, Seona." He waited until she opened her eyes. "Have ye heard of a thing called handfasting?"

She frowned. "Is that like a broomstick marriage?"

"Not quite," he said, though it was uncomfortably close. "It's an old custom. My parents did it. They were handfast a year and a day before they wed in kirk."

It wasn't a deception, he told himself. They'd have a real wedding—perhaps on the journey north after she was free. Then she would be his, waiting for him in Boston. Waiting for his uncle to die and free him, too.

He fetched a shaky breath. "It's a way for us, Seona. But first, let me do this proper." Afraid his legs mightn't hold him for the duration, he knelt. The damp soaked cold through his breeches as he took her trembling hand. "Will ye do me the honor of becoming my wife?"

"Ian, please." She tugged at him, trying to pull him up, then dropped to her knees too. "Master Hugh won't let us."

"He need never know." He'd find a way to keep both promises, to his uncle and to her. The only thing that mattered now was whether she would have him.

"But I'm a—"

He touched his lips to hers, silencing her.

"No matter where or how I found ye," he said after the kiss, "were ye the queen of Sheba and above the lift of my eyes—I would love ye."

Her eyes were wide and drowning green. "You love me?"

"Aye." He took the comb from his pocket, brushed back her hair, and slid it in, trailing a finger across the fading bruise at her temple.

She raised a tentative hand. "Is it fitting?"

"It suits ye." He touched the comb as though it were a diadem. "Will ye accept it as an earnest of all I mean to give ye—even if I must hold it in keeping for now? Will ye be handfast with me?"

Some constriction within her seemed to loosen its hold. She spread her hands against his chest, ran them over the shoulders of his coat and high around his neck. Their touch was chill, but her mouth turned up to meet his was warm and sweet.

"If you want me . . . I will. But how? When?"

Ian smiled against her kiss, then told her.

21

Ian was there at the hollow ahead of her. So was Munin, perched up in a birch tree that leaned across the pool. The raven was eyeing Ian, who stood at the water's edge eyeing it back. "Is it ye, Cousin," he asked, "come to stand witness for us?"

Seona barely heard him above the water falling, splashing over pebbles, green and brown. Munin gave no answer as she stepped from the birches into sunlight. "You making friendly with that old bird?"

Ian started, turning to stare like she was coming to him out of a dream. When she stopped before him, he said, "Your eyes . . . they really are all the colors of the water."

He'd spread an old quilt in a grassy space among the rocks. A knapsack, canteen, and his rifle lay to the side. He wore his good blue coat. His hair was bound in a proper tail, shining like wheat in the sun. Ashamed of her shabbiness, Seona looked at the ground. "Water's clear. It don't have color."

He crooked a finger under her chin to raise it. "But it does."

His hand was warm. She leaned her face against it and wondered could he hear the pounding of her heart. If her eyes were pools, then his were smoke in an autumn sky. She wanted to fly away into them and be swallowed up whole.

"Ye got away all right?"

Ian had left the farm in the milky-blue of dawn, saying he was bound for the Reynolds'. Seona had slipped away as soon after as she dared without a word to anyone, heading through the wood, where the mist hung thick until she'd climbed up to the hollow, above it. She hadn't dared go near the kitchen, afraid if she saw her mama, she'd spill it all, what they planned to do. "They'll 'spect I've gone off to draw. Long as I'm back afore too late . . ."

Munin glided down to a nearby stone, trying for their attention. Ian paid him no mind. He'd brought the comb. "May I?"

She'd shaken out her braid once she was well into the wood, coming to him with her hair loose like he'd asked. She nodded and he moved behind her, gathering up the hair at her temples, his touch tingling her scalp. She felt the comb slide in snug at the back, against the curve of her head. When he stood in front of her again, he held a circle of tiny white blossoms, last of the season, their stems woven into a crown.

"A bride should have flowers, aye?" He fit the circlet on her head and stepped back. His smile made porridge of her knees, but somehow they bore her up as Ian led her to a birch tree, where the ground sloped toward the ridge. He held aside a branch and she ducked under it, holding her flower crown to keep it from tumbling.

The tree was actually two, splitting out from each other at the base. Leaves like bright coins quivered around them and lay in a carpet at their feet. They were curtained in gold, tucked away from the world in a space big enough to stand up in, little wider than her arms might have reached stretched full.

Ian stood close, smelling of sun and fresh-cut wood. He held her hand, rubbing his thumb against her wrist. Shy of the wanting in his eyes, she slid her gaze away. A breeze quivered the golden leaves on stems as slender as the hold she had on her calm.

"I don't know what to do."

The corners of his mouth started to curl. "First I . . ." His smile vanished. "I meant to bind our wrists for the handfasting but didn't bring anything for it."

"Turn round," she said. He stared down at her, quizzical. "We could use your ribbon."

Relief flooded his face. "Good thinking."

He turned his back to her. Reaching up, she did what she'd wanted to do since the night of the Reynolds' cornhusking, loosed the ribbon and spread his hair in waves across his shoulders, letting it run through her fingers.

He faced her again, features framed now in

every shade of gold from flax to barley. He rubbed a hand over his hair, mussing it some. "Ye don't mind?"

"I like your hair down."

"Ye do?" he said in plain surprise, then bent to kiss her. His lips lingered, soft as the fluttering in her belly, yet behind the softness she sensed something strong, deep enough to drown her, but so sweet she wanted it to. "Something we've in common then."

He took her hand and with the other looped the ribbon round their wrists. Twice he nearly had it tied but it slithered from his grasp. She helped with her free hand, laughing until their fingers worked together and the ribbon bound them wrist to wrist.

For a second Seona feared what was coming and thought she might tear free and run from the hollow. "This—this is what your parents did?"

His eyes warmed. "Aye. They were handfast in secret—like us."

"Why in secret?"

"Mam was the only daughter with three elder brothers and one much younger—Callum, who sailed with us from Scotland. Mam had the raising of Callum and the keeping of my grandda's croft in Aberdeen."

Seona's fear was easing as he talked of his parents. They spread their fingers and linked them, palm to callused palm.

"Da's Highland-born, from a place called Glendessary, but he went to Inverness to apprentice himself to a bookbinder. That's where one of my Lindsay uncles met him. I suppose the family thought an acquaintance with a lad hailing from the wild Highlands fine and good, but when that lad took a shine to their sister . . . they were having none of that. Mam was old enough to marry, but they insisted she was needed at home. True enough. But so was their wanting to wed."

"She liked him back?" Seona felt foolish in asking, like a child caught up in a story. Inverness. Glendessary. Aberdeen. There they were, hands bound and clasping, yet she felt like he stood across some wide river trying to tell her what was over on his side. He'd seen so many places she never would. Scotland, Boston, the wilds of Canada, everything in between.

A leaf fell between them, landing on her hand, a splash of yellow. Ian turned their palms so it dropped into the cup of their fingers.

"Aye, she liked him back," he said, and with a look she felt down to her toes, he crossed back over to her side of that river. "They slipped away on a market day to be handfast. Then Da went back to Inverness. Mam went back to milking the goats. They met when they could, the family none the wiser, 'til six months later Mam got with child. Then there was a great fizz and kebby-lebby—as Mam puts it—but in the end they let her go to my da, and Callum with her."

His eyes, grown distant in the telling, now focused on her. She heard him pull in a breath, saw his chest swell with it. "How is it done?" she asked, with a fresh jolt to her nerves.

"I'm meant to speak my vows to ye. Then ye'll say yours to me."

"What vows?"

Sunlight through the leaves speckled shadows across his face but didn't hide his rising color. "Your intent to have me as your husband—if ye haven't thought better of it by now."

Though his eyes were teasing, Seona hoped he wouldn't guess how much she'd thought better of it, and worse of it, and chased herself in circles half the night over it. Shutting out every argument and prayer, she squeezed his hand. "I mean to have you."

"Good." He closed his eyes briefly. "Reckon I'll go first, then?"

Before she could say a word, he fetched a breath and started in, sounding like he'd practiced the words.

"I, Ian Robert Cameron, take thee, Seona, to be my wife. To provide for thee and defend thee, to be faithful unto thee in sickness and in health, in plenty and in need, in sorrow and in joy, while we both shall live. And hereto I pledge thee my word."

Seona blinked away tears. All this he was promising her, a woman of no account? How had it come to this? Yet there were his eyes, shining with tenderness and wanting. His mouth smiling. His hand bound to hers. She was shaking and knew he could feel it. His words echoed in her heart. *To provide . . . defend . . . plenty and need . . . sorrow and joy . . . while we both shall live.*

She ached under her ribs, wanting to say them back to him and something more. *Something more* . . . "You didn't mention the Lord. Seems like you ought to, time like this."

"Aye. Well . . ."

It troubled her, the way he seemed to cast about for something to say. He was raised going to meeting. He'd said so. He was friendly with John Reynold, who spoke of the Almighty as easy as he breathed. Surely Ian believed, like Malcolm had taught her and her mama to believe.

"I might have mangled the wording a bit," he said at last. "It's years since I've heard the wedding service conducted. I ought to have said *in the sight of God*—is that what ye were missing?"

She'd never heard a wedding service in her life but didn't think that was the heart of the matter. She gulped down breath and somehow found the courage to ask, "Are you a child of God, Ian?"

He laughed, though it sounded a little strained.

"If ye mean do I believe in the Almighty, aye, of course I do. Did ye think me a heathen?" The puzzlement lifted from his brow. "Ye'll have heard the injunction against being unequally yoked. That's it, aye?"

Yoked. Did he mean like a pair of oxen?

"I was baptized Catholic as a bairn in Inverness," he hurried to add. "Again after we joined my father in Boston. Only then it was the Presbyterians." He nodded toward the pool, beyond the birches. "They do say third time's lucky. I'll do it now if it sets your mind at ease."

He was making light, but Seona didn't feel light. If they were going to do this, be married, she wanted to know she shared with him something more than *believing.* But how to put into words the longing that pressed against her breastbone was beyond her. Maybe he didn't have words for it either. Maybe it was something they'd have to learn to tell each other.

"You don't have to do it again."

"Good," he said and with his free hand gave her hair a playful tug. "Now that's out of the way . . . are ye ready?"

It didn't feel out of the way, but she nodded. In that moment she wanted Ian Cameron—more than she wanted to draw. More than she wanted breath. More than she feared the notion.

"I, Seona," she began, forming each word with care, "take you—thee—Ian Robert Cameron, to be my husband. . . ." What all she said wasn't a match in prettiness for his words to her, but his face shone with an eager joy as she finished. "To be your wife in plenty or want, happy or sad, while we both live. That is my promise."

The tears on her cheeks surprised her. "Did we do it? Are we married?"

He kissed each knuckle of the hand bound to his before kissing her mouth, soft at first. Then he pulled her closer and kissed her until she had no breath.

She reckoned that meant *yes*.

The contents of the knapsack he'd filled that morning littered the quilt between them—a buffer of restraint, rapidly diminishing. Half an apple pie. Cold chicken. Biscuits fit for the house table. Ian was halfway through the repast before noticing who was devouring most of it. Perhaps Seona's nerves were working on her by stealing her appetite. He was suffering the reverse. He ached to touch her again.

Conscious of her watching, he took off his coat before he went to fill the canteen at the pool. The raven was back, hopping along the rocks at the creek's edge.

"Our witness," he said, settling back on the quilt.

Seona drew her knees up. He noticed a small tear in her skirt, yet to be mended. The shift beneath had ridden up, exposing skin at the bend of her knee. He brushed it with a fingertip. Her hand came down to cover the hole.

Munin opened a silent beak, one eye cocked at Seona. "Look at her now," said the bird, with all the suggestion of a courting swain.

"I am looking," Ian said. "She's beautiful."

"So are you," Seona said.

"Me?"

His surprise made her blush. "You used to be so skinny, like a heron in a creek. But even with your knobby knees you looked like an angel to me."

He stared. She wasn't teasing. "Not ye, too!" He fell back onto the quilt with a groan. "My manly pride is crushed. On my wedding day, no less."

Her laughter, low and musical as the falls, was worth the theatrics. "Someone else said that?"

"Oh, aye. Cecily Reynold for one." He grasped both hands full of his hair. "Because of this. But Cecily wasn't the first."

Though no longer the towhead he'd been in childhood, he'd worn his curls cropped at eighteen, when he left Boston with Callum. "It was my uncle's partner in the fur trade, a Frenchman called LeJeune. He took one look at me, pretended to swoon over my curls, and never called me aught again but *Gabriel*."

"Gabriel." She mimicked his French inflection perfectly, then fell to giggling.

"Go on then. Laugh." He clasped his hands across his brow and closed his eyes. Sunlight came warm through his eyelids. "It's why I let my hair grow, to be rid of the curls."

"Gabriel," she said again. Then softly, "My angel."

He rose up on his elbows. She'd been leaning over and the movement brought them close. Her hair spilled dark against his shirtsleeve, more tightly coiled than his had ever been.

"Not that I've aught against curls. Generally speaking." Sitting up straight, he ran his hand down the length of her thigh as he kissed her. His fingers found the small rent in her skirt again. Again her hand came down.

"I wish I had a nice gown—for today."

He took her hand in his. "Ye will, Seona— many of them. But they don't matter now." He turned her palm over and brushed his lips across it. "I have what I want."

Moments later she made a sound that might have been pleasure or protest. He pulled back from their embrace, searching her face. "We don't have to do this now if ye don't want to."

Seona took his head between her hands. "Do you want to?"

"*Yes.*"

Smiling at his earnestness, she moved her fingers to his neckcloth. She unwound it and folded it atop his coat. Then she spread open the neck of his shirt. Cool air touched his skin, then warmth as she slid her hands beneath the linen and laid her cheek to his chest.

"I hear your heart."

"Not mine." He held her, burying his face in the fall of her hair. The circlet of flowers had fallen away, but their fragrance lingered, sweetly intoxicating. "Not anymore. It's yours."

22

The shouting reached her on the path, halting her as if the breeze coming off the ridge had turned to ice and frozen her to the ground.

"Seo-naaa!" Esther came into sight and spotted her. "Seona! Where you been? Master Hugh done sent us out to holler you home."

Esther raced down the path, skirt flying, yet she seemed to move too slow for running, so slow Seona had time to think of Ian, gone to the Reynolds' so they wouldn't return together. She pictured him at Miss Cecily's table, thinking her home safe, nobody the wiser to what they'd done. Fear shot through her.

"Why the fuss? I'm allowed to go off and draw on a Sunday if I take a notion." Would Esther see she had no lead, no paper?

The girl barreled into her. "It's Mister Allen! His missus got that baby coming. Your mama wants your help catching it."

She'd scant time to welcome relief before they reached the stable-yard, thrown into shadow by clouds blown in on the breeze that really was chilling now. Zeb Allen stood with his horse in a lather, haggard and distraught. Lily clasped her simples box while Jubal saddled a second horse, one of Master Hugh's.

"I ought to have come sooner. Rebecca didn't think she'd need—" Zeb Allen passed a hand over his mouth, as if to rub out what more he might have said.

Lily caught sight of her. "Seona, get ye to the house and fetch the pass Master Hugh's writing us."

Seona went, with a dread in her chest that twisted hard at the door of Master Hugh's room. He was at his desk, sifting sand over a freshly inked paper. She clasped her hands to stop their shaking, afraid what she and Ian had done must show on her face.

"They found ye, I see." Master Hugh was a big man—every Cameron male she'd ever seen stood tall—but now his long bones seemed stripped of flesh, like he was being eaten from within. He folded the pass and held it out. As she took it, his hand closed over hers. "Tell Zeb they've my prayers, for what they're worth."

The blue of his eyes was lighter than Ian's, faded, haunted with old griefs. She knew he was thinking of his first wife, who died birthing their baby girl.

"I wish I'd known her," Seona said, then wished she'd held her tongue, but Master Hugh's eyes went soft, even as the pain in them deepened.

"So do I. Stay as long as ye're needed. I've sent provisions, something to set on Zeb's table." He gave her hand a squeeze and let go. "Away wi' ye, lass. The woman's suffering."

Lily was in the saddle when Seona reached the yard. Jubal hoisted her up behind. Through years of being hired out as midwife, her mama had learned to keep her wits on a horse. Seona clung to her waist as they splashed across the creek and broke into a smoother gait out on the road, following Mister Allen.

She shut her eyes and was back under the birches with Ian, sunlight dazzling through yellow leaves, nothing but his body holding her to the earth. . . .

"Where ye been all the morn, girl-baby?" Lily asked over the noise of hooves and creaking saddle.

Seona pretended not to hear. "This one gonna be a boy or girl, Mama?"

Lily most often guessed right, but she didn't answer for a spell. In the silence dread bloomed. "Boy," she said finally, the word bitten sharp, borne back on the wind.

The Allen cabin lay over the ridge, a mile by winding trails, farther but quicker by road. It was past midday when they reached it, down a track through cornfields where cattle grazed on stubble. In a fold between the hills Zeb Allen had built two snug cabins for his brood, a covered dogtrot between. There the younger Allen children clustered. From one of the open cabins came the mewling of a newborn.

"Thank God Almighty," Mister Allen said before a moan tore through the air.

The eldest girl, Katy, came out to the dogtrot holding a bundle. Above it her face was white and scared. "Pa? I done caught this'un, but Ma's paining again."

Another moan from within the cabin worked like a shove on the oldest Allen boy. Stumbling in his haste, he took their horses' reins as they dismounted, calling to his brothers to come down to the barn, leaving Katy and little Ruthie, who had a fist jammed in her mouth.

Lily passed her simples box to Seona and took the baby from Katy. "Mister Allen, take Ruthie into the other cabin. I'll need Katy with me."

Mister Allen halted Lily with a hand to her arm, too shocked to look at the infant. "If the babe's come, what's ailing Becky?"

"Likely it's twins." Lily's smile was less reassuring than it might have been had Rebecca Allen not cried out just then. A weak, desperate sound. Ruthie gave a hiccuping sob. Mister Allen scooped her up and carried her off.

Inside the cabin where Missus Allen labored, a fire blazed in the chimney hearth. The warm air reeked of birthing, woodsmoke, and sweat.

"Two babies," came a strained voice from the dimness, confirming Lily's guess. "First nigh killed me. Second's like to . . . finish the job."

Half the cabin was taken up with bedsteads.

In the middle of one Missus Allen lay, clad in a sopping shift, fists pressed to her belly. The oilcloth spread beneath her to protect the corn-husk tick was blood-covered.

Seona set Lily's box on a table, while Lily laid the infant on the other bed and unwrapped its swaddling. "Where's the caul?"

Katy pointed at the baby. "That's all that come out."

Lily took the girl by the shoulder and turned her toward the door. "Ye did fine, Katy. Go now, fetch us some more water. Seona, come wash this baby so I can see to Missus Allen. When ye finish, set more water to boil on the crane."

Seona tried to put away memories of the birch hollow while she did as Lily bid her—noting in passing that this newest Allen was, in fact, a boy. She tried not to stare at Missus Allen with her big belly and her face screwed up in pain, while Lily told Seona what the trouble was. The afterbirth hadn't come, which could be causing the bleeding.

"Or could mean the twins shared it," she allowed. "If the second comes fast, it'll be all right. I think."

But it didn't. Missus Allen's pains came and went. She lay in a fretful doze between, bleeding out slowly onto the tick, while they used every scrap of cloth they could find to mop the flow. At last, sometime after nightfall, there came a gush as a second water broke. They got Missus Allen off the bed and onto an old birthing chair one of the children had fetched from the barn, and for a time they thought the second twin would come. But still it didn't.

"Turned catawampus," Lily said after another check. "Feet first."

Seona did what she could to hold Missus Allen upright, feeling the woman strain until her face purpled and the cords stood out in her neck. She subsided with a whimper, the color draining from her face, leaving her white and heavy in Seona's arms.

"Mama?" she said over Missus Allen's shoulder and realized she was weeping.

Crouched on the floor between Missus Allen's knees, Lily said, "Feet are coming. Push, Rebecca. *Push.*"

But they couldn't rouse Missus Allen again to push.

Finally Lily looked at her. "Seona, help me get her to the bed. Then go fetch Zeb."

Clouds had come up thick, blocking the stars. Seona stood in the cabin doorway, staring at the face of the firstborn twin framed in his wrappings, features scrunched like a fist. Waking to hunger, she reckoned, but there was no chance of feeding yet. Her breath misted in the chink of light from the near-shut door behind her. It was too cold to be standing there with a newborn, but the night air at least was clean. No smell of blood. Even so it held a scent beyond the tang of woodsmoke pouring from the chimneys. Cold, familiar, but she couldn't name it.

Mister Allen had come at her fetching, talked with Lily, wept over his wife, then gone with his sons to bring in the cattle for the night. He hadn't come back. Seona felt pity for his helplessness. They were all helpless. Lily had tried to pull the second baby from Missus Allen. It wouldn't budge.

"I've seen it once with a breech. Head's gotten hung up inside. She's lost so much blood I just don't think . . ." Lily put a hand to her mouth, pressed hard, then said, "Anything else I was to try would only worsen her suffering and Mister Allen says don't. She's in God's hands now. His will be done."

Grief clenched Seona as she glimpsed Katy Allen through the half-open door across the dogtrot, lying awake on a pallet with Ruthie nestled close.

Snow. That's what she was smelling. The first flakes drifted through the faint light from the cabin. Snow, when that morning she and Ian had lain beneath the birches with the sun shining golden through the leaves.

She went back into the cabin with the baby in her arms, praying for his poor mama's release.

Mixed in was a terrified plea that she hadn't already sealed herself to the same fate. She put a hand to her belly, blameless-flat from hip to hip. It wouldn't stay so long, not with many more days like today. Then what they'd done in secret would be made plain, like with Ian's parents.

And then . . . what was it he'd called it? They'd have themselves a kebby-lebby.

Snow in October. It was more in keeping with Massachusetts weather than what he'd expected of Carolina. Two nights had passed since its falling and it had yet to melt. Ian warmed his hands at the brazier he'd set up, then made another circuit of the shop, stooping for bits of wood to feed the flames. Time might as well have stopped when he returned to the news of Rebecca Allen's childbed and Seona's attendance. Apparently it meant to continue in abeyance until he had her back. In his arms, if he could manage it.

At his workbench he picked up a chisel, its blade in need of honing. He put it down and fingered a length of pine board marked for dovetailing. His head jerked up as the door swung open, letting in the cold. And Rosalyn, expression as guarded as his own must be.

"Do you mind my company, Cousin?"

He did. But saying so would only further strain relations with the girl, with whom he had to go on living, like it or not.

Rosalyn made up her own mind, shutting the door to stand inside the shop. "It's some time since I was in here."

He knew exactly how long it had been—the day she discovered Seona's secret.

"What d'ye want, Rosalyn?"

She rounded the workbench, hair pinned high, artful curls trailing down her neck. "I never apologized for my behavior at the springs. I don't expect you'll ever . . . But never mind. Will you at least forgive me, Cousin?"

Forgive her. For drugging him and attempting to seduce him into marriage? For endangering his uncle? His every fiber rebelled at the notion but the last thing he needed now was further family strife. He could give her the words, however empty. "I will."

Rosalyn waited, expectant. "Have you something to say to me?"

He ought to have known she wouldn't shoulder the blame for that ugly scene alone. What could he say that wouldn't sound an utter falsehood?

"I regret . . . my treating ye roughly."

Rosalyn gave him a smile that once would have dazzled him senseless. Now it only made him wary. Had his aunt compelled her to this, or was it her own notion?

Seeming satisfied, she left without his asking. Let them play their games. None of it mattered now. He had his uncle's promise. All he needed was his da's support. He'd written before they left the inn and posted the letter; it would be weeks before he heard from Boston. But he had Seona. Unless those hours at the birch hollow had been an enchanting dream.

Could it take this long to catch a bairn? He'd expected Lily would stay a night or two to make certain the new bairn thrived but assumed Seona would have returned once it was safely born.

He stared through the window at the snow-laced forest beyond the garden pales. "For pity's sake, lass, hurry!"

The words were still on his lips when two figures, one leading his uncle's horse, emerged from the trees at the head of the footpath that led to the Reynolds'.

He was out of the shop in an instant. Seona was wrapped in the arisaid, her face within its folds drawn with fatigue and strain. He halted, leaving a careful pace between them.

"What's happened?"

"Missus Allen died," she said in a voice small and cold. "I'm to ask will you set to making a coffin and get it over the ridge to Mister Allen by morning? Mister John's gonna do the burying. We came home the long way, past their place."

He thought his chest would burst with the inrush of feeling—a frozen stab of grief for Zeb Allen at odds with the blood-warm joy of Seona standing before him again. Until she started walking away. Lily had led the horse toward the stable with no more than a glance at them, her face haunted with grief.

He reached Seona in two quick strides. "Wait. Seona . . . come into the shop." He dropped his voice until it was hardly audible above the crunch of snow beneath their feet. "We can have a moment."

"I can't." She slipped in the snow and he steadied her, but she pulled free. "I'm sure the washing's done piled up."

"Hang the washing."

"I mean to." She quickened her pace.

Ian halted. Seona kept going and didn't look back.

There was pine board enough for a coffin. While Ian worked, he tried to reason away his dismay. What had he expected? That Seona would fling herself into his arms the moment she saw him, devil take all watching eyes? But what if more was amiss with her than sorrow or caution? Did she regret what they'd done?

The hammer missed its mark. His thumb exploded in pain. Pressing it, throbbing, to his lips, he strode from the shop.

The washhouse door was unlatched. Closing it softly behind him, he was enveloped in warmth and the harsh smell of lye. Seona had her back to him, prodding the kettle's steaming contents with a stick. She was dressed as she'd come to him in the birch hollow, the same skirt with its tiny hole. He was behind her, reaching for her, when she spoke.

"Please . . ."

"Seona?"

She dropped the stick with a splash, crying out.

He drew her away from the rising steam, turning her wrists, seeking evidence of scalding—and found it, a spattering of bright-pink marks on her skin. Then he registered her face. She'd been weeping.

"Come here," he said. He thought she would resist him, but when his arms went around her, she molded to him, pressing her face into his chest and sobbing as if her heart would break. He held her, torn with her grief, relieved to have her in his arms.

"Were ye praying?" he asked and heard a muffled affirmation from the vicinity of his chest. "For the Allens?"

"And for you."

"Me?" He pulled back, needing to see her face.

She pressed a fist to her breast, as though to stifle a pain there. "Ian, will you heed the Lord?"

"Will I—?" He was baffled by the question.

She took hold of his arms, beseeching. "When Missus Allen died, Mama said we do what we can, then bow to the Lord's will. Are you bowing? Do you know His voice when you hear it?"

Something like panic knotted in his throat. "I believe in the Almighty, Seona. I thought ye understood—"

"I believe in George Washington but I don't *know* him." She was hiding nothing from him now. The veils were stripped clean from her eyes, yet he couldn't bear what was revealed. The naked pleading. The doubt.

"What would ye have me say? I've done things, Seona. I doubt the Almighty's terribly keen on knowing *me* these days." He'd disappointed her. If only he knew what she needed from him. "I know *your* voice. Isn't that enough?" He bent to kiss her with the fire he'd contained since they parted blazing up.

She stiffened. "Not here. They'll know."

He let her go, wishing the whole world would disappear so he might have the freedom to hold her, love her. "What happened at the Allens'?"

"Mama couldn't save Missus Allen."

"That I know. But the child?"

"It was twins. One lived. One never got born."

His gut felt as though a fist had landed there. "Is that what this is about? Ye're afraid the same will happen to ye?"

The idea was enough to chill his blood.

"No . . ." Her eyes pooled with tears. "Yes."

Thought of a child and the host of complications it would mean for the plan of freedom he'd yet to share with her filled him with dread. Ought he to tell her that plan now? He'd meant to wait for word from Boston. No sense in raising her hopes until he was certain. But meantime . . .

"Seona, if it's a bairn ye fear . . ." He forced the words out like a breath he couldn't spare. "Then I won't touch ye again that way. For now."

Her eyes flicked to him, startled. Relieved?

He put his hands to her shoulders, his lips to her brow. "Is that what ye want of me?"

Don't say yes.

"Yes," she said and stepped from his embrace.

23

The cabin was dark. Soon Malcolm would lead them up the ridge to the clearing by the burying ground to pray. No lantern would be lit until they were among the trees. If the moon was bright, not even then. Lily had wrapped herself against the chill. "Get your shawl, girl-baby. We're starting."

Seona sat on her cot, barefoot in her shift. It was too dark to see Lily's face. "I ain't going this time, Mama."

"Feeling poorly?" Lily's hand found her forehead. "Ye've not been yourself these past days."

Seona pulled back from her touch. She was sick, just not in the way she let on. It was four days since they'd come back from the Allens'. Ian had kept his word and stayed away. She didn't know how much longer she could stand it. "Headache, is all. Don't feel up to going. Go on afore the others leave you back."

"Go up to the kitchen for some bark tea."

"I will."

Lily left her, unhappily. Seona waited. When she figured they'd all passed through the orchard and started up the ridge, she wrapped herself in the shawl Ian called an *arisaid* and stepped outside.

Up at the house a candle burned at Ian's window, a halo of yellow. Tempting as a will-o'-the-wisp. A glimpse was all she got before a voice spoke from the dark.

"Evenin', Seona."

"Will!"

He came out from under an oak. She pulled her shawl tighter. Cold seeped up through the soles of her feet. "Why didn't you go with the others?"

"Ain't messing with that Jesus twaddle now." Will's voice was colder than the air as he dropped into a mocking chant. " 'Ride on, King Jesus, no man can hinder me—' " He broke off with a scornful breath. "Seems men hindered *Him* aplenty—to His death. Same's they hinder me."

"Jesus? He didn't stay dead," she said, forgetting for a moment that candle in the distance.

"You think so? Then what you doing hanging back?"

"My head's paining me. I'm going to fetch something for it."

Will moved closer. Moonlight caught the sheen of his eyes as his hand curled hard round her wrist. He jerked his chin toward the lighted window of the house. "Uh-huh. Mind how you go, girl—and what I said about them white men."

With a small shove he released her, opening his hand like he was flicking off dirt. Then he turned his back.

• • •

She stood beneath the breezeway, in the cane-shadows where a few late roses clung. Ian was at his desk, face golden in the candle-glow. At first he was writing something. Then he set aside the quill. She watched through the window as he bent his head, raked fingers through his hair. Her heart squeezed tight.

Among the canes she found a rose, past its glory and fading. She broke its stem and it fell open in her hand, colorless in the night.

Her head jerked up when Ian snuffed the candle, plunging the window into darkness. Fear rushed in, clawing at her, urging her back to the cabin. Just as she made up her mind to go, the back door opened. Ian stepped out. He started toward her, quiet in his stride, but she could feel the tension in him as he neared. She didn't make a sound; still he halted, a shadow framed in the breezeway arch.

"Who's there?"

The hope in those words washed over her. "Me," she said.

He had her in his arms so fast it took her breath. He groaned, then found her mouth with his and gave her his warmth. His hands crept below her shawl. "What are ye doing here in the cold—in naught but your shift?"

He slipped off his coat and put it round her, warm from his body, smelling of buckskin. The half-breed coat. She reached her arms around him, the rose crushed between them, its scent mingling with their breath. "I wanted to see you."

"Seona . . . I cannot eat, sleep, or work for this wanting. I said we wouldn't . . ." Ian bent to kiss her again; his lips against hers smiled. "But would ye?"

An urge to tell him *no* rose, but she knew she wouldn't say it. She'd chosen this night's path when she'd stayed behind alone.

The heat of him was like a fire. She pressed closer. "Where can we go?"

He took her hand to lead her, but she stumbled, feet gone numb from cold. He scooped her into his arms along with their wrappings. Along with the rose. She clung to him, clutching it to her breasts, as he stepped from the breezeway. Turned. Turned again.

He made for the house.

She scarcely breathed while he shut the back door, hoisted her against his chest, and started up the stairs. She felt his heart drumming as he went careful, straining to make no sound. He set her down in the passage and they half fell into his room, a tangle of limbs and coat and shawl.

Seona breathed in air that smelled of him and the candle he'd snuffed. He eased the door closed. They stood listening but heard no voices. No hurried footsteps.

Moonlight slanted through the window, falling across the bed. Ian led her to it, then slipped round to the other side to draw the hangings. She put a knee on the feather tick. Across it he reached for her, but she whispered to him, *"Wait."*

Taking the rose between her hands, she scattered the petals over the sheets, then let him draw her down among their sweetness.

Seona's back protested as she bent for another bedsheet. Down the double clothesline, linen flapped like a wedge of white geese hurrying south. She was hidden between the lines save for when the wind gusted. She hoisted the sheet into place, then dropped her arms and was rolling her aching shoulders when hands slid around her waist. She stifled a yelp.

"Easy," Ian said. "It's me."

He stroked the small of her back, thumbs pressing firm into aching muscles. Her legs went weak, but there was a buzzing in her ears like a swarm of frantic bees. *We can't. Mama or Esther or—God help—the mistress could come along any second.* But she didn't pull away.

"Will ye come to me again tonight?" His mouth touched the curve of her shoulder, making her shiver. She leaned back against his chest and shook her head.

His body jerked. "D'ye mean it?"

Again she shook her head. He relaxed against

her, bending low until his beard stubble rasped her cheek. "Say it, then."

"I will . . . if you shave first."

He nuzzled her with his bristles, then pressed a kiss to the corner of her mouth. "I'll do that."

He gave her shoulders a squeeze, then slipped between the sheets, quiet as he'd come.

She'd thought Lily asleep when she rose, quiet as she could manage, and crossed the cabin. It was too dark to see more than the outline of her mama's cot, but when Seona reached for the cabin door, a dark shape loomed between.

"Mama! You gave me a fright."

"Not half the fright ye're giving me." Lily took hold of her wrist. Her hair was down, tangled in her grip. Seona was about to say she was going to the necessary when Lily said, "I saw ye today, hanging out the wash. Girl-baby, don't go to him."

"Mama, let go."

"Is he making ye do this?"

"It ain't like that. He promised—"

"White men's promises have a way of dying on the vine." Lily's hand slid down and clasped Seona's, urgent, beseeching. "I'll stand by ye. We'll tell Master Hugh."

"Tell him what? Why oughtn't I to go, when *you* went?" Something reckless had taken hold of her tongue. "What happened between you and

Master Hugh? Anyone can see he cares for you. Why didn't he ever claim me?"

The questions rolled off her lips and clung there like tears.

Lily's hand went cold, then slipped away. Seona reached for her but she pulled back into the shadows. Beyond the cabin door Ian waited, and she knew her mama wouldn't stop her going now. Still she stood rooted. "Why, Mama?"

"Because," Lily said from the darkness. "I never asked him to."

Ian reached for a candle, then changed his mind and closed the shutters. It was dark save for the hearth embers. He added wood. Barefoot, he paced the floor, casting glances of mingled longing and fatigue at the bed. Would she not come after all?

If you shave first. He rubbed his smoothed chin, a smile tugging, until he minded the mute refusal that had preceded her teasing reply. Though retracted, it had shaken him. The deuce of it was he'd brought this on himself. He'd been on his way to the shop when he glimpsed her through the swaying sheets. He'd risked discovery—for a promise he might have secured any number of safer ways with the application of a little patience.

Would she not come? Or could she not? Perhaps Dawes had been abroad and caught her out.

Across the room in an instant, he wrenched

open the door. Seona stood in the passage, hand raised as though to tap. Weak with relief, he pulled her into the room and shut the door. He snatched the taper off his desk and took it to the hearth to light.

She'd brought another rose. She must have searched long for a proper bloom but in vain. Candlelight revealed the brown-edged petals, bitten by frost. He set the taper down. Started for her. Stopped.

"Why did ye first say *no?*"

He hadn't meant it to come out so sharp. Or at all. No emotion registered on her face though he searched it hungrily. They were back to how it had been between them weeks ago, when he couldn't fathom her, couldn't reach her. *Had* he ever reached her? Uncertainty shook him.

"D'ye not wish to be with me?" He tossed the wilted rose onto the counterpane, then took her face between his hands. Candlelight coppered her skin, throwing the bones beneath into sharp relief, heightening her resemblance to Lily. She seemed to him as remote as her mother as well.

"Don't tell me what ye think I want to hear. Tell me what's true . . . here." He pressed his hand flat above her heart, wanting desperately to understand it.

It beat swift beneath his palm, a struggling, trapped thing. She didn't raise her eyes. "Mama saw us today. Out by the wash."

He swore softly, then drew her into his arms. The night's chill clung to her clothes, her hair. "Will she speak of it to my uncle?"

"I don't reckon. It might cause trouble."

He frowned at the bitter reply. They'd been handfast less than a fortnight and already the strain of secrecy was tearing at them. Turning from her, he planted his hands on the desk, resolve hardening like a weight in his chest. "I'll do it. I'll tell him I've taken ye to wife, that I'll have no other whether he bequeaths Mountain Laurel to me or no. And when he's freed ye, we'll leave—together."

Silence. He turned back. Seona was clutching her shawl tight, knuckles white.

"Master Hugh means to free me?"

"Aye. He does." This wasn't how he'd planned to do it, but he told her now of the bargain struck at the springs, the signed agreement. Her promised freedom. "We're waiting on my da to say he'll welcome ye. I believe he will, Seona."

Her eyes were wide. Stunned. "And you didn't see fit to tell me 'til now?"

He drew closer, speaking low, willing her to understand, to trust him. "When I pressed my uncle for your freedom, I was prepared to let ye go to live in Boston while I stayed here. And then . . . we came back, and I saw ye again— and knew I couldn't send ye away with nothing spoken between us. I didn't want to lose ye."

"But you will. If what you say is true."

"Only for a time. 'Til my uncle . . ." Until his uncle died. He'd thought it a hundred times yet still couldn't voice it. "Then I'll find a man to oversee the land. Not Dawes. John Reynold, maybe. I'll come back to Boston. I'll marry ye."

A line had formed between her brows. "We are married."

"Before a minister, I mean. So none can dispute it. Ye could pass, easily."

She blinked at him. "Pass?"

"For white. Not that I care about—"

"But if you tell Master Hugh what we done," she cut in, shaking her head as if to clear it of everything save what mattered most to her, "he might change his mind. Send you away and keep me here."

"D'ye think I've not considered that?" Since returning from the mountains, he'd thought it through from every possible angle—from letting things play out as agreed upon, trusting Robert Cameron and the General Assembly to come through for them, to defying his family's sensibilities and living with Seona openly, his wife by common law, to stealing her away and making for the frontier. Leaving behind the complications of kin, lands, laws.

The latter option was gaining fast appeal. If he took Seona away, without the blessing of the General Assembly or his uncle, it would have to be Canada and Callum and little hope of ever making things right with his da.

Could he live with that, if he had Seona?

It hurt to see her now, wrapped in her shawl, face bowed in shadow. Unable to bear the constraint between them, he drew her to the bed. The rose he'd tossed onto the counterpane might have wilted, but its perfume was still potent, stirring memories.

"I told ye of my mother's brother. D'ye mind that?" He followed her glance toward his quilled coat, hanging by the door. She nodded. "Callum has a wife. She's Chippewa. Full blood. They were married by a French priest ten years ago. They've three little boys. He's never told my parents." He recounted for her his shock the day he first rode into the trading settlement with his uncle to see the trio of black-haired boys racing toward them, shouting their greeting. *Noos abi! Daddy's home.*

"Your cousins?"

"Aye."

"And no one in your family knows?"

"Only me. And ye now."

Seona sat in silence. Ian turned her chin so her face caught the candlelight. Her eyes pleaded. "Can't we keep on in secret like your uncle?"

"Callum isn't living with his wife under the noses of his kin." He touched her face, but she pulled back.

"He's ashamed of her?"

349

Ian felt a stab beneath his breastbone. "Seona . . . listen to me. 'Tis naught to do with shame but with a man protecting what he cherishes. I spoke of them so ye'd see there's more for me than Mountain Laurel or Boston. More for us, if ye'll go with me."

"You mean run away? To Canada?"

"If every other avenue closes, aye."

"With Mama not knowing what's become of me?" Panic made her voice rise.

He put his fingers to her lips. "I didn't say we *would* run. But I have to do something before the truth is plain for all to see—not just Lily."

When he took his hand away, she shook her head. "It won't be plain . . . if we stop."

He nearly laughed. "We tried that, remember? Bid me stop my heart beating. It'd go easier."

She bit her lower lip, a gesture of awareness that drew him irresistibly. He leaned close to kiss her, but again she pulled away.

"D'ye not trust me to keep ye safe?" he asked.

"When you can't see where to put your foot next?"

Her lack of confidence burned. "So ye don't trust me. I haven't exactly earned it, have I?"

"It's the Lord we need to trust."

He strained to keep his voice low. "Ye'd have me wait, then? Do nothing?" He pressed his fingers to his temples and sighed. "It oughtn't to surprise me. Ye're used to having your decisions made for ye."

"I best go back."

She was off the bed and heading for the door before she'd finished speaking, but he'd seen the hurt in her face. He caught her before she reached the door, pinning her in his arms.

"Seona . . . I'm sorry. I shouldn't have said that. I spoke in frustration, but it wasn't with ye."

She might have been a woman carved in stone, indifferent to his touch. "Maybe it's true. Maybe I can't think for myself."

"It isn't true. Listen. Ye were a wee girl when ye picked up that slate. Ye thought it was forbidden, yet ye did it—kept doing it all these years and look what's come of it. We've given beauty to people neither of us know and found our way into each other's souls. Haven't we?"

He wanted her to agree. *Needed* her to. In silence he held her, despairing that he'd harmed her with his ill-chosen words, until softly she said, "It was your likeness."

"What was?"

"That first time, with the slate. It was while you were here I found it. I hid under the kitchen lilacs and drew your face."

His heart leapt, then eased into rhythm with hers. He was awash in a sense of connection with her so powerful it left him trembling, as though they'd been this way forever, mind and heart entwined.

"Flesh of my flesh," he whispered against her

351

hair, then pulled back to see her face. The candle cast a sheen against the moisture on her cheeks. "There's a way for us, Seona. We'll find it." He traced his thumb across the curve of her lip. "Stay with me. I won't tell my uncle yet."

He'd have promised the sun, the moon, any star of her choosing, to go on holding her, to let the sweet, reckless tide they'd held at bay sweep over them. He bent his mouth to hers, and she was living woman in his arms again, pliant and warm.

24

A crackling beneath his ear woke him. Opening his eyes to blinding sunlight, Ian squinted and raised himself to an elbow, shedding stray leaves and twigs. Some yards off, a figure bent to lift a stone from the earth. "John? What's the time?"

John Reynold staggered upright with the stone, found his balance, and headed for the field's edge. With a grating chunk he dropped it onto a pile—which had grown since Ian last saw it.

"Sleeping Beauty of the Wood awakens," his neighbor said, sauntering over, features mild with amusement. "You nodded off whilst I was recounting our Robin's latest prodigy, so I wrapped what you didn't eat. If you're lucky, the ants haven't got it."

A haversack lay in the shade of the shedding maple under which he and John had paused to eat their dinner—a good two hours past, judging by the sun. "Ye shouldn't have let me sleep."

"You looked to need it. Still do."

Ian minded the image staring back from the glass that morning, that of a man who'd tasted little of sleep in days. Stifling a grin—and a yawn—he hauled himself to his feet, determined to make up for time squandered.

It was a good day for the work, chill enough

for laboring in shirtsleeves under a sky of aching blue, glorious against the autumn patchwork of the hills. He felt John scrutinizing him as he set to grubbing out the nearest stone with a long-handled spade.

"What is it has you fagged? Something troubling you?"

"No." Ian tossed the stone onto one of the cairns marking the field's boundary, then turned his face into his shoulder to blot away a trickle of sweat. "Unless ye count a peddler stopped over with a wagon full of house-clutter my aunt doesn't need and my uncle cannot afford. Which won't stop the women buying their trinkets and fancies, mind."

"That'll be Gottfriedsen, out of Salem." John moved past him, scouting the torn earth and matted grasses. "He's passed through with his wares since before the war, I'm told. Stay for supper. Cecily and I will walk you home. She'll want a look."

"Aye. I'd appreciate it." Ian inserted his spade beneath a stone and with a grunt pried it free. Sunlight cast the field in bands of gold, each alive with the flutter of insects. Ian's shirt clung in patches. His hand came away slick when he wiped his neck.

John was watching him still. "Cecily misses Seona's company. Especially after the loss of Rebecca Allen . . ."

Hefting the stone spared Ian the necessity of a reply. He heaved it onto the cairn, which shifted with a clack like giant marbles. He'd meant to give Seona a few hours with Cecily while he worked with John, but the household had been in high fettle that morning, his aunt and cousins eager to spend the day examining the peddler's wares. Seona had been needed to help prepare a dinner to mark the occasion. Taking her away for the better part of the day would have roused protest.

He loosened another stone but didn't bend to wrest it free. "Listen . . . I spoke too careless of my uncle's affairs."

John was quick to raise a hand. "Dinna fash, as you Scots say. It stays between us—depend upon it. Lend your back to this one?"

As John levered a large stone from the earth with his pick, Ian got his fingers round its edges, gripping through moss and clinging earth. He hoisted it free, muscles knotting with the effort.

His first indication of anything amiss was John's cry.

He stepped back by instinct even before he saw the banded canebrake in the hollow the stone had capped. As the snake rattled its warning and tightened its coils to strike, John lunged backward, caught a heel on a tussock, and went down.

With the strain of it arcing like fire across his

shoulders, mouth open in a roar, Ian wrenched the stone above his head and slammed it down.

"It was half again my arm's length and thick as my fist." Seated on his uncle's dressing bench, Ian described the canebrake at his uncle's request, though by his count the man had heard the tale at least twice already. "It missed John's shin by a breath when it struck."

He'd have made no mention of the incident at all had John and Cecily not recounted the episode to the family the previous evening, casting Ian in the role of dragon-slayer. Practically asleep on his feet, he'd endured the attention from his kin, acknowledged the purchases the womenfolk had made and the peddler who sold them—a diminutive, elderly Moravian, grateful for the offer of a bed in the stable for himself and his mule—before escaping to his room.

"I once saw a slave die of a canebrake's bite." The fire had overwarmed his uncle's room, yet Hugh Cameron sat filling his pipe at his desk, robed in a banyan wrapped snug. "Ugly business. The Almighty bethankit for keeping ye, lad. And Reynold, forbye."

Ian rose to bring a splinter of kindling from the hearth. Uncle Hugh set it to the pipe's bowl, drew, and grunted satisfaction. Ian snuffed the kindling and sat again, watching thin smoke ascend from its charred tip. "Uncle, have ye penned the petition for Seona's manumission?"

Ledgers cluttered the cherrywood desk. So did scattered quill scrapings and the canebrake's severed rattles. No freshly inked letters. No document bearing Seona's name.

"I didna see the need as yet, since Robert hasna written."

"It's the General Assembly will take the longer. I'd hoped ye'd petition at the November session."

His uncle eyed him narrowly. "And do ye hold to it, should the assembly grant her freedom, that ye'll see the lass to Boston and return to me, content?"

"I mean to, Uncle . . ." Clenching the bit of kindling, burnt black at the tip, Ian steadied his breath. "But is there no way Seona may return to Carolina? No way around the manumission law . . . even if she returned as my wife?"

His uncle stared, momentarily blank. "Did ye say *wife?*"

"I did, sir."

"What are ye saying? Ye and the lass . . . ?" Uncle Hugh gripped the arm of his chair, suspicion flooding his gray face with color. "Have ye gone and done the very thing ye nearly came to blows with Pryce over?"

Heat prickled Ian's face. "No, Uncle. It wasn't like that. She came to me full willing."

"Wheesht!" Uncle Hugh flung up a hand. "I

dinna want to hear what the pair of ye have done—
and all under Lily's nose? She must no' ken or—"

"Aye. She does."

His uncle nearly dropped the pipe, spilling
flakes of dottle in his lap. "Lily kens . . . and
never a word of it to me?"

"Ye're surprised at that? After all ye've denied
her?"

Uncle Hugh brushed the dottle to the floor, the
motion not brusque enough to cover the shaking
of his hand. "Ye've precious little room to be
setting yourself up as judge, Nephew. Have ye
got a bairn on the lass? Is that what has ye hell-
bent to free her? Ye'll have *your* child born free?"
He barked a mirthless laugh. "Confound us all,
lad, if ye have. Your auntie will be vexed."

A rap on the study door made Ian start, then
blanch as his aunt's voice rose, sounding sore
vexed already. "Hugh? I must speak with you.
The matter is of urgency!"

Without awaiting reply, Lucinda swept in,
halting in the center of the room. "We've searched
everywhere but they are simply vanished!"

Ian felt the blood leave his face. "Who's
vanished?"

"Not *who,*" Lucinda said. "What. We've been
robbed—shamefully and brazenly robbed!"

Having run from the washhouse to the stable-
yard, Seona stopped short at sight of Ian's roan,

358

hitched to the fence. Ian straightened from tightening the saddle girth, head lifting toward her though she hadn't called his name. She forced herself to walk, eyes lowered, until she reached his side.

"Seona. I was about to come find ye." Shadows rimmed his eyes, but they were clear and fixed on her with an almost-giddy light. A far cry from the panic she was trying to bridle.

"Esther said you're going after him." Already every slave had been summoned to stand while the house was searched, then the cabins, outbuildings, and stable, with nary a trace of the missing house plunder to be found. The mistress reckoned "that little peddler" had crept in during the night and taken back the things he sold her.

"Aye," Ian said. "I don't wish to, but I cannot let such thievery go unanswered."

"Mister Gottfriedsen's been peddling through these hills since afore I was born. Why would he turn thieving of a sudden?" It was absurd, to Seona's thinking. But then Mister Gottfriedsen had always traveled with kinfolk. This time he'd been alone. Had other things about him changed?

"Jubal says the man was gone before dawn," Ian said. "Bound for Salisbury, then north to Salem. I mean to catch him this side of the Yadkin."

His rifle was snug in its holster. She watched him slip a pistol into a saddlebag. "Why you?"

"I wouldn't trust Dawes to get farther than the first crossroads tavern. Best he see to the barn, as he's meant to do."

A wind in the night had torn another patch of roofing from the tobacco barn where the crop still cured. It needed fixing without delay.

The oaks shading the stable-yard rustled. Seona shivered in the crisp air. Her sleeves were wet from washing and clung cold to her skin, smelling of lye.

Ian tied the saddlebag and faced her. "Seona, I need to tell ye—"

"Cousin Ian!"

They wrenched apart as Miss Rosalyn bore down on them, gown hoisted above the stable-yard's filth. She sidestepped a pile of droppings, the swish of her petticoat disturbing a swarm of flies, and made for Ian, holding out a folded paper.

"I've accounted for the stolen items. I'm concerned most particularly with the brooch Mama purchased for my chemise gown. It's ringed with seed pearls, with a case embossed in gold—the only item of true quality that perfidious little tinker—"

"I know what it looks like," Ian said with thinly veiled impatience. "Have I not spent the past three hours helping ye search for it and the rest?" He took the list and tucked it in the folds of the buckskin coat draped over the saddle.

Miss Rosalyn's eyes narrowed on his back before she glanced aside at Seona. "Why are you lingering? If you've finished the washing, go help in the kitchen—if they can bear the stink of you."

Ian whirled from the horse and closed his hand over Miss Rosalyn's arm. "Seona's waiting for me to speak to her about our work—on the desks for Stoddard."

Miss Rosalyn yanked her arm free. "Oh, aye?" she said, miming his way of speaking. "By all means, don't keep Seona waiting. She does look prodigiously fagged. Which reminds me, I overheard a most peculiar thing this morning that I've yet to puzzle out."

Seona knew that cat-in-cream look coming over Miss Rosalyn's face, but Ian didn't, else he'd have stopped her mouth instead of asking, "And what is that?"

"I heard Esther telling Maisy that when she last stripped the sheets from the upstairs beds, she found yours full of rose petals, of all things." Miss Rosalyn pretended to peer close at him. "Come to notice, Cousin, you're looking every bit as fagged as Seona these days."

"Grubbing stones the day long will do that to a man." Ian made a gesture that showed his blistered palm. "If that's all, I'm in something of a hurry to bring back your wee baubles."

Miss Rosalyn's chin rose. "I imagine you are,

361

but don't pretend it has anything to do with me."

"I won't, then." Ian sketched her a bow so curt it did for a slap, before heading for Seona. His eyes beckoned and she followed, Miss Rosalyn's glare jabbing her back like a roasting spit.

Inside the shop Ian lit neither lamp nor candle but drew her into the wood-scented shadows and his arms.

"She knows," Seona said.

"She only suspects. But never mind Rosalyn."

Cold was seeping into her, like a door gusted open, exposing her to a bitter wind. In the dimness she couldn't read his eyes, but the mouth that had been hard-set against Miss Rosalyn was soft now, smiling.

"I'd nearly decided I must steal ye away after all, but after my aunt barged in with her news, then left . . . I couldn't leave ye like this had my uncle not said what he did then."

"Ian . . . what?"

He kissed her briefly, shushing her. "Let me finish and ye'll understand. Ye know we agreed Uncle Hugh would grant your freedom if I stayed here at Mountain Laurel? I thought he'd change his mind after I told him how things stand with us—aye, I told him about the handfasting," he said hastily, adding, "but there's no cause for worry. We talked it through. He's going to write the petition anyway, while I'm gone on this errand. Ye won't have to go to Boston alone, Seona. He's going to let me go with ye."

"Why?" After everything, all the worry, the secrecy, it sounded too good to believe. "Why would he?"

"Because he's willing to hold Mountain Laurel in trust for a son—my son—instead of me."

She was suddenly off her feet, whirled around in his arms. Ian laughed as he put her down.

"He hasn't exactly given his blessing, but he won't prevent it. We can be together, Seona."

She put a hand to her belly. She'd had the oddest feeling while he spoke, like a tiny weight had dropped between her hips and rooted itself there—gone the next instant as shock washed over her. "Our son?"

"Of course, *ours*." Ian grasped her shoulders, unaware his hands were all that kept her upright. She could see him better now, see the blue of his eyes searching hers.

They'd disturbed a cricket, hidden in the wood shavings on the floor. Its chirping filled the shed, steady as a clock's ticking. Seona wanted to run to Master Hugh and beg him to free her mama with her. Lily had never asked anything of him— and she'd got nothing. Ian had pressed. He'd hounded. And look what had come of that. Or was promised to come of it.

But she'd known herself Hugh Cameron's slave far longer than she'd thought herself his offspring, and promises to slaves were no more to be trusted than shifting sand.

Wasn't that what they all kept telling her?

"At least my uncle's set himself to do what's right in the end," Ian was saying. "How he's borne it all these years, his own daughter—"

"And Mama's daughter," she said. "What about her?"

"Seona." He took her face between his hands, tender, certain. "We won't abandon Lily. But I haven't the means to care for them all—yet." His thumbs moved over her cheeks, her lips, like he meant to set her features to memory. "We needn't work it out this minute. There's time. But do me the one thing—don't speak of it 'til I return. Not even to Lily."

Seona's thoughts darted like wasps, stinging so she didn't know which way to turn. No one had asked if she wanted a son of hers to be a master, an owner of other women's sons, as if the only blood in his veins would be white blood. How could Ian want it? Was he even thinking beyond the two of them being free? Thinking they'd maybe only ever have daughters?

Still she heard herself give the answer he wanted. "I won't."

"I'll be back in a day," Ian said. "Two at most. We'll be all right, Seona. I'll take care of ye."

Her insides twisted at his words, but she could see his mind was set. She didn't know how to change it. He kissed her, fierce and full of longing.

"Bide a bit, aye? Just 'til I've gone."

He left her there, and she did as she was told.

The cricket was silent now. Only her heart beat in the dark, loud enough to muffle the sound of his going.

25

He reached the Yadkin after nightfall, too late for crossing. The next morning the ferryman assured him he'd poled across a peddler, evening past, but hadn't got his name. In rising hope of soon dispensing with his unsavory errand, Ian ascended the muddy road westward toward Salisbury. By midday the sky had darkened with clouds. Hope had dimmed with the daylight, while bewilderment grew. Every merchant he spoke with in town was certain Gottfriedsen hadn't been seen in Salisbury for at least six months. The man had crossed the Yadkin and vanished.

Back on the muddy main street, mood as grim as the brooding sky, Ian hitched Ruaidh outside a two-storied frame structure, the inn he'd saved for last. A fire and a scattering of lamps lit the low-beamed taproom. A haze of pipe smoke hung in air ripe with smells of ale and bread, abuzz with dinner conversation. The rail-thin figure languidly polishing cups behind the cage bar mightn't have budged since Ian clapped eyes on him weeks ago.

As Ian crossed the sanded floor, Jonas Sprouse eyed his quilled buckskin coat. "You were dressed the tradesman last I saw you. This getup better suits, you don't mind my saying so."

"Suits me better too, truth be known."

"How'd that gift for your lady suit?"

"She agreed to be my wife." Only half-suppressing the grin even the present frustration couldn't quench, Ian took a seat on a vacant bench. Sprouse brought him a brimming pint. Groans and laughter erupted from the fireside as a dice game broke up. Gottfriedsen was patently absent from the tavern crowd, but nothing would be lost in asking.

"A Salem peddler, come from east of the Yadkin?" Sprouse said once Ian explained his errand. "Didn't catch his name but there's a fellow hereabouts might answer your description."

Ian's pulse quickened at the news. "Where do I find him?"

"Parlor." Sprouse nodded toward the taproom door. "Across the passage yonder."

Ale forgotten, Ian snatched up his hat. The door to the parlor, a public room, stood half-open; Ian rapped once and pushed it wide. Three men, seated at a pedestal table stacked with ledgers and an inkpot, swiveled toward him. Spying the shortest of the trio, Ian's hope was finally dashed. Short of stature the man was, but unlike Gottfriedsen—whom Ian minded as frail, old, and clean-shaven—the figure rising from his chair was square-built and bearded, the skin across his cheekbones weathered red. "Your pardon, gentlemen. I thought to find someone else."

"Vait you, *mein Herr*." The risen man advanced with a purposeful air, his width giving the impression of a boulder rolling Ian's way. "Who is the someone you think to find?"

Ian nearly drew back at the wave of brandied breath that reached him before the man himself. "A Salem peddler, name of Gottfriedsen. A wee fellow. Looks like a stiff wind would knock him flat. He's traveling alone, with a wagon and mule."

"I am myself of Salem—and this Gottfriedsen I know!" At the man's hearty answer, there was a stir at the table. One of his companions laid aside his idle quill and sat back with folded arms. The other fished a pipe from a coat pocket and began filling the bowl with an air of resignation.

Ian, however, was instantly keen. "He's here? In Salisbury? Where might I find him?"

The man's bearded mouth bowed downward as he shook his head. "You vill not find him *here*. Herr Gottfriedsen is not in Salisbury."

"What's got you staring at the fire like Lot's wife? Get them dishes in here."

Seona jumped at Naomi's command, pulling her unseeing gaze from the hearth. Steam from the wash kettle glistened on Naomi's face. Lily had a half-scraped platter in hand, poised over the slop bucket. Both eyed her, standing in the kitchen doorway with the plates she'd carried from the big house in her arms.

"Tired, I reckon." She set the dishes on the workbench.

Naomi turned back to scrubbing. "Who ain't tired, I'd like to know? Scrape them plates. Then slop the hogs and be done for the day."

Seona didn't take the grumbling to heart. Naomi was worried. Ally had been sent to the mill to fetch lumber for the barn roof. Jubal would have gone, but Juturna had a touch of colic and Master Hugh wasn't about to let him leave his prized filly ailing to go fetch wood. Ally knew his way to the mill and back, had a writ pass tucked in his pocket. He could handle the wagon and team just fine. But he'd never been sent to Chesterfield on his own to deal with Pryce's people.

"Jackdaw should've gone hisself," Naomi muttered as Seona took up the first plate to scrape.

No one said a word to that.

Seona's nose had gone over fickle. As the scraps spattered on the mess of cobs and parings in the slop bucket, the stink rose up like something rotten. Her belly heaved. A thousand evenings she'd done this task without such bother. She shut her eyes and swallowed. A thousand evenings of Naomi bent over the wash kettle. A thousand evenings of Lily busy wiping the same plates, putting them up in their same place. The fire's pop and snap. The spice of onions and garlic and cloves and nutmeg mixing with the damp-leaf smell coming through the door. It was so aching real and precious and *hers,* she could have wept.

"Ye've been quiet today, Seona. Feeling puny?"

Lily hadn't used that word with her since she was a knee baby. It pushed her nearer to tears. "I'm all right, Mama." She scraped another plate and stacked it for washing.

"Moping over Mister Ian gone, more'n like." Naomi had her back turned, bent to her scrubbing. "After all we done spoke on the matter."

Silence weighed heavy.

Naomi turned a frown their way. "What's got you both shut up tight as hogsheads? Seona, you done something to vex your mama?"

Seona opened her mouth, teetering on the edge of spilling everything, but words to tell how she was going to be Ian's free, passing-for-white wife fled. In their place anger bloomed, a red flower filling up her mind. "Mama, tell me one thing. Is Master Hugh my daddy?"

Behind her came a crack, as Naomi dropped a plate.

Seona spied Esther down the carriage drive, staring toward the mist that marked the creek's snaking course through the darkening wood. Ally was late getting home. It was cold in the stable-yard and she'd left her shawl in the kitchen. She wasn't going back for it.

Go slop the hogs like Naomi asked was all her mama had said to her question. Naomi had said nothing at all. Not that Seona needed them to. When Ian came back, all the secrets would be out. And what then? Were they to go on through the winter, sneaking round to be together? Or was she to move into Ian's room like a proper wife, sit at table with his kin, suffer their sour-pickle gazes while they waited for the papers that made her free?

At the hog pen she hefted the bucket to the fence rail and dumped the leavings over the side. Slimy peelings and scraps spilled like vomit into the trough, nearly setting her to retching. The sow and her big shoats heaved themselves up to come shoving and squealing to feed.

Seona swallowed hard and left them to it, trudging back through the dusk, tiredness in her bones, unaware right off it was Esther's screaming she heard. The shriek blended with the shoats kicking up a squeal over their supper. Then she heard her name in it.

"Seona-a-a!" Esther came pelting up the lane with petticoat hiked and skinny legs like sticks beating the ground. "Fetch my daddy! Ally's down by the crick lying in the wagon!"

She halted, frozen with dread, but still making no sense of Esther's words. "Ally's what?"

As she reached her, Esther stumbled. Seona flung aside the slop bucket to catch her.

The girl's eyes were edged in white. "There's blood all over—he hurt bad, maybe dead!"

Ally wasn't dead, but as near to it as he'd come since getting mule-kicked as a boy. Master Hugh didn't look much better. He'd come down to Naomi's cabin and they'd all backed out of his way except Lily, busy cleaning Ally's striped back. Seona watched him. Seemed like though he stood among them in the flesh, part of him was gone away. Like a man struck dead on his feet, before his body crumples.

Then he seemed to shake himself and come back from wherever he'd gone. "Was it Pryce, or another, did this?"

"Mister Pryce laid the lash to him," Malcolm said. He sat with Naomi at a rickety table, close by the door. Naomi's lips were pressed so tight Seona doubted she could part them without cracking her face wide open. She was mindful of her own back pressed against rough logs, their edges pushing into her flesh. Smells were still loud in her nose. Blood and sweat and vinegar, the tobacco sweetness that clung to Master Hugh, all conspired to gag her. She wanted out of there if only to breathe, but she held the lamp for Lily to see by.

Esther leaned against her, crying tears for Ally,

who'd hollered at first touch of the vinegar wash, then passed out cold. A mercy.

"Who was it brought him home?" Master Hugh asked. "He couldna have driven the wagon. Esther, ye spied no man near it?"

Esther jumped when addressed. "No, sir. I ain't seen nobody. Just Ally."

Master Hugh glanced at Seona. Something flickered in his eyes, and she wondered what he truly thought of her going away with Ian. Was he looking at her and thinking *daughter?* Or was he thinking about her being the one to finally give him his heir? She did not want to ask that.

"White . . . man."

They all started and turned to the cot. Ally's deep voice was muffled against the ticking, making them all lean forward to hear.

"Was a white man . . . brung me home."

Finished washing the wounds, Lily went to the table to pound herbs in the mortar for a poultice.

Master Hugh knelt near Ally's head. "What happened, Ally? Can ye tell me?"

The lamplight caught the flutter of Ally's lashes. "Mule . . . done it."

Master Hugh's lips thinned. "No mule laid these stripes to ye."

"It was on account of a mule, he means," Malcolm said. "He's told us that much. A man come to the mill had a mule take to fashing, and Ally's way wi' horses is kent. Mister Pryce called him to come deal wi' the creature so they could be getting on wi' matters."

Ally's voice came thick. "I telled 'em . . . don't have no truck with mules."

A grimace tightened Master Hugh's face. "I ken it well, Ally."

"Mister Pryce, he go red-faced . . . Men lookin' on . . . Told his mill slaves get hold of me. One hiss at me, saying . . . 'Don't fight—it make him meaner.' "

"Did ye fight?" Master Hugh asked.

"Yes, sir. Ain't never been whupped afore. It *hurt*." A shudder went through Ally.

Esther gave a little whimper and gripped Seona's arm tight.

Master Hugh wiped a hand over his mouth, pressing hard. "What did Pryce do wi' ye, after?" he asked after a pause.

"Said . . . get on home, tell why I got my lickin'. But I couldn't climb up on the wagon. I fell . . . woke up in the dark."

A cabin in the slave quarter, Seona guessed. Or a shed out of the way. Someone had taken pity.

"Was a white man bending over me," Ally said. "And Thomas."

"Ian's Thomas?" Master Hugh asked.

With all the focus on Ally, Seona had clean forgot about Thomas still being at Chesterfield. The mill wasn't near the cooper shop, but word of such doings would have spread like a crop fire.

"Yes, sir. I hear the white man say he drive me home. Hear Thomas tell him where to go. That's when I knew . . . it'd be all right."

Esther wiped her streaming nose on the sleeve of her shift. "It ain't all right, Ally. It ain't!"

Seona squeezed her hand to hush her, but Master Hugh paid her no mind. "What of Thomas? Did he ride home with ye? Surely it's time for him to be back."

More than time, but after the scene at the mill, Gideon Pryce would have been in no fit mood to dole out traveling passes. Knowing Thomas, he'd risk it without one, especially in the company of a white man. Had he? If so, where was he now? And who was that white man? Not John Reynold, if Thomas had to tell him where to take Ally. Besides, Ally knew Mister John.

Then she wondered, Might it have been the Quaker Thomas once told her about? The one who meant to help him? Thomas had never named him.

Master Hugh sought the same answer. "Did ye hear talk between Thomas and this man who brought ye home? Anything to tell who the man might be?"

Ally's back quivered beneath the web of welts, but he said no more. Finally Master Hugh stood to go, pausing in the doorway when Malcolm asked, "Ye'll go to Mister Pryce?"

"Aye. Tomorrow." Plainly Master Hugh hadn't

strength to mount a horse tonight. Seona hoped he would come morning. She hoped even more to see Ian come riding in to take care of this mess. Of everything.

Master Hugh said something more. She heard Dawes's name but missed the rest, for just then Ally spoke again. She took a step closer to the cot, Esther moving with her like an extra limb.

"What did he say, lass? Did ye hear?"

Seona raised her eyes to Master Hugh, who'd turned back as well. "Yes, sir. But I don't take his meaning. He said they—Thomas and the white man—was talking about the Garden."

Master Hugh frowned. "The man was a gardener, d'ye mean? Pryce's gardener?"

Seona shook her head. "No, sir. The Garden, like in the Bible. Ally says he heard Thomas and the white man speak of Eden."

26

Mist hung low in the hollows east of the Yadkin River as the day folded in. Despite sporadic horse and wagon traffic on the road, Ian had had solitude for thinking, for casting ahead to the future, and for looking back. He'd had time to think about his uncle's startling offer. Himself for Seona's freedom, or a son for both. Most would call it a father's duty to see a son well-settled. His da had tried his best with him, let him go three times. First to his indenture to Pringle, cabinetmaker. Then to Callum Lindsay, frontiersman and fur-trader. Then to Hugh Cameron, planter. Owner of other men.

But is not the slave trade entirely at war with the heart of man? And surely that which is begun by breaking down the barriers of virtue, involves in its continuance destruction to every principle . . . The words remained emblazoned upon his mind. Was any amount of land or inheritance worth that price? Perhaps he and Seona *should* run. . . .

He'd nearly forgotten Gottfriedsen and the stolen goods until he found himself at the crossing of the Cape Fear road, which cut north toward Salem. If he were to make for Mountain Laurel, he must continue east over the Carraways.

Ian drew Ruaidh to a halt. What if the peddler had

changed his mind after leaving Mountain Laurel, had made directly for Salem instead of Salisbury? Had Salisbury been a ruse to begin with? An echo of Seona's bewilderment reverberated through his thoughts. Gottfriedsen was a familiar bird, his roost well-known. The peddler he'd mistaken, sight unseen, for Gottfriedsen had been struck with hilarity by the error.

"Traveling alone? Herr Gottfriedsen? I vould not think he had the courage!"

"What makes ye say so?" Ian had asked.

"Herr Gottfriedsen is . . ." The man had stroked his beard, searching for the appropriate appellation. "*Ängstlich.* The mouse that flees at shadows."

A canny mouse, indeed.

There came a rustle in the nearby undergrowth, the startled *chit* of some night creature. Though the hills he traversed were far from the mountain frontier, still he was smack in the middle of a good-sized track of virgin forest, its isolated farms no hindrance to the roaming of bear and catamount—neither of which he'd relish meeting after nightfall.

Ian leaned forward in the saddle, breath a barely perceptible plume in the twilight. Gottfriedsen had gained a day on him, but he mightn't yet have reached Salem to tidy away all trace of his thievery. Finding out meant a day's travel north, at least another back.

Ian ground his teeth in sudden, dual resolve. He couldn't be the one to provide his uncle an heir, but he'd give him back his womenfolk's trinkets. Then he would go, taking with him the treasure his uncle had failed to value. If Callum wouldn't have him back, with all his rash promises broken and a runaway wife at his side, it was still a vast frontier stretching across the west. Two people could fall into it like drops in an ocean, never to be found.

"I'm sorry, Da," he whispered and turned Ruaidh onto the Salem road.

Cold air stirred, raising gooseflesh up her legs, as Seona shut the back door and stood listening, heart banging at her recklessness. Only the faint ticks and pops of old timbers settling broke the house's slumbering hush. She knew those back stairs, which ones creaked, how to come up them quiet as a cat. Once in Ian's room, she slipped between his cold bedsheets, drawing the hangings shut. Pulled into a trembling ball, she curled her hands round her icy feet. And held her breath.

Silence eased her fear as warmth stole into her limbs. Cosseted in clean linens and feather ticking, she pressed her face into Ian's pillow and breathed the smell of him.

Deep in the night hours, huddled there like moths in a cocoon, he'd told her how it would be in the North. The home he'd build, maybe near a frontier village. Someplace they could go on working together, making crops, making furniture . . . babies. She would draw whenever she pleased.

She'd shook with disbelieving laughter at that last bit, thinking free folk must have more hours in a day than slaves heard tell of.

"I see it, Seona," he'd said. "Our life. See it so clearly I could hold its shape in my hands."

She'd tried to hold it too but found the notion slick as moss on a river stone. No matter how she came at it, the shape slipped from her grasp.

Her hand slid between the sheets, shocked to feel the cold instead of Ian's warmth.

Wilt thou go with this man? The line from a story Malcolm had told them over the years popped into her mind. An old story, set in Bible times. She couldn't remember the names of those doing the asking or the answering, but that girl that got asked? She had known her mind.

And she said, I will go.

Had that girl never worried she wasn't fit to live in her man's world? What did Seona know about being the wife of a white man? She'd seen what went on between the mistress and Master Hugh, that cold battle of wills cloaked in brittle smiles when folk like the Pryces were by to witness. Almost from the start it had been that way.

There was Miss Cecily and Mister John. What they had, that was worth trying for. Miss Cecily and Mister John were matched like two fine horses, mind and heart. *And spirit.* For all her asking, she wasn't sure Ian knew what it meant to be a child of God. Seona wondered if she knew. Did she believe the Lord was watching over her lot? Was that faith her own, or did she have faith in her mama's faith? In Malcolm's?

Wilt thou go with this man? Had she a choice? She was his wife now. For better or for worse. Those were the words they'd promised. A wife had to do what her husband wanted. Like a slave her mistress. Didn't she?

Seona clutched the pillow, murmuring a prayer to hold back the dark of unknown threatening to sweep her away. "Thy will be done, Lord. Thy will be—"

The click of the door latch cut off plea and breath alike. For a second she thought it was Ian come home in the night, creeping like she'd done so as not to wake the house.

Cautious feet skirted the bed. Booted feet, and heavy. *Not Ian's.*

She didn't know how she knew, but she cringed under the counterpane, braced for the hangings to be yanked aside. Those on the window side hung open a crack. A shadow moved across the strip, so close the hangings stirred.

A boot scuff told her the man had paused in front of Ian's clothespress. Hinges creaked. Cloth whispered as garments were shifted. The man muttered under his breath, too low to catch words or recognize the voice. Was it Jackson Dawes? Master Hugh?

The search moved to Ian's desk: a rattle, a jiggle-and-scrape, a click as a drawer slid open. That desk had a locking drawer. This man knew how to pick that lock. Or knew where Ian kept the key. Papers crinkled for a time before the drawer slid shut and the lock clicked.

A key then.

The shadow loomed. Seona's heart slammed like a frightened rabbit's until she heard the turning of the door handle. When she could bear it no longer, she sat up and parted the hangings.

She was alone.

She kept her calm until she was outside. Then she broke and ran. She was passing the kitchen breezeway when hands shot out of the dark trellis tunnel and grabbed her. Strong fingers splayed over her mouth. She squirmed in the tangle of her shawl, freed an elbow, and jabbed it into a set of ribs. The hand over her mouth slipped. She bared her teeth to bite it.

"Relax, girl," Thomas hissed in her ear. "It's me."

She wrenched loose, furious. "What do you call yourself doing?"

"Trying to pin a wildcat, seems."

Seona fixed him with a glare, wasted in the

dark. "You're meant to be at Chesterfield. Was it you come into Ian's room?"

Thomas grasped her arm and towed her into the kitchen. A faint glow came off the banked coals in the cooking hearth. Seona felt her way around the worktable while Thomas scraped bare an edge of hearth embers. A brighter glow splashed his scowling face red.

"Might as well saunter through the front door at noon as go sneaking in the back by night," he said. "You and Ian the only ones think no one sees."

"It's not how you think." Seona gripped the edge of the table, feeling a splinter prick her palm. "Ian's my husband."

"Husband?"

It jarred, the way Thomas flung the word back at her. Like he'd never heard it before. "We're handfast. It's binding for a year and—"

"I know how handfasting works. I grew up hearing the same tales of Scotland as Ian." When she stared, dumbfounded, a smile played on Thomas's lips like he was laughing. "And here's me thinking Ian must've told you the truth long since."

"What truth?"

"About me. I'm no slave. I was born to a free woman and I've known *Mastah* Ian since I was eight years old."

Seona stood speechless while Thomas told

how his daddy saved Ian's daddy on a battlefield somewhere up north during the war. How afterward Thomas and his daddy—his mama having died—came to live with the Camerons in a part of Boston called North End. How he and Ian grew up like brothers, their daddies working together in the bookbinding trade.

As he talked, she quietly broke inside. Ian had kept this from her. Let her go on thinking Thomas was his slave. After all his talk of trusting?

"Why?" she asked. "Why come here pretending?"

Thomas grinned, eager, like he'd hoped she'd ask. "My daddy acted like his life started the day his master died and freed him in his will. After a time I quit asking about his slave days but I never stopped wanting to know. Couple years back I met some folk, call themselves *abolitionists*. It's slavery they want to see abolished—all of it, everywhere, but especially places like right here and deeper in the South. So do I, but I needed to see for myself how bad it is—before I decided what to do about it. But I couldn't come even this far on my own. When Ian came back from the wilds and the letter came from Hugh Cameron, I saw Providence was handing me the chance."

Seona clenched her arms over her ribs, afraid the brokenness would cut her from the inside if she didn't squeeze tight. The things Thomas told her that day in the herb shed after Dawes had roughed her up. Talk of running. She'd thought it was the bitterness talking, like it did for all of them when things got bad. But Thomas was no slave.

"And Ian went along with it?"

Thomas chuckled. "Not at first. He played me a game of cat and mouse from Boston nigh to Maryland. When he couldn't shake me, he brought me along to muck it up for him. That's my guess—though I doubt he knows it himself. Not yet."

Seona was trying not to breathe, to keep the jagged bits inside her still. All those stories from Ian's childhood . . . how many had he told her, all the while cutting Thomas out, careful as her mama snipping pieces for a gown?

"What did you tell Ian you meant to do?" she asked.

"Told him the truth. That I wanted to see if what I'd heard and read about slaves in the South was true. Now I've seen. I'm ready to act."

So many things about Ian made better sense now. Why he let Thomas speak to him so uppity. And those lines he'd crossed with her, like he never even saw them. He'd been living a lie. He and Thomas both. Her thoughts were dazed and bruised, like her body had been after Dawes caught her under the poplar tree.

"How long has Ian been dallying with you?" Thomas asked.

The question pulled her head up sharp. *Dallying.* She didn't believe it. Not this part. "Ian loves me. He—"

"This ain't Scotland, Seona, and bedded ain't wedded. Not for a slave, which is what you are— in case you need reminding."

She struck with her open palm, catching him across the mouth.

Thomas flinched. Then his eyes softened, reflecting back the hearth glow. "Reckon I deserved that. But I hate what slavery's done to our people," he said with renewed fervor. "To *you*. Making you desperate enough to trade your purity for freedom—my bones ache with hating it."

Trading her purity. Was that what he thought she'd done?

"If it's freedom you want, there's other ways— without compromise." Thomas took her by the shoulders. "There's something you need to hear. Come with me down to the creek. He— someone's there waiting on me."

How many folk were creeping about Mountain Laurel this night?

"Who's waiting? That Quaker? We know from Ally you had a white man helping you at Chesterfield."

Thomas stepped back. "Come see. Then decide how you want to be free. It doesn't have to be Ian's way."

"What about Mama?"

"I told you I'd take her, too. But you got to decide. Tonight."

Her heart rose into her throat. If there was a chance she could see Mama free—not someday maybe, but *now*—along with herself, did she dare dismiss it out of hand? What harm could there be in going to see?

Wilt thou go with this man?

The question echoed in her mind, even as she nodded and Thomas smiled. And suddenly, like a random spark spit from the hearth, she remembered. *Rebekah.* That was the name of the girl in the story who'd said, *I will go.*

27

Even from a distance Ian knew the small, lumbering, high-bowed wagon for Gottfriedsen's. With his pistol shoved into the back of his waistband, he overtook it swiftly, bringing the roan to a halt across the wagon's path. The startled peddler jerked back on the mule's traces. With a jangle and clank of wares, the wagon creaked to a standstill, wheels sinking into the miry clay road. The backdrop of wooded hills made the man perched on the box seem even smaller than the slight, diffident figure Ian recalled sipping tea in his aunt's parlor.

"Mr. Gottfriedsen. I'm sent to detain ye."

Wary blue eyes peered from the chink between felt hat and woolen muffler. Like a terrapin venturing from its shell, the man poked a red-tipped nose from the muffler's folds. Recognition cleared his expression of alarm, if not puzzlement. "Ah—the nephew of Hugh Cameron who kills the snake. In his goodwife's parlor I make your acquaintance, *ja*?"

"Aye, and ye stand accused by that lady. Of thievery."

Gottfriedsen's eyes rounded. "I—she—what are you saying? Of *thieving* you accuse me?"

Ignoring the show of bewildered innocence, Ian

reached into his coat for Rosalyn's list. "I've an accounting of purchased items that vanished with your leaving. Ye may assist me in returning them or—"

"No!" The peddler's head wagged furiously. "There is no thievery. As *Gott* sees me."

"Or," Ian resumed, "I'll lash ye to the nearest tree while *I* do the searching. I cannot promise to be tidy about it, so if ye value your wares—and your time—ye'll save us both the trouble and produce the items."

The mule stood placidly, puffing plumes of breath. The peddler gaped. "You—the nephew of Hugh Cameron—would *rob* me?"

Ian drew Ruaidh level with the peddler. Before he could reach for the man, Gottfriedsen scrambled off the wagon, in such haste his round-brimmed hat tumbled to the mud. Ian vaulted from the saddle in pursuit, pistol drawn, but Gottfriedsen merely scurried to the wagon's rear and flung wide its painted doors. Lifting placating hands, he stepped back from Ian, who towered over him. "For these things on the paper, you look. You will not find."

"I had better *find*—or have their price back in coin." Feeling absurdly like an actor in a stage play—the villain, at that—Ian gestured with the pistol. "I want ye in there with me."

The elderly man ducked his head, features set in indignation, but complied. Grunting, stiff joints popping, he hoisted himself into the wagon. Ian climbed after him into a narrow confine of hanging tin and rag-wrapped stoneware, of crates and chests with innumerable drawers. Light fell across the clutter to a corner where blankets rested on an upturned crate. There Ian took a seat, pistol aimed, and consulted his list. Halfway through Rosalyn's description of the brooch, the little man's head began to bob.

"Ringed with the seed pearls, *ja*. To the pretty daughter I sell."

"She claims she paid your price—"

"She did."

Ian held up a hand. "But she left the brooch in the dining room with the things my aunt purchased. During the night ye entered the house, took back the brooch, a mold for six candles, a snuffer—" he consulted the list—"and a pierced-tin lantern, and were gone ere the theft was discovered."

Spots of color flushed Gottfriedsen's sunken cheeks. "Why would I do such a thing? A false accusation!"

"So ye say."

"I will show!" With small, half-flinching motions, the peddler took down the nearest chest, removed his mittens, and began rummaging within. The chest was stocked with soap. When the scented stuff lay heaped on the floorboards, Gottfriedsen turned the chest up for Ian's viewing. His hands, red with chilblains, were shaking.

"You see a brooch? *No* brooch." He swiped a coat sleeve beneath his nose, reached for another chest, and began the process again.

There were countless places in that wagon to stash an item as small as a brooch, places the uninitiated might never find—without dismantling the conveyance down to kindling.

"Mr. Gottfriedsen," Ian began, but the man had stilled.

Slowly Gottfriedsen faced him, blinking at a thing in his hand. Moistening chapped lips, he placed the brooch he'd sold to Rosalyn between them on the wagon's floor. He lifted his bewildered eyes only briefly to Ian, before he launched into motion again. Ian half rose, but the man seemed hardly aware of him as he stood to examine his pierced-tin wares, dangling from the wagon's roof tree.

The peddler took down a lantern and set it beside the brooch. Gray light edged his stricken face, and as he spoke, Ian's own indignation crumbled.

"My sister's son . . . he has the broken leg what is slow to mend, and I am not having the memory so good now. 'Do not go alone on the road,' they tell me, *mein Familie*. A few more weeks, they tell me, the leg is mending. But a few more weeks is snow, *ja*? And the living must be made."

The corners of Gottfriedsen's mouth clenched in a spasm of restraint. "Maybe I do this . . . this thieving, but it was by mistake. My mistake. For it I am sorry."

It was awkward business, witnessing a man confronted by the indignities of his declining years. Ian had had his fill of it with his uncle. To find it here on the road when he'd sought a thief was strangely disheartening. He handed over the list. As the little man searched his wares, Ian studied the back of his head, bared without his hat. Silvery hair ringed the base of Gottfriedsen's skull, wisping over ears red with cold.

Having gone from wanting to arrest the man for theft to pitying him in a matter of minutes, Ian rose, returning to the peddler what dignity he could. "I see that it was a mistake, sir. We've all made them, aye? Take your time."

At the front of the wagon Ruaidh stood communing with the peddler's mule in a cloud of mingled breath. Ian retrieved the man's fallen hat and turned it over in his hands. The brim bore a streak of mud. He wiped it on his breeches, then stood beneath the gray sky in the pine-scented air until Gottfriedsen descended the wagon.

The peddler insisted on seeing the parcels into Ian's saddlebag himself. Holding out the battered hat, Ian cleared his throat. "Ye'll forgive my giving ye a scare?"

"*Natürlich*—of course." Gottfriedsen took the hat and offered him a self-deprecating smile that somehow made Ian feel worse.

"May I ask your given name, sir?"

"My name?" the peddler said, seeming surprised. "*Ja.* That much I recall. It is Karl."

With Karl Gottfriedsen and his wagon behind him, Ian opened his mind again to Seona, their future. He'd no hope of reaching her by nightfall. The sky had already begun to darken. Seized with resentment at the shortening days, at the slogging mud, at his aunt and cousin, he held Ruaidh to a trot. One more night and he'd be with her and they could stop pretending.

Despite the chill and wasted days, the miles and threatening clouds, the thought brought a sense of release. He was smiling when the *kier* of a hawk caught his ear. He sighted the bird circling above, dark against the lowering gray.

When he looked again at the road ahead, he saw the riders coming. Two of them, shapeless hats shoved low, cantering their horses. They broke stride as they neared, slowing to a trot. Assessing glances skimmed the roan, the rifle in its scabbard, the half-breed coat he wore. A clash of eyes with the nearest rider . . . and they were past, the slog of hooves receding in the widening gap.

Their faces stayed burned in Ian's memory:

hungry, calculating faces. A vision of Gottfried-sen's bared and vulnerable head flashed across his mind.

He brought Ruaidh to a halt and turned in the saddle. The riders were gone round a bend in the road. After a moment's indecision he continued southward. A quarter mile. A half mile. Trying to put the peddler out of mind.

Another harsh *kier* tore the air, sounding like a cry for aid. And he knew. His conscience wasn't going to let him go in peace.

Ian swore and wheeled the roan, heading back the way he'd come at a gallop.

He'd found Karl Gottfriedsen perched on his wagon like a treed possum, a rider to either side of the mule's traces. The peddler had been cowed enough to hold his tongue when Ian hailed him as *Uncle* and made show of continuing the journey to Salem as companion and guard. Which, in the end, was exactly what he'd done.

Though he'd imagined finding her watching for him, there was no sign of Seona as, days later than promised, he rode up the leaf-drifted lane of his uncle's farm. He hitched Ruaidh, dropped the saddlebags on a bench, and peered into the stable's depths.

"Jubal? Ye there, man?"

There was no answering hail. Smoke from the house chimneys hung in the damp air. A gray thread wafted from the kitchen roof. Aside from such evidence, the place might have been deserted, but by the time he'd turned Ruaidh out to graze, he'd sensed the watchfulness, heavy and still, like the breathlessness before a storm breaks. Leaving saddle and bags outside the stable, he strode up to the house.

In the entryway he paused. The same storm-charged atmosphere prickled the hairs on his neck. Movement down the passage caught his eye. Maisy and Esther stood outside his uncle's door, bent toward the room as iron filings to a magnet.

"Maisy? What's amiss?"

His voice crackled along the passage and struck the pair like a bolt. They sprang apart as a rumble of voices rolled like returning thunder from his uncle's room—three voices, four.

Maisy and Esther scuttled from his path. In the doorway he stopped.

Inside the room were his kin, arranged in a frozen tableau. A fire blazed in the fieldstone hearth, gilding their faces, imprinting each upon his mind—the pained, waxen features of his uncle, risen from his chair; his aunt in the center of the room, face frozen in fury; Rosalyn, mouth pulled into a moue of distaste; Judith, teary-eyed with distress. And in the midst of them Lily, hair unbraided, on her knees and clinging to his uncle in supplication.

Uncle Hugh's shoulders bowed. One hand stirred as though he would touch the sleek black head at his knee. "What more would ye have me do, Lily? I've sent Dawes—"

"Please." Lily rocked on her knees, clutching at his uncle. "Don't let Mister Dawes be the one to find her."

Her. The word jangled through Ian, ringing with identity though no name was uttered, freezing limbs and tongue.

His aunt, immune to the immobilizing power of the word, grabbed hold of Lily's arm. "Promise her nothing! Jackson will find them—or he won't. I wish this one was out of my sight as well." She gave Lily's arm a wrench, then drew back her hand as if to strike.

Ian had no memory of crossing the room, only of his aunt's wrist jerking in his grasp. He loosed her and reeled back.

"Someone tell me what in blazes has happened!"

Rosalyn came toward him, hand extended absurdly in greeting. He stared at it, then at her face. "Where is Seona? What have ye done?"

Rosalyn halted, face contorting with incredulity. "What have *I* done? I daresay we all know what you've done. You and your half-breed doxy!"

The blood beat in his head like a drum. "Where—is—Seona?"

"That is not at present known." Lucinda had

taken Rosalyn consolingly by the shoulders. The two faced him together. "We've had word from Chesterfield. Your boy has run. It would appear he's taken Seona with him."

Ian felt those words strike his heart like fangs. Then the slow spread of their venom. *Thomas.*

"But I just saw Black Huzzah in the stable. Why didn't . . . ?" He didn't finish the question. If Thomas had been his slave, then the horse would have belonged to Ian. Was Thomas continuing the ruse even now, whatever he was up to? But why Seona? Why would *she* have gone?

"What proof have ye Seona's with him?" he asked instead.

"One of my gowns is missing." Rosalyn shook in her mother's hold, small fists clenched. "And a pair of Judith's shoes. Both were in the washhouse yesterday, and we know who does the washing."

Loathing and satisfaction distorted the features Ian had once thought beautiful.

"I don't believe a word of this," he said, though the ground beneath that statement was more than a little shaky now. "What have ye done with Seona?"

"It's true—"

"How dare you imply my daughter—"

"Please!" Silence fell at the astonishing sound of Judith's voice raised, imploring. "Why didn't you tell him everything at once?"

Ian fixed on her now. "Everything? What else is there? Judith—tell me."

Judith's voice faltered. "T-Thomas left a letter addressed to you. It said . . . it said—oh!" She crossed to his uncle's desk, snatched up a folded paper, and thrust it at him. "Read what it says."

"You wanted proof." Lucinda's voice rang with triumph. "Perhaps you'll trust your own eyes—and recall it was you brought him here. You've yourself alone to blame for this!"

Before he recognized the script or read a word, Ian knew the paper—a page trimmed from Thomas's journal. The poison was spreading, striking deeper. He dropped to his knees, taking Lily by the shoulders. If a scrap of hope remained that it was some misunderstanding, that Seona hadn't left them—left *him*—Lily's devastated eyes unraveled it.

"This smacks of forethought," Lucinda said. "Did I not tell you, Hugh, no good would come of his bringing a strange Negro into our home? If he cannot manage even one slave, how will he—?"

"*Wheesht*, Aunt!" Ian broke in. "Thomas was never my slave."

"Then whose is he?" his aunt snapped, an instant before the truth registered. Ian watched the horror of it blanch her face.

"No one's. His father was Oliver Ross, Da's

partner in his shop. Thomas is . . . like a brother to me." Or he had been. Once.

A recoil of silence met his words. Uncle Hugh sank into his chair. Judith's hand went to her mouth. Rosalyn turned to her mother, shock giving way to matching horror.

Lily's was the only face devoid of reaction, but her eyes still held their desperate appeal. "I don't know what she's thinking, Mister Ian. I thought it was you she wanted. But please . . . don't let Mister Dawes be the one to find them."

He minded Seona's bruised brow, uncovered in the shop when he gave her the comb. "Has Dawes hurt her before?"

"I'd have had the man hangit had he touched her!"

His uncle's outburst drew everyone's attention save Lily's. "She'd bruises fading when we come home from the springs. Said she fell in the wood. Now Pete and Will are telling me that's not what happened."

"Lily," his uncle said, lurching forward in his chair. "Tell me what they've said."

While Lily told a tale that raised the hairs on Ian's neck, and skeptical protest from his aunt, Ian stood in their midst, braced and beset. All that had seemed solid beneath him was shifting, despite his attempt to hold it steady. And he knew the thing inside him now, spreading its red venom. It was rage.

• • •

He went straight to the cabins to see Ally, recovered from Pryce's lashing enough to sit up and tell his tale. But when the name *Eden* was spoken, he corrected no one's guess. He didn't say this Eden had a first name and wore the Quaker gray.

While Jubal saddled his uncle's sorrel, leaving Ruaidh at rest in the paddock, Ian leaned against a stall, forehead pressed to folded arms, dizzy with weariness, while Uncle Hugh—as much enraged as Ian now concerning Jackson Dawes—related the events of the past few days. The morning following the whipping, Pryce had ridden to Mountain Laurel to inquire after Thomas, gone missing from the cooperage at Chesterfield, and to offer the price of the lumber Ally was sent to fetch as recompense for his "damaging."

"As for Thomas," Uncle Hugh said, "we'd settled the matter that he'd no' been seen hereabouts, and so I told Pryce."

"Pryce knows nothing of Seona missing?" It felt like glass breaking in Ian's chest, speaking her name.

"He didna hear it from me. 'Twas after his going Lily came seeking the lass, and no' 'til Esther ran to the Reynolds' without fetching her home did we find the letter left for ye and put her together wi' Thomas gone missing."

Ian nodded, but his mind spun with another

400

possibility. Gideon Pryce wanted Seona, had made it known he would take her in trade for his uncle's debt—and been refused. Had the man stolen her, creating an elaborate subterfuge involving Thomas to cover the act?

He might have plunged down that path of reasoning had it not been for Ally's memory of Eden. It smacked of forethought, his aunt had said. More than she could know.

Jubal led the sorrel out, ready to ride. Lily appeared as Ian mounted, marks of weeping on her face, and handed him a satchel of provisions. He met her look of pleading with a wordless promise. He would do everything in his power to find them.

Dawes, his uncle told him, had ridden northwest along the creek, thinking that the route Seona and Thomas had taken.

"Have ye aught for me to tell the man, when I see him?" Ian asked, though words weren't what he had in mind for his uncle's overseer.

"Oh, aye," Hugh Cameron said, face set with a fury that matched Ian's own. "But it can wait. Bring him back to me. He's done here and I'll have him ken it well. As for Seona and your . . . Thomas, pray God ye find them safe."

"Do that," Ian said, turning the sorrel's head toward the road. But for all his rage against Dawes, there was another that went deeper. "And God save the soul of Thomas Ross when I do."

PART IV

November–December 1793

I have played the Fool, though some may say I come late to the Acknowledgment. Are you praying for me, Da, you and Mam? Am I fighting Heaven's will, as well as yours?

28

At midday Ian dismounted to study the trail. The telltale prints in the moist earth he'd followed since yesterday were only hours old now. Dawes's horse had a shoe working loose; his pace had slowed. Ian pulled his hat low and remounted, rifle across his knees, pressing on through ranks of hardwoods dripping from last night's rain, while high clouds pushed along on chilling air.

Though he'd long since left the course of Mountain Laurel's creek behind, the sun was setting when he heard the faint burble of another. He left the trail, guiding the sorrel down through hazel and bare-limbed ash, across a sandy crescent to the water. While the horse drank, he crouched to fill his canteen, scanning the bank by habit.

A patch of sunlight showed the cloven prints of deer in the sand. The handlike impressions of a raccoon. No mark left by a woman's slender foot. Or a man's.

He corked the canteen but didn't rise. Nor did he glance at the saddlebag that held the crumpled letter, written in Thomas's familiar scrawl:

I hoped to find in you an Ally, as of old. But if ever we saw face-to-face, now it be through a Glass darkly. I mean to bring her away with the others. Leastwise she will have the Choice. Freedom, at a kinder Price than you exacted.

Face and gut burning at memory of the words, Ian checked the priming pan before shouldering his rifle, then headed back up the wooded slope. It was hours since he'd passed the spot where Dawes had finally stopped to tend his horse's shoe. The man wouldn't be far.

A quarter mile on he heard the clank of metal, perhaps a spoon against a pot. Smoke scented the chill air. He dismounted, rifle in hand, and led the sorrel forward until he spied the glow of flames.

Dawes had camped below a rock outcrop that jutted from the forest like the wall of a castle ruin, its crumbling surface studded with lichen. A few yards from its base a fire licked at the underbelly of a pot hung from a tripod. The man's horse grazed a short way off.

The breeze shifted, carrying the aroma of salted pork on the boil. The sorrel, scenting something different and not to its liking, jerked its head with a violence that wrenched the lead from Ian's grasp. As he lunged to recapture the panicked horse, he caught movement on the rock's high lip, fifteen feet above Dawes's head. The twitch of a tawny tail.

It was the space of a heartbeat, his hesitation. In that space the catamount leapt.

Ian let the sorrel go, swung the rifle to his shoulder, braced, and fired. Ears ringing, he plunged through fraying powder smoke to find Jackson Dawes laid out flat, the catamount sprawled atop him. The man's barrel-sprung chest heaved beneath the animal's inert weight. As Ian moved into his stunned field of vision, his voice came strangled with terror.

"Get—get it off me!"

"Hush your noise, man. It's past harming ye." With some regret at having thwarted nature's course, Ian propped the rifle on a log set back from the fire, where the pot's contents bubbled undisturbed.

Ears to tail-tip, the catamount had to be eight feet long. Blood stained the animal's neck a bright scarlet. Ian grasped a heavy foreleg above the elbow joint, preparing to roll it off Dawes. The animal's scent enveloped him like a musky breath as his fingers dug through blood-slick fur, pressed into flaccid muscle, and met with a thumping pulse—an instant before what he'd thought a carcass revived to spitting, clawing life.

Ian staggered backward, wrenched free his hunting knife, and made a desperate slash. The blade skidded through hide and muscle before a swipe of claws spun him to earth with an alarming strength. He landed facedown, inches from the fire, still clutching the blade. Pain seared his shoulder and he was on his back again. He twisted under the cat, scrabbling with the knife, seeking room to thrust. A maw opened wide, spiked with white. His fingers slipped beneath the cat's jaw. For an instant its throat was bared. Ian drove the blade at it. Blood spurted, hot, salty. Still it had him, clawing, biting, silent in its killing.

A musket cracked. Heat licked across his hip and the animal's weight sagged.

Ian heaved himself toward the flames, rolling the catamount into the coals, overturning the tripod and its contents in a searing tumult.

Smells assaulted him first: spent powder, charred cloth, singed fur, the metallic tang of blood. Something had him by the legs, trying to drag him off. His body convulsed and he opened his eyes, wild with panic until he saw that Dawes had pulled him from the fire's remains and was beating at his legs with a blanket. Ian tried to snatch it and nearly swooned. Pain knifed through his left arm and chest. Burns seared like a horde of stinging insects swarming over his legs. He might have been skewered to the earth for all he could move.

"The cat?"

Dawes released him, breathing hard. "You stuck it. We both shot it. Ain't dead by now, it ain't no natural painter-cat. Shrieked like a banshee into the wood after you rolled it through the fire—and my supper."

Bright pinpoints darted through Ian's vision as he raised his head. The kettle lay on its side, contents smoking in the scattered embers. Dropping his head, he sucked in breath as pain washed him in fiery waves. He heard Dawes reloading the musket.

"You're bleeding fit to puddle. Can you sit?"

Ian managed it, lip clamped between his teeth. Dawes's musket ball had grazed his hip. The scoring it left seeped scarlet, but the blood soaking the torn left shoulder of his coat concerned him more. He hoped some of it was the cat's.

"Help me get this coat off."

Peeling away the heavy buckskin was torturous, and Dawes wasn't gentle. The shirt beneath was saturated. Gingerly Ian pulled the shredded remains away from his flesh but couldn't see the extent of the wounds in the failing light.

Dawes dropped the ruined coat. "How bad is it?"

Ian closed his eyes, fighting off a numbing swoon. "Nothing vital."

"Then I'll see to the fire."

"Do that. And . . . my canteen." Memory clenched him. Raising his head again, he made out a solitary dark shape: Dawes's picketed mount. No sign of his uncle's horse. "The sorrel . . . it spooked."

The overseer muttered oaths as the kettle was righted, embers raked, deadfall added until a fire blazed again.

Bracing himself, Ian peeled away the damaged shirt and by firelight examined the cat's work. His coat had absorbed some of the mauling. Still it was bad. Scratches ran in furrows from his collarbone down across his chest. Blood streamed where claws had snagged deep. A set of punctures high on his shoulder showed dark and round, but the bleeding there was less alarming than that of his left arm, gashed below the swell of the shoulder muscle. A tide of crimson flowed past his elbow, writhing in snakes to his wrist. He pressed his fingers to the lips of the gash. Blood seeped through unstanched.

His heart gave a thump, then slammed against his rib cage. He swayed, banged the back of his head, and realized he was sitting nearly against the rock face. In tiny increments he shifted until the lichen-crusted stone supported him, while his vision spun—black, red, black again.

"This'll sting a mite."

Before Ian could speak, frigid water sluiced his arm and chest, running in a reddish gush to spatter his burnt breeches. The shock of it stole the breath for screaming. Fresh blood welled and streamed in the water's wake.

"Whisky," Ian hissed when he could speak.

Dawes stepped back, clutching the canteen. "Ain't got none."

"Aye, ye do. Whisky—or whatever ye have. Now."

Dawes thumped down the canteen and produced a flask. Ian shut his eyes, bracing himself. "Pour some over the worst of it."

"Now that's plain wasteful."

"Do it . . . or yours is the next throat I stick."

"I'm mighty feared," Dawes said dryly but obliged.

This time Ian did scream, muffled through clenched teeth. His next breaths came in gasps, as if he were drowning in the whisky's honey-smoked fumes. Between them he rasped, "Bind my arm—use the shirt. Bind it tight."

The result was crude, but at least it drew the wound closed and lessened the bleeding, though the linen bloomed scarlet within seconds.

"Reload my rifle."

His head fell back against the rock and he must have swooned. Next he knew, Dawes was dropping a blanket over his battered torso. The overseer laid the rifle across his burned thighs and mumbled what sounded like "Going for the dang-blamed sorrel," before stumping off into the trees.

Ian roused again—he'd no notion how much later—to see Dawes leading the sorrel into camp. A huge carcass, golden in the firelight, draped the saddle.

"Is the horse sound?" His voice cracked, coarse as scuffed gravel.

"Scratched a mite. Found the painter-cat too— dead." Dawes rolled the carcass into the firelight, challenge in his eyes. "I shot it last."

It took a moment for Ian's brain to process the implication: Dawes wanted the scalp bounty. Nodding curtly, he groped for the rifle, which had slipped while he dozed. He dragged it back across his legs. When his bags and bedroll landed beside him, he forced his eyes to focus on his uncle's overseer, his brain on why he'd tracked the man.

"What are ye doing out here, Dawes?"

Firelight caught the startlement on the man's rough-hewn features, hastily quenched. He jerked at the ties of Ian's bedding and rolled it out. "Trailing runaways, what else?"

"Why here?"

"There was sign they come this way."

Beneath the blanket Ian's limbs shook, from shock as much as cold. "What sign?"

"They was anxious to get off quick. Left prints that dumb buck Ally could've followed."

"I've seen no tracks." He'd not seen so much as a toe-print to confirm the direction Dawes had been hunting.

"Rain washed 'em out. But I met a farmer said he drove two runaways off his place. Bedding down in his corncrib, they was."

A lie. But the knowledge didn't prevent the jolt to Ian's heart at the mental picture the words created. Dawes retreated to his side of the camp. Ian began the excruciating process of lying down. "Ye met . . . a farmer . . . ye say?"

"That's right. Back a ways, near that cart track. You'd have crossed it today. Man said the buck he chased off was dark-skinned and the woman looked near white. Lots of hair . . . pretty thing." Dawes coughed and spat into the dark. "Took to her own kind in the end, huh?"

Ian fought back bile as his grazed hip took his weight. There was truth mixed in the lies. There had been a cart track. No knowing if there had been a farmer. Rifle cradled in the crook of his uninjured arm, he raised his head. Above him stars shone through a webbing of branches, brittle and cold. He closed his eyes. "There is no trail."

Across the fire, Dawes cursed. "I lost it, all right? Come the morning I aimed to backtrack."

Ian's eyelids flickered. "Come the morning . . . we head back to Mountain Laurel. Ye're off the hunt."

If there had ever been one.

"Reckon when there's light enough we'll see," Dawes muttered after a prickling silence.

While his uncle's overseer broke camp in the gray dawn, Ian secured the blood-stiffened quilled coat behind the sorrel's saddle, pulled a blanket over his shoulders, and fumbled for a grip with his right hand. He could feel the heat coming off his mauled flesh. Though there was plenty light enough to see the wounds now, he couldn't bring himself to unwind the makeshift binding. The worst of the bleeding seemed to have stopped.

"Can you ride?" Dawes asked, the first he'd spoken since rising.

Ian mounted the horse one-handed and settled in the saddle, jaw clenched against the pain bursting stars across his vision. "I can. Let's start."

He'd slurred the words, but he stayed upright.

The day commenced cold. The rising sun did little to warm it. The first real bite of winter since October's snow had clamped down in the night, making the breath of man and horse condense like smoke. Pain spiked with every jar of the horse beneath him. A drumbeat throbbed behind his eyes.

He collapsed to his knees when they dismounted to camp in the lee of a pine-clad slope.

Dawes watered the horses at a stream, while Ian stumbled to the saddlebags. The bindings had worked loose, exposing his wounds. Some bled afresh. Others gave off a fouler seepage. The flesh surrounding the deepest gash had swollen, tight and red. The gash itself emitted a sickly smell. He tied the crusted linen around his wounds as best he could manage.

The following morning he mounted again but rode for long stretches half-blind to the trail that skirted wooded ridges or crossed open stretches cut by ice-rimed rivulets. When he jerked back to clarity, it was to blazing pain, sickening weakness, and despair. Seona and Thomas would be miles away, their trail cold.

When the sorrel stumbled, jolting him half out of the saddle, he hauled himself upright but lost the blanket. It slid to the ground and was left behind. No matter. He was so warm. . . .

Ahead Dawes's slouch hat blurred. Ian's head rocked forward with a snap. He clenched his knees to stay upright but it was no good. The sky heaved and the earth came crashing up.

The air was gone out of him. He was sprawled beside the sorrel's hooves, eyes full of hurrying cloud, until the face of Jackson Dawes blotted out the view. His heartbeat juddered. Pain reached for him. Bleeding onto the red Carolina clay, he closed his eyes and let the dark tide pull him under.

29

Fire raged in his flesh. In his bones. Voices spoke and shadows moved beyond the burning veil. A cup rim touched his lips; trickles of water briefly quenched the flame. Then he burned again.

And again.

At last he woke, no longer burning, but with a bruising weight on his chest. His mind dredged up a word for the weight. *Saddle.* Had he fallen from a saddle? Had a saddle fallen on him?

Awareness that he was abed took on substance. He was under a roof. There was no saddle. With that realization he expected the weight to lift. When it didn't, he longed to let it press him down into oblivion, preferring the fire. Memory had awakened. It tore at him like a hungry raven, eating at his vitals.

"Seona." It came out a rasp, half-buried in the sweat-soured pillow on which he lay.

"Hush, Mister Ian." A whisper in his ear. A touch on his hand. "I ken ye loved my girl-baby, but hush now."

Loved? He had. Did. Would always. But had Seona loved him? Had she done anything at all without his leading?

The answer welled like blood from a wound, spilling into a gulf of doubt.

Others were in the room. A murmur separated into his cousins' voices. He moved his head, opened his eyes, saw them in the doorway.

"He's waking," Judith said.

"With you hovering over him like a mama hen," Rosalyn replied.

"You may have a turn. I didn't think you wished it."

"He has you and Lily—and we all know he's had Seona. What need has he of me?"

Ian turned his face from them. His left arm was bound to his side, keeping it immobile. He clutched at Lily with his free hand, ignoring the pain the movement caused. Words ground out of him, broken things. "What would ye have me do? Tell me, Lily, and I swear I—"

"Ian? We've been terribly anxious."

Judith's face swam into view. Lily's hand slid from his grasp. "Judith. How long . . . ?"

"Since Dawes brought you home?" Judith asked. "Eight days."

Eight. Seona was a fortnight gone. A fortnight free. Was that all she wanted in the end, to be free? Or free of him?

They'd touched each other's souls—he *knew* they had—spun between them the merest thread of connection. Then he'd rushed in with his passion and his outrage, trampling that fragile filament without knowing what he did. He'd cajoled, persuaded, promised—taking what he

417

wanted, convincing himself she gave it freely. That she wanted it too. Truth opened beneath him like a pit. Seona hadn't loved him. She'd obeyed him.

Water poured. Turning dull eyes, he saw Judith tipping pitcher to cup. Lily wasn't in the room now. Had he dreamt her?

Judith propped him up and arranged the pillows behind him. He was naked beneath the covers. As he settled back gingerly, taking the cup in his free hand, he saw her cheeks were aflame at this sickbed intimacy.

"Is there news?" he asked.

"Not that we've heard. Papa Hugh hasn't let Mr. Dawes go looking again."

"Dawes?" He'd taken a sip of water. It choked him going down. "He wasn't sent packing?"

Judith took the cup from his unresisting hand. "Mr. Dawes swears he never touched Seona. The field hands lied."

Ian swore. Judith flinched. He didn't care.

"Judith, will ye help me?"

She colored bright again, glancing at the room's chamber pot. "Do you need—? Lily usually . . ."

"Not that. I need to get to Hillsborough."

She straightened, no longer mortified but alarmed. "Ian, you mustn't leave your bed again. It's only been a day since you tried. That's why Lily bound your arm." When he stared at her blankly, she said, "Jubal found you sprawled in the stable with a saddle on your chest. Don't you remember?"

There had truly been a saddle? Aye . . . he minded it now. Like a fractured dream. He'd left his room in the gray of dawn, barefoot and half-clothed, determined to ride for Hillsborough, to search out the Quaker, Benjamin Eden. Or that had been his fever-muddled plan. He'd made it to the stable unobserved, managed to lead Ruaidh from the stall, but hadn't been able to lift the saddle. A fresh realization gripped him.

"Today, Judith—what is the date?"

"The eighteenth November."

The General Assembly session had passed. Had his uncle bothered petitioning? Did it matter now? A growl of frustration caught in his throat.

Judith hovered, fretful. "Ian—are you in pain? Shall I call Lily back?"

From downstairs came the clink of cutlery. The table being laid, for what meal he'd no notion. The gray light at the window might have been dawn or dusk.

He stared at his hand, splayed on the counterpane. The fever had wasted more than his time. He felt frail. Exhaustion reached for him as he spoke. "There's someone I know in Hillsborough. A Quaker. He may have helped them." Though he hadn't said their names, his cousin's expression grew pained. "What is it ye're not telling me, Judith?"

"No, I was only remembering," she said, then gave him a wistful smile. "When we first came here, Rosalyn and Mama and me, I thought Seona and I . . ." She trailed off, shaking her head. "I just wish things might have been different."

The weight on his chest pressed him tenfold. A straggle had fallen from the coil of Judith's hair. He lifted a heavy hand and tucked it, clumsily, behind her ear. "I know ye were drawn to her, and she to ye, as lasses. She told me."

Judith blinked, looking sad but pleased. "I'm glad she remembers." After a moment's hesitation she ventured, "Ian, do you know where to find this Quaker?"

"If he's still in Hillsborough, aye." He and Thomas had ridden with Benjamin Eden to the home of his cousin, with whom the man had meant to bide. "Why d'ye ask?"

"Could you not post a letter?"

Of course. At the rate he was mending, a letter might reach Hillsborough faster. Even if it didn't, the exercise would ease the frustration of doing nothing.

Judith read the relief in his face and rose, smiling. "I'll just fetch my lap desk."

While rain pelted the window, Hugh Cameron took up the letter that had come in prompt reply to Ian's, posted scarcely two weeks past, and read aloud:

420

"I knew of this matter pertaining to the Jars of Clay, with which our mutual Acquaintance was concerned. I met with our Acquaintance lately at the Mill at Chesterfield, by Providence's Design, and was able to aid in the Return of the unfortunate Soul there most cruelly misused. I regret that a Child discovered the Wagon's Burden, but I did not wish to show myself to thee or thy Kin, for it was during this aforementioned Meeting with our mutual Acquaintance that the Subject of the Jars of Clay was newly broached, and my Aid enlisted for a proposed Plan for their Transferral. We set Time and Place, but our Acquaintance failed to keep the Assignation. Until thy Letter, I had presumed a Change of Heart or some Impediment to his Plan had prevented. I must now conclude that he has undertaken the Endeavor without my Aid. I wish them Godspeed and every Kindness on the Journey and regret I cannot be of further Help or Intelligence to thee in seeing these Vessels come safe over Jordan. Yours &c . . . A Friend."

His uncle let the letter fall to the desk and studied Ian, banyan-clad in a bedside chair. "For a folk with claim to plain speech, the fellow speaks in riddles. I take 'our mutual acquaintance' to be Thomas. But this . . ." He tapped a finger on a line of script. " 'Jars of clay'? What the devil does he mean by it?"

"Earthen vessels." When his uncle's frown deepened, Ian quoted, " 'We have this treasure in earthen vessels.' From the Epistles—Judith guessed it straightaway."

The name of one particular vessel remained unspoken, though it might have been scrawled in the moisture condensing on the windowpanes for all her presence filled the room.

His uncle pushed the letter across the desk. "The fellow admits having no notion where the pair of them might be, and ye've done all ye could to find her—minus a public hue and cry."

The last thing either of them wanted was a manhunt that might further endanger Seona, so no broadsheet had been printed, no descriptions posted at the county courthouse or tavern. Apart from that, had he done all he could?

Ian hunched his shoulders, feeling the itch and pull of healing wounds, the weakness of wasted sinew. "I'm at a loss where to go from here."

His uncle arched a brow. "Ye're fit to go nowhere, lad. Though I see ye havena given up the notion."

"Have ye?"

"Perhaps 'tis best we do. Best for Seona, if this is her choice. But before ye set some ill-considered course, there's a thing or two I'd say to ye."

They were come to it at last, the *get thee hence* part. He couldn't have made a bigger mess of this chance to make something useful of his life had he set out to try. Ian braced himself to receive his uncle's dismissal, wondering how soon he'd have the strength to obey it. The silence between them was a lifeless weight, despite the patter of rain and the fire's noisy crackle. Into it his uncle spoke.

"I've the letter from Robert at last."

"From Da?" Ian said, startled out of resignation. "When?"

"Four days since. John Reynold brought it when he stopped to look in on ye. I dinna think ye kent he was here."

"No." He was still sleeping far more than was normal, his body healing. Ian wondered how much John had been told about Seona, how much he'd guessed, what he must be thinking. But at that moment it mattered less than what his father had to say.

"What was Da's answer?"

"Ye were right about the one thing. He's agreed to open his home to Seona. Lily as well, if she wishes it."

Ian swallowed back his frustration that such grace could not now be received, but it was some moments before he could speak. "Have ye told Da that you mean to send me away?"

Uncle Hugh's gaze was unflinching. "I havena written back. What I tell Robert when I do, that I'll leave to ye."

"What d'ye mean?"

"*B'fhearr leam gu fuirichidh tu, a charaid.*"

Ian's jaw hung slack as he translated the words. *I would have you stay, O kinsman,* his uncle had said.

"With a few matters straight between us," he added. "Lucinda urges I insist on the publishing of marriage banns. She'd see ye wed to Rosalyn, so the land stays with her line as well."

Ian couldn't help his grimace. "Does she think me more likely to manage her daughter than her slaves?"

Uncle Hugh ignored the bitter remark. "I'll not force ye to a marriage ye dinna want. But if ye choose Mountain Laurel, then ye'll give yourself to it, body and soul. No more half measures." Something like a smile twitched his uncle's whitened beard, but there was no humor in it. "Now that ye ken the cost."

Ian opened his mouth, changed what he meant to say twice. Finally shook his head. "I cannot give ye answer yet."

"Good," his uncle said. "I dinna want a hasty answer. I'll write to Robert of Seona, if ye think Boston's where Thomas might take her. I'll ask him to do what he can to find her, give her shelter if—"

"No, Uncle." Ian sat up straighter, wincing. "I'll write that letter."

Beyond the window thunder rumbled. Rain came in a sudden spate, a gray curtain cutting them off from the world beyond the streaked panes. With a pull in his chest, Ian wondered for the hundredth time where Seona was, if she was warm, dry, if they'd found kindness on their journey as Eden wished them.

Seeing those same thoughts in his uncle's eyes, he felt a fleeting kinship with the man that went deeper than blood—a kinship of suffering, self-inflicted.

His uncle rose. "See to it, then. And, Ian, dinna leave room for doubt, whatever ye decide—for as I stand here breathing, after this there willna be another chance."

His sister's desk rested under canvas on the workbench. Ian pushed aside the covering, exposing the carved front panel, and trailed his fingers over the delicate vines that coiled like Seona's hair. Twisting and treacherous, like the doubts that entwined his memories.

Seized by grief and something darker, he grabbed for the nearest tool—an adze—and swung, but instead of bringing it down on the desk, at the last second he hurled it through the shop's open door, past the nose of the figure who stepped into view.

Judith cried out, hands flying up in defense.

"Did I hit ye?" Ignoring the throb of his mending arm, Ian snatched up his knapsack and rifle. Pulling the shop's door shut behind him, he stepped outside and reached for Judith, who cautiously lowered her hands.

"I'm all right." Her eyes darted to the knapsack. "You missed. But . . . where are you going?"

"Away." He was desperate for distance between himself and his kin, whom he couldn't avoid, and the slaves who seemed bent on avoiding him. Grief hung over the kitchen-yard like a pall, a reproach heaped upon him. Lily hadn't returned to tend his wounds since he'd clung to her, begging for . . . what? Direction? Absolution?

"Not for good," he added when argument rose in Judith's eyes. "Ye see I've not saddled Ruaidh? Or packed up my shop?"

Not yet.

His cousin did not appear reassured. "Away where? To look for Seona?"

His jaw tightened. "No."

"The Reynolds'?"

"No, Judith. Just away. I need solitude, aye? And time—to think." To come to terms with what he'd lost. And the choice his uncle had set before him. To decide no less than the course his life would take.

Judith followed his glance toward the wood. "You're going to do your thinking up on the ridge? In this weather?" The clouded sky wasn't weeping rain presently, but it would again, and soon. "But you aren't yet well, Ian."

"And never will be if I let ye go on cosseting me." She flinched at that. She'd been the one to tend him in Lily's place. Brought his meals. Sat with him while he ate. Read to him. Left him only when he feigned sleep.

He sighed. "Judith . . . I'm grateful for your kindness, but ye'll be kinder still to let me go without a fuss. I'll be back. I promise."

She reached for him, but he stepped aside, leaving her hand raised to empty air. He turned from her worried eyes, making for the trees.

"Ian?"

Boots squelching the sodden ground, he paused but didn't look back. "Aye, Judith?"

He heard a sniffle, but her voice was steady. "If you must go . . . then go with God."

30

In the distance dogs were barking. Seona huddled where she hid, praying they hadn't been set loose on her. Mister Gibbs, the sawmill overseer who'd paid his *scant hard-earned last coins* for her, didn't keep dogs, but the planter he worked for did. She'd seen them sniffing round the mill that time she toted over victuals, forgotten back at the cabin in the tall pines. Mister Gibbs had taken what she'd brought and scowled her off, back through the pines to her work.

Those lanky hounds had eyed her meaner still.

Her empty belly threatened to heave at the thought. Clapping a hand over her mouth to keep from gagging, she shut her eyes to better hear that barking. Angry-sounding, but too far-off to be concerned with her.

Besides, it was raining. That made it harder for dogs to track a body, didn't it?

Peering through dripping leaves clinging dead to limbs, she tried to see down the track she'd followed in the night, but with the rain and fog drifting about the patchy woods, there was little to see in any direction.

She hunkered in tight, poked by branches, bone-chilled and soaked with the drizzle that had fallen since before she found the thicket, just after dawn. What she wore was little shield to either cold or wet. She could see her skin in spots through the threadbare homespun. She no longer had her own petticoat and short gown. Missus Gibbs had taken them off her straightaway, saying no slave of hers was going to parade around her kitchen-yard better dressed than she. Seona wore the woman's shapeless castoffs over her shift.

At least she had back the shawl that had been her own, the old arisaid, taken from the kitchen, where Missus Gibbs left it lying.

Craning her head, she peered with longing at the abandoned cabin off through the trees, a bit down the road. She hadn't dared go inside it. Too likely a place for a runaway to hole up. And what if it wasn't abandoned? What if someone returned and caught her there?

The far-off barking stopped. A musket fired, making her jump. The report echoed until it was swallowed up by rain-patter. A hunter, must be.

Out of exhaustion she dozed, to be jarred awake by the clop of horse's hooves. She didn't move, though her cramped limbs cried for it. Her nose was running. Rain dripped down her face while her heart drummed thunder. The horse snorted as it passed, but the rider had a hat pulled low, his mind apparently on getting wherever he was going. He didn't notice her. Didn't feel her watching him.

No one else came along the road, but Seona was too chilled to sleep again. She thought of eating the hunk of bread she'd tucked inside her gown when she fled in the night, but truth to tell, for the past two weeks she'd barely kept down a bite as she dragged herself from chore to chore around the cabin-yard.

Missus Gibbs worked her dawn to long after dusk, cooking, scrubbing, boiling wash, hanging wash, putting dry wash back on squirming little bodies, chasing after those same bodies—all six of them save the littlest that wasn't hardly crawling yet. Between chores she was wiping noses and bottoms, pushing food into mouths, toting babies around when they cried from teething or skinned knees or a yanked braid or a slapped face. There was always quarreling in that cabin. Always someone wailing their head off.

With another baby starting to show, Missus Gibbs had looked as spent as a candle set to gutter when Mister Gibbs ordered Seona down off the wagon that carried her to his cabin, there to stand in the pine straw–covered yard for his wife to approve.

As if the woman was going to turn away another set of hands to work. Seona had known right off this was where she'd be staying. Until Ian found her. She'd clung to that hope and borne it nigh a month, waiting for him to come, before

430

she'd grown desperate enough to run in the night and start on her own for home. Or try to.

What else could she do? She'd prayed he'd get back to Mountain Laurel, learn what happened, and track her down quick. Then they'd go get Thomas and be home safe and it would all come to light what the Jackdaw—Miss Lucinda, too, she was sure—had tried to do. But Ian hadn't come. Lying in her cold corner of the kitchen cabin with her thinning memories for warmth had grown a torment. Memories of that dark workshop, Ian telling her he was going to do this last thing for his kin; then he and she were going away together. *Man and wife.* And something about a son one day being master at Mountain Laurel, but she found no comfort in that, so she set that part aside, holding to the memories of his arms around her, his body pressed close. Shelter. Home. *Warmth.*

Surely he *was* searching? Maybe he was finding Thomas first. Thomas had been sold off before her, to men making up a slave gang to take back east. She'd memorized every word those men said in her hearing, in case it was the only means they had for finding Thomas—once Ian found her. But Thomas had no idea where she'd wound up. He'd been hit over the head when the Jackdaw dragged them off that night, knocked clean out of his wits. Not until they were miles away, trussed in the bed of a wagon, had he come round to understand what had happened. There'd been no chance to find out what he'd had in mind to do, who he'd wanted her to see. They'd not been allowed to talk to each other.

She'd been a fool to listen to him in the first place. All those doubts about Ian he'd tried to sow in her thinking . . .

Even so, she'd lost hope in waiting. She'd finally taken her chance in the night and made a few miles at least, before the dark lifted. The rain had let up some with the morning, but the sun never showed. She thought it was still close to midday when hunger like she hadn't felt in weeks cut through every other worry. It gripped her belly sudden and hard, her mind even harder.

Before she half knew what she was doing, she'd wolfed down the bread she'd taken from the Gibbses' kitchen, soggy bits and all. When she kept it down—wonder of wonders—she figured she best move while there was something in her belly to lend her strength.

She was south of Mountain Laurel. How far south she didn't know. It had been more than two days by wagon, but had it been three, four? They'd traveled down one main road. The Cape Fear, she thought. All she need do was follow it back north, hiding as best she could. She'd no food now but she could last a week without. Longer even. Maybe she'd find something.

That old cabin. There could be a garden over

yonder, or the remains of one. Something overlooked. She could dig up a turnip. A potato.

Hunger assailed her again, until all she could think on was potatoes and turnips hid like treasure in moist red clay. She wouldn't care if they were covered in dirt. She'd eat them straight from the ground. Her mouth watered.

It came into her head to wonder at the fierce hunger, when all this time she'd had no appetite. She'd put it down to this frightening thing that had been done to her, to her fear of the Gibbses, and to missing Ian and Mama, her desperation to get back to them, all the unknowns lying between. What if it did have to do with Ian, only not as she'd thought? What if there was someone else she had to be worried about now?

She shoved that thought deep down, fixating instead on thoughts of food. She had to wait for dark. The days were shorter now, this one clouded thick. She could last. If only every minute wasn't a torment.

Maybe she could slip out of hiding, hunt around behind the cabin, out of sight of the road. . . .

Best stay hid and hungry. But *potatoes*. Or carrots. There might be *carrots*.

She couldn't stand it anymore. She left her hiding place, snagged, begrimed, moldy as a mushroom sprung up after the rain.

She didn't make it to the cabin, much less spot a fallow garden, before they rushed out at

433

her. They'd been concealed behind the structure, waiting all the while. No dogs. Just Mister Gibbs and another man she recognized from the sawmill, brought along to help hunt her down.

Seona screamed, but Mister Gibbs's big hand clamped over her mouth, cutting off the sound. Arms like barrel staves pinned her tight no matter how she thrashed.

"Be still now," he said into her ear. "Or I won't be gentle."

She'd been too panicked to be still. Now she throbbed with the bruises his hands had left on her face, her arms, even around her neck, where finally he'd squeezed until she'd no breath left to fight him. They'd dragged her down the road to where horses waited, got her up on one, and brought her back.

"How far'd she get?" Missus Gibbs asked in her worn-thin voice as Seona was yanked off the horse and deposited in the yard. The children clutched at their mama's skirts, noses running in the evening's chill. Staring like she was some battered animal their daddy had brought home.

One of the littlest raised a hand and waved.

"No more'n five miles." Mister Gibbs planted a boot in Seona's backside and gave a shove, knocking her to her knees. "Jones seen her creep into a thicket near his place, round first light."

Missus Gibbs strode forward and snatched the shawl off her shoulders. "This is mine."

Seona had no time to react. Pain rippled over her scalp as her hair, come unbraided in the night, was wrenched up hard in Mister Gibbs's fist. She cried out from startlement as much as from the sting.

"Ought to have covered this hair better. Jones knew you right off by your description gone round. Stupid girl." Clutching at the man, neck twisted to ease the pain, she heard him tell his oldest child, "Bring me them shears of your mama's. Now."

Put up your hair, girl-baby. . . .

How many times your mama got to tell you?

She struggled. "No! Please, I'll braid it up!"

The man knocked her in the head. The blow stunned her long enough for him to do the deed.

Next she knew, her hair was lying in hanks in the pine straw and she was being hauled toward the nearest tree. Where the rope came from, she never saw. He put it tight around her hands and tied her standing, rough bark pressed into her face, the world spinning dizzily. He pulled down the shoulders of her short gown, ripping out the pins, driving a few into her skin.

She hadn't been strap-beaten since that time she and Miss Judith blacked their eyebrows, and never with the strength of a man's arm. After the second blow she screamed. After twelve there

435

was some commotion behind her. The blows stopped. Rough hands released her bonds and she slumped to the sandy ground. Pine needles poked into her shoulder, the side of her face. Her back was on fire.

Mister Gibbs said, "Leave her, Betha. Let her lie and think on what she done."

How long she lay there shaking head to foot—thinking of nothing—she didn't know. After a while the three oldest children ventured near, a row of dirty feet blue with cold in her swimming vision. She didn't want them gaping at her. She should sit up. Cover herself.

Instead she turned her head to peer up into the face of the oldest child, a boy. He poked her arm with a chilled bare toe.

"You oughtn't to have done it, Show-nee. Daddy whips bad girls."

His sister, second-born, gave him a shove. "Boys, too! He tanned yo' backside just t'other day."

He shoved her back. "Shut up."

"*She* look like a boy now," said the third-born, hunkering in front of Seona to jab her shorn head with a finger. This one wasn't out of shifts yet. Seona only knew him for a boy from having wiped his backside often enough. "She shakin'. Look."

"Babies, move off." The petticoat that had been Seona's, hemline spotted with new scorch marks, swished into view. Little feet vanished. She winced when Missus Gibbs touched her back but didn't cry out. She wouldn't. Not again.

"I'm sorry for it, but you brung it on yourself," the woman said, voice low. "You best mind him from now on. Now get up. Come to the kitchen, let me clean these welts. Couple of 'em bleedin'."

Between the shaking and the fire lacing her back, Seona was a long time getting to her knees. The woman gripped her arm and half hauled her to her feet. Seona clutched the front of her gaping gown, took two steps toward the cabin that served for a cookhouse, then doubled over to vomit onto the pile of her shorn hair. This sickening was different than those before. It was deep and violent, seeming wrenched up from her soul. She heard the children squealing in disgust.

Missus Gibbs hadn't let go her arm. When she straightened, the woman peered at her, frowning. Her face pinched up tight.

"Ain't got time to tend you after all," she said, as if something had changed her mind. "You missed supper. Go to your bed 'til I need your help putting these young'uns down for the night."

The woman left her at the cookhouse, clinging to the doorpost.

"Wrap your head in something," she tossed back over her shoulder. "It's unsightly."

Fingers trembling, Seona reached up and felt the cropped hanks springing out thick from her head. Curling more tightly than they ever had long. *Some great-granddaddy of yours likely made the Middle Passage—same as mine. But you got Indian in you, too ...*

Whatever she was—Cherokee, African, or something else entire—how had she imagined for a moment that she could be the wife of a white man?

"Ian," she whispered, aching for him all the same. What would he think when he saw her now? If he ever saw her again.

There beside the hearth was the ratty quilt she'd been given to sleep on—so old she dared not wash it for fear of its falling to pieces. A fire was burning low. Seona got another stick of wood onto it, then fell onto her pallet, wishing it were her grave.

Hers, but not her baby's.

31

The fire sputtered its smoke through the dripping pines that enclosed the cleft in the ridge, deep in the hills above Mountain Laurel. Ian had chosen the spot for its seclusion. Though chill and wet, the only knocking came from the occasional woodpecker, the only voices those of crows and ravens, the nightly hoot of owls. But solitude had brought Ian no nearer the decision he needed to make. He felt run aground, the weight of grief, regret, and longing beneath his ribs dragging at him like an anchor.

The scent of roasting rabbit, snared that morning, failed to quicken his appetite as he sat cross-legged before a brush shelter, letting his thoughts skitter like leaves down a well-worn trail.

If he left Mountain Laurel, where was he to go? What was he to do once he got there? He'd money left from the sale of the desks, the new batch in the making. He could finish them and with the proceeds start over somewhere as a cabinetmaker; a hardscrabble life to begin with, but he could bear that. He was less certain he could go on crafting furniture and bear the constant reminder of—

He took a mental step back from Seona, as from the cracking of thin ice.

Taking the rabbit from the flames, he arranged the meat on damp leaves to cool, then ran a hand through his hair. His fingers caught in a tangle of sap, yanking painfully.

Perhaps he was unsuited for civilized life. There was the frontier and furs to be taken still—maybe Callum would have him back.

A raindrop struck the top of his head, tracing a cold line down his scalp. Clouds trundled by like wool-heavy sheep grazing the treetops.

" 'The Lord is my shepherd,' " he murmured, then fell mute. Those words had no place on the lips of such a wayward lamb.

Other words came to mind, spoken by John Reynold that sultry summer day Ian returned the shoat, the day he discovered the birch hollow, the raven, and Seona . . .

Memory cracked the ice again. He scurried back.

What was it John had said? Something to do with vision, a thing his neighbor possessed in spades. Ian raised bent knees, sharp-boned beneath loose buckskin breeches, tattered now with spots scorched through, and pressed his brow against them. Then he had it.

Without vision the people perish. Uncertain if that was Scripture—knowing John, it likely was—he lifted his head and stared down the sloping forest aisles, past pines and laurel thickets, dark and evergreen, past leaves plastered in rain-matted mounds, brown among tumbled gray stone. "Give me vision, then, or I perish."

His stomach growled. For the first time in days he felt the stirrings of hunger. He tilted back his head, mouth quirked at this blunt answer to his prayer.

Eat, the glowering heavens might as well have rumbled.

The rabbit was cool to the touch. With his knife he carved away the roasted flesh, while his mind moved on to the third of his options: stay in Carolina, accept his uncle's offer—one with an onus of expectation he didn't think he could bear. Yet here he sat wrestling with it as though his soul were tethered to the place. Did he think Seona might return? Or was it that it still bore her presence and those who grieved her absence?

Stop it. She's gone. Let her go.

Ian thrust a stick into the settling fire, then reached to massage his healing arm. At least he wasn't cold. Aside from two wool hunting shirts, he'd the buckskin coat. Someone had attempted to work out the bloodstains and repair the tears, but the quillwork was shredded beyond restoring. He touched the rows of stitches high on breast and sleeve, a mirror of the scars he bore beneath. He'd left his finer clothes behind, as well as the homespun he wore for shop and field.

Three sets of garments. Three lives from which to choose. Tradesman, planter, frontiersman.

There was something in each that appealed, but something that repelled as well.

The rain pelted down with resolve. He crawled inside the shelter and pulled a woven mat across the opening. He'd a letter still to write, one he'd been composing in his mind, off and on.

Dear Da—he might pen—*I have squandered another chance at settling to a useful life. I am no longer worthy to be called your son. Make me as an apprentice in your shop. . . .*

He'd write no such drivel, but he must write something. And soon.

In the dark of the shelter Ian laid his head to sleep, perishing beneath the weight of fruitless thought. *Where there is no vision . . .*

Vision. He could try a vision quest, after the manner of the Chippewa. Such ceremonials were solitary affairs, but he'd once stumbled upon a glade where a boy and his father were preparing for one. He minded cedar boughs laid upon the ground, ringing a brush shelter. Four sticks tied with bits of colorful cloth, their purpose unknown. The boy's startled eyes staring at him from a blackened face.

On a fragile thread of hope he drifted toward sleep, wrapped in his old camp blanket, with its comforting smells of horse and smoke.

He dreamt of Seona. Peril threatened but he couldn't reach her.

She is a lithe shape slipping through shadow and

442

mist, through brush and bramble that lets her pass but claws his flesh as he pursues, until not just shoulder and chest but thighs and belly are striped in red. She isn't alone. Thomas runs beside her. This enrages him, driving him on despite the lashing. A swamp spreads before them. Thomas slips and falls into it. He struggles and sinks deeper. Seona implores him to help, but he doesn't help. His heart is a stone that swells and bursts from him, a rock that's taller than he is. Seona stands atop it, disappointment in her eyes. He tries to reach her, but the rock that had been his heart grows as he climbs it. Small and high above him, Seona shakes her head in sorrow and turns away . . .

He started awake, breath coming in pants. Clutching his belly like a man gutshot, he curled inward around his grief. His breathing quieted.

The noise of panting didn't.

The sound came from beyond the shelter. Rhythmic, steady. Not human. He reached for the rifle but stilled with his hand on the cold barrel, nostrils flaring at the pungent, incongruous whiff of *wet dog*.

The dogs—Charlie Spencer's, he presumed— were gone before he emerged from the shelter next morning and found their tracks in the mud. He saw no sign of Spencer, at least not in the moist earth surrounding his shelter. But Spencer might have been more careful than that. Hoping the man hadn't been trailing his dogs close, Ian went about his preparations for the vision quest.

The nearest to cedar he found by his camp was juniper, but he made a ring of it for his quest. He blacked his face with soot, sat on the cold ground in the ring's center, and settled in to wait.

On the second day of his vigil he began to suspect himself of folly, his quest of futility. By the third day he'd lost all doubt on both scores. Desperate, he persisted.

Early on the fourth day he saw the raven, eyeing him from the crest of a nearby stone. He couldn't be certain it was Munin. If so, would the bird speak without Seona by?

He ground the heels of his hands into his eyes. Weak from hunger, he'd been dreaming of her again on the edge of sleep. This time she'd come seeking him, saying it was a mistake. She hadn't meant to leave him. With hands and lips she touched his scars, weeping for each one.

Ian shifted, sore from sitting. "If ye've come to reproach me, ye needn't bother," he told the raven, voice graveled with disuse. "She made her choice."

"Ye've taken to conversing wi' the birds, Mister Ian?"

Ian's scalp crawled with shock, but when he spoke, he sounded calm. "Only the one."

Behind him a stick snapped. The raven took wing.

Ian turned.

Malcolm stood below him on the slope, braced on one side by Ally, on the other by John Reynold.

They sat on boughs gathered from the juniper circle, Ally with a bundle clutched to his chest. While the fire blazed, Ian devoured the last of the sweet rolls his neighbor had brought, shamelessly licking his fingers.

"John, your wife is an angel of mercy. I feel almost human." He rubbed a hand over his stubbled face, palm coming away smeared with soot. "Though I cannot be much to look at."

"You aren't," John agreed with a cheerfulness that almost rang true.

In the firelight Ally's teeth gleamed as he grinned. "You don't want to be white no more, Mister Ian?"

Malcolm shot a hushing look at his grandson.

John cleared his throat. "Cecily hoped you'd be ready to extend your appreciation in person."

Though Charlie Spencer had left no sign of his presence, he had, in fact, found Ian's shelter—so they'd told him—and gone down the ridge to tell John of his discovery. John had gone to Uncle Hugh, who'd blessed this deputation.

"I don't know what I'm ready to do," Ian said. "My uncle wants me to stay, though God knows why after—"

"Best do as he wants, Mister Ian," Ally blurted, smile vanished. "I ain't wanting Mister Pryce as mastah—I rather it be *you*."

Ian frowned at the anxious outpouring. "My uncle isn't about to sell ye to Chesterfield, Ally. And I'd rather ye called no man master."

"Got to be somebody." Around the bundle he clutched, Ally wrung his big hands.

"We ken ye dinna want the yoke Master Hugh means to place on ye," Malcolm said. "But as to what makes Ally speak so of Gideon Pryce . . . Who d'ye think Miss Rosalyn is like to wed, if no' ye? And if ye go, leaving your uncle wi'out an heir, into whose hands does Mountain Laurel pass?"

Pryce's—or whomever Rosalyn married. Had the old slave come to entreat him as the lesser of two evils? Ian wouldn't ask whether Malcolm knew of his uncle's debt and to whom was owed the greater portion. Without a male heir to assume those debts, part of Mountain Laurel would fall into Gideon Pryce's hands upon his uncle's death, marriage or no. And what, aside from livestock, was easier to turn into cash than slaves?

He'd asked himself, Could he live with what he would become if he stayed? Now he wondered, Could he live with himself if he left?

He hunched his shoulders, feeling the yoke begin to settle. It was anything but light. "D'ye know what ye're asking of me?"

"Probably better than ye do, Mister Ian," Malcolm said.

He raised his head when John stood. Ally put down the bundle and lumbered to his feet. "Ye're going so soon?"

"Not quite yet. Malcolm has a thing yet to say to you. We'll be waiting, just out of hearing." John grasped Ian's shoulder in farewell. "You're not alone in this, Ian, whatever you decide."

A wind moved down the ridge, stirring the trees to creak, rattling the few clinging leaves as the crackle of their footsteps diminished. What light filtered through the trees was dim. The fire cast a ruddy sheen on Malcolm's seamed face as he stared into it.

"Seona told ye about that old raven?" the old man asked.

"She did," Ian said. "It's to do with Seona, what ye have to say to me?"

The old man had to be cold and paining. He gave sign of neither. " 'Tis to do with Seona, why ye're up on this ridge freezing your bum to the ground?"

Ice of a different sort broke under Ian. The waters rushed up to engulf him. "It is."

It was all to do with Seona. Why should he deny it?

Malcolm's breath flowed out in a sigh and he let Ian see his grief at Seona's loss. But there was something deeper in his careworn face, something vital, like strong bone beneath ravaged skin.

"How d'ye do it, Malcolm? How have ye made your peace with . . . ?" He groped for words to finish the question. *Enslavement? A wasted life? The sheer burden of living?*

"Peace, or the kind I'm thinkin' ye mean," Malcolm said, "comes only one way. Or it doesna come. Through the lordship of the Almighty."

Ian ground his teeth. "Tell me something, Malcolm. Can ye read?"

"No, Mister Ian. I canna."

"Then how d'ye know about the Almighty?"

Malcolm's face beamed with pleasure, as if it was a question he'd long waited to be asked. "When I was a young man still, Naomi just a bitty lass, there came a traveling preacher riding circuit through the backcountry. Auld Master Duncan let him preach to us—in English. But I was stubborn. I held out surrendering my will, thinking I was already under one master's thumb and didna need another. But it wasna more chains the preacher meant to heap on me. 'Twas freedom from chains he preached."

"And so ye gave your heart to God." Ian waved away the rest of the predictable tale. "Nothing changed, did it? Ye still toil for a master." For a Cameron.

"Ye're wrong, Mister Ian. Everything changed because *I* changed."

448

Go with God. Judith's words to him, days ago. He'd dismissed them as simply a thing pious people said. Was there a reality behind them?

How was it done, then, this going-with-God business? How did one divine where the Almighty was headed when the aims of men and women, even his own heart, were a mystery at best? At worst, a deceit? Easier to guess where a star might fall.

He frowned at the circle of juniper, broken and scattered now. No guidance to be had there. Not for him.

Malcolm stirred to rise. Ian rose to aid him. The man was so slight it was like pulling a child to his feet.

"Ye can read the Scriptures backward and forward, Mister Ian, but if ye dinna ken the voice of the Lord who inspired them, all the printed words in the world willna matter. Ye willna see if ye dinna believe." Malcolm didn't release his hand but turned it over in his knobby grasp. Ian's knuckles were raw from the cold, cracked and threaded with blood. "Lily has a salve, for when ye come back."

"Am I coming back?" Ian pulled his hand free and bent for the bundle Ally left, meaning to give it to the old man.

"That's for ye," Malcolm said. "From Master Hugh."

Ian drew a chest full of air, sharp with the promise of another frost. Perhaps even snow.

Thoughts pounded in his head. Thoughts of duty. Thoughts of escape. Could he put aside betrayal and guilt, stay for the sake of his uncle's slaves?

He wasn't that noble. Nor that good.

"Lily had a thing for me to tell ye."

He swung his attention back to Malcolm, stooped over his cane. "Lily?"

The old man's eyes softened. "When ye woke from the fever, ye asked her a question, did ye no'?"

He'd not thought of those first moments of waking, after the catamount's attack, since he left for the ridge. Memory of them returned, vivid with the urgency he'd felt, the certainty that Lily held the answer he'd been seeking. "Aye. I asked what she wished me to do. She didn't answer."

"She does so now."

Footsteps rustled the fallen leaves. Ally and John, coming back to take the old man home in triumph. Ian shut his eyes, as though that would make the hearing of it easier.

"What does Lily ask of me?"

32

Lily had one word for him. *Stay.*

The message from his uncle, though wordless, echoed the appeal. Contained in the bundle Ally brought were Ian's best suit of clothes, brushed clean, and his razor and strop. It was time to come down off the ridge and make his choice known.

The following morning he took a brand from the fire and set it to the shelter. He watched the structure catch and blaze, collapsing onto itself in a smoking ruin, as a bank of low cloud moved over the Carraways, promising more rain.

Obscured in thickening mist, it seemed just another stone thrusting through the leaf-mulch in a fold of the ridge. Ian nearly strode past it before its smooth regularity registered. Not a natural stone, nor just the one. A group of stones he'd taken for the bony knuckles of the hillside assumed their true identities. He'd blundered into a graveyard.

No boundary separated the cluster of headstones from the surrounding forest, but the markers appeared tended. He rounded the nearest and read the name chiseled into its face:

Miranda MacDonald Cameron
12 October 1736 Scotland
2 July 1771 Randolph County, NC
Beloved Wife

He crossed to a weathered marker, that of old Duncan Cameron, Mountain Laurel's original settler. Completing the half circle was Aidan Alexander Cameron, born 1757. Below his son's name, Hugh Cameron had engraved a longer inscription than that on his wife's headstone: *As for the light of mine eyes, it also is gone from me.*

Ian groaned, closed his eyes, but the words remained, bleak and indelible.

He started to back away, yet something compelled him to leave the graves altered from how he'd found them, as if removing the windblown twig from old Duncan's resting place or uprooting the tangle of weeds obscuring the base of Miranda Cameron's headstone could break the timeless spell of sorrow that overhung the place.

The weeds were brown and draggled. The sodden earth released them without struggle, but Ian let them slip from unfeeling fingers. Another name was chiseled into Miranda Cameron's stone, below the words *Beloved Wife*. With shaking fingers, he brushed aside the last of the weeds.

Seona Cameron
2 July 1771–3 July 1771

The bairn had lived a day. Briefly enough to be buried with her mother. Long enough to be named—the name Lily would, years later, give *her* daughter. In hope that his uncle would accept her, bearing the name of his first wife's child?

"Seona—" His lips clamped over the name, like the forcible closing of a wound.

He was stumbling in his haste to leave when the first haunting calls broke the stillness. He halted, gazing at the treetops that grasped at the mist with skeletal fingers. The calling of the wild geese echoed, muffled and refracted, as they passed unseen above him.

When the cries faded, only the dead were left behind. Ian hoisted rifle and knapsack and went down the ridge to face the living.

In an empty horse box in the stable he stripped and bathed, then changed into the garments his uncle had sent. While Jubal held a cracked glass fetched from his own cabin, Ian scraped away his beard, conscious of the slave's eyes shining in the light of a horn lantern, watching him, apprehensive. Ian wiped his face, then tied a neckcloth at his collar.

While Jubal gathered up glass and basin, Ian brushed self-consciously at his blue coat. It no longer fit him snug, yet his chest felt constricted. His hair was tailed tight enough to sting his scalp.

His buckled shoes pinched. "Will I do?" he asked his uncle's slave.

Jubal paused, giving him a once-over. "Now you will, Mister Ian."

Mouth tucking wryly, Ian eyed the buckskin breeches and quilled coat, crumpled in the straw. "Will ye do me the one favor more?"

Jubal shifted his burdens to add the garments. "Want me take 'em to the washhouse?"

"I want ye to burn them."

His answer surprised the man. "You sure 'bout that?"

"I am." He reached for Juturna, who thrust her seal-brown muzzle through the slats of the neighboring box. Over her bout with colic, the filly promised to make a bonny tall creature, a credit to her blood. Ian stroked her silky nose, minding her birth and the hope of those days.

He'd been right about the two-faced Janus.

"Devil take this dithering," he muttered. He'd do what he must and leave thinking for later.

"You be staying on, then, Mister Ian?" Jubal finally asked.

Ian bent his head in the direction of the house. "I suppose I'm about to find out."

No one in the house had marked his return, not like the slaves beyond its walls. Ian had felt their watchful presence all the way to the back door, though he never glimpsed them. *D'ye see, Lily?*

454

he'd willed her to hear in the dripping silence of the yard. *I can keep a promise.*

The weight of that promise rooted him to the floorboards outside his uncle's room. At the other end of the passage, Maisy stood at the parlor doorway, holding a tea service, as though waiting to be called in.

Rosalyn's voice carried down the passage, but it wasn't to Maisy she spoke. ". . . said they found Cousin Ian, but *I* think he never means to come down off that ridge. He'll turn into some outlandish recluse with a beard down to his belt. Years from now Judith and I will tell tales of him to scare your grandchildren, Mama."

"Must you say such things?" Judith's admonishment was quickly drowned.

"Must you so readily overlook the fact he lied to us all?" his aunt countered. "He deceived us about Thomas."

"*And* Seona," Rosalyn interjected. "Yet he'd the audacity to speak ill of Gideon. He's no better, the hypocrite. Well, Mama? Do you still think it wise I refused him?"

"Refused?" Judith said. "What do you mean?"

"I mean, ninny, that Gideon made me an offer of marriage in August, but Mama bade me hold him off until Cousin Ian arrived."

"I will concede," Lucinda said, "that may have been a miscalculation. Still, Gideon hasn't ceased his attentions nor bestowed them elsewhere. Has he?"

"Phyllida would have told me, if so." Rosalyn's voice rose. "And really, what does it matter if Gideon dallies with a servant from time to time? It's to be expected—"

"Modulate your tone, Daughter," Lucinda cut in. "You'll wake your papa."

"Your papa," a tired male voice rumbled, "is verra much awake. And surprised to learn a daughter of his house had an offer of marriage made her—four months past. Would ye care to tell me why I'm just hearing of it now?"

While voices rose, Ian started resolutely down the passage. Maisy, engrossed in the conflict beyond the parlor door, startled at his approach, rattling the tea service. Ian took the tray from her unresisting hands. It was a full tea with a plate of Naomi's ginger cake. The spiced aroma clenched his stomach as he made his entrance.

Silence fell, as sudden as if he'd tossed a rock into a pond of croaking frogs. He set the tray on a table and bowed to his uncle's wife. "Auntie, will ye have sugar to your tea?"

Uncle Hugh threw off a lap robe and rose from his chair, appearing more than a little relieved. "Lad, welcome home. I see ye got the clothes I sent."

Scrutinizing his appearance—a far cry from his cousin's prediction, he hoped—his aunt's expression thawed minutely, the frostbite of shock giving way to speculation. "If we're to have this conversation now, let us do it *with* our tea. Maisy? I'm sure you're still there. Mr. Cameron has made his dramatic entry. Cease your skulking and come serve."

While the housemaid obeyed, Ian stood in the center of the room, eyes on his uncle. "I've come to give ye my answer, sir."

"So I see," Uncle Hugh said, matching him in formality. "And what might that answer be?"

"That I do mean to stay . . . since ye'll have me."

There was no immediate response to the declaration. No sound save the snap of burning logs in the hearth, the clink of dishes as Maisy served cake. The faces of his kin turned to him, the chinaware plates suspended in white hands, were a blur. What was sharp and immediate was his heart, pounding fit to burst free and flee the stuffy parlor.

His uncle's gaze held him, pale and clear. "Ye're resolved upon it, then? I'm glad of it, Nephew—"

"Begging your pardon, but I've conditions. If ye'll permit me to name them."

Lucinda set down her tea. "Conditions?"

Ian felt the sweat gathering on his brow. "For one, I'll not ask any man to perform a task I haven't set my own hands to. I'll work alongside your people, Uncle, learn every chore and task, no matter how menial."

His uncle nodded. " 'Tis how I began."

Though meant as approbation, the words produced an inward shudder. Ian had but to look into his uncle's eyes to see his future. The man he would become.

"Ye said *conditions?*" Uncle Hugh prompted.

"Aye, sir. I mean as well to—" There was nothing for it but to push the words past the croaking strings of his throat. "I mean to ask for your daughter's hand in marriage . . . with your blessing."

In the hearth a pine knot popped, a sound like distant musket fire. It was nothing to the tension that crackled in the air as heads bent forward and eyes bored into him.

"That wasna a condition of mine, ye'll recall," his uncle said.

There it was, his way of escape. But even the possibility was a thing he must deny himself lest in some future moment of weakness he take it.

"No half measures, Uncle. Ye said that too."

Hugh Cameron lifted a hand to his beard, then swept it in a gesture of concession. "Verra well. Ye've my blessing. But had ye no' best be asking the lass will she have ye?"

Ian had the grace to flush. "Aye, sir."

He turned to face his cousins, seated side by side in matching chairs. He felt oddly removed from his body, so that it didn't seem *his* eyes that swept their faces and rested upon Rosalyn, with her golden hair and cornflower eyes and lush mouth parting in expectation . . . then moved past her to fix upon her sister, plain as a sparrow in a gown of gray. He took a step, wondering whose legs moved him, whose hand grasped and raised the small white hand of his younger cousin. *Kneel,* he told himself but couldn't get the message to the appropriate limbs. He stood like a puppet with its strings pulled taut. "Judith—"

"Judith?" Lucinda and Rosalyn exclaimed together.

Judith's face was lifted, her mouth fallen slack. He was aware of the rustle of skirts as Rosalyn rose and went to her mother. "Judith may have him, Mama. After all, I believe I shall marry Gideon Pryce!"

The dismissal barely registered. The pressure of the small hand in his increased, tentative, questioning, a tether to a body bent on carrying him through this ordeal. "Cousin—will ye consent to be my wife?"

Judith shut her mouth. The shock in her brown eyes softened. A light sprang into them, wavered like a candle's new-lit flame, then steadied. Something inside Ian thawed, flowing toward the serenity of that flame.

Judith set her tea on the table by her chair. He blinked, and she was on her feet in front of him, the neat parting down the crown of her head barely level with his chest. He'd expected her to appeal to her mother for guidance. She didn't. She looked at him, quite composed.

"Yes, Ian," she said. "I will consent to be your wife. With all my heart."

PART V

January–May 1794

Unsteady and profitless though he remains, dare this Prodigal look back from whence he's come? Would you be watching for me?

33

Gooseflesh prickled over Ian's legs, standing the hairs on end. Ignoring the chill, he splayed his hands on the windowsill, pressing his forehead to the frosted glass. Snow had fallen with the dark, but the clouds were parting now, drifting east. The thin blanket of white magnified the moon's sporadic glow. Down by the oaks the slave cabins hunkered beneath snow-laced boughs.

"Seona." Her whispered name scalded the frigid air. Was she safe this bitter night? Imagination knifed through him: Seona and Thomas entwined in some distant hayloft, clinging to each other for warmth. He gripped the sill so hard its joints creaked.

Behind him bedding rustled. "Husband?"

With frost-melt trickling down his brow, he left the shutters thrown wide and crossed the room to slide his legs beneath the still-warm bed linens. Moonlight cast a colorless sheen on Judith's features as she sat up.

"Why were you at the window?"

He drew in his gates, a fortress besieged. Something inside him had shattered in the act committed not an hour ago. It took all his will to ignore the caged thing beneath his ribs that mourned and raged. "Did I hurt ye?"

She'd come to him innocent of the marriage bed and he'd tried to be gentle—until his mind burst with a flood of memories and the woman in his arms had ceased to be Judith. He reached now to touch her; ever so slightly she shrank from him.

"Mama said I wouldn't like it."

The ice around his heart cracked with shame. "I'm sorry." He touched her face, warm beneath his chilled fingers. He lingered on the hollow of her neck, his thumb on the rapid pulse at her throat. She tensed.

Seona had welcomed his touch with a desire as eager as his own. So he'd thought. But Seona wasn't the only one who could pretend.

"It doesn't have to be painful."

"I—I thought it was supposed to start with kisses?"

She'd noticed. He hadn't kissed her, afraid a touch of her mouth would melt the illusion he'd clung to. "Would ye like it to?"

Silvered moonlight showed her wavering smile. Her nod.

He bent dutifully, trying not to notice the small lips, the inexpert hesitancy. Trying not to think of Seona. It was like trying not to breathe. Already he was losing sense of time and place as his mind raced back to the fire of autumn.

Judith winced, a small gasping sound, and it was winter again. "Ian, I—I want to like it."

He could feel her trembling and rolled away from her. He'd tried to forget what he'd seen in her eyes as he made his offer of marriage, again when they spoke their vows in his uncle's parlor the previous evening. He'd convinced himself she'd consented in the face of Lucinda's unbending will—one of her daughters would claim Mountain Laurel for herself and her children. But there was more to it for Judith. He was past denying it, and now their future lay before him, bruising in its clarity. Whatever hopes she had for their marriage, he was going to trample them.

Seona had torn apart his soul in leaving, like a dovetail joint holds fast under stress, forcing the coupled pieces to break at a weaker point. He'd nothing but jagged splinters to give his wife, fit only to pierce and wound.

She'd never known such cold. Never mind winter was all but past; it might as well have been ice, the March air against her face, the ground beneath her feet, as she peered up at the strip of stars above the track cut through the pines. Hope had fled her world, taking every warmth from earth, flesh, soul. Ian hadn't come for her. Which was why she was standing in the dark, barefoot and without provision, teetering on this reckless edge. She had to leave that place. Before the Gibbses discovered her secret.

Twice now she'd run. The second time had come once she'd stopped denying she was with child. That had gone worse than the first time, for all she'd better planned things. The beating she'd got had left her fearing she'd lose the baby. She hadn't, but once she'd healed enough to work again, she'd been too afraid to try a third time.

She'd still had hope then Ian would come for her.

She was nigh five months along now. What had been a thickness in her middle was getting harder to hide. Her shapeless clothes and the old shawl she'd been given, wrapped around her even in the kitchen's warmth, had kept her secret from the Gibbses, but yesterday one of the children— thankfully out of her mama's hearing—had eyed her and said, "You gettin' fat, Show-nee."

What would happen when the baby was too big to be taken for a little extra weight? Bone-thin as she was otherwise, how would she hide it?

She took another step away from the cabin-yard, mind spinning with its endless questions. Where was Ian? Why hadn't he come? Couldn't he find her, or had he given up trying?

Maybe he never looked at all. Maybe Thomas was right.

Such thoughts lurked around every corner, waiting to sting and claw. It was getting harder to fend them off.

Angry, she strode forward into the night until

her bare foot came down on a sandspur and she stifled a yelp. She pulled up her foot, found the wicked thing, and yanked it from her flesh. What was she doing walking off in the night with nothing but the clothes on her back? She hadn't planned to run. She'd gone out to use the privy and just kept going.

She wrapped her arms tight around herself, finding no warmth. *Lord, I don't know what to do. Please . . .*

Staying and leaving both were a risk, but tonight she risked more by leaving. Turning, she walked back to the cabin-yard. She was passing the woodpile when a stick cracked—not under her foot. She veered toward the wood and started picking up pieces.

Missus Gibbs's voice came out of the dark. "What you doing out here?"

Seona straightened, cradling kindling. "Woke up cold. Thought I'd get some wood . . ."

The woman moved closer, her face in the starlight hollow-eyed. "Don't do it," she said.

"Don't bring in wood?" Seona asked, pretending she hadn't understood.

"He'll hurt you bad, you try it again."

Instead of the warning Seona had expected, it had been pleading she heard in the woman's tone. "I'm just getting in wood."

She tried stepping around Missus Gibbs, who stood on the path to the cookhouse, but the woman shot out a hand and clamped her arm hard.

"I know you're carrying. Is it his?"

Seona halted. For a second she thought to go on playing dumb, mutter something about carrying wood. That wasn't what squeaked out of her mouth. "No, ma'am, it is not. But does he know?"

The grip on her arm released. "Iffen he did, you wouldn't need ask."

The woman sounded worried. Seona swallowed. "How long have you known?"

"Since you ran that first time."

She hadn't even been sure then. *Mama would have known too, before I did,* she thought, and it rankled that this woman could remind her in some way of her mama, who she missed so deeply right then she had to bite back a sob. Or was this woman just pretending she'd known?

As if she could read Seona's thoughts—again reminding her of Lily—Betha Gibbs turned toward the cabin full of sleeping babies, then ran a hand over the one soon to join them. "You think I don't know what a woman breeding looks like?"

Nothing Seona could say to that. Only one thing mattered. "You going to tell him?"

The woman was silent a stretch, then said, "Long as you stay put, no."

But he'd know, by and by. Should they hide

468

it the whole nine months, there'd be no hiding a newborn from the man, even among his own brood. "Will he take my baby?"

Silence again. Cold and dark.

"I don't know." This time Seona was certain the woman lied. She knew what her man would do. Or thought she knew. "Go tend the fire. Might as well get breakfast going since we'll all be up early." Missus Gibbs was talking fast now, as if to prevent more questions. She gave Seona a push to get her moving. "He talk of taking the wagon into Fayetteville for some things. Said we can all go. You too. Ain't leaving you here alone, and I'll need your help with the babies."

Ian sighted down the rifle at the painted target fastened to a tree at the field's end. He was reasonably certain of hitting the mark. The target wasn't moving. Neither was his aim, despite a few swigs from the flasks passed round since the morning's militia maneuvers. From among the line of spectators perched on the split-rail fence behind him, someone gave a catcall. Someone else whistled. In the face of Ian's stillness, the ribbing died. He released a breath and fired.

A lengthy pause as the powder smoke drifted. Then a shout of affirmation carried down the field. A dead-center strike. A clamor rose as a crowd of men and lads came surging to congratulate him.

"You won it, man!"

"You've hawks' eyes, Cameron."

"It's that dang widow-maker rifle," a slurred, morose voice cut in. "Puts our muskets to shame."

At Ian's side, Charlie Spencer muttered, "Go suck your sour grapes in private, Dawes."

Ian turned to see his uncle's overseer stalk off the shooting field. An uneasy truce had reigned between them the last few months. Dawes had kept his head down, gone about his work, given no reason for complaint—until three days ago, when he'd disappeared on one of his drinking binges. Ian was revisiting the notion of sending him packing, but he wasn't about to let the ill-tempered man's reappearance spoil the muster-day festivities.

"I'll have another go," he offered, grinning and relaxed, "should one of ye care to loan me a brown Bess."

A hand gripped his shoulder as a smooth voice said, "Your uncle's man couldn't hit my barn at twenty paces—even sober." Gideon Pryce held out the shooting prize, a polished black powder horn, its cap engraved in silver. An eye-catching piece to judge by the warmth of bodies pressing close. "Yours wasn't the only rifle fired today."

Pryce held the rank of captain in the local militia, though a colonel had ridden to Chesterfield to direct the county muster and record the

470

names of recruits, Ian's among them. Requisite maneuvers had been dispensed with while the morning's mist lay over the trampled field.

"And it doesn't even leave the family," Pryce added, nodding toward the house, where Rosalyn watched from the garden's edge.

Hugh Cameron had agreed to Pryce's renewed offer of marriage, made during the celebration of Ian and Judith's nuptials in January. Past the militia's exemption age, Uncle Hugh was back at Mountain Laurel, no doubt ensconced fireside with pipe and brandy. Since the wedding his uncle had retreated from the farm's daily managing, leaving the responsibility in Ian's hands. Not that there was a great deal to manage in winter— acreage to clear, soil to enrich, seeding beds for the new tobacco crop to prepare.

Ian slipped the horn into his shot bag.

Off toward the veranda, Chesterfield's slaves were busy setting out food. Searching for the dark head and quick stride of John Reynold and failing to find him among the crowd, Ian shouldered rifle and bag and trudged up the field. He hadn't seen John since the wedding. Sometime during that interminable day their neighbor had spoken of an intended trip south. To Fayetteville, Ian thought.

Judith met him near the garden, the voices of the gathered crowd swelling around them. "How did you fare, Ian?"

"Middling well," said Spencer, who'd come

up the slope with Ian, then chuckled at Judith's crestfallen expression. "Your husband whipped us all from here to Sunday—Mrs. Cameron."

Judith beamed. "Was there a prize?"

"I'll show ye later." Ian gestured at Reverend Wilkes, who had officiated at their wedding, now awaiting their attention from the veranda steps. They gathered at the foot of the steps while the man pronounced a blessing over the dinner that spanned tables running the veranda's length.

They filled their plates, then found a seat on the veranda steps. Ian ate, sporadic in his conversation with those nearby, smothered by Judith's hovering—did he need more to drink, a fresh napkin, another slice of sweet potato pie?

"Ian, would you care for some?" Judith held a linen napkin on which rested a triangle of shortbread. "It's from our kitchen."

He'd never refuse Naomi's baking. "Aye. Set it down, then."

She stood at the foot of the steps, expectant. Suppressing a sigh, he picked it up and took a bite. Frowning over the dry texture, he chewed, tried to swallow, and choked. He grabbed for his cider and washed the crumbly mass down.

"What did Naomi do? Toss in wood shavings for flour?"

Judith's face stained radish-red. Wordless, she backed away from the steps, bumped into

Zeb Allen, apologized, then hurried off into the crowd.

"Jud—" Ian tried to call, but a dry bit caught in his throat. Coughing, eyes watering, he slipped the offending shortbread over the veranda railing and into the waiting jaws of one of Charlie Spencer's less-discerning hounds.

"Naomi didn't make that, Mister Ian." He looked up to find Lily at his side. "Miss Judith's been coming to the kitchen for days to practice. Ye praised Naomi's shortbread in her hearing, said it reminded ye of your mama's. She wanted to make it for ye."

He might have imagined the mild reproach in Lily's voice, but the guilt that smote him was real enough. Breathing imprecations at himself, he went after his wife. She wasn't with her mother, nor had she joined herself to any of the knots of women scattered across the veranda.

He spied a flash of mousy hair, across the lawn among the ornamental shrubs.

"Judith!" He caught her up behind the shrubbery and turned her toward him, wincing at her tears. "Ye meant to do me a kindness and I spoilt it. I'm sorry."

Judith bit a quivering lip. "I suppose I best stay clear of the kitchen."

"No . . . it was a fine attempt."

"Really?" Her eyes held hope. "Ought I to try again?"

He started to reply, then heard a familiar voice calling his name.

"Judith—a moment." He ducked round a shrub and scanned the yard. John Reynold was making his way down from the veranda, searching the crowd, creased and mud-spattered as though he'd ridden a great distance. "John! Here, man."

Spotting him, John made for him straight as a plumb line, concern evident on his face.

"Is it Cecily? Robin? D'ye need Lily?"

Heads turned near the garden, distracted by the small scene. John took Ian by the arm and steered him back into the shrubbery. "They're well. I've been to Fayetteville."

"Aye, I thought so. Ye missed the morning muster—"

"Ian, I've seen her." John's eyes held his, intense. Urgent. "I've seen Seona."

His friend might have brained him over the head, so stunning was the utterance of her name. "What?"

"Seona," John repeated. "In a wagon full of children, heading out of Fayetteville. At first I wasn't sure—her hair was covered—but once I knew my eyes weren't playing me tricks, I followed at a distance and saw where she was bound. A plantation about three miles outside of town."

The words washed over Ian, a flood of syllables without meaning. "Fayetteville? That's south. Days south. She's away north—"

474

"Ian." John's grip tightened. "She's on the Cape Fear River."

Ian jerked away. The garden, the milling crowd beyond the tall shrubs—his own flesh—none of it felt substantial, as though the universe were in the act of flying apart at the seams. And he with it.

John's hand steadied him. "I'd never tell you like this if I thought for an instant I could be mistaken. I'm not. It was Seona."

His gut knotted. "And Thomas?"

"I don't know. I saw no sign of him."

Dazed still, he was seized with sudden conviction—and the need to act on it. "I should tell Uncle Hugh. Get some things. Papers . . . proof."

"And a fresh horse if you can spare one," John added.

Bit by bit Ian was gaining possession of himself. He felt his feet, planted on the garden path, and his face, hardening with resolve. "Ye've been gone, John. Cecily will want—"

"But of course John will go." Cecily was there, Robin on one hip, though he hadn't noticed her approach. "You will together bring Seona home. This has been decided."

Relieved, Ian leaned down to kiss her cheek. Only then did he notice Judith, silent at his side. Her expression told him she'd heard it all. He'd no words to allay the distress in her eyes or the foreboding in his heart. "Judith . . . I must."

She firmed her chin. "I know. I—I'll go home with Mama, in the carriage."

"Aye." *I'm sorry,* he wanted to say again but couldn't. He kissed her forehead briefly. Then he was away like an arrow loosed.

34

Though a ragged turban swathed her hair, a glimpse was all it took to banish whatever lingering doubt might have remained. Seona wasn't free, wasn't with Thomas. Wasn't in Boston or anywhere to the north. She was enslaved to strangers, spreading their wash over a thicket to dry.

Waves of emotion crested and crashed through Ian as he rode beside John Reynold through the towering longleaf pines—elation, rage, relief, regret. Black Huzzah and the pack mare trailed behind, hoof-falls muffled in sand and pine straw. The air bore the tang of turpentine. Distant shouts and the chunking grind of a sawmill, somewhere off through the trees, made it clear the mill's overseer, in whose possession John had seen Seona, wouldn't be found at home—home being a listing cabin with a smoking chimney and a yard littered with children.

Seona hadn't noticed their approach. One of the bairns, having crawled to her, was attempting to pull itself up by fistfuls of her dragging skirt. She bent to detach the child, who latched on to the wash basket, nearly tumbled into it, then set to wailing when Seona rescued the wash from grubby fingers.

Another child stood and shouted, "You let Billy alone, Show-nee!"

Their arrival was spotted then, and the lot of them set up a howl, *Mama* being the sole distinguishable note in the chorus. This drew a woman with a bairn in her arms, another swelling under her apron, to the cabin doorway. She stepped outside, moving with the distinctive waddle of advanced pregnancy.

Not until then did Seona turn their way, petticoat in one hand, child grasped in the other.

Across the sandy yard she saw him and went as still as stone. Then she let go child and petticoat both and came running.

"I regret the inconvenience, Mr. Gibbs," Ian told the overseer, who'd come from the sawmill to confront the unexpected claim on his recently acquired slave. Gibbs and his wife had their heads bent over the document pertaining to the birth of Seona, one light-skinned, green-eyed female offspring of the slave Lily, belonging to Hugh Cameron of Mountain Laurel. "But she was never sold. She ran, though she's still my uncle's property."

Seona looked at him blankly. A command from Gibbs's wife had halted her short of reaching Ian, but not before he registered the hollowed eyes, the too-sharp cheekbones, the ill-fitting gown and petticoat that even at a distance stank of sweat and fear.

Gibbs shoved the paper back at Ian. "Reckoned 'twas too good to trust, cheap as she come—though 'tweren't cheap to me." He glared from Ian to John Reynold, who'd dismounted to add his witness to Ian's claim, then shot a scowl at Seona. "I ought to contest this but . . . maybe it's for the best. Betha needed a hand with the young'uns, but last thing in this world I need is another mouth to feed."

Before Ian could ask why the man had purchased a slave, that being the case, he was distracted by Mrs. Gibbs, who'd covered her belly with her hands, as if to shield her child from its father's bitter words.

"As I said," he began, "I regret—"

"Regret ain't worth spit to me!" Gibbs snapped. Mrs. Gibbs flinched as her husband's hand rose, but he reached for Seona, shoving her at Ian. "Reckon you're the one to blame. Take her, then, and get off my place!"

Seona staggered against Ian. As he caught her, he saw the bruise fading on her cheek, another set on her wrist. The aftermath of a hard-gripping hand. He looked up, seeing red, as Gibbs pushed past his wife.

The woman latched on to his sleeve. "Eben, ain't nothin' you can do?"

"Forget it, Betha. Work's waiting on us both." Shaking her off, the man stalked off through the pines.

Ian took the pack mare's reins from John, ready to help Seona mount, then noticed the brood of children staring at him, grubby-faced and grave. "Dey takin' Show-nee away?" one asked, but Mrs. Gibbs had her mouth pressed too tight to answer.

He made the decision on impulse. Motioning Seona to wait, he led the saddled mare to Gibbs's wife. The woman's eyes were bruised with fatigue, their color the soft gray of a dove's wing. They peered from her worn face without expectation or hope.

"She's called Cricket," he said and put the reins into her work-ruined hand.

It was John who rode beside Seona as they turned the horses northward, John who learned Thomas never set foot on that plantation. Ian heard them conversing, John asking his questions, but kept Ruaidh too far ahead to join in. He couldn't think past the different set of questions roaring in his head. Those first moments in the cabin-yard spun through his mind. Had she meant to fly into his arms? He hadn't expected that. But why wouldn't she be relieved to see him? Since her bid for freedom had failed, better slavery to his uncle than to strangers. At least at Mountain Laurel she had Lily, everything familiar. But she'd left it all once. Left *him*. For Thomas? Why else? How could he have been so blind to her true feelings?

He'd thought he'd put these bitter questions to rest, but they burned in him still. He lengthened the distance between them so he wouldn't hear her weary voice, John's consoling replies.

Toward evening two riders approached on the road. Between them trudged a line of slaves, men and women, faces bronzed with red clay dust. Ian's mouth, gritted from hours of riding, went drier as with faint hope he scanned their passing ranks for Thomas.

His attention lingered on the last in the coffle, a scrawny woman with cropped hair gone white. Every few steps she stumbled, dragging at the woman next in line, who strained to bear her up by their linking chain.

He didn't meet the gaze of the rider in the rear.

What was he to do about Thomas? Should he even find him, he hadn't money enough to buy him outright and no proof of his status; his free papers had vanished with him, taken from the desk where Ian had kept them locked away.

Pity had robbed Ian of the mare. He'd only Huzzah with which to bargain now. And no more pity to spare.

"Steady on—Seona!"

John's shout jarred Ian from his brooding in time to see Seona, dismounted, dashing back down the road to where the slave coffle had halted in a mill of confusion. Bodies parted to reveal the woman at the coffle's end slumped on

481

the road. One of the riders had dismounted and was prodding her to rise. When she didn't, he kicked her in frustration.

Seona ran into their midst, tripped on her trailing skirt, and sprawled over the fallen slave. As John grabbed Huzzah's reins, Ian heeled the roan into a canter and swung down as the slave trader made a grab for Seona.

"Get your hands off her—she's mine!"

The man whirled, hat knocked askew in the scuffle. He reached up to clap it straight, glaring at Ian from beneath an overhanging brow. "Yours, is she? Then get her in hand!"

While dirty bare feet shuffled around them, Seona hovered over the fallen slave, hands cupping the woman's head, staring into her face.

Ian bent over Seona but didn't touch her. "Seona, let her be. Come away now."

She raised her eyes to him. "Ian . . . it's Ruby."

The force of her imploring gaze hit him square in the breastbone. Instead of pulling her off the prostrate woman, he went down on a knee beside her. "Ruby?"

"Esau's Ruby. You played with her boys, that time you came to us."

A boot scuffed the dirt beside him. "For pity's sake, man—"

"Give us a moment, aye?" Ian snapped.

The slave was conscious, breathing heavy through dirt-caked nostrils. She lifted suffering eyes to him. *Ruby was a pretty gal,* Lily had told him. Emaciated, filthy, and exhausted, there was no beauty left this woman, nor hint that she had ever possessed it.

"Is that her name, then? Ruby?" he asked the scowling trader.

"Do I ask their names? *Worthless* is what I call her."

"Yes, suh," came a shaky voice at Ian's knee. "I's called Ruby." The woman frowned at Seona. Her lips drew back from what remained of her teeth. "I know them eyes . . . You Lily's girl-baby, ain't you?" The woman's own eyes flicked to Ian. Her dusty brow furrowed deeper. "You done got you a white man? He a good man?"

"He is, Ruby. He'll help you."

When Seona looked at him again, pleading, Ian knew he'd been wrong. He still had pity to spare.

The coffle departed, leaving Ian grappling with the fact that the crumpled heap of humanity in Seona's arms belonged to him—and he now had even less hard coin to spare. Ruby had proved slightly more than worthless to the trader, after all. "Can she sit a horse, d'ye think?"

John, kneeling by the woman with a canteen, reassured him with a nod. "They can double on Huzzah."

"My boys." Ruby's hand gripped Seona's arm. "Sammy, Eli . . . they with you still?"

483

"Ruby . . ." Tears tracked Seona's face. "Master Hugh sold them off a few years after you. We don't know where they wound up."

Ruby hung her dusty head. "Mastah Hugh. Ain't never think to hear that name no more in this life. He still drawing breath?"

"He is," Ian said, thinking it time he joined the conversation. "I'm Ian Cameron, his nephew, and I suppose ye . . ."

"I be yours now . . . Mastah Ian." Ruby seemed to notice the bruise on Seona's cheek, her ragged clothes. "You free now, Seona, or . . . what?"

Seona glanced at Ian as if expecting him to answer. When he didn't, she said, "We're going home, Ruby. Can you get up on that horse with me?"

The woman's eyes rolled white with dread. "Can't see that comin' off good. T'ain't no other way?"

"Only shank's mare," John said. "And we've far to go."

John aided the slave to her feet. Frightened and growing voluble, she peppered Seona with questions about Mountain Laurel and its people, questions Ian had no wish to hear. He focused on Ruaidh, checking cinches that were perfectly adjusted, until they were ready to mount up. He was coming over to hold Huzzah's bridle when Ruby balked, leaving John standing with his hands cupped to give a hoist into the saddle.

"Then I ain't goin' back there—no sir, no ma'am!" Ruby stood on the verge like a wind-bent scarecrow. "Leave me die right here on this road. I can't go back there—not while *he* there."

Ian turned on Seona. "What the devil did ye say to her?"

She took a step back. "She asked about Mister Dawes. I told her he was there that night but that you must know about it now, so it's all right—"

"All right?" He was struggling for calm as the wound of her betrayal broke open afresh. "D'ye know what I've just done for ye? Likely thrown away any chance of buying Thomas out of slavery—if I can find the wee fool! Does that not concern ye at all? Or did ye use him, too, 'til he no longer served a need?"

"Ian," John cautioned.

Seona shook her head. "Use him?"

"Aye—did ye?" Three sets of eyes stared at him as if he'd grown horns. Fine then. He'd behave like the fiend they seemed to think him. But he'd have his answers.

Taking Seona by the arm, he marched her off the road, headed for a break in a thicket beyond the verge.

"Where are you going?" John called after them. "Ian!"

"Bide ye there, John. We'll not be long." He shouldered his way through the thicket, dislodging twigs. Seona resisted as he dragged her up the wooded incline beyond, limping on bare feet, but his grip on her was iron. He sloshed through a trickle of creek, then halted and yanked her around to face him. And he kissed her. It was a mouth-bruising kiss, until he woke to the feel and taste of her and the anger went out of him. He cupped the back of her head, then tugged at the rags that covered it, wanting his hands in her hair, wanting all of her.

She twisted away. "No—"

He jerked the rags loose and buried his fingers in her hair, but the feel of it was wrong. Very wrong. He pulled back, catching her by the shoulders. And stared, dumbfounded.

Her hair was gone, hacked away to ragged ringlets.

He released her and she staggered, catching herself against the nearest tree, its bark a peeling, mottled white. He'd paused at the edge of a birch grove. Around and above them leafless branches trailed the downy tails of winter catkins.

He wouldn't—*would not*—let himself recall the gold of autumn. Not while dismay and grief were running riot through him, colliding off his ribs, squeezing his heart—for the months that lay between them, for doubt and betrayal and pain, and—irrationally—for the loss of her glorious hair.

"Did ye do that to yourself?"

Seona bent for the fallen rags and wound them

round her ravaged head. "Mister Gibbs did it, after I ran the first time."

"Seona—" But he could find no words to render a single thought in his head. *I love ye. And ye're lost to me. Lost.* There was but one thing left to ask. And one thing left to tell her. He chose the lesser of those evils. "Thomas. Where is he?"

She told him what she knew in a voice as pale as winter. Thomas had been sold to a man headed east, a man buying slaves to build some sort of waterway through a swamp.

"A canal, he called it."

"Did the man have a name?"

"O'Sullivan. I made sure to mind it, in case it might help."

"O'Sullivan? D'ye know how many Irishmen there are back east? How many swamps, for that matter?"

"No. But I know this one's name. Dismal Swamp. Ian, why . . . ?"

She didn't finish the question. She'd a look about her he recognized, as though she gazed at him across a sea of incomprehensible loss, baffled that it should be there. He stared helplessly back at her across that sea, with the one difference. He could name it.

"Seona, I have to tell ye . . . I'm married."

Color drained from her face. "To me."

As she said the words, he sensed the fraying thread still linking them. Betrayal, abandonment, separation, even marriage to another hadn't unraveled it completely. His fingers curled convulsively, as though it were a thing he might latch on to. "Never legally. After ye left, we—Judith and I—were wed. She's been my wife these two months and more."

Seona didn't blink. Her expression didn't alter. Tears tracked the grime on her cheeks like water over stone. "Oh," she said, then linked her arms across her belly as if containing a spilling wound.

The sun had set. The road was a patch of lighter gray beyond the darkening wood. John Reynold was quick to register Seona's expression when they emerged. Whatever he saw seemed to reassure him. Still Ian said, "We talked, John. That's all."

"Of course. I didn't think—"

"John." Ian didn't wish to know what his neighbor had or hadn't thought. He couldn't bear another moment of this. "Ready to ride?"

John halted him with a hand. "I've talked to Ruby. It's your uncle's overseer has her terrified. Something the man did nearly twenty years back."

Minded of Lily's revelations last autumn at the inn concerning Ruby's man, Esau, and Aidan Cameron, Ian frowned at the slave, clutching again at Seona, who seemed barely aware of her now. "Can ye do me a favor, then, and shelter

the woman 'til I return? I'll pay ye for her keep."
Somehow.

John's brows rose. "Of course. But where do you mean to go?"

"I know where Thomas was taken." True only in the broadest sense, but he hurried on, sensing impending protest. "Don't try to talk me into going back with ye, John. I won't. Not 'til I've found him." He had Ruaidh's reins in hand, ready to mount. "I must take Huzzah. He's all that's left to barter. I'm sorry to strand ye with one mount—"

"Never mind that." John grasped Ian's shoulder. "Listen to me. Seona's safe, and what harm was done her will heal, by the grace of the Almighty. Go for Thomas for his sake, but for your own . . . remember mercy."

His neighbor had read the hunger for vengeance in his heart.

Ian swung himself into the saddle. "I don't like to disappoint ye, John, but that's a promise I cannot make."

35

Making his way eastward across half the state, then locating the canal works amidst the timbered sprawl of coastal swampland aptly named Great Dismal, proved simplicity itself compared to finding one particular Irishman among the warrens of shanty camps dotting the snake-infested landscape. Every other white male Ian encountered, it seemed, was Irish; a disproportionate number of those answered to O'Sullivan.

The fourth O'Sullivan bossed a slave gang for the southern portion of the state-straddling canal project, their ranks hired from neighboring plantations or—more hopeful to Ian's purpose—purchased outright with company funds. O'Sullivan's gang was employed in a yard some distance from the diggings, splitting off shingles from the massive cypress and juniper being felled along the canal route. Others stacked the riven boards on horse-drawn carts and guided them away, rattling along corduroy causeways.

"Bound for the nearest navigable ditch in this pesthole of a bog," O'Sullivan explained. A mosquito landed on the man's bull-like neck. He dispatched it with a slap, leaving it stuck to his flesh in a bloody smear. "'Tis vexing early for the skeeters."

The weather had warmed nearer the coast, bringing on an early hatching of the insect hordes, but Ian hadn't come all that way to talk of mosquitoes. He turned the conversation to the hands that did the labor, giving a description of the one he sought.

"Ah . . . *him*." Eyes gray as winter seas were frank in their scrutiny of Ian, stained and bedraggled after days of rain and road dust. "And what would yourself be wanting with the sorry likes o' that boy?"

"He ran off from me November last," Ian said with matching bluntness. "Got himself taken up and sold without my leave—to an Irishman by name of O'Sullivan, bound for these parts." He swept a hand at the camp, teeming with workers, flora crowding dense and green on all sides. "His name is Thomas Ross, and he's mine."

"Thomas he's called, right enough." O'Sullivan's Irish lilt softened. "But would you be coming round t' calling me a thief, Mr. Cameron?"

"Nothing of the sort," Ian replied in kind. "Ye couldn't have known how the matter stood." He glanced beyond the hodgepodge of open-sided pole sheds and rickety shanties that made up the shingle camp, to the shingle cutters themselves. He didn't see Thomas among them.

O'Sullivan's voice snapped his attention back. "I expect you'll want to see the blighter." He shouted to one of his gang, then stumped off.

Surprised by, and faintly suspicious of, this sudden cooperation, Ian followed, boots squelching through a porridge of mud and wood chips—not toward the yard but down a path between slope-roofed shanties, pausing before the last in the row.

"Boy claimed he'd no skills at all, didn't he? But when I set him to cutting, 'twas clear as me granny's blue eyes he'd handled a piece o' wood before. I put the rest under his charge, and *that* was when me trouble started."

Hit full force by the stench from within the shack, Ian suppressed a gag and followed the man inside. At first he thought the dirt-floored shanty deserted, save for a heap of rags in a corner, speckled with what appeared to be inkblots. The heap moaned; the blots took wing to buzz about in agitation. The fat body of a fly struck Ian's hand.

Breathing through his mouth, he crouched and turned the prone figure's unresisting head, revealing Thomas's face, gaunt but recognizable even in that gloom. The heat of fever radiated off his skin, but Ian had barely time to utter an oath of dismay before he saw what had been done to Thomas. His head had been shaved to the scalp in a strip running ear-to-ear, another from forehead to nape, forming a cross.

"'Tis how we mark the troublemakers." O'Sullivan's voice punched the fetid air. "But he's nay trouble t' anyone now, is he? Audacity's no guard against the ague."

Ian's scalp prickled as if the swarm of flies had descended to crawl on him. The putrid air was liquid, bathing him in sweat. "Ague? Not yellow fever, then?"

" 'Tis no such catching thing." O'Sullivan sounded appalled by the suggestion. "Swamp fever, is all. But once they go down with it, most aren't worth their feed again. Nor the cost o' physicking. Not slaves, anyway."

Thomas's eyes rolled behind their lids. He moaned again but didn't waken.

"Ye mentioned trouble," Ian said. "What sort of trouble has he caused?"

"Only inciting half me gang t' go slipping off t' the gators. Not a one made it past a day before the dogs found 'em." O'Sullivan scratched at the small bite mark rising on his neck, dislodging the dead mosquito stuck there. "One named *him* the instigator, so I took him off the yard and set him t' digging—and prettied up his woolly head."

The scenario had promptly repeated itself. Within a week's time two prime ditchdiggers made a break for the swamp's interior.

"Never went off task himself, mind," O'Sullivan said. "But 'twere *him* right enough—putting notions o' freedom in their fool noggins. Had him strapped, hoping it would do for him. 'Twas the next day he came over fevered."

Ian stood, a motion O'Sullivan took as cue to exit the reeking shanty. Ian followed him out onto the path and the relatively breathable swamp air.

"Still want him, now ye've had a look?"

"I've no papers to prove he's mine." Nor free papers to prove Thomas was no slave. Ian gave a jerk of his chin. "That black horse though, tethered with my mount—ye'll take it in trade, with its saddle and tack?"

Thomas, if he survived this, wasn't going to be pleased with him for trading away his horse.

Neither, it seemed, was O'Sullivan. The man drew himself up, neck inflating like an indignant bullfrog's. "What sort of thieving pirate do you mark me for? I'll not be taking a fine piece o' horseflesh for a good-as-dead slave, and you saving me the trouble o' putting him in the ground."

"Ye'll take a shilling for him, then, and write me a proper bill of sale." A shilling he could spare, though little more.

The Irishman raised a sardonic brow. "You'll be after driving a hard bargain, won't you?"

It began to rain, a drizzle that cast a pall over the camp, turning afternoon to dusk.

"If ye've paper and ink to hand," Ian said, dispirited and beyond cross, "let's be about it, aye? And I'll beg of ye a few of those cedar poles I saw in the yard, so I can haul my shilling's worth out of here."

In a village south of the canal works, Ian found a tavern with a proprietor who could tell ague from yellow fever and allowed them a space in his stable for the night. Ian inquired after a physician and a lad was sent to fetch a Dr. Rawlins, could he be found. He saw to the horses, then settled in the straw next to Thomas, whose stink was an assault on the senses, overpowering the stable's pungency. He'd lost more flesh than it had appeared in the shanty. Sweat poured off him as if it were the heat of summer.

"In for a shilling," Ian muttered, drawing up his knees and laying his forehead to them.

Straw rustled and he whipped his head up. Thomas's eyes were open wide, fever-blind in the lantern light. "Seona . . ."

Ian heard his own breath, unnaturally loud. The guilt and longing that had clotted Thomas's voice might have been his own. He lurched to his feet.

Outside, the air was thickly damp. Ian heaved lungfuls, trying to ease the clench of jealousy around his heart. What had gone on under his nose all those months? How had he not seen it?

The yard behind the inn lay thick with night shadow, until from the direction of the tavern a light intruded. Another lad, dressed in breeches and rumpled shirt, came striding toward Ian bearing lantern and case, spectacles glinting in the swinging light. At the stable door he set down his burdens and briefly jerked a hat from atop a mop of curly brown hair.

"Dr. Marcus Rawlins," the lad announced, beginning to roll up his shirtsleeves. "I'm told there's a man here needs my attention?"

Stripling though he appeared, the doctor knew his business. Muttering at sight of his patient's shorn head, Rawlins counted Thomas's pulse, listened to his breathing, looked inside his mouth and under the lids of his eyes, then with practiced efficiency stripped him of fouled shirt and breeches.

The sight of Thomas's back was a shock. O'Sullivan's strapping had been vicious enough to break the skin.

Rawlins set about making an infusion with a cinnamon-colored powder Ian recognized for Jesuit bark. Raising Thomas, they managed to get most of the liquid down his throat. Water was then sponged over his flesh and dribbled between his peeling lips.

"I'll leave you some bark," Rawlins said, brusquely tidying away his powders. "Keep him bathed and cool. Get as much water down him as you can. If he wakes and will eat, feed him. Dose him again come morning. If you've spare clothing, cover him decent, else wash out those filthy rags. Can you manage?"

"Aye," Ian said, taken aback by the man's

terseness. "Thank ye . . . Doctor." The title felt absurd on his lips. Rawlins couldn't be older than nineteen.

Ignoring the thanks, Rawlins shut his case and stood. Lantern light reflected off his spectacles, obscuring tired eyes. "Be thankful I've another patient nearby or your man might have been dead by morning."

Ian rubbed a hand through his unbound hair. "I haven't coin to pay ye but can offer one of the horses. The black. A fine animal, sound as you'll come by."

Rawlins's glance took in the horses, the saddlebags heaped nearby. "And how distant is home for you, sir? A day's journey? Two?"

"More than two."

Rawlins's mouth tightened. "Doubtless you'd make *him* walk. I cannot in good conscience take your spare horse and jeopardize the life I'm meant to save." The physician glared up at him, not the least intimidated by their substantial difference in size.

Ian drew a calming breath. "I'll give ye something for your services, all the same." Struck by inspiration, he went to his shot bag, untouched since the muster at Chesterfield.

Rawlins left the stable with Gideon Pryce's silver-ornamented powder horn slung over his shoulder. Ian watched the absurdly young physician vanish into the night, wondering was it something in the local tea-brown water that made these swamp dwellers stubborn as mules.

When he returned to their corner, Thomas's face still gleamed with unhealthy sweat, but his eyes were open, swiveling to take in the stable rafters illumined by lantern light. They shifted, settling on Ian, flaring in recognition.

"Welcome back." Ian settled in the straw and began pulling off a boot.

Frowning, Thomas blinked. "You're not a dream. How did you . . . ?"

"Spirit ye from under the nose of your Irish overseer?" Ian pulled off a second boot. "I didn't. I bought ye."

Thomas's eyes flared again. His cracked lips twisted. "You enjoying this . . . Mastah Ian?"

"Not much." Not at all.

Thomas raised a hand to the marks shaved into his head. He started to speak, then went still. The pulse beat fast at his throat. "Seona?"

Ian tensed. "Aye. What of her?"

Moisture gleamed in Thomas's eyes. "I lost her."

"And I found her. Or John Reynold did. He was in Fayetteville and happened to spot—" Struck by how close he'd come to never knowing she hadn't gained her freedom, his mouth hardened. "She's chosen ye over me, has she?"

Thomas met his glare. Unrepentant. "She never got the chance."

"She left with ye!"

"She was taken with me. Not the same."

Ian opened his mouth, then shut it as understanding shimmered at the edges of his thoughts. *Taken.* Seona hadn't left Mountain Laurel willingly, despite all the evidence to the contrary? Thomas's note, the stolen garments . . . Even as it blasted his soul with a warmth he hadn't felt in months, he flinched from the notion, unwilling to embrace it. Thomas was lying.

"Someone forced ye to go? That's what ye mean me to believe? Forced the pair of ye?"

"You said you found Seona," Thomas said. "Didn't she tell you?"

"No." The denial came too quickly.

"Or you didn't let her."

He hadn't, and now his gut writhed like a nest of snakes as doubt assailed what he'd thought was bitter truth. "Ye left that note! I know your hand, Thomas. It was ye wrote it. Ye meant to take her away."

"It was. . . . ." Thomas closed his eyes. "And I did."

Ian gripped him, merciless. "Don't ye dare sleep! Tell me what happened that night or so help me, I'll sell ye to the first dupe fool enough to buy ye—for half the shilling ye cost me."

That roused him. Fixing Ian with a bleary glare, Thomas asked, "You bought me for a *shilling?*"

"I did," Ian said. "So start giving me my coin's worth—now."

After another long drink from Ian's canteen, Thomas obliged. "I hadn't meant to speak to her at all that night, but she was hiding in your bed when I slipped in to find where you'd put my papers. Thought I heard breathing but was too set on getting out without being caught to pull back the hangings to see. I waited near the kitchen and sure enough, out she came on my heels. I told her I was leaving, wanted her to come too. Knew I'd some convincing to do, but we hadn't got past the washhouse before the Jackdaw caught us."

During the long recitation Thomas's voice had sunk to a rasp. Ian reached again for the canteen and put it to his lips, supporting his head while he drank. He still couldn't half believe the tale. "D'ye tell me Dawes subdued ye both single-handed and took ye off my uncle's land without rousing anyone to see or hear? Ye didn't put up a fight? For yourself or for her?"

"Never got the chance. Must have come out of the dark . . . clubbed me over the head first thing. I woke trussed in a wagon driven by men I'd never seen before, bound and gagged. Even after they took that gag off me, they kept watch so we didn't talk. Seona managed to tell me just the one thing before O'Sullivan took me off. It was Dawes."

The shock of it had his head spinning. Why

would Dawes abduct and sell Seona and Thomas, then lead them all on a wild-goose chase, pretending to hunt them down? Surely his uncle knew nothing of it. But what about . . . ?

Shock was passing. Some of the spinning pieces were falling into place. The robbery that had sent him away from Mountain Laurel for days, chasing down a peddler. It hadn't been a robbery, true enough. Nor had it been a mistake. It had been very much intentional, though not on the part of Karl Gottfriedsen. "Lucinda."

"Maybe," Thomas said. "Probably. I never heard her named. Maybe Seona did."

"Sounds as if Dawes had a buyer ready," Ian said, struggling to reason past the rage. "O'Sullivan?"

"He came into it later . . . pure chance."

Ian shivered, though the stable air was by no means chill. Recalling one piece to this puzzle Thomas hadn't yet offered, he asked, "And where does Benjamin Eden come into it?"

The hesitation was brief. "He doesn't."

"It was Eden drove Ally and the wagon back to Mountain Laurel, after Pryce beat him. Ally saw him. Heard his name spoken."

"Ally got it wrong."

Ian's jaw tightened as he clenched his teeth. "Ye're lying to my face, Thomas. I've a letter from the man. He admits intending to aid ye in helping slaves to run. Ye'd an assignation with him that night. Ye were taking Seona to meet him."

"Sounds like you got it all figured, Mastah Ian." Thomas shifted under the blanket and winced, closing his eyes.

Pity and fury surged. "Why did ye have to meddle? I meant all along to see her free. I thought she lov—"

"Loved you?" Thomas's breath came labored now. "How could she know . . . a slave? How could *you?*"

Regretting his revealing words, sickened by the bitter truth in Thomas's, he said, "I'm sending ye back to Boston. Soon as ye're fit to go."

Thomas didn't blink at that. After a pause long enough to prick Ian with concern, he asked, "And Seona?"

"She stays at Mountain Laurel for now." Memory of Seona running to him across Gibbs's yard filled his mind, with new and gutting import. Thomas had said she hadn't made up her mind to go with him before Dawes intervened. Would she have stayed, given the choice?

What if Thomas had it wrong, and she'd never for a moment meant to leave Mountain Laurel, or him?

Then Ian was the one who'd broken their vows. Not Seona.

36

Light from the cabin licked over the doorway where Seona stood. She hadn't moved since Esther rushed up to say Ian was come home with Thomas, who looked about half-dead. Thomas had been brought to their cabin instead of the big house. Her mama had come to tend him. Seona had watched the to-and-fro like it was all a dream, until Esther came panting out of the dark again.

"They stewin' like to boil up at the house, Seona. Mister Ian sent me for to fetch you."

Lily spared attention from Thomas, lying fevered on her cot. "Go on, girl-baby. It's going to be all right. The Lord is—"

"I know, Mama." *Watching over our lot.*

Her lot was grief and it hurt all over. In her chest. Her throat. Low at the back of her head. Grief was the burden in her belly too. She was hiding it still with her own winter clothes layered on, the drawstring petticoat let out to its full extent, and a shawl—an old blanket—wrapped just so. Like the head-rag hid what was left of her hair.

So far only Lily and Naomi knew her secret. Maybe that was all about to change. Maybe that was why she was being sent for.

Heaviness dragged her steps along the track. *Sent for.* Was this how it was to be, Ian handing down orders from the house, sending to fetch her like a proper master would?

That proper master's wife was coming down the passage as Seona came through the back door. She'd avoided Miss Judith since her return, feigning ill the one time she'd sought her out at the cabins. Esther had heard Miss Lucinda berating her daughter for it, telling her a master's wife shouldn't make friendly with the servants. "Especially *that* one."

Maybe Miss Lucinda was right. It wasn't lost on Seona that she carried inside her what was meant to be Miss Judith's. Meant to be . . . or would be? She trembled before the girl who once read her stories. Who blacked her eyebrows and giggled at the silliness. Who cried and pleaded when Seona got punished for it. Who could take from her the very child of her body to raise up for her own, if she wanted and Ian was willing. And why wouldn't Ian be willing? The child was his.

She dropped her gaze before Miss Judith could meet it.

"You're wanted in the parlor, Seona," Miss Judith said, then passed her by and started up the stairs.

"Ye've the evidence of your eyes, Aunt. He made a botch of it—didn't even see the papers burnt proper. I found them in the ashes." Ian's coat cuffs and tails were begrimed, his hair down in straggles, unwashed. Esther had told them how he'd run to Dawes's cabin soon as he flung himself off his horse. Jubal tried to tell him Dawes was gone, lit out for parts unknown, but he'd acted deaf.

Seona hung back in the parlor doorway while Ian thrust the burnt remains of whatever he'd found—Thomas's free papers, she reckoned—under Miss Lucinda's nose.

"Tell me where Dawes is hiding, Aunt, or so help me—"

"Hugh!" Miss Lucinda snapped at Master Hugh, sitting in his chair by the fire. "Will you say nothing while your nephew threatens me?"

Master Hugh appeared unmoved by the appeal. "Ye've held your *wheesht* about Dawes, letting me think he was about the place. Answer the question Ian put to ye."

Miss Lucinda's mouth tucked in like she'd taken hurt. "I held my *wheesht*, as you put it, to preserve your health and peace. Jackson has always returned from his truancies in the past."

"How long has it been?"

"No one has seen him since the muster—or admits to it." Miss Lucinda spied Seona in the doorway. "There's the one to question! Come, girl. Tell what you know. I hadn't a thing to do with your misfortunes of late."

Ian turned, showing her his face for the first time since he left her, John Reynold, and Ruby on the road north of Fayetteville. It was a leaner face, and agonized. Across that river spread between them again, his sunken eyes reached for her as he said her name. "Seona . . . Thomas was knocked senseless that night, but ye weren't. Did my aunt have anything to do with your being taken?"

Aching for his arms to do what his eyes were doing, she took a step toward him.

Confusion crashed over her and she halted. He belonged to Miss Judith. Married by law. He oughtn't to be reaching for her, even with his eyes. Nothing could span that river now.

She looked to Master Hugh. A shock it was, seeing him after months. He seemed aged a year, maybe two, for each. Pity and resentment tangled in her throat. Would he want to know she carried another child of his blood? Would he care any more for its well-being than he ever had for hers? Still she spoke to him as if he'd been the one to ask. "I never saw Miss Lucinda that night, nor heard her name spoke."

"You see!"

Apart from Miss Lucinda's vindicated outburst, there was silence. Seona lifted her eyes to the painting over the mantel, the one the first mistress painted long ago. Water flowing over mossy rocks. Yellow birches. Could she but step through those put-on colors and disappear . . .

Ian's voice pulled her back. "Seona, are ye sure?"

"I never saw Miss Lucinda, nor heard her name spoke." She'd nothing more to say. What she suspected hardly mattered.

"Verra well," Master Hugh said. "Ye can go, lass."

No one had said a word about her baby. Her secret was still safe. She would keep it so, for as long as she could.

"Very well?" Miss Lucinda's face was all bone and stretched skin as she glared at her menfolk. "Her word satisfies you, where mine does not?"

Seona fled the parlor, not wanting to hear more. Let the white folk fight it out among themselves. She wanted her mama.

Ian burst out the back door in time to see Seona start down the kitchen breezeway.

"Seona, wait!" He plunged after her, thinking she meant to ignore his plea, and all but collided with her in the near dark of the arching trellis, where she'd paused. Her arms were crossed below her breasts, fingers clenching the ragged blanket that wrapped her so tight it hunched her shoulders. "I tried to find ye when first we knew ye gone. I did try, Seona. I was injured. There was—"

"A painter-cat. Mama told me. She said you near about died of it."

Her voice was lifeless. No hint of pardon or concern. It was all he could do not to pull her into his arms. "Still I oughtn't to have given up, let myself believe ye didn't want to be found. Between that blasted note, the missing gown and shoes, and Dawes—if ever I set eyes on him again, he's a dead man. That I promise ye."

She unlocked her arms and touched him, a grip on his hand that sent a thrill surging through him. Until she spoke. "No, Mister Ian. No more promises."

Pinioning her hand in his, he tried to pull her closer. She tugged, trying to break free.

"Seona, please . . ." He took her forcibly in his arms, holding her tight against him, an arm snaked around a waist no longer slender. Her body had changed, grown full in the belly. But she was so *thin*.

He'd a moment of surprise, another of confusion; then blinding comprehension rocked him.

He backed away, clinging to her still, a hand spread over the unmistakable curve of her pregnancy. "Seona?"

Darkness cradled them. An eternity passed. Then she said, "It's yours."

"It . . . You—" Joy exploded through him, robbing him of speech. There was a child. His. Theirs. For a moment he could only breathe and wonder. Then he remembered Judith, and guilt and remorse heaved against his joy like a bitter wave. "Do they know?"

"Mama and Naomi do," she said. "Reckon others suspect."

Not his aunt. Not his uncle. Not yet. And Judith . . .

What his kin would say or do warred with the sheer wonder of the life inside Seona, one he welcomed with all his terrified heart. Did she?

Thought that she might feel otherwise left him shaking.

"I swear to ye, Seona, I'd never have forced ye to be with me if I'd believed that's what I was doing. This child—our child—was conceived in love. My love at least. Everything I promised beneath the birches, I meant. I'll keep ye—"

She pushed away from him. "Keep me? Do whatever—punish me like Mister Gibbs—but I will never be *that* to you."

He stared at her shadowed face, stunned, until her meaning registered. *That*—his mistress, kept in plain sight behind Judith's back. A second family, a shadow family, seen but unacknowledged. For a sickening moment he understood how such a thing might come to be. And be borne. Then what else she'd said hit him. *Punish me like Mister Gibbs . . .*

"What did the man do to ye?" Rage boiled up in him, unreasoning. He wanted to hear every word of it, for his heart to be flayed raw by all she'd suffered. "Seona, tell me."

Perhaps she wanted that too, for she spared him no detail. She told him how she'd run from the Gibbses, how they caught her and hauled her back, cut off her hair as punishment, then tied her to a pine tree and beat her with a strap. She'd run again, and again they'd hauled her back and strapped her worse. " 'Til I feared they'd beat the baby out of me. I didn't run a third time."

The ache in his chest robbed him of breath. He could hardly speak. "Seona . . . I am so sorry. For—for everything."

"Even for Miss Judith?"

Before he could utter the emphatic reply that leapt to his tongue, the back door opened. Lamplight speckled through the trellis onto Seona's face. She closed her eyes, hiding their anguish. "Let me go, Ian. Let me go to Mama."

"Seona, that you?" Maisy's voice. "Miss Judith asking for you. She up in her and Mister Ian's room."

Wretched with guilt, Ian met the glint of Seona's opened, frantic eyes. "I'll see to Judith. But first . . . Seona, we have to tell them."

"I do. You don't."

He frowned in the darkness. "Ye said it was mine."

"It is. You the only man . . ."

510

"Then what? Ye're saying I could refuse to claim it? I won't do that."

"No matter Miss Judith's feelings?"

His chest constricted with the magnitude of what he'd done, with this sundering of his heart. All their hearts. "No matter what," he ground out. "I won't be like my uncle."

He reached for her, but all he caught was the ratty shawl she'd worn. Rather than be kept another moment with him, Seona had slipped out of it and let it tumble to the breezeway stones.

When she was gone, he took it up and pressed it to his face, breathing in her scent, until the worn wool lost the fleeting memory of her warmth.

Judith was abed with a book, a small volume he'd seen her read from often. A candle burned on the bedside table she'd added to the chamber's furnishings.

Ian shut the door and crossed the room. "What did ye want with Seona?"

"I've hardly seen her since she returned. I think she's avoiding me." Judith marked her place in the book and set it aside. "What is that?"

He saw in her eyes that she'd recognized the shawl, knew exactly what, and whose, it was. Wondering what had happened to the old arisaid she'd worn, come down from his uncle's first wife, he dropped its pitiful replacement on the chair.

"Ye didn't answer my question, aye?"

"I wanted to talk with Seona about . . . what happened to her."

"I can tell ye. She ran from the man who bought her, trying to get back to m—to Mountain Laurel. They hacked off her hair as punishment and laid a strap to her."

She'd stopped running, given up the hope of freedom for the sake of their baby. She *wanted* it. He clung to the realization as he peeled off his travel-stained coat and dropped it on the floor, tugged his reeking shirt over his head, and crossed to the basin to wash the worst of the road grime from his face and hands.

"I'm so sorry for her suffering." Judith's tearful voice jerked him back to their room, the stomach-churning fact of their marriage. "Is Thomas gravely ill?"

"He'll live." His expression in the glass turned grim; he'd not forgiven Thomas for his part in their abduction, for luring Seona out into the dark that night, though he'd suffered for it. It had been a difficult journey west through the Piedmont, but Thomas was stronger now than when Ian had found him in that swamp shanty.

"As for Seona . . . a beating isn't all of it." Better Judith hear it from him than a gossiping house slave. Or worse, her mother. Still he took the coward's tack, speaking with his back turned. "She's with child."

He heard his wife's convulsive swallow as he wrung out the rag, dripping water noisily into the basin.

"Was she . . . *forced?*" Judith barely got the word out.

Ian caught his haggard reflection in the glass, seeing lines around his eyes he'd never noticed before. "Thomas would say so."

"Ian, I don't understand. Did Thomas see it happen?"

"No. The bairn's mine." He moved to a chair and stood one-legged, attention riveted on removing his boots and stockings. From the corner of his eye he saw his wife's face, pale, stricken.

"I see." Another swallow. "Will it be—? Do you intend . . . ?"

"I've no answers to give ye. I only just learned of it myself." Ian set his feet to the floor. His flesh still clung to the feel of Seona, of the bairn beneath his hands—tangible proof of their union. "Ye needed to know, Judith, but can we not talk of it tonight? Please."

He grasped for a way to stall further, to put off joining his wife in their bed. But he'd ridden hard for days, caring for Thomas along the way. He swayed where he stood. Oblivion would be sweet, since solitude was denied him.

He snuffed the candle and shucked off his breeches, then slid between the linens.

Oblivion proved disobliging. Memories of Seona tangled with glimpses of a future fraught with unfathomable complication, while his body longed for release of another kind. It might have been an hour later when he heard a wakeful sigh beside him.

"Judith?"

She reached for him readily, as if she'd been waiting. He sucked in a breath at her touch, mind in an uproar, lips pressed tight over a forbidden name.

"You don't have to ask permission, Ian."

Though her voice was barely audible, he heard the pain of longing in it. As deep as his own, but infinitely purer. He reached for the hand lying on his chest, not knowing whether he meant to clasp it or push it away. Then he closed his eyes and turned to her embrace.

Three days passed before Ian thought of Ruby, and not until she was mentioned at table. John Reynold had taken the *quaking sack of bones,* as Rosalyn christened her, home to Cecily until Ian returned to deal with her as he saw fit.

One look at the woman, washed and decently clothed, winding yarn and rocking six-month-old Robin's cradle with a skinny foot, and Ian saw fit to leave well enough alone. John made no objection, for the time being; Cecily, not surprisingly, had taken a liking to Ruby, who'd greeted him warily when he entered the cabin but bid him farewell with unconcealed relief that she'd been allowed to stay put.

"How fares Thomas?" John asked him on the cabin porch.

"The fever's lifted but he'll need time to recover his strength. I mean to send him north as soon as he does. Her too," Ian added, nodding toward the cabin. "Unless ye'd rather I didn't?"

"We would never hold her in bondage—you know that. But you'd make certain she has a place to go? Some means of living?"

Ian nodded, having no idea what such arrangements would entail. Deciding on a means to see Thomas safe out of Carolina had proved difficult enough. He'd yet to inform Thomas of his plan; though Thomas was in no condition to abscond with himself in a fit of pique, one could never be too chary with him.

John regarded him, more questions in his eyes. Chary of them as well, Ian took his leave before his neighbor could speak Seona's name, but he felt that searching gaze until the wood swallowed him up.

Spring had hold of the landscape. Redbud shimmered its pink lace through the dark pillars of budding hardwoods. Ian was too preoccupied to appreciate the sight. His head teemed with thoughts of crops to sow, livestock to tend, slaves to oversee, and the promised desks for Stoddard—the proceeds from which he desperately needed—calling from the shop.

And his kin. They all knew of the child now, and he bore their varying degrees of dismay or disdain—and Rosalyn's smug air of vindication—with as much composure as he could muster. While his uncle seemed to withdraw from them daily, for Judith's sake Ian had settled into a brittle civility with his aunt. As for Jackson Dawes . . . Ian never left the house now without his rifle.

Palming the stock, he scanned the trail for places a man might lie concealed, but no one lurked behind rock or tree.

Soon his thoughts flowed back into that current that flooded his waking mind and swept a reckless course through his dreams at night. Far from hounding his uncle about Seona's manumission, he now shied from mentioning it. Thought of his child born free yet sundered from him by so great a distance as Boston was no more bearable than the notion of a child born to him enslaved. Like a man caught behind a veil, he went about only half-seeing, making a dozen small decisions every hour that affected those around him, but never coming near *that* decision.

Emerging from the wood moments later, he saw Seona, bent over a toting basket outside the washhouse. Before he could think, he was striding toward her, wet grass pulling at his boots—until the sound of retching behind the garden pales checked him.

"Miss Judith, let me help ye." A breathless sob answered Malcolm's soothing voice. "There now . . . 'tis easing off, then?"

When Ian looked toward the wash line again, the basket lay abandoned in the grass. Seona had seen him and fled.

"I'll have eaten something disagreeable," Judith said, clearly mortified that he'd heard her in an act so unbecoming as vomiting into the peavines and come into the garden to investigate. Half-moons hung beneath her eyes, dark as bruises. She'd never been the picture of blooming health, but how long had she appeared so peaked?

Guilt stirred in Ian's chest. Perhaps her malady wasn't physical. Her long-suffering silence was another reminder of the choice looming over his heart.

"There's no need to tire yourself," he said. "I don't see your sister sullying her hands in the garden or anywhere else for that matter." Rosalyn was often away to Chesterfield now, reveling in the grander living that would soon be hers. The wedding wasn't until June, yet there seemed no end to the urgent matters requiring Jubal to escort her to the neighboring plantation at the most inconvenient of hours.

Judith tucked her hands into the folds of her skirt. "I enjoy the garden. It's peaceful."

She'd retreated to its peace often of late. "I'm guessing ye've been out here all the morn. Ye should rest."

Judith flicked a glance at Malcolm, who'd turned to hoeing a nearby bed. "If that would please you, Ian."

Her swift compliance irritated him. He bridled the unreasonable reaction. "At least ye've something gives ye peace," he murmured as she went, and wished he hadn't driven her from it. A dithering fool he'd seem, though, calling her back.

"Ye say that, Mister Ian, as though ye hadn't as much yourself." Leaning against the handle of the hoe, Malcolm regarded him from the shadow of a tattered straw hat.

It seemed an age since they'd spoken more than a word in passing. Not since the cold day on the ridge, when another impossible choice faced him. Malcolm and Lily had gotten their way. He'd stayed. But Malcolm hadn't suggested he bind himself in marriage to one of his uncle's stepdaughters. That choice had been Ian's, a safeguard against abandoning yet another course.

Wedlock, in truth.

He studied Malcolm's face, lined as an aged map, as though in it he might discover the path to his wife's soul. "Does Judith speak much to ye, Malcolm, out here in the garden?"

"She doesna mind a stretch of quiet, your wife," the old man said. "But aye, she does speak to me."

"What about?"

"Mainly what she's been readin'."

"That Lowlander poet she fancies? Burns, isn't it?"

"She hasna mentioned a poet." Malcolm twisted the hoe, turning moist earth with the blade. " 'Tis from the Psalms Miss Judith's been readin' of late."

Surprised, Ian asked, "Any psalm in particular?"

Malcolm didn't pause his work. " 'The Lord is the portion of mine inheritance and of my cup: thou maintainest my lot. The lines are fallen unto me in pleasant places; yea, I have a goodly heritage.' "

The old man had dug the hoe deep again before Ian found his voice. "Does she think she has that now? Or she hopes for it?"

Surely the latter. He'd brought the lass little but disappointment and misery.

The richness of manured earth came up to fill his nose as Malcolm turned the soil. "Miss Judith isna different from any other soul. She's wanting that goodly heritage the Almighty has for her."

A goodly heritage. Exactly what he'd come to Mountain Laurel hoping to find—or create. The yearning stabbed deep. Then he looked at the old man laboring before him, seeing him as if with new eyes. "And ye? Is it what ye hope for too?"

Malcolm gave a rattling chuckle. "I have it already, as I told ye once."

Ian frowned. "Malcolm, ye haven't even a cup to fill. Ye own nothing—not the clothes ye stand up in. They belong to my uncle."

He regretted his words—what need had he to point out the bitter obvious to a man who'd lived it every day of his long life?

"Hugh Cameron isna my master."

It was more unexpected than the reply that had launched them down this thorny trail. "Ye came to him when old Duncan passed—along with the rest." Ian gestured, taking in house and outbuildings, the fields rolling up to the sheltering ridges of the Carraways.

"Aye, that's so," Malcolm agreed.

"Then . . . ye don't think of *me* as your master?" He would be, should Malcolm outlive his uncle; the man seemed as durable as a stick of hardwood, despite swollen joints and stooped back.

"Dinna take it amiss, Mister Ian," Malcolm said with the faintest of smiles. "I dinna see ye that way either. I ken well enough your uncle has his papers telling the world he can bid me work for him, wi' no more thought for my well-being save what keeps me fit for his use. But d'ye ken your uncle isna master over my soul?"

"Of course."

"Do ye then?"

"That's what I wanted for Seona before—" He couldn't keep the pain from his voice. "I wanted to give her freedom, body and soul. I want that still."

And he wanted this man to believe it.

With evident effort, Malcolm bent to pluck a stone from the soil. "Whether ye see this or no, Mister Ian, ye never had it in your power to give her that. 'Tis your own soul's freedom ye should be worrit over."

Ian stared at the bent neck, the skin creased and sagging, at the twisted brown fingers grasping the hoe. "My freedom?"

Malcolm tossed the stone onto the garden path. "Every man makes himself a slave to someone or something. Your white skin doesna spare ye that." The old slave straightened with an audible creak. "And my brown skin doesna mean I canna choose what masters me. In the way that matters most, I am free."

Ian ceased hoping for sleep to quiet his longing. He listened to Judith's breathing, assured himself she slept, then slipped from bed and took up his boots, waiting until he was on the back steps before pulling them on.

He oughtn't to be doing this. For a moment he fought the pull, but his heart wasn't in the struggle. His heart was very much in favor of plunging off the steps into the night. He followed its will, past the kitchen-yard, down the track under a starless heaven, until he stood in the shadows of the oaks.

An acorn dropped, rattled down a cabin roof, thudded to earth. An owl called from the orchard.

He moved closer, creeping over last year's mulching leaves, stepping round a broad trunk, and came in view of Seona's cabin. Sweating now despite the night's chill, he crouched against the tree, refusing to heed the scream of conscience telling him being there was a betrayal. What choice had Seona left him? If she'd only stop running from him, let him talk to her. The child was his. Did that not give him some right to approach her?

Perhaps she would come out to use the privy.

He tucked his hands beneath his arms for warmth. Clouds cleared. Stars glittered in patches. The cabin door never opened.

The first trill of birdsong drove him back to the house, where he pushed his clothing under the bed and crawled between the sheets, careful not to let his cold limbs touch his sleeping wife. He lay staring at the bed hangings taking form in the graying dawn, frustrated over the night's fruitless watch. Eager for night to come again.

He knew the voice of his master now.

37

April 1794

Outside the privy beneath the leafing oaks, Seona hesitated. Instead of going back inside the cabin, she tread the cool ground to the edge of the track that skirted the plowed field beyond, where the night sky opened wide. Orion in his glittering belt stared down at her, minding her of years back when Miss Judith read her stories of the belted star-man. Ancient peoples thought he was a hunter or a giant. *They didn't know God put the stars in the sky,* Miss Judith had said.

Now Seona reached out to those heavens and let her heartache flow, streaming from her eyes, through her open mouth in wordless appeal.

"He thinks I never wanted him," she'd told Lily and Naomi the morning after Ian brought Thomas home and learned about the baby. "He thinks I went along with it 'cause he expected me to."

"Best he go on thinking that," Naomi had said. "He married to Miss Judith. Ain't no changing it. Best leave things as they be."

Things as they be couldn't stay so forever. Day after day she waited to know what would be done with her and the baby growing inside her. Night after night she listened for a voice whispering hope. God wasn't cold and distant like the stars He'd made. He wasn't so high and set apart He couldn't understand her pain. Her fear. Surely.

"You were a man, too," she whispered. But God-become-man was a mystery hard to keep hold of, like water in the hand. Comfort spilled through her fingers as Orion watched, uncaring. How was she to live within sight of Ian and Miss Judith together without it shredding her soul to ribbons? What was she to do if Ian took her child but sent her away?

There was no answer. Shivering in her shift, she turned to go back to the cabin. A twig snapped as she moved.

A rustle of leaves brought him into the starlight—Orion himself, barefoot and fair-haired, linen shirt glowing as if with its own light. His hand closed over her arm, cold as a star.

"Don't go." His breath wasn't cold, but warm on her brow. She couldn't see his face but didn't need to. Her heart minded every plane and hollow. "I've waited for ye, Seona. I cannot bear it, watching ye from afar. Not touching. Not speaking."

Exactly what Orion might have said, could he speak. But this was Ian, and his whisper fed her soul. He cupped her head, fingers combing deep through her cutoff curls. He drew her to him, pressed her head to his chest, and she thought how easy it would be to let the longing sweep her away. To forget Miss Judith up at the big house, lie down with him beneath the oaks, and take back what was theirs.

His breath raised gooseflesh down her neck. "Our marriage was real to me. But if ye spoke those vows and shared my bed because ye thought ye had no choice . . . then say so."

Had she thought that? Ever? She couldn't think now, not with him so close. "You can't be coming to the cabins like this. You have a wife—"

"Ye're my wife!"

His hold on her tightened, and like a wife her body had the memory of his, long muscles, wide shoulders, the hard planes of his chest. Her arms went around him, feeling his ribs and the line of his backbone through his shirt. Was he starving himself? Starving for her like she was for him? Then his mouth was on hers, warm and wanting and sweet.

Stop. The word seared through her, hissing as a falling star. Planting her hands on his chest, she pushed, breaking the kiss, and stepped back.

Ian stood tense as a painter-cat ready to spring. "I've tried to do what I must, Seona, but I cannot love her. Only when I'm near ye can I feel."

He held out his hand. She stared at it, afraid her heart would come bursting free to meet him halfway and they'd take the fall together.

Then he said, "I'm leaving tomorrow. Thomas is going back to Boston."

The breath went out of her like she'd been punched. It was a thing she'd never thought of, not in all her worrying. "You're going too?"

"Part of the way." He came a step closer. "Stay with me now. Let me be near ye—for an hour. That's all."

It seemed so little to ask, yet she knew if they took an hour, they'd want the night. And another. But if she went on holding him off, how soon until that love he professed wore thin? How soon until he started thinking of taking from her what was his to take? A fierce maternal need propelled her toward him, but only a step, before a knowing clear as light filled her. If she gave in and became what he wanted her to be, she'd be giving to him by pieces what wasn't his to take now—her soul. And she wouldn't save her child.

It felt like walking blind off a cliff, even knowing it was God asking it of her. Still she said, "No."

"Seona." His reaching hand was white in the darkness. "Please. Ye've my child inside ye, and my soul ye own until time should end. As I thought I owned yours. Do I?"

He was baring that soul to her now. The nakedness of it, and its poverty, was more than she could stand. She stepped back, shaking her head. "Master Hugh might own me on a paper, but my soul is God's." And God's alone. Master Hugh was slipping away from them. She'd just denied Ian. There was no other covering left her, save the only one she'd ever truly had. "Go back to Miss Judith. Don't come down here again."

She ran for her cabin, acorns skittering under her feet, a hand muffling her sobs.

Benjamin Eden met them on the Cape Fear Road two days north of Mountain Laurel, driving a two-wheeled cart pulled by a bay horse. The man himself was immaculate in his plain Quaker garb as he halted his conveyance in a flood of morning sunlight. "There is an inn not a mile farther where we may find accommodation," he told Ian. "Thee will bide the night with us?"

"I will not," Ian said. Though assured by his uncle no harm would befall Seona in his absence, he was anxious to return.

The Quaker nodded, accepting his curt refusal, then addressed Thomas, not yet fully recovered and visibly drooping after the long ride. "Thee is resolved upon returning north, Friend Thomas?"

"He hasn't a choice, as I explained in my letter." Dismounting, Ian removed a bundle tied behind Ruaidh's saddle. "Provisions." The offering was accepted. Ian laid a hand to the cart's wheel. "Swear to me that ye'll not let him turn back."

Eden's brows lifted. "Thee knows little of Quakers to bid one swear an oath. I shall see Thomas reaches Philadelphia and supply

527

introduction to those who can aid him on his journey. With that thee must be content."

"Still fretting over me?" Thomas asked from the saddle.

"Aye," Ian ground out. "Ye worry me no end. Go back to Boston or stay in Philadelphia—just keep your brown hide out of the South." Ian dropped his voice as he turned back to the Quaker. "Convince him to give over the notion of freeing slaves, for his own good. What can one man hope to do?"

Eden smiled at that. "Nothing, if he does not try."

Overcome with a sense of failure in the parting, Ian studied Thomas, who was staring down the road, face as shuttered as any born slave's. He wasn't gazing northward, where his journey would take him, but back along the road they'd traveled, as if he'd taken Eden's words to heart.

"Thomas," Ian said, warning in his tone. Their ruse was known. Even if Ian wanted him there, Thomas wasn't welcome at Mountain Laurel. His kin had made that clear. As had Thomas his opinion of Ian.

Thomas had made no secret of his disappointment upon learning of Ian's marriage to Judith—or of his resentment for Seona's sake—accusing Ian of having fulfilled every dark prediction gleaned from the slave narrative he once more carried in his satchel. But he hadn't

528

wasted breath arguing to remain. Ian had thought him come to his senses at last, at least about his own disastrous sojourn in the South. Now he found himself nearly as certain Thomas's equanimity on that point had hidden another agenda—the same one he'd had all along.

Of the two of them, Thomas's had always been the more reckless courage.

But responsibility for this friend once closer than a brother was passing out of Ian's hands. He'd have to trust Benjamin Eden to do the sensible thing.

Aware of Ian's scrutiny and likely his doubts—if not his guilt—Thomas pressed his mouth in a tight line before he murmured, *"Aonaibh ri chéile."*

Let us unite. The embittered reminder shot heat into Ian's face. Regret and frustration choked whatever words of warning, or farewell, he might have made.

Thomas glanced down from the saddle, his gaze cold, unreadable. "I cannot imagine we ever will unite. Still . . . reckon I owe you a shilling, Mastah Ian."

Home after days on horseback, Ian paused outside his room, halted by the all-too-familiar sound of Judith's retching. He started to open the door, but Lucinda Cameron's voice on its other side froze him: "You've made a habit of losing your breakfast—supper nigh as often—for how long now? All of April to my reckoning, and here it is May. You're thin as a rail."

"I've been too ill to keep anything down."

"When was your last monthly?"

"Mama."

"For heaven's sake, you're a woman married."

"I—I don't remember. Why?"

"Because, Judith, you aren't ill. You're *breeding*. My guess is three months gone."

Ian didn't hear his wife's reply. He barely made it to the top of the stairs before his knees gave way and he sat down.

When at last he descended, Lily was coming from his uncle's room, tray in hand. Taking her by the arm, he steered her into the warming room. Garden greenery soiled her apron. She smelled of mint and rosemary.

"Master Hugh has a cough starting," she said. "I'm on my way to make a chest plaster. There something ye need, Mister Ian?"

"Aye, Lily. I need ye to tell me what my uncle's choice has done to ye."

Light from the warming room window should have shown her age. She had to be past five and thirty, yet her complexion was still smooth, the bones beneath carved of a timeless grace. A grace with a wildness to it, alluring, mystifying. What power over a man might she have wielded with that allure, twenty years ago?

"I see ye caring for him, day after day," he pressed. "Ye're bound to it—I know that. But is it out of that duty alone? D'ye care for the man at all?"

Lily set the tray on a sideboard and regarded him. "No, Mister Ian. Not in the way ye mean."

He searched the dark depths of her eyes but could read nothing of the soul they shielded. Was this what he could one day expect of Seona, should he make the choice his uncle had made? This calm, unreachable acceptance? Did he risk losing her piecemeal by not letting her go? Letting *them* go? Or could he somehow raise the child as his own, fully acknowledged, without taking it from Seona? Treat them with dignity, keep them near—but separate, for Judith's sake?

" 'Cast out the bondwoman and her child.' "

He drew breath, staring at Lily. "What did ye say?"

" 'Tis what will be said, Mister Ian, if ye do what it is I reckon ye're thinking of doing. There'll be some with brass enough to say it to your face. Ye maybe have the courage to face that. Seona may have it. But what of Miss Judith or her child?"

Judith's child. Lily knew; midwife that she was, she could read the signs as well as could his aunt.

"Lily. Did ye never think of running away? Of taking Seona and leaving?"

The sigh that came from Seona's mother might

have started at the root of her soul. "I came to the edge of doing it a hundred times."

That caught him by surprise. "What stopped ye?"

Lily regarded him with something like compassion, and he saw the choice had been simpler for her than for anyone else caught in this tangle of bondage and kinship.

"Where were we to go," she asked, "the two of us alone?"

Hunkered in the tree-shadows under the oaks, Ian watched his uncle's slaves file toward the flowering apple orchard, lying like a ribbon of mist beyond the cabins. They moved in silence, carrying no visible burdens. He crept to the edge of the oak grove in time to see the last of them swallowed in a fall of blossoms. He'd no notion where they were bound in the middle of the night; yet stronger than suspicion or alarm, the ever-present ache of isolation swelled at their going. They were a circle closed, into which he could never find welcome. Even his child was part of that circle. One of them.

No longer seeing the night around him, Ian stared down the passage of years at a curly-haired youth, fair and clean-limbed, with a face uncannily his own. But the eyes that gave him back his stare were cold, the features blank. The lad turned his back, showing him a livid web of scars.

A breeze stirred, clammy against his skin.

Alone at the edge of the grove, Ian watched the last of the apple blossoms disturbed by the slaves' passing drift to the ground like snow.

Before the final one settled, he'd risen to follow.

He emerged from the orchard alone, thinking he'd lost them among the gnarled boughs and silvery petals, until a flash of movement caught his eye—there and gone in the starlight. The slaves had issued from the orchard farther to the west, making for the ridge.

Guided by a glimpse of shirt or kerchief, he crept in their wake. The ground sloped upward as he snagged through thickets, blundered through spiderwebs, tripped over roots. Higher up the ridge, the pinpoints of a pierced-tin lantern sprang to light. The figure in the lead held it aloft to illumine a footpath, which they'd been following all along.

Scratched and muddied, Ian made his way to it and afterward gained ground on the slaves, strung out along the upward-winding path. From the front of the procession, a male voice chanted low. Snatches floated back, borne on the breeze that whispered through the laurels.

> *"I know moon-rise, I know star-rise,*
> *Lay this body down.*
> *I walk in the moonlight, I walk in the*
> *   starlight*
> *To lay this body down."*

He followed, passing through the insect-humming dark, echoes of half-forgotten Scripture thrumming an undertone through the chant: *And the Lord spake unto Moses . . . say unto Pharaoh . . . Let my people go, that they may serve me.* A sense of being swept along in the wake of exodus lay heavy on him, though he was sure this nocturnal wandering hadn't to do with some sort of mass escape. Not of the body.

Something stirred in his chest, unnamed, insistent. One more ache among the many. He gave himself to the pull of it, ceasing to wonder.

> *"I go to the judgment in the evenin' of the*
>   *day,*
> *When I lay this body down."*

They were come to a level stretch, a notch running behind a shoulder of the ridge. The slaves had reached the farthest headstone before he recognized the place. The graveyard of his kin. Beyond it the lantern veered aside. The slaves passed shadowlike into a clearing separated from the burying ground by a scrim of dogwood spotted with blossoms, disembodied in the starlit dark. Discarded petals lay on the ground, a shroud for the dead.

Ian cast about for a place of concealment. There

was none, save the stones rising from the damp earth in straight-sided ranks. He crept forward, chose a grave, hunkered behind it.

A fire was lit—so quickly there must have been wood laid by for the purpose, sheltered from the damp—while Ally seated his grandfather on a stump chair. The slaves gathered near, ringing the small blaze, now and then one of them feeding it more fuel.

After a time Malcolm prayed, though few heads bowed and fewer eyes closed. Before the old man ceased speaking, a hum like bee-drone rose. A rich alto voice—Naomi's—crooned a low note, and the singing began again.

"Jesus Christ is made to me
All I need, all I need;
He alone is all my plea.
He is all I need."

It had been Ian's impression that the slaves sang unreservedly at the autumn's corn-shucking. He'd mistaken skill and long practice for abandon. This blending of voices, clapping hands, stomping feet, was unlike anything he'd have thought them capable of, restrained as they were by day.

His surprise reproached him. He'd seen early on Seona's spirit struggling to free itself, finding outlet in her clandestine drawing. Had he assumed she was the only one among his uncle's slaves who possessed such hunger?

There was Ally, voice booming like a drum as he shuffled to the song's rhythm. Beside him Naomi swayed with palms raised high. Malcolm, normally stooped, had risen to his feet and now stood straight as a garden pale as he sang, doubtless a sacrifice of praise.

There were the field hands, Pete and Munro. Across from them Lily, graceful as her name as she harmonized with Seona.

> *"Jesus is my all in all,*
> *All I need, all I need,*
> *While He keeps I cannot fall,*
> *He is all I need."*

These were the floodwaters dammed behind the masks they showed his kin. Washed in the flow, an urge came over Ian to join in, to lift both hand and voice.

He didn't. The one was heavy as lead, the other strangled mute.

> *"He redeemed me when He died,*
> *All I need, all I need,*
> *I with Him was crucified,*
> *He is all I need."*

The headstone that hid him smelled of decay. He longed to recoil to his feet, plunge in among the living, soak up whatever it was that gave them joy. That gave *her* joy.

Sparks from the fire fountained upward, obscuring his view of Seona. When they vanished, his chest constricted at sight of the growing bulge beneath the knotted tails of her shawl. Seona shut her eyes and joined in a new song.

> *"You may talk of my name all that you*
> *please and carry my name abroad,*
> *But I really do believe I'm a child of God*
> *as I walk in the heavenly road.*
> *O, won't you go with me? O, won't you go*
> *with me?*
> *For to keep our garments clean."*

What was it his uncle's slaves grasped of the Almighty to make them throw off their fetters and worship like this? How much could they understand, forbidden even to read? Ian knew Holy Writ well enough, had spent plenty of Sabbaths in a pew. Yet it hadn't been enough to capture him, heart and soul. Instead he'd run from the Almighty, thinking his failings an insurmountable barrier to grace.

The vision that had propelled him on this midnight trek flashed through his mind, this time with deeper revelation. Had it been his and Seona's future child grown he'd seen . . . or was *he* the lash-marked boy, the son who turned from a longing Father in whose image he was made?

Perhaps two fathers, only one of them on earth.

"Da," he whispered to them both and bowed his head against the gravestone while the slaves sang on.

Seona got up off her knees to find only Malcolm left in the clearing. He must have sent the others on without a word while she'd been lost in prayer and weeping. The fire had sunk to embers.

"Mama and the others go and leave you?" She held out a shawl-draped arm. "Reckon we can make shift to get down off this ridge, if we take a torch."

Malcolm made no move to rise. "The Almighty and I have further business tonight, lass. But mind ye take a stick and beat the path as ye go. There be snakes."

"Who's gonna knock those snakes in the head for you? Or you aiming to sprout wings and fly down off this ridge?"

In the fire's dying glow Malcolm smiled, stubborn as the stump he sat on. "Go on now. Though did ye lay a few sticks to the fire first, I'd be obliged."

No use arguing. Sooner she did as he bid, sooner they could both get off that ridge. She laid the wood and left, but she didn't go far. Malcolm might be set on solitary praying, but she wasn't about to leave him there with a thousand roots and stones ready to throw him down in the dark and break his old bones. Never mind snakes.

A mosquito whined near her ear. She swiped at it. Waited.

The baby grew restless. Her bladder was full enough to take unkindly to being squirmed against. She was about to head back to the fire when Malcolm's voice lifted.

" 'O, won't you go with me? O, won't you go with me?' "

It was a comfort, his creaky voice chanting that song—but he did go on for a tiresome time, repeating the line like he was calling someone to the fire.

A beat before the shadow rose up from the graves, she understood what was happening and clapped a hand to her mouth to keep from blurting Ian's name. As if it rang like a bell inside her, the baby kicked hard. She squeezed her thighs tight, willing it still.

Malcolm was looking straight at the standing shadow. " 'O, won't you go with me? For to keep our garments clean.' "

Ian must have been outside the cabins again when they started for the ridge. How many nights since he caught her outside had he waited there? But if he'd come up the ridge for her, why stay behind after she pretended to leave? He could have caught her on the path by now and . . .

Her heart seized with hope. She didn't know why he'd come, but she hoped she knew why he stayed.

Malcolm stopped singing and stared into the dark beyond the fire's reach. "Ye aim to keep me waiting the night long, Mister Ian? Or will ye come into the light?"

Not a twitch from the shadow hovering among the graves.

"The Father's been waitin' for ye to come home. Spirit's calling. The Son blazed the trail. All ye need do is walk it."

There was a tussle going on, unseen. It made the night air press down, damp and heavy as a coming storm. Then with the snapping of twigs the tension broke.

Ian stepped into the clearing.

Seona's heart wrenched at sight of him in the firelight, tall and drawn, hair tangled, shoulders hunched in what she read as shame. Then his head lifted and in his face was something else, bright and fragile as a nest-egg. He folded up before Malcolm, going to his knees.

"Tell me, Malcolm. Tell me of your Jesus."

Malcolm showed less surprise than she might have done, had Ian Cameron put that question to her. *Your* Jesus?

"Surely, Mister Ian, ye've heard the gospel afore now?"

Firelight bathed Ian's cheek, shining off his

tears. "Aye, but I want to hear it from ye. Tell it to me the once more, as *ye* know it. Please."

Turning her back on the two men she loved most in the world, Seona made her way down the ridge alone. She wanted to be at Ian's side, to lay her hands on his head and welcome him into a new kindred. But it wasn't her place. Nothing that happened in that clearing was going to change that.

Her foot caught on a root and she landed hard on her knees, scraping her palms. The pain jarred loose a sob, but she stood and kept on, walking away from Ian one step at a time, clinging to thought of the arms that welcomed him home this night. Those same arms held her too, and no height or depth, no man or angel, was going to change that either.

PART VI
June–October 1794

"O to Grace how great a Debtor daily I'm constrained to be! Let Thy Goodness, like a Fetter, bind my wandering Heart to Thee." I stood a lad beside you and sang those Words—or pretended to—more times than I can recall. They were yours then. Now I can in Truth call them mine.

38

Just in from the fields, Ian barely glimpsed the departing rider before the curving lane took the familiar form from sight. He washed quickly in a bucket outside the stable, stripped off his work frock, and went up to the house in his shirtsleeves. His uncle's door was open, his uncle abed, Lily seated in a chair drawn close.

Ian advanced into the room, frowning between them. "Uncle, was that your solicitor just leaving?"

Uncle Hugh made no answer. Lily rose and came to Ian, urging him toward the door.

"Lily, I need to speak to—"

"Ye can't, Mister Ian, unless ye want to speak of Aidan. His mind's cast back."

Ian threw a vexed look at the bed, recognizing the haze in his uncle's eyes. Had the solicitor found him so? As Lily shut the door behind them, he asked, "Why wasn't I sent for when the man arrived?"

"I was with them," she began, but footsteps on the front stair drew Ian's attention. When he turned back, Lily had fled catfooted to the back door and was gone in a swish of homespun.

The skirt that skimmed toward him from the front stairs was made of finer stuff. Though the gown's line was long and loose, its tiny puffed sleeves bared Rosalyn's arms nearly to the shoulder. As she reached him, Ian got an eyeful of its neckline, cut low and gathered in tight below the bosom. While he wouldn't call the pale fabric sheer, she clearly wore no normal stays beneath it.

He wrenched his eyes up. A smirk curved Rosalyn's mouth. "Admiring my new gown? It's a Grecian style."

"Is there no more to it? Have ye a kerchief or a shawl or . . . something?"

Rosalyn's brittle laughter broke off when he blocked her attempt to step past him. "Pardon me, Cousin. I wish to speak with Papa Hugh."

"To what purpose?"

"I've purpose enough. Let me pass."

"I meant there's no point."

"Oh." Her face fell in disappointment. "One of his spells?"

"Not that I'd have let ye in to see him regardless. Rosalyn, the gown's unseemly."

She wrinkled her nose at his sweat-darkened shirt. "Which are you then, pot or kettle?"

No surprise the smell of honest work offended her. "Is there something *I* can do for ye?"

Rosalyn raised her chin. "I meant to do something for you."

"And what is that?" he asked warily.

"Relieve our family of this wretched state of

affairs you've created. I mean to ask Papa Hugh for Seona as a wedding gift. She'll come to Chesterfield as my maid. You can keep the child. I suppose you mean Judith to tend it alongside hers?"

Had Ian not been stunned immobile, he might have slapped her.

She speaks from the bitter well of her upbringing, and you are not her judge. In that suspended moment, the admonition seemed to come from a source apart from himself. Clinging to restraint, he said, "Ye'll ask my uncle no such thing."

Rosalyn arched a brow. "Afraid he'll oblige me?"

"He has more decency than that."

"And I do not, you mean? You've thought the worst of me from the beginning."

"Rosalyn—"

"Oh, Cousin. It no longer signifies." She dismissed his opinion with a wave. "But so you know, I wouldn't have taken Seona away to spite you. I'd have done it to spare my sister."

"And if ye did," Ian said, "it would be ye in Judith's place. Or d'ye not know at all the man ye're marrying?"

Spots of pink bloomed in Rosalyn's cheeks. "Of course Gideon would sire half a dozen pickaninnies on her! What is that to me?"

"I'd think it would be something to ye." He'd

spoken with a gentleness that surprised even himself, given the shock that had coursed through him at her admission. It certainly caught her off guard; he saw the glitter of tears in her eyes, but she let not a one of them spill.

"I don't give a fig how many slaves Gideon beds, because he'll never want anything so preposterous as to *marry* one or claim one of their brood as his own."

Anger, astonishingly, had gone clean out of him. What remained was pity—for the facade she was prepared to wear lifelong in exchange for wealth, comfort, and position. "Ye've made your choice, Rosalyn. Let me make mine."

Her mouth curled in disdain. "You and Papa Hugh—cut from the same cloth, the pair. You'll pretend to give up Seona, but you won't, and you'll sacrifice everyone's happiness on the altar of your pining heart. And that, Cousin, is a greater wickedness than anything Gideon can lay claim to. So go ahead. Keep your doxy tucked up in her cabin, favor Seona and her brood as I know you will, and while you're at it, crush my sister's heart—though she's ninny enough to let you do it and bear her shame in silence."

She flounced away in her revealing gown, returning down the passage. Ian hadn't moved when she turned to mount the stairs, a waiting target for her parting shot: "I hate this place. It never was my home. Aside from Mama, I'm finished with the lot of you!"

After a wash and change of clothes, he stretched out on the bed—and smelled it as his head touched the pillow. *Roses.* The crash of memories brought him full awake. Fishing beneath the pillow, his fingers closed on the fragrance's source: a muslin pouch, cinched and tied.

What misguided notion had possessed Judith to scent their bed with roses?

The thing that tied it gave away its purpose: a double lock of hair, gold and mouse-brown, twisted together. A love charm. Had she snipped the lock of his hair while he slept?

You'll pretend to give up Seona, but you won't.

He'd not let Seona near Gideon Pryce for a moment, could he prevent it, much less surrender her defenseless to the man's appetites day and night. But were his own motives in wanting her near more pure?

Cast out the bondwoman and her child.

He couldn't. He hadn't the legal right, not until his uncle's death. Had his uncle ever petitioned the General Assembly? If not, he could press him again to do so. But the child would have to leave North Carolina with Seona. His child.

He flinched from the notion.

"What, then?" he said aloud, desperate for the answer even as he feared it. "What must I do?"

That answer dropped like a stone into his storm-tossed spirit, sending out ripples that left still water behind. He was to do nothing, as Rosalyn predicted he would do. He was to wait.

Could he have heard right? Or was this merely what he wanted to hear?

It was still there, clear, emphatic. *Wait.*

Was this how the Almighty spoke to a man? This small voice, this peace that made no earthly sense?

He was still holding the pouch when Judith came into the room. Laden with a tray, she turned her back to shut the door, giving him time to shove the charm under his pillow. He started to get up to help her, but she set the tray carefully on the bed.

"I didn't mean to disturb your rest. I thought we'd sup in here."

A simple meal, soup and bread—but he wouldn't be forced to sit across from her sister at table. For that he was grateful.

"Are ye well this evening?" he asked her, constrained and formal; she appeared tired as she drew up a chair.

"Mama says the sickness should have passed by now." She gave an embarrassed shrug and spread a napkin over her knees, then eyed the soup with some trepidation.

Ian reached for the bread to break it. "Try some of this first. Lily hasn't told ye anything's wrong, has she?"

Holding a chunk of bread, Judith peered at him over the rim of her cup. "Would she tell me?"

"Aye. She would. Lily wouldn't do anything to harm ye or the child."

The child. He hadn't yet called it *his* aloud.

Favor Seona and her brood as I know you will . . . Rosalyn had joined them regardless, it seemed, still speaking bruising truths into his soul. He did his best to banish her but ate with little conversation for her sister, who seemed content with the silence. Before Judith finished her soup, Ian lay back on the pillows, the scent of roses sweetly painful, but roused at the clink of dinnerware and took hold of Judith's hand.

"Leave it. Would ye like me to read to ye?"

Her face brightened. "Burns?"

Ian smiled wryly but capitulated. Judith liked him to read the man's romantical works, *Poems, Chiefly in the Scottish Dialect*, with his faint accent ridiculously broadened. "I can manage a verse or twa. But first . . ."

She was reaching for the volume when he withdrew the love charm. Her eyes held mortification. "Oh . . . you weren't meant to find that."

"I know. I'm sorry ye felt ye had to resort to old wives' foolery to . . ." *Gain my affection,* he couldn't say, reproached by the yearning in her eyes. "How did ye know what to use?"

"Maisy's mama, back in Virginia—she was a

conjure woman among Daddy's slaves. Maisy told me what to put in it. It's not just roses." Judith bit her lip, misery in the sag of her shoulders.

Ian leaned across the bed and brushed a straggle of hair from her face. He didn't ask what else was in the pouch. "We'll find our way without such things. All right?"

Judith raised her eyes, searching his face. Firming her small chin, she took the muslin pouch and with unaccustomed decisiveness threw it onto the hearth. A symbolic gesture; they'd have no fire in the room again for months. He'd make certain the thing was gone by morning.

Despite the cold hearth there was a new warmth in the room. Outside the day was fading. Ian lit a candle while Judith settled on the bed.

"I marked where we left off. 'My Father Was a Farmer.' "

"Aye, right." Ian lay beside her. Pitching his voice to mimic his mam's Lowland speech, he began the poem of the son who left his father's farm to seek an easy fortune. " 'My father was a farmer upon the Carrick border, O / And carefully he bred me in decency and order, O . . . ' "

In the middle of the fifth stanza, as the son left off his failed schemes and returned to work the soil—*to plough and sow, to reap and mow*—Judith interrupted him.

"Do you like being a farmer, Ian?"

"Aye, lassie. I like it weel." He'd answered flippantly but hearing the words out of his mouth knew them for true. He stared at his hand, splayed on the page, noting new calluses from spade, ax, and plow. Minding the slaves' lighter steps coming in from the field that evening, he said, "Today's Saturday."

"And tomorrow the Sabbath," Judith said. "Though there's no meeting for us to attend."

"There is . . . if ye wouldn't mind a bit of manure on your shoes."

"You mean the Reynolds'?"

He'd surprised her with the notion, but why not? He'd yet to tell John of what happened on the ridge, the night he followed Seona, Malcolm, and the others. Time he did so.

"Would ye come with me tomorrow to worship with our neighbors?"

Tiredness lifted from Judith's face. "I'd like that, Ian. Yes."

39

Seona set the basket of herb cuttings on the worktable, then waddled to a corner. Sweat streamed down her face as she lowered herself onto a stool. Her temples throbbed with the heat. Her back had pained her fierce since the wee hours and her belly felt tight as a prized hogshead.

"Mama, I want this baby out of me."

Lily put aside a wiped plate and came to kneel in front of her.

Naomi dropped pone into a pan, already preparing supper though dinner was barely past. "You hungry, Seona?"

"No room in me for a bite." Wincing at a pain beneath her ribs, she pressed the spot until her belly shifted. "How can it move in there?"

Lily's eyes held sympathy, but there was no more relief to be had from the fidgety little so-and-so bent on kicking her insides to jelly than there was from the swelter of a July afternoon.

"Is he moving as much as a few days ago?"

He. "It's a boy, Mama?"

"We'll see." Lily gave her a secretive smile, then waited for her question to be answered.

Seona sighed. "Maybe not quite as much. Why?"

"They don't move as much right before their time. Sometimes," she added at Seona's pointed look. "It's always different, girl-baby. Is the pain like it's been the past few days?"

"Just the backache." She didn't bother saying how much worse it was today, how she longed to have someone knead her back like bread dough. Lily's hands moved over her belly in circles, pressing gently. Soon those hands would catch her baby—a comfort, but one as thin as skin. Underneath it, fear stirred, as rooted inside her as Ian's child. She closed her eyes.

"Give her some water. She's red as a beet." Naomi's voice seemed to come from far away.

Lily pressed a horn cup against her hand. Seona took it, drank long, and came up for air like someone drowning. Lily took her hand and guided it low, to where her belly curved under. "Here's the head, turned and ready. Not long now."

Naomi's voice floated above them. *Malcolm needed to come in for his dinner afore the flies swarmed it. Would Lily step out and give a holler? Had Esther eaten afore she went to the field with dinner for the hands and Mister Ian? Were Miss Judith and the mistress done at the house table? What a job of work keeping hungry mouths fed . . .*

Seona had seen Ian heading out at daybreak with the field hands to sucker the tobacco plants. She pictured him working down the rows, skin browning and hair bleaching in the sun, toiling for a future she couldn't begin to hope in. Where did she fit into that future? Where did her child fit? Her chest ached with a love so mingled with grief she feared they'd never untangle. Like skeins of wool snarled together, red and black . . . blood and dark waters flowing away to streams and rivers and an ocean she would never see . . .

Her head fell forward, yanking her back from a doze. The baby moved, stretching her until she felt ready to split. Pain burned above her hips. Voices spoke around her, the sound like tumbling water, like the falls in the hollow where the birches grew. Yellow shimmered across her vision, dazzling as those leaves in the sun.

The touch of a wet cloth on her face shocked her eyes open. Hands grasped her, holding her upright.

"Are ye all right, *a leannan*?"

Seona blinked into a face framed in lambs' wool, felt the dry touch of old man's skin on her hand, her face. "Malcolm? Did I swoon?"

"Like to do so again 'less you leave this stifling kitchen." Naomi thrust into view, hands planted on broad hips. "I asked Miss Judith could you go down by the creek for a spell. She said—"

"I said it would be fine."

That voice cleared the last of her daze. Naomi

stepped aside and there was Miss Judith, white-faced under her garden hat, setting down the dirty plates she'd brought from their table herself.

Lily and Naomi thanked her. Seona kept her eyes lowered until the scuff of well-shod soles told her Miss Judith had gone.

Ian ate with his uncle's field hands in the tree-shade above the farthest tobacco field, admiring the view down the green rows stretching nigh to the far-off creek-bottom. Esther was gone, scampering back over the heat-shimmered fields like a rabbit to its burrow. In addition to the usual fare, the girl had brought pastries, tiny pies bursting with sugared apples. Enough for all. Naomi could cook a toad to perfection, but her pies were something to transport a man. The field hands had whooped at the sight.

Ian gave thanks as he finished his dinner, hearing Pete, Will, and Munro already back at their labors, voices lifted in song. A few yards off, Ally bent to snap off the suckers—extra unwanted stems—and stuff them into the sack dragged behind him, big head covered by a kerchief, like the one Ian wore beneath his hat.

After the suckering, more work waited. They'd cleared new acreage before the planting. The mature trees had been girdled the previous year, making the grubbing easier. The underbrush was piled for burning, larger trees rolled together, awaiting his sorting eye. He'd noted a maple he wanted milled, maybe for a cradle. They'd be needing cradles. And more desks. Edward Stoddard had taken the second batch away in June, the day after Rosalyn's wedding.

Waving off an onslaught of gnats, Ian set to work along his row, the slaves' singing a hum on the blistering air.

> *"Stop an' let me tell you what Samson done,*
> *He looked at the lion an' the lion run,*
> *But Samson killed that lion dead*
> *And the bees made honey in the lion's head."*

Their blended voices made Ian aware of how solitary his existence had become, though he was surrounded by kin and his uncle's slaves from sunup to sundown. He'd turned inward, straining for the faintest echo of a guiding word, unwilling to move lest it be in a wrong direction. Like the summer heat, his inaction weighed on everyone. At night the very timbers of the house seemed to hold their breath in apprehension, awaiting answer to the question: what would he do when the child came?

> *"Samson said, 'An' if I had my way,*
> *I'd tear this buildin' down.' "*

For a time Ian stopped thinking and focused on the work, stooping, grasping, snapping, eyes peeled for black widow spiders, ears tuned for a canebrake's rattle. The smell of tar and leaf. Heat pressing on his sweating back. The next plant down the row, and the next . . .

From the corner of his eye he saw her, a distant shimmer in the baking air, wading the shallows near an old willow tree that leaned weeping curtains over the creek.

His rhythm faltered. He reached for a sprout to snap and his hand came away with a good broad leaf that should have been left to mature. He stuffed it into the sack and straightened, staring. Why was she so far from the house?

"Mama say it be a trial for her, this heat." Ally had come up even with him, one row over, face glistening in the sun.

Ian blinked, blinded by the sting of his own sweat. "It's a trial for all that breathe."

The singing had stopped. The others had seen him looking—and the object of his interest.

Ian forced himself to turn from the wading figure, but as he did, the memory of Seona's name, chiseled in weed-grown granite, flashed across his mind. He was helpless to stop death should it come for her or the child. If it came, it would be soon.

Since that night on the ridge he'd promised himself—and the Almighty—he would keep his distance, but there were things he needed to say to her, things he wasn't prepared to live out his days on earth having waited too late to speak.

He squinted through the wavering heat. Listening.

Do not fear to go to her.

He stared down the long field at her distant figure, testing the impulse. Could it be?

Go to her.

Ian untied the sack at his waist. He stripped off his gloves. He made his way to where he'd left his rifle, removed his field tunic—so tar-coated it nearly kept its shape—slung the rifle over his shoulder, and started down the slope without a backward glance.

It was a long trudge through the heat, down through the tobacco and across a fallow field that ran level to the creek, each stride kicking up dust and grasshoppers, heart winging heavenward in broken snatches of prayer.

Speak through me. Comfort her. We're dry, thirsty. Send Your rain. . . .

At the water's edge Seona shaded her eyes and saw him coming. He made for a point upstream near the willow's shade, where insects overhung the water in fretful clouds. Setting the rifle on the rocks, he untied the kerchief from his brow and used it to wash, tasting salt and dust and bitterness as the water ran down his face.

A breeze stirred the willow. The broad creek

rippled over stones. The air smelled of baking earth. Surprised by distant thunder, he saw in the west a cloud bank building. Felt the weight of it in the air. Rain coming.

From his cupped hands he drank, then shouldered the rifle and stood.

She'd washed her hair in the creek and left it uncovered. It had grown since he'd seen it, the longest of the springy curls pulled to her shoulders by their damp weight.

He came on, pulse going at a gallop.

She waded to the bank, clad in her shift, and halted in the shade of an overhanging maple to watch his approach.

"I know what happened on the ridge," she said. "I'm so glad."

They sat on the maple's exposed roots, side by side, but not touching.

"Seona, I need to say a thing to ye." He read the joy in her eyes. Sorrow, too, like the amber mingled with the green. "What was meant for evil, God will turn for good."

"Did you mean to do evil by me?"

"No," he said with feeling. "But I did. And grieve that I did. I'd grieve the more if what I've done caused ye to mistrust the Almighty or to doubt He has good plans for ye. He does, Seona. For me. For all of us. Ye tried to tell me but I wouldn't listen. I wanted what I wanted, thought

I knew what was best, and found a way to make it happen. But I understand it now, what ye tried to tell me—or I'm learning to. *His* will be done. In the end, that will prove to be what's best."

She looked away, leaving him wondering could she accept such words from him, belated as they were. She more than he had to bear the consequences of his rushing ahead of God. He would help her do so, however he could.

But keep me from bringing my wife more pain.

He passed a hand over his hair, dislodging the thong that bound it, then noticed she cupped something in her hand. "What's that ye've found?"

Her fingers uncurled. An arrowhead no bigger than his thumbnail lay in her upturned palm. He took it, turning it over. Its flat sides were silken, polished by the creek's flow, but the tapered edges and tiny notches still showed the chiseled marks of its knapping.

"Ally used to spy those in the field or the creek and give them to me."

"I mind your wee basket." The breeze quickened, a murmur passing along the creek bank, leaping its waters and rushing away. Thunder rolled up from the west. He closed his fist over the arrowhead and sought for words. "I pray daily for the Almighty to show me what I must do, how to right my wrongs against ye. I've kept my distance because—"

A damselfly darted past his nose, startling him. It landed on the slope of Seona's belly, where it glinted like an azure jewel, gossamer wings folded in repose. The words he'd meant to say knotted in his throat. *Because of the vows that bind me to Judith. Because I couldn't come near ye until now and be sure of holding to them, even in my mind. And if not for Him who restrains me, I'd break those chains with the strength of Samson and flee with ye this moment.*

The sultry breeze lifted Seona's hair. The damselfly flitted away.

The gulf between them ached.

"It wasn't you stole me away," she said, gazing at the rising clouds. "That was someone else's evildoing."

"I ought never to have doubted. If only . . ." *If only.* He clenched his jaw, alarmed at his soul's propensity for going its headstrong way. The choice was his to make, moment by wrenching moment. *Not my will.*

Seona's hands moved over the child, then rubbed at her lower back. She appeared to be in discomfort.

"Have ye thought on a name?" he asked.

She glanced at the crown of his head. "Gabriel?"

Laughter came as a relief. "Dark or fair, the bairn's bound to have ringlets."

"Poor thing." She lifted a hand to her hair in

563

mock dismay. Short as it was, it seemed to spring out from her scalp, the coils dancing wildly on the breeze as they dried.

As he gave her back the arrowhead, thunder reverberated in a clap. With it Seona winced. He thought her merely startled, until the pain in her contracted features registered. Pain and dawning awareness.

"Seona?"

As the last of the thunder rolled away, she stared at him, eyes dilated to a blaze of green.

"Ian . . . I need Mama."

40

They made it a dozen steps before her water broke, soaking her shift. Seona sucked in breath, clearly gripped in pain. Ian kept his arm about her, his heartbeat thudding in panic, as the first pelt of rain struck his back. Thunder rolled. "The house?"

She shook her head. "Too far."

He fought a rising panic, trying to think. They needed shelter, fast. *The willow.*

He dropped his rifle and, grunting with the effort, swept her into his arms and headed back along the creek. Hair whipped across his face and stuck there, plastered by the rain. The heavens opened as he reached the willow, soaking them in seconds. Seona turned her face into his chest as he shouldered through clinging, silver-green fronds.

Below the willow's tangled roots, the bank formed a sandy slope, wide enough to lay her down. The air was close, thick with the tang of rotting leaves and the storm's coppery scent, but the tree's canopy filtered the rain. He touched her face, brushing back straggles of wet hair. She grasped his hand as if to push him away, then clung to him.

"I need *Mama*."

So did he. Could he make it to the house and back? Was there time? Could he leave her?

Thunder rolled over them, near enough to tremble his flesh. As it faded, his head jerked up. He'd heard another sound amidst the rumbling. A voice.

"I'll be right back." Bursting through the willow's lancet screen, boots churning sand and stone, he saw Ally coming through the gray downpour, shirt plastered to his hulking frame, dinner-plate hands cupped at his mouth.

"Mister Ian! I come down to see—"

"The bairn's coming!" Ian flew toward him, slipping, staggering. "Get Lily! And, Ally—hurry!"

Ally halted, gaped, then turned to lumber back along the creek, picking up speed until he was running. Ian retrieved his rifle, then thrashed his way back through the willow. Seona's face was contorted in pain, shift clinging wetly to her belly and thighs.

"Ally's gone for your mother. I'm staying." Lightning split the sky. Seconds later, thunder cracked. Ian counted the increasing seconds between flash and rumble. Counted the decreasing seconds between her pains. "How is it come so sudden?"

Seona released a gasp. "My back's pained me bad since early morn. I didn't realize . . . Will Mama get here in time?"

He didn't know. "Whether she does or not, we'll manage." He shoved wet hair from his face, trying for a reassuring smile. "I've seen this done, aye?"

Her eyes melted into his, full of memory—until her mouth compressed over another pang.

Ian scoured his own memories for everything Seona had done for Cecily Reynold—most of it had involved a kettle and soap and a fire and a deal more comfort than they had to hand. He'd need to tie the cord with something once the babe was out. Hair straggled into his face and again he pushed it back. What had happened to—?

"Here." Seona uncurled a fist to show him the bit of crumpled leather, tangled around the arrowhead. Never asking how she'd come by it, he took the whang and bound back his dripping hair. He'd know where it was when the time came.

"What can I do for ye now?"

Seona twisted and rose up on her elbows. "I want to sit up."

The slope of the bank was wrong for it. His thoughts raced through possibilities and came up with . . . *sand*. He scooped it with his hands, piling it behind her in a makeshift bolster.

"That help?"

She lay back on the incline, nodding. Brushing sand from his palms, he knelt in front of her. She grasped his forearms, fingers digging. Rain drummed around them, pattering on his head. He hovered over her, giving her the shelter of his body. A dozen more pangs crested before her features sharpened with purpose; she was bearing down.

Panic seized him. "Already?"

She nodded, lips pressed too tight to speak. He wrenched at his shirt, yanked the sodden fabric over his head, and spread it between her thighs. She clasped her hands beneath her knees and bore down, crying out for the first time, a bone-deep grind of a cry that juddered through him. He saw the bairn's head. "Seona—it's coming!"

She moaned low in her throat and sank back against the sand. He waited for the next push. And waited. Seona sank her teeth into her lip but showed no evidence of strain.

"Ye're nigh there!"

Her body was rigid, fighting the urge, refusing the final push.

Lightning flashed. Truth struck him with the force of the following thunder. He gripped her shoulders. "I will not take this child from ye. D'ye hear me? Look at me!" She opened anguished eyes to him. "I will never take it from ye, Seona. I swear. Now push!"

Tears spilled down her cheeks, but with the next pain she bore down. Lightning flashed once more as Ian moved to cradle the emerging head. Seona pushed again as thunder rolled, loud as the cry tearing through her. Before the rumbling ceased, the bairn had slid into his hands.

"He's so *small*."

Seona raised her head, fixing him with incredulous eyes. "Small?"

Ian couldn't quell the grin he'd worn since placing their son into her arms. Though the bairn was properly severed from the cord that had bound them, Ian's breeches were scarlet from the blood that had gushed from the afterbirth he hadn't tied off correctly on his first try. Just now he didn't care. The bairn was out of her and they'd all survived the exodus.

"Look at him," she breathed.

"Aye." Splotched and wrinkled, puckered as last year's apples, still he was a bonny lad. A hand flailed, splayed like a tiny pink star. Ian caressed the tender palm with a fingertip, delighted when the bairn took hold. Seona closed her eyes, mouth working, tongue seeking moisture from dry lips. "Ye're thirsty."

Ian extricated himself from his son's grasp and went to the creek. As Seona drank from his cupped hands, the willow stirred around them, a silvery soughing that blended with the falling rain, the water's rushing flow. Ian's eyes were drawn back to his son, alive, breathing.

A touch on his bare shoulder stole his breath. Seona's fingertips traced the scars above his collarbone, the marks that scored his chest, the ugly gashes carved below the swell of his shoulder. She'd never seen them before. He raised a hand to finger the cropped hair clinging to her neck. Acknowledgment.

The ache in his throat made speech an effort. "I should try and make myself presentable. Right now I look like the one who birthed the bairn."

Kneeling at the creek's edge, he wrung out the kerchief to scrub his breeches, while behind him their son made noises like a kitten's mewl. Ian stilled, listening. He could have shouted for joy. Or wept with grief. In case either display was imminent, he stood and passed through the willow, ostensibly to see if Lily was in sight.

She wasn't. For the moment he was glad. Then he noticed the silence beyond the creek's rushing. The kitten-mewls had ceased. Seized with concern, he swept aside the leafy curtain, hurrying back to them. And halted to stare.

Seona had loosed the neck of her shift and put the child to her breast, pressed close in a soft-boned embrace, her features caught in an expression of tenderness deeper than he'd ever seen. He didn't move until she raised her eyes; then he came and knelt beside her and put his hand on his son's head, gently encompassing the tiny skull.

"Blood of my blood," he said. Seona's eyes flashed an agony of longing, then closed. He touched her, felt her trembling with exhaustion as she strained to support the bairn's weight. "Shall I hold him?"

Her eyes fluttered open. She hunched her shoulders over their son. "He ain't done sucking."

"Greedy wee mannie," Ian said gently. "I expect he's earned it."

Another quiver ran through her. "Ian . . . I'm cold."

The appeal tore at him. He'd no fire for her, no place dry for her to lie, naught to wrap her in but his bare arms. He dug away some of the sand from behind her, brushed himself clean, then settled her between his knees and eased his arms under the bairn, entwining them with hers.

Sweat sprang up between them, but the soft, wet rhythm of the child's sucking went undisturbed.

"Better?" *He* wasn't sure it was better. With his arms full of his son and his son's mother, it hurt him to breathe. But she nodded.

"Ye did well, Seona," he said against her wet hair.

"So did you."

He hadn't expected that. "Me?"

"You didn't swoon when his head crowned. Saw a new daddy do that once."

A quiver ran through them both, this time of laughter. His heart beat against the curve of her back. Over her shoulder, he watched the babe suckle.

Daddy. His hand caressed the crook of Seona's

arm and the soft little rump it nestled. They were a riot of hues: amber, mottled pink, sunburnt bronze. Of the three his skin was at present darkest, the hairs of his forearms bleached pale.

The hair. A sprinkling of flaxen swirls, damp from birth, capped his son's skull.

"Gabriel," he whispered. "What d'ye think? Will it suit?"

"Yes." Her legs trembled between his, muscles jerking in small spasms. A shudder ran through her.

"Be easy, Seona. I'll hold ye both safe."

A sigh went out of her as at last she surrendered herself and the child to his embrace. His skin was slick with moisture, the touch of her like the touch of his own flesh, the child's weight seeming there in his arms one second, gone the next, as though the boundaries between them had dissolved. Hollow as a gourd, replete as the swollen creek, he breathed the smells of rain-drenched earth, of sweat and birth and effort expended. He watched his son suckle himself into a stupor. Beyond the embowering willow, rain still pattered. Moisture trickled from his hair, running down his face no more heeded than his tears, even as footsteps on the stones beyond the willow's shelter reached his ears.

His uncle was among those waiting at the cabins when they came up from the creek. Ally carried

Seona. Lily walked between them, arms full of Ian's ruined shirt and her simples box. Ian carried his rifle and his son, cleanly wrapped in a tiny blanket prepared for him. Naomi hurried forward as Ally ducked into Seona's cabin, but Hugh Cameron hung back, staring at the bundle in Ian's arms.

"Uncle, I've a son—and ye a grandson. Would ye care to see him?" Save for a tightening of his mouth, his uncle's expression didn't alter. "Ye'll hear his name at least. It's Gabriel. Gabriel Robert Cameron."

Indifferent to paternal pronouncements, Gabriel Robert Cameron emitted an ominous squawk.

With a tightening in his chest, Ian gave his son into Lily's keeping, lingering for a last glimpse of the scowling little face. Then he stalked past them all—gawking slaves and stone-faced uncle alike. He might have swept past his wife as well had he not run headlong into her rounding the kitchen.

"Ian!" She stepped back, sweeping his bare chest and stained breeches with alarm. "I was resting during the storm and had to dress. Mama said . . ."

"It's a son," he told her, voice shaking. "They're both well. But I'm not fit company just now. Might ye have Maisy bring water to me in our room?"

Judith lowered her eyes. "Of course."

He'd not thought the band around his chest could squeeze tighter, but his wife's dashed expression made it constrict his ribs like a barrel hoop. Ian put a hand to her cheek. "We'll talk, aye? But I need time. Don't wait supper on me."

Alone in their room, he propped the window sash high. A rush of warm air, rain-freshened, belled the curtains inward. He shucked off his breeches, then pulled on a clean pair. At a tap on the door he said, "Aye, Maisy."

He rubbed his hand across his face as a bucket thumped against the floor.

"Mister Ian?" Maisy came deeper into the room, holding out her hand. A small object nestled in the folds of her palm. "Lily—Seona, more like—say you meant to have it."

When the door shut, he curled his fist, pressing the arrowhead into his palm as he'd done last on the creek bank. He'd lost track of it. How had Seona not? He needed no token to remember, but it suited his heart to have it, to hold when he thought of his son.

By all that was holy—*he had a son.*

"Gabriel . . ." He'd thought he'd done this grievous thing, released them both. But that was before he held them against his heart.

Ian went to his knees, then laid himself out, arms outstretched, the weight in his chest pinning him to the floor. "I couldn't abandon her. *Them.* But if anything done this day wasn't of necessity, rather for my own need . . . search me, forgive me."

The curtains billowed. Air moved across him head to heels, gentle as the brush of fingers. *As we forgive our debtors.*

His hands fisted in resistance, but there was no mistaking the Scripture that had come into his mind. Nor what it bid him do. He summoned the image of his uncle, withdrawn in rejection of the bairn . . . because all that was embracing in him had died years ago, with *his* son. With Aidan. Hadn't he caused it to be chiseled into granite, for all to read? *The light of mine eyes.* Had Gabriel died this day, had Seona not survived, what would Ian have seen in his uncle's eyes? A reflection of his own gutted soul?

He let bitterness against his uncle go. What lay within his power was his own heart and his choices in the coming days.

"If it be possible—I ask to be near the child, to see him grow. See the lad he makes. And the man." He paused, drawing strength, as the tears pooled beneath his cheek. "But be they near to me or far, for as long as I have breath, they shall be mine to see whole and lacking naught in my power to provide. Mine to shield. Mine to love."

If only in the silence of his soul.

When he opened his eyes, light streamed through the west-facing window like liquid gold. His heart thumped steady against the floor.

His thoughts drifted back over the hours past, fingering the indelible moments like strung beads, anxiety burnished away in prayer. The future would be there to meet them, with its paths to choose. For now, that moment, he knew what he must do.

Ian rose, washed, and finished dressing. He combed and bound his hair. Peering into the glass above the basin, he tied his neckcloth. Then he slipped the arrowhead into a coat pocket and went to find his wife.

"Mama Josephine professes herself positively shocked at his conduct." Rosalyn's disparaging tone carried from the dining room. Ian halted in the adjacent warming room as she pitched her voice higher, mimicking Josephine Pryce. " 'I would think he'd show more concern for the mother of his heir than a half-breed got on a slave.' We'll see what everyone has to say once what Cousin Ian has done today makes the rounds. Imagine, attending her himself—under a *tree*—then standing half-naked before Papa Hugh and claiming the child. He really is a perfect savage, your husband."

"He's nothing of the kind." Judith's voice was surprisingly firm. "I'm sure it was a terrifying ordeal."

Lucinda sighed. "How much simpler it would be had the plague of a girl died of it."

"Mama!"

"Did the thought never cross your mind, Judith? Still, your stepfather now has an iron hold on his nephew."

"What do you mean?"

"She means," Ian said, stepping into the doorway, "that Gabriel is your stepfather's property, as well as my son."

Rosalyn nearly dropped the glass raised to her lips, but Lucinda's composure went unruffled. "Listening at doors again, Mr. Cameron?"

Ignoring the pair, Ian extended a hand to Judith. "Will ye come with me?"

"Your wife hasn't finished her supper," Lucinda said coolly.

Though Judith's plate was hardly touched, she pushed back her chair and rose awkwardly to her feet. "Even so, Mama, I am quite ready to be excused."

"I had no idea my sister meant to visit today." Judith shut the door and faced him, pale with apprehension. "How much did you hear?"

"Enough." He moved numbly to the bed, kicked off his shoes and swung his feet onto the counterpane, then patted the space beside him. "Come rest with me."

Judith sat gingerly on the edge of the tick.

"That won't do," he said and slid an arm beneath her knees to bring her full onto the bed.

He removed her shoes and dropped them onto the floor with his. Lying down again, he rested his head on the slope of her belly. Her heart was tripping like a rabbit's.

"Can ye feel it moving now—the bairn?"

"If I lie still for a bit." A tentative hand rested on the crown of his head. The room was warm, despite the open window. Sweat sprang up beneath her fingers but he didn't pull away. "Ian? What was it like?"

The bed hangings moved in a current of air. He knew what she asked, but words eluded him.

"A miracle?" she said.

He drew an audible breath, minding their long-ago exchange about Cecily Reynold's childbed. He'd made her blush and been amused at the doing of it. "Aye, a miracle."

As if on cue, he felt a nudge against his cheek.

"There. Did you feel it?"

"I did." He waited, but the child didn't stir again. After a moment he heard himself speaking. "I was in the field when I saw her, away down at the creek. I felt . . . a compulsion, I guess, to go and speak with her. I don't know by whose leave she came to be there, but when I realized her travail had come, I thought to bring her back— she wanted Lily, not me—but the storm broke over us."

He told the rest quickly, while Judith's pulse beat beneath his ear. When she didn't speak at once, he was struck anew by the stillness of her, the composed patience he'd once taken for lack of substance, but which he knew now as a capstone over a depth he'd only begun to fathom.

The child stirred again. He closed his eyes, reaching out to it, suddenly longing for the connection.

Sometime later Judith shifted. He roused, confused as to where—and with whom—he lay. The room had dimmed. He'd slept through the sun's setting, dreaming of water and willows.

He raised his head and looked at his wife. She was awake. She'd been watching him sleep. "Shall I light a candle? Read for a bit?"

"Could we stay like this a little longer?" she asked.

"Am I not heavy on ye?"

"No. I like it."

The summer hangings swayed like willow boughs in the watery dusk. He drew breath, forcing it past the ache. "Then we'll stay."

Beneath his ear her heartbeat quickened. He felt a tug at the base of his neck, then the spill of his hair as the ribbon he'd tied it with came loose. Judith's fingers combed the damp strands.

Memory of sun-browned fingers, of green eyes and tumbled curls, took him strongly. Nothing but a veil as thin as the hangings lay between. He could snatch it aside, let his heart go winging . . .

"It was me."

Judith's words called him back to the darkening room. "What was?"

"I told Seona she could go down to the creek today."

She spoke as if in apology, yet gratitude burned the backs of his eyes, a gratitude he couldn't express, for entwined in the joy, the grief, and the cleansing was the indelible memory of *oneness*. Fleeting, bittersweet. Released.

Judith must have felt him quiver, though he tried to suppress it, face pressed against their unborn child. Her fingers slid down his temple, brushing the moisture on his cheek. "Ian—I'm so sorry for your pain."

"Aye," he said, when he could speak. "But I more for yours."

"He's perfect, Mama. Don't you think so?" Seona watched from her cot as Lily knelt on a pallet, changing Gabriel's first clout.

"First of ten thousand," she'd said, whipping a rag over his nethers in time to stem an arcing fountain, then laughing. "Little man's already showing off."

Seona was warm, a pleasant dew of sweat on her skin. Her clean shift clung to dips and curves that were strange now, flaccid, no longer taut and round. She watched Lily brush Gabriel's cheek with a knuckle. "You mind me being that tiny, Mama?"

" 'Course I do, girl-baby."

She winced as pain stabbed through her—her insides going back to their rightful shape. "Was it hard, birthing me?"

"The easiest childbed's a job of work. Ye know that. But I forgot the pain once I held ye."

Lily gave Gabriel, snug in his clean clout, into Seona's reaching hands. She laid him on the cot where she could stare at his face by tallow-light.

"I ain't forgot yet," she said softly. She minded it in flashes. In every flash was Ian, carrying her, kneeling over her, gripping her arms while she split asunder. Holding the messy little body of their son. His long limbs wrapping her like the sweetest of blankets. The smell of him on her skin.

She felt the push of darker thoughts, hovering like the muggy night air, and saw in Lily's eyes the grief she longed to hold at bay. An instant before she burst into tears, Esther popped up in the cabin doorway.

"Hey, Seona. Miss Lily. Can I see that baby?"

Instead of a sob, laughter broke in Seona's throat. "Come on, then."

Esther knelt by the cot as Seona loosened Gabriel's swaddling. "He's so white!" the girl blurted, then covered her mouth and giggled. "Well, pink really—but he's still perty, with them tiny fingers and ears. He got ears like Mister Ian!" She bent over and cooed. "Look there, he done opened his eyes. You think they gonna be blue, Seona? What was it Mister Ian called him? Some angel name. Gabriel! Ga-a-abriel . . . you hear me talkin' to you, baby?"

Over Esther's head Seona and Lily locked their gazes, hearts spilling over as abundantly as the girl's words.

41

Outside John Reynold's barn, Ian watched his wife engage in conversation with the womenfolk of a family newly settled in the area, while he communed in solitude with the corn, grown up to the door-yard like the previous summer. John came out of the barn, Robin bouncing in his arms, and strode over to him. "Before you go, Ian, we need to speak of Ruby."

Guilt had smote him the moment he'd arrived and set eyes on the woman. "Forgive me, John. Until today she'd gone clean out of my reckoning."

"You've had your distractions of late," John allowed.

"Still, I'll write the petition today. See her manumitted. Meantime tell me what's needed and—"

John held up the hand not busy with his fidgety son. "I'd hoped you hadn't written it, actually. Ruby doesn't wish to be manumitted. Not yet."

Taken aback, Ian spotted his nominal slave, appearing more robust than when last he'd seen her, herding the Allen children and those of the new family toward a plate of sweet rolls set out on the cabin porch. "Why not?"

"Seems she had two sons your uncle sold?"

"Sammy and Eli. What of them?"

"She's insisting her boys will come back to Mountain Laurel to find her, one day."

"Has she reason to think so?"

"Not that I can ascertain. But she believes it. With all her heart."

Ian frowned, watching the woman. "Has she spoken of what happened before? With my cousin and her man, Esau?"

"No, though Cecily's tried every charm in her considerable arsenal to coax it from her." Robin kicked, wanting down. His father gave his clouted bottom a genial smack. "Still yourself, rascal. If I let you run amok while your mother's busy, we'll both get an earful of French."

Robin pouted, then relented, giggling, when John poked his belly. "He's barely toddling without a finger to clutch," he told Ian, "but thinks he should be racing about with the big lads."

Ian watched the interplay, arms aching for his own son. He spotted Judith again, but she wasn't showing signs of leave-taking. Just as well. At least here he had distractions.

"Ian, you look as if you've the weight of the Carraways on your shoulders."

A little taken aback, he searched his neighbor's solicitous gaze. "Ye know the weight, John. Ye just preached me a sermon on it, aye?"

"Did I?"

Ian quoted the words still seared across his heart. " 'No man can serve two masters: for either he will hate the one, and love the other; or else he will hold to the one, and despise the other.' "

"I was speaking of serving God rather than mammon."

"Not about women?" Ian blurted, then ran a hand over his mouth, face ablaze.

John didn't laugh. He studied him, head cocked in that listening way of his. "True. Other things than monetary gain can crowd the Almighty from our hearts. Or those He means to be our first loves on this earth."

"Didn't ye speak on that?"

"Not directly. But if you heard it, receive it from the Lord."

"And do what with it? He's my *son*. And she . . ." Ian dropped his voice, though no one was nearby. "What do I do?"

John shifted Robin and put a hand to Ian's shoulder. "The Almighty will show you in His time. When He does, you'll know. And it will be right. For everyone."

"How can ye be sure?"

"Because, brother, He does *all* things well. Leave it in His hands."

Despite the ache, Ian felt a smile tug his lips. He liked this man calling him *brother*. "It's more what *I* might do that worries me. What if I cannot obey?"

John's eyes warmed. "I've no fear on that score,

in no small part because you do. So tell me, how is Seona? And your son?"

"They're well—far as I know. I haven't seen Gabriel save from a distance since the day he was born." But to say his name aloud to this friend who'd stood by him through it all was a small healing.

"That's nearly a month." John's eyes held compassion. Ian thought he meant to speak.

Before he could do so, Judith was there, ready to depart.

She was silent on the walk home, despite his efforts at conversation. They paused at the back door, Ian intending to go to his shop. For solitude to pray. To wait.

"Ye'll have a wee rest, then?" he asked her.

"I think so." Judith's hand went to the swell of her belly. She was due in a little over a month yet was smaller than Seona had been that far along.

As if summoned by his thoughts, Seona stepped from the kitchen, Gabriel in her arms. Down the rose-scented breezeway her eyes locked with his. Then she stole a glance at Judith and slipped off to the side. Leaving a heavy silence behind.

Judith put a hand to his arm. "I heard what you said to Mr. Reynold. I've prayed on it the whole way home. I can't bear to watch your heart break, Ian. Go and see your son. You've my blessing to do so."

He covered her hand with his, as if to trap the words—until he could believe she'd said them. He searched her eyes for indecision.

Either he will hate the one, and love the other . . .

"I trust you, Ian." Judith slipped her hand from beneath his and went into the house.

Seona had settled it with herself that first Sabbath day Ian came to visit Gabriel. She wouldn't stay to spy. She'd hand him over so Ian could sit on the cabin stoop and hold him on his knees or take him off walking like he'd done this warm September day. She'd go on with whatever she was doing—usually scrubbing out clouts, folding clouts, or hanging clouts on the line—and let them have their time. But today, when her breasts grew heavy with the need to feed her baby and still Ian didn't bring him back, she left the washhouse to go looking.

She found them in the curing barn. Except for some swallows nesting in the rafters, at first she thought it stood empty, doors open, gutted in the late-summer heat. The tobacco harvest was days away from filling it again. When she peeked inside, all she saw were bands of sunlight lancing through the siding, cutting up the dimness like a new striped shirt. Then Ian stepped into one of the bands, arms full of Gabriel. The air around them danced with the dust of last year's leaf. He was talking to the baby, the murmur of his voice a river flowing sweet across her breaking heart.

". . . maybe not as good a crop even as last year, though I can make it better. I've studied on means to improve the land, restore it. But I won't plant cotton. I'll take care of ye without going to that." As he bent his lips to the curve of Gabriel's brow, Ian turned and saw her.

She wondered did he know how he dazzled her. How the sunlight made crystals of his eyes, like there was no gray in them at all, only blue, clear and pure. Pulled like a tethered lamb, she crossed the empty barn, the tobacco smell a tickle in her nose, until the three of them shared the same spill of sunlight. Her need was plain. He put Gabriel in her arms. What had passed between him and the baby lingered on his face. A softness. An ache. Hope.

"Thank ye, Seona." Pain flickered in his eyes. She sensed he wanted to touch her, maybe say something more. With a breath like a groan, he moved past her, doing neither.

When she knew he was gone, she kissed Gabriel's brow where he'd kissed it. Breath filled her chest like she'd been running, deep and ragged.

Lord, please. She left it at that, not knowing what else to pray. Seemed just when she'd steadied herself with a few days passing, keeping out of his path, Ian would come for the baby and with a single look send her reeling again.

Gabriel let out a squawk. She sat on the tail of a cart shoved off to the side, held him against her, and watched the swallows swooping high among the rafters.

Lily and Maisy had tidied Judith, taken away the soiled linens to boil, even left the window propped to the mild October afternoon. Judith lay in the center of the bed beside the bundle swathed in embroidered blue. Her labor had lasted through the night and into the following day; the bairn had come at last as the parlor clock struck the hour of three.

Ian's breeches bore the stain of fieldwork. His shirt hung in grimy wrinkles, open at the neck. He caught his image in the glass above the washstand. A good portion of his hair had escaped its tail. He tamed the tangle, then washed his face and toweled dry.

Judith's eyes opened as his weight sank the tick. She tried to sit up, but pain creased her brow. Instead she pulled aside the bairn's wrapping. "Want to see?"

"Of course."

And he'd thought Gabriel small. She was a wee elfin thing, their daughter. Her eyes were open, nearly invisible brows knit above them, as though she puzzled over some thought beyond her comprehension. He brushed a fingertip against her cheek and the little brows arched in surprise. She was beautiful.

"I hope a daughter isn't a disappointment?"

"Not at all." Ian smoothed back Judith's hair, still damp with the sweat of her labor. "She's a bonny girl. Like her mother."

As if to protest this exalted estimation, the bairn crumpled her face and mewled.

Judith stroked the back of his hand. "So brown," she said, then smiled. "Would you like to hold her?"

"I'm filthy, Judith—my shirt."

"Take it off." She'd bid him go about his labors while she tended hers, else he'd have stayed perched on the stair just outside the door throughout her travail. Lily, Maisy, finally even his aunt, had insisted he'd be of more use in the fields helping the hands bring in the last of the sun-dried cornstalks.

Absurdly self-conscious, he tugged the stained garment over his head. While his arms and face were sun-browned, his chest and belly were the color of pale buckskin. "All right," he said and scooped his daughter into his arms, by now well-practiced at the maneuver.

The weight of her was surprising, bitty as she was. As he met her solemn stare, what rose in him was something apart from what he'd felt with Gabriel, as if this tiny girl-child, despite her security of birth, would prove the more vulnerable of the two. He held her as if she were porcelain, giving her the shelter of his body, and promptly fell in love.

And in that moment he knew, with gut-wrenching surety, that Seona would leave Mountain Laurel. Gabriel with her.

But not yet. Let there be a little more time. . . .

Tears pooled in Judith's eyes, running into her hair. He had to break the moment or he would break. His voice cracked as he said, "What shall we call her?"

"Miranda . . . if that's agreeable."

He studied his daughter, considering. "Miranda Cameron." Spoken aloud, the name evoked a memory: cold granite, wreathed in mist. "Wasn't that the name of—?"

"Papa Hugh's first wife."

"You want to name the lass for her?" With infinite care he laid the bairn on the bed beside her mother. "Ye never met her, Judith. Why would ye want our daughter to bear her name?"

"I've seen her," Judith said.

A chill prickled the hairs on his arms though no breeze came through the window. "What d'ye mean, *seen* her?"

"In Papa Hugh's room. He has a little portrait. She was beautiful."

As often as he'd been in his uncle's room, he'd never seen a portrait of the man's first wife—

though there was no reason he mightn't have one tucked away somewhere. Still, doubt gave him pause. The name might be less agreeable to his aunt. And to his uncle?

No matter. If Judith wanted the name, she'd have it. "And so will our Miranda be. Beautiful."

Judith closed her eyes. "If she looks like her papa."

He eased his weight off the bed and knelt beside it. "I don't deserve ye," he whispered, head bowed over her small hand. "God knows ye don't deserve me."

There was no stir of movement, only Judith's voice drifting into sleep. "What has deserving to do with our blessings?"

Two striped kittens, one orange, one gray, follow him down the row of ripened corn, twisting round his ankles, threatening to trip him. Exasperated, he faces the whiskered duo and addresses them in Callum Lindsay's broad speech. "Awa' wi' ye. Canna ye see I've the crop tae put up?"

The kittens mewl. Somewhere a hammer commences to bang. Someone is dismantling the corncrib. He'll have nowhere to put the corn . . .

He started awake, blinking at the washstand across the room. He was abed beside his wife . . . who'd just borne him a daughter. *Her middle name will be Grace.*

The thought crystallized as he fixed the time

by the window's light. Sunset. And it was his daughter doing the mewling, the sound he'd dreamed was kittens', so soft and unobtrusive it hadn't disturbed Judith's exhaustion.

The banging had followed him into waking too. He lifted his head, then let it sink back on the pillow, too tired to care. And too troubled.

Hours earlier, before returning to rest beside his sleeping wife and daughter, he'd found his aunt and uncle in the parlor. Hugh Cameron had appeared confused when Ian announced his daughter's name; then understanding eased his brow.

"Miranda. 'Twas Judith's choice?" Smiling but distant-eyed, his uncle had stood and crossed the parlor, passing Ian by.

Lucinda had been less sanguine. "Miranda Cameron is dead!"

His uncle hadn't even flinched. Ian had likewise ignored his aunt. "Uncle, wait. I need to speak with ye about Seona and my son."

It was time to make his decision known, no matter how grievous the speaking of it.

His uncle had paused in the passage. Illness of heart and mind had left him shrunken from the imposing figure who'd emerged from the stable's gloom to greet Ian that late-summer day, more than a year past, but there was a steadiness about him Ian hadn't seen for months, as if something he'd long wrestled over had been resolved— much as it had within Ian.

"Seona has been my care for nigh twenty years," his uncle said. "Lily much the longer. I ken ye think I've no' done well enough by them, and ye may well be right, Nephew. But I've at least made certain ye willna repeat my mistakes."

Alarmed, Ian had grasped his uncle's arm, disconcertingly thin beneath the sleeve of his banyan. "What have ye done?"

His uncle had pulled away. "Never ye mind. In time ye'll ken. Your place now is wi' your wife. Go to her."

Hugh Cameron had seemed less to walk away than to drift, like the ghosts that had so long haunted him. Ian had pressed his teeth into his lip to stem the bitter words flooding his mouth. As though he'd heard them anyway, his uncle had paused at the door of his room.

"Ye maybe think, too, I've taken no account of your conduct since ye came back to us, last winter. I have, lad. And I've no worries leaving Mountain Laurel in your hands, to do wi' as ye see fit. I trust ye."

The banging's sudden cessation jarred Ian from the memory. Voices had replaced it—one molasses-thick, the other high and sharp. Both urgent.

He was out of bed and pulling on a shirt when Judith roused. "Ian? What . . . ?"

"Yet another stramash of some sort. I'll see to it. I think our Mandy's hungry."

"Mandy?"

The name had slipped out, but he found it suited their wee lass. "Aye, if ye don't mind it." With a fleeting smile at her shaking head, he stepped into the passage.

Footsteps clattered on the stairs. Maisy, round-eyed and breathless, met him on the landing.

"Mister Ian, come quick! Ally saying the hands done run off toward the creek and it's your Thomas taken 'em. Come back like Moses to lead 'em over Jordan!"

42

Ian had taken time to step back into the room for his rifle and tomahawk before leaving at a run for the creek, thinking all the while it couldn't be Thomas. It wouldn't be.

But there was no mistaking the players in the creekside tableau that greeted him as he came through the trees, despite the gathering dusk. It was indeed Thomas Ross. And holding him at musket-point was a filthy, bearded Jackson Dawes.

Ian had tomahawk in hand, ready to throw, as the man whirled to see him coming. Dawes shifted the musket, aiming instead for him.

Thomas charged, ramming Dawes's shoulder as the musket fired. Ian heard the ball whine past his ear. Half-obscured in powder smoke, Dawes threw off Thomas and bolted for the wood spreading upslope along the creek.

Hot with rage, Ian drew back the tomahawk, but Thomas lunged across his path, grabbing his raised arm. He staggered to a halt, catching the rifle that flew forward off his shoulder.

Thomas locked eyes with him across the blade between them. "Well-timed, Ian. The man meant to abduct and sell me yet again. Looks like he could use the proceeds. Or never tell me your uncle's taken him back?"

Ian jerked his arm free. "Never mind Dawes. Ye're meant to be in Boston!"

A shiver of leaves in the windless air drew his attention to a nearby thicket. Dark faces peered out, heads pressed close. His uncle's field hands: Pete, Will, Munro. A woman and boy he didn't recognize.

Thomas spread his hands. "Eden took me north to Philadelphia as promised. Introduced me to some folks who were pleased to help me from there."

Dawes, still running, had reached the trees. A calm corner of Ian's brain noted the spot where he plunged into cover. "Help ye? Not back to Boston, I take it."

"To set the captives free. Unless you aim to stop me."

The half-hidden faces watched them, some terrified, some defiant. Likely the woman and boy were those Thomas knew from Chesterfield. Ian was of no mind to hinder their escape, but his uncle's farm was doomed to fail without men enough to work it.

Breathing hard, he glared into Thomas's challenging gaze as frustration and alarm at the knowledge filled him . . . then drained away, leaving the sweetest sense of release he'd known since coming to Mountain Laurel. As if he were himself one of that huddled company in the thicket, a step away from freedom, a desperate certainty came surging through his soul. *If failing's what it takes to set us free . . . give them wings.*

Ian shoved the tomahawk into his belt. "Tell me, Thomas. When have I ever stopped ye doing a blessed thing ye set yourself to do?"

"Never yet." There was the slightest easing of Thomas's shoulders. "I hear you're a daddy now. Twice over. My congratulations."

Ignoring the remark, Ian jerked his chin at the woman and boy. "Think Pryce will let them go without a hunt?"

"I'm betting I can keep Amy and Jo a step ahead—if you don't dither in giving me your blessing."

His blessing? "That still means something to ye?"

"It does." The challenge bled from Thomas's features, and Ian saw he meant it. He didn't want permission to follow his reckless scheme—he needed none. He wanted Ian's approval.

There passed between them then a rush of feeling Ian had thought lost forever. "*Aonaibh ri chéile,*" he said and held out his hand. "Get ye gone then, and God keep ye."

"And you." As Thomas gripped his hand, Ian felt something hard pressed into his palm. He grasped it and looked down. A shilling.

Thomas backed off, teeth gleaming in the dusk, then slipped into the brush.

Ian heard feet splash in the creek shallows but

didn't stay to see them cross over. Pocketing the shilling, he gripped the rifle and headed upslope after Dawes.

The man had left a heedless path, skirting field and orchard. The harvest moon was rising over the ridge, crickets singing in the grass, before Ian spotted him silhouetted on the back steps of the house, musket slung at his shoulder. In the doorway stood Maisy, holding a Betty lamp, evidencing no surprise at the sight of the long-vanished overseer on their doorstep.

Maisy disappeared inside, to be replaced by Lucinda Cameron. Ian crossed to the garden palisade and, rifle cradled, crept within range of their voices.

Lucinda descended the back steps. "Where is he?"

Dawes's breath came short. "Don't know—didn't come after me."

"He saw you? Why are you here? Have you discovered the source?"

Ian frowned, uncomprehending. *The source?*

"I was coming to tell you," Dawes said, "but came across that boy of his first—with the field hands and some slaves from over Chesterfield, I think. Making a run for it."

"We are apprised of the situation," Lucinda said. "I've sent Jubal to inform Gideon. But the loss of a few hands hardly matters—not if you've found it. Come inside before you're seen."

Alarm coursed through Ian. Pryce would be after Thomas and the runaways he shepherded within hours, unless Jubal took his time bringing word. The man was canny enough to give them a lengthy start, if he was so inclined; Ian couldn't be sure he would be.

Lucinda had stepped back into the doorway, Maisy giving her room. The lamp's light moved to the dining room. Dawes raised a foot to the bottom step.

Ian crept forward to the last fence pale, a plan forming.

"Is it too much to hope my nephew's doxy and her brat have gone with them?" Lucinda asked, motioning Dawes inside.

Dawes moved up another step. "Not that I saw."

"How I wish I'd left well enough alone last autumn," said his aunt. "Let her run off with Thomas, as it seemed was her aim, and saved myself the trouble of getting rid of them both."

"I'd have gotten that buck again," Dawes said, "if not for—"

The import of their words burst through Ian, but he was already rushing the door. Lucinda saw him in time to move out of his path, too late to utter warning before he rammed a shoulder into Dawes's back and shoved him bodily into the house.

Dawes slammed into the frame of the warming room doorway, but momentum sent them barreling through, banging sideboards, sending dishes crashing. In the dining room Maisy had set the Betty lamp on the table's edge. She sprang back with a cry as they staggered in, a tangle of grappling limbs.

Ian had meant merely to apprehend the man and force him to face his uncle. Now, as Dawes fell over a chair, rage at what the man and his aunt had done to Seona, to Thomas, to them all, consumed reason and restraint.

"Get up, Dawes! Ye've a thing or two to answer for to me."

The overseer kicked himself free of the chair. Lurching to his feet, he looked wildly for his musket. Ian had dropped his rifle in the scuffle as well. At the back door? In the yard?

Fury showed red through the dirt ground into Dawes's face. "I only ever did what *she* bid me do." He jabbed a finger toward the warming room door, where no doubt his aunt hovered. " 'Get rid of the pair of them,' she says. But it all goes to blazes when that self-styled preacherman Reynold went nosing about in Fayetteville. I had to run for the hills, while she's living it up in the big house, cooing her innocence, letting me take the blame!"

A smile stretched Ian's lips. "No doubt she has. But it's ye I mean to deal with now."

He saw it in Dawes's eyes, the choosing of fight over flight, an instant before the man came at him like a bull charging. Ian landed a fist to Dawes's gut, then was borne down in a grappling hold. He took a chair with him in the fall, entangling his assailant long enough to scramble from reach. Dawes was up again fast. Ian's fist crashed into teeth; then he was thrust back toward the window. Dawes grabbed the Betty lamp from the table.

"Jackson!" Lucinda screamed.

Ian dodged the lamp. It hit the window with the tinkle of breaking glass and a gush of cooler air as he rushed at Dawes, who went staggering against the opposite wall.

The smell of lamp oil was strong above the man's sour stink. Ian's grip on Dawes's ragged shirt slipped. The sleeve was saturated.

He was aware of Lucinda's voice, shriller than before . . . an unsteady light behind him . . . a spreading warmth at his back. Then Dawes heaved him around and the light was in his face.

The window curtain was in flames, floor to ceiling.

He shoved Dawes aside to reach the fire, but the man tripped over the fallen chair and went sprawling up against the flames. The curtains fell, crumpling in a fiery heap over Dawes's legs. The overseer swept them aside; the fire caught his oil-soaked sleeve. Flames flowed up his arm, alive and molten.

Ian tackled him, intending to beat out the flames. Dawes threw a fist, catching a blow to Ian's head that dropped him to his knees. The man was ablaze—screaming obscenities, thrashing. Reaching up, Ian snatched off the table linen, the smell of burning cloth and hair sharp in his nose. "Be still, man! Let me—"

Dawes let out a bellow and struck him again. Intentionally or not, Ian never knew. Engulfed in flame, the overseer half fell, half ran from the room, roaring in agony.

Ian lurched to his feet. Lucinda caught his shirt as he tried to pass her. "The fire!"

It struck him then, with skin-crawling horror: Dawes's bellowing had ceased, but the roaring hadn't. The carpet had taken flame, as had the florid wall papering. Smoke curled at the high ceiling. He took his first harsh breath of it, expelled in a violent cough.

Lucinda gaped, eyes reflecting flame. Ian shook her. "Get my uncle! D'ye hear me? Get my uncle and get out!"

She bared her teeth at him and slapped his face. Gathering her skirts, she swept out through the parlor. Too panicked to be stunned, Ian beat at the flames but quickly realized the fire was beyond such measures. He dropped the scorched linen and raced through the warming room.

Lily was at the door, breathless. Down the passage his uncle's door was still shut.

"Lily! Get my uncle!" He was on the stairs, grabbing for the banister. "Get him out of here!"

When he burst into their room, Judith was on her feet, pale and barefoot in her shift. "Ian, there was shouting, and I smell—"

"Fire! Wrap Mandy. Cover her face. Can ye walk?"

"I . . . I think so." Judith stared at him, frozen.

"Move, Judith!"

With a cry of alarm, she moved. Ian hauled his saddlebags from under the bed, then jerked open the desk drawer and stuffed its contents into the bags. At the press he snatched out clothes, his, Judith's . . . Seona's drawings . . . all went into the saddlebags. He slung them over his shoulder.

Judith was ready, the baby bundled in a tiny quilt. He hustled them into the passage, but Judith hesitated at the stairs, gasping at the heat funneled up from below. The gasp became a cough. She swayed. Ian swept her up as she clung to the baby. Smoke rose up the stairwell.

At the foot of the stairs he caught sight of Lily stepping from his uncle's room. Seen through the haze of panic and smoke, there was something absurdly serene about her. She didn't seem affected by the smoke stinging his eyes, strangling his throat. He might have been seeing the ghostly imprint of her standing there on a day long past, calmly awaiting instruction. Then his uncle was in the doorway, handing something to her.

"No time for that! Get out!" Believing they'd

heard him, that they'd be on his heels, he lunged through the door with Judith in his arms. He staggered onto the lawn, sucking air in gulps, nearly tripping over the rifle he'd dropped earlier.

Naomi huddled back by the garden pales, staring. "Miss Judith all right? The baby?"

Ian set Judith on her feet, but she crumpled, clutching Mandy. The saddlebags tumbled in a heap beside her as he caught his wife.

Seona ran out of the dark, Gabriel in her arms. "Where's Mama?"

Ian whirled toward the house, expecting Lily and his uncle to be there, safe out of the fire. There was no sign of either of them. Flames licked at the open door.

Seona clutched at him, terror in her eyes. "Ian!"

Behind them Naomi was taking charge. "Fetch clouts from the washhouse, someone. Miss Judith's bleeding and I can't tell how much in this dark."

"Help them, Seona. I'll find Lily!" Ian pulled loose and raced to the front of the house, past windows bright with leaping orange, thinking they might have escaped that way. In the loop of the drive, among a heap of gowns and bedding and sundry rescued effects, Lucinda stood barking orders at Maisy and Esther.

"Get everything back from the house—shift it over the shrubbery! No, wait, we might make another—"

"Uncle Hugh!" Ian bellowed over the fire's swelling roar. "Where is he?"

Lucinda's face held a savage resolve. His uncle was nowhere to be seen. Nor was Lily. Down at the stable? But the stable was dark. And there was Ally, lumbering up into the light of the burning house. Ian shouted, "Is my uncle at the stable? Lily?"

"No, sir. Jubal gone to Chesterfield and ain't nobody else there."

Ian lurched into a run again, eyes streaming, back around the house. He found them by the garden as he'd left them, Naomi and Judith, now Malcolm with Mandy in his arms. Seona came rushing from the washhouse, still holding Gabriel, arms full as well of clouts and linens. Staring past him at the burning house, horror on her face, she screamed. "Mama!"

He turned as Lily came leaping through the flames barring the door. She fell on the steps, picked herself up, and ran, the hem of her skirt aflame.

Ian bore her down, beating at her skirt as they hit the ground. The smothering weight of the fabric aided him, but his hands were scorched before the flames were snuffed, leaving a ragged hem of smoking char. Lily hadn't made a sound but clutched to her heart the thing his uncle had given into her keeping: a flat, leather-bound bundle.

His uncle. The sting of his hands was nothing to the pain that gripped his chest. He took Lily by the shoulders. "Where is he?"

Lily's eyes held the calm of shock. She shook her head.

Ian wrenched to his feet and took two running strides toward the wall of flame that had been the back door, before a weight plowed into him from behind. Brawny arms encircled him, pinioning his own. He twisted and fought, but he might have been locked in irons.

"Loose me, Ally! He's in there!"

"Mister Ian, can't you see?"

The windows of his uncle's room were alive, lurid with flames, bathing the yard in a hellish twilight. The fire had spread to every room belowstairs.

"No." Ian slid down in Ally's arms until his knees struck earth. Transfixed like the rest of them, he watched the floor of his and Judith's room collapse. With a swell of noise like cackling laughter, the fire reached upward, engulfing garret and roof.

As sparks sprayed high, bright as fireflies against the night, Ian watched in helplessness as Hugh Cameron's house became his funeral pyre.

43

"It was a few steps to the door," her mama said, "but he wouldn't take them."

They numbered four at the kitchen worktable, each red-eyed, faces blank with loss. Ian had come in last, finding Seona there with Lily and Malcolm. His blistered hands were salved but his poor face . . . one eye swelled half-shut, a bloodied knot on his brow, lower lip split. Tears had tracked the grime on his cheeks.

As cold came down the ridge in the night and the ground whitened with autumn's first hard frost, they'd watched over the dying house, drifting off one at a time to see to hurts, to babies, to Miss Judith. Drifting back to stand and watch the last of its walls standing fall with a whoosh like a final breath, leaving timbers poking up like black ribs between the chimney stacks.

Ally had gone down to the stable in the dark of morning. He was there still, seeing to the stock—his now to tend, what remained.

Lucinda Cameron hadn't waited for daylight to shake the ash of Mountain Laurel off her shoes. Soon as Jubal came back from Chesterfield, she'd had him hitch up the carriage and off they went rattling to Miss

Rosalyn in her grand abode. She'd taken Maisy and Esther too.

"They're mine," she'd said, standing by the carriage while the plunder from the fire was stowed. "Maisy and Jubal came with me from Virginia and were never Hugh's. Ask Judith, if my word counts for naught."

Miss Judith, worn from childbed, fear, smoke, and grief, had been asleep down at the cabins, and what Miss Lucinda said was true enough. Ian seemed relieved to see her go. Esther had been so dazed by it all she hadn't said a word. Seona had kissed her but hadn't cried at the parting. She wasn't ready for that grief.

She was glad now for the bundle her mama had placed on the table once Ian joined them, its leather worn in the light of two candles. A needful distraction.

"He meant it for ye," Lily said, looking at Ian in the gray of morning. "Will ye open it?"

Clumsy on account of his burns, Ian unwrapped the bundle. Seona leaned forward, understanding Master Hugh in death less than she'd done in life. What could've been of more value to him than his own self?

Ian's hands trembled as the last flap of leather peeled away. *Papers.* Her heart sank at the sight. What had she hoped for?

"It'll be his will," Ian said in his smoke-ravaged voice, but he didn't break the seal of the top paper or take up any beneath it. He moved them aside. There *was* something besides papers. Two tiny portraits set in oval frames.

" 'Tis his wife," Malcolm said, as if there'd never been more than one to claim the title. "Miss Miranda. And, sweet heaven—that be Mister Aidan."

Miranda Cameron's hair had been dark, but with a touch of warmth in it, as if it might have glinted bronze in the sunlight. That wasn't what held Seona's stare. It was the eyes. The woman's eyes—and those of her dark-haired son—had been painted as green as her own.

Seona wanted to snatch up the two bright ovals and run with them out into the dawning light, to stare at the painted faces no bigger than the palm of her hand. But it was for Ian to touch them first.

He lifted his eyes to her. "Look at them, Seona. I was wrong. My uncle—" He cleared his throat, a painful sound. "He couldn't claim ye as his child because he wasn't your father."

"No, Master Ian. He wasn't."

People tended to pay heed when Lily spoke. Maybe on account she kept so much to herself. Or maybe this time it was what she'd called Ian—the first of them to call him what he was now. *Master.* But there was something more. Something had changed in her eyes. Something long sealed was cracking open. "The same hand painted both of these," she said, touching the

610

portrait of Aidan Cameron with a fingertip. "Mister Gottfriedsen."

"The peddler?" Ian asked in surprise.

"Aye. But Master Hugh had them done at different times. Hers was first," Lily said of the face of the woman who'd raised her from a weaned child. "She died afore Aidan was a man grown. This one—" again she brushed a fingertip over Mister Aidan's face—"was finished just afore *he* died. He was eighteen years old," she added, turning to Seona, "your daddy."

"Mama—" Seona's throat shut tight over a dozen things she might have said. Her eyes didn't know where they wanted to rest—on her mama, on Ian, on that young man's face staring from the table. That green-eyed face with its straight nose and its Cameron chin. Her face.

"It wasn't Aidan who hurt Ruby in the fields that day," Lily said, "and it wasn't Esau who killed Aidan. It was Jackson Dawes."

Seona shut her eyes, trying not to see the body they'd found after the fire. They still didn't know where the Jackdaw had hid himself all those months or why he'd come back to see Miss Lucinda, though Ian had told them of their puzzling words on the back stoop. Maybe it no longer mattered. He could no more trouble them.

"Ruby took that knowledge with her," Lily said, "when Master Hugh sold her."

Sold for the reminder she was of what Master

Hugh had done to Esau. And what he thought Esau had done to Mister Aidan. And what he'd thought Mister Aidan had done?

"Ruby told me the truth the night John Reynold brought ye home, Seona," Lily said. "Not that I needed her to. I knew your daddy would never have tried to hurt her. Aidan had gone out to the fields and taken his musket and happened to see Dawes trying to have his way with Ruby. Aidan tried to stop it. In the scuffle his musket fired. It might have been an accident. But there was Aidan dead and the only one Dawes could blame was Esau, who'd come running at the shot."

They were silent for a time, staring at each other round the table. Then Ian asked, "Did my uncle know, at the last? Did ye tell him the truth of it?"

Lily met his gaze. "Your uncle never stopped carrying his grief and guilt or his doubt about Aidan. Least I could do was put to rest his doubt."

Half a lifetime of it, and needless.

"Didn't he know his own son?" Seona asked the table at large, thinking it would be her mama who answered. But it was Ian.

"It takes only the hearing of a reproach, false or no, to forever mar a person's character in your thinking. No matter how ye try to forget it. I know . . ." He paused, then shook his head.

Seona frowned, wondering what he'd meant, thinking for some reason of his Boston kin. Of his daddy, Mister Robert, who would have to be told his last living brother was gone.

It was then she felt it—sudden and warm as encircling arms. They were there, *her* kin. The woman and the young man. As vivid in her mind as ever Master Hugh had been, as Lily and Ian and Malcolm were to her now. She thought if she raised her hand, she'd touch a sleeve or a face she couldn't see. *Daddy.*

Then like a breath exhaled, the sense of them was gone. She blinked at the faces around her. Ian was staring at Lily like he was trying to read her thoughts. But that was a trick only her mama knew.

"I understand the doubt," he said. "And the grief. But why did my uncle carry guilt over Aidan?"

Lily sighed, and Seona reached for her hand. There was more truth to tell.

"Master Hugh and Aidan quarreled. I'd told Aidan I was carrying his child." Lily laced their fingers together. Seona hardly breathed. "Aidan went to Master Hugh, asked him to free me. We were going to leave Mountain Laurel, make our way in the world. Aidan wouldn't own slaves. He'd set his mind to that." But Aidan had come away furious from that talk, making little sense to Lily at the time. "I suspected Master Hugh refused me my freedom in order to keep Aidan here. I never knew for certain. Aidan said he needed to get his thinking straight, then he'd come talk to me. He went out to the fields and came upon Ruby and Dawes . . ."

"And my uncle never told ye, all this time, why he refused?" Ian rubbed his neck, then winced and laid his blistered hand on the table.

"After Aidan died, he never spoke of him again," Lily said. "Except those times his mind slipped and he forgot."

Ian frowned. "Did he know ye were carrying his grandchild—before Aidan died?"

"Maybe. I don't know," Lily said. "He did soon after."

They sat in silence, and Seona heard more than one belly set to growling. No matter their griefs, old and new, time kept moving on, and the living with it. It was getting on to breakfast time after a long and wakeful night.

Ian picked up Master Hugh's will but set it aside in favor of a paper underneath. He stared at it as if, for him, time had all but stopped. Without a word to prepare them, he started to read.

"Whereas Hugh Cameron, of Randolph County, has by his petition represented to this General Assembly, that he is desirous of procuring the emancipation of Lily, a woman of mixed blood, and her daughter, Seona, heretofore his property, as a reward for their Meritorious Services:

Be it therefore enacted by the General Assembly of the State of North Carolina, and it is hereby enacted by Authority of the same, that from the passing of this Act, the said mixed-blood women, Lily and Seona, the property of Hugh Cameron, be emancipated and forever set free from slavery, and henceforward be called and known by the names of Lily Cameron and Seona Cameron."

The meaning of those words worked over them in breathless silence.

"Mama," Seona said, still gripping Lily's hand.

"Does it say more?" Malcolm asked.

"'Read three times and ratified in the General Assembly, the nineteenth day of July 1794.' And here at the bottom . . . 'A true copy, by Ruffin Lewis Puryear, Secretary.'" Ian's broken mouth trembled as he added, "It's dated a week before Gabriel's birth. Ye were already free that day, the both of ye."

Lily was gripping her hand hard enough to hurt. Seona squeezed back, unable to speak.

Ian smiled at her, shakily, and a drop of blood beaded on his lip where it had split. "God bless the pen of Mr. Puryear."

"Amen," Malcolm said into the silence, as Naomi came through the door with Gabriel riding her shoulder.

"Daddy," she said, taking in the sight of them. "What we got to be *amen*ing on this dark morning?"

Seona laughed, then clapped a hand over her mouth. Not until she saw Ian's hand shaking did it hit her what else this meant. Six months from the middle of July. Before the spring they would have to go, she and her mama, and Gabriel with them, though he'd been born free.

Ian had promised. He would never take her baby.

His eyes were reaching for her, full of that very knowledge—reaching across the table like he'd pull her to him. But that work-worn space was a distance neither he nor she could cross, no matter they were both free persons now.

There was no more *amen* in her soul. She took Gabriel, who was waking hungry, and left the kitchen.

44

Gold and scarlet canopied the graves on the ridge above Mountain Laurel. The solemn conversations of fellow mourners making their way down the footpath drifted back to Ian, alone at his uncle's grave. A simple cross marked the raw mound beneath which Hugh Cameron rested near his wife and children. In time there would be a proper stone for this kinsman who had welcomed him, flaws and all—had offered him a settled life and legacy, flaws and all. Though heir to his land, chattel, and heartache, unlike his uncle he clung to a more enduring light than the shades of thought and memory. One that time and distance, even death, could not extinguish.

He breathed the crisp air, no longer tainted with the acrid ghost of burning, and said, "I'll tend what remains, Uncle. For my time."

Whether or not that proved a lifetime, God would make it clear in His time.

"Fois sìorruidh dha anam." Rest in peace.

It was then he heard the wild geese call and knew he'd been waiting for the sorrowing sound in that place of grief and his rebirth. He watched the break in the trees, expecting to see an arrow of dark shapes crossing the gap of blue above the graveyard clearing.

There was only one, winging its lonely way southward.

Charlie Spencer was waiting on the path when Ian started down the ridge, a skinny hound pressed against his knee.

"Ye needn't have lingered," Ian told him, though he nodded appreciation of the gesture. Which, it turned out, was a good deal more besides.

"Meant to tell ye sooner," Spencer began, "but with the fire and whatnot . . ."

Ian was reminded of the disconcerting emptiness that loomed over the ashen scar where the house had stood, broken by naked chimneys rising from the earth like withered trees. Naomi and Lily had swept and scrubbed Dawes's old cabin—in which they found Rosalyn's gown and Judith's shoes, the very items Lucinda Cameron had, nearly a year ago, blamed Seona for stealing. Though besides that they had only what came out of the fire or had been in the washhouse, Judith and Naomi had found bedding and candles, a washbasin, a basket for their daughter's bed, sacking for curtains at the single window. The Reynolds, Zeb Allen, and other neighbors had given what could be spared. And more, Ian was sure.

"Tell me what?" Ian asked, brought up by Spencer's hesitation.

"Well. See . . . it's to do with that rascal,

Dawes—though I oughtn't speak ill of the dead."

They'd buried Dawes as well. Not among Ian's kin. "What of him?"

"It's a thing best seen. Bit of a trudge." Spencer waved toward the ridgeline curving between Mountain Laurel and John Reynold's land. "But ye need to clap eyes on it."

"Can ye give me a notion, Charlie? There's a dinner commencing below."

"Try this for notions." Spencer opened a palm shiny with calluses. Cupped in it was a thing Ian had never in his life set eyes on—not in the raw.

High above the birch hollow, in a tight draw near the stream's source, they found where Dawes had been living rough in a makeshift shelter. Of more interest to Ian were the scars of recent digging along the creek bed, spaced as methodically as the terrain allowed. All the excavations were abandoned a few feet in, save one; a tiny natural cave had been expanded to a tunnel large enough for a man to hunker down and enter. It ran some ten feet back into the ridge. Along one wall, between layers of white quartz, flowed a narrow glittering vein.

"That what I think it is?" Spencer asked, stooping to peer into the widened crevice as Ian ran his hand along the bright seam.

"Given I've never seen a gold mine before, I think so."

Behind him Spencer let out a throaty whoop. "I heard tell of the Almighty giving water from a rock, but this is something else entire!"

Crouched in the tunnel, the scent of raw earth in his nose, Ian was busy linking a chain of seemingly random memories into a pattern that finally made sense. *Ally used to spy those in the field or the creek,* Seona had said of the arrowhead he'd carried since the day of Gabriel's birth.

Arrowheads and pretty stones. Ally must have found a bit of gold in one of the streams that cut the hills—a bright thing, a pretty thing to give a little girl. Seona put it in her basket and there in the garret it stayed, until the day that basket spilled its treasure under Lucinda's shrewd eyes.

Dawes must have tried his hand along every feeder creek on Hugh Cameron's land, in search of the gold Lucinda hoped lay hidden under the earth of Mountain Laurel.

"That's what he was coming back to tell my aunt, the night of the fire. 'The source,' I heard her say. He never confirmed it." Ian hadn't given him time.

Spencer scratched at his stubbled beard. "Notice yet whose land it's on?"

It took a moment for the implication to register. Though Ian hadn't paid scrupulous heed to the boundary markers set down in his uncle's ledger the year a parcel of land was sold off to pay expenditures, he recalled enough to gauge where it was they stood and on which side of the boundary stream the gold vein ran.

"I do." For the first time in days Ian felt a gladness of heart. "Let's go tell him."

They met John and Cecily, toting Robin, on the path headed home. John's face showed relief at sight of Ian with Spencer, but their muddied clothes and dirt-streaked faces raised a brow. "We've speculated as to where on earth you two had vanished. Perhaps we ought to have been asking ourselves where *under* the earth?"

Cecily shot her husband a flaring glance. John's amiable expression froze. "Ian, forgive me. That was thoughtless."

"Hit the mark, though," Spencer said.

Ian shrugged aside the reminder of sorrow. "Never mind it, John. Charlie and I—we've something to tell ye both."

John and Cecily received the gold nugget, and the news of its finding, with laughing skepticism, which faded to stunned silence once they realized Ian was in earnest. "Ye did once say as ye'd like to plant trees, John, should the Almighty drop a bounty from heaven into your arms. This one's from the earth, but no less from His hand."

Spencer went with the pair, still lost in wondering joy, to see Cecily home, then to show

John the site of his newfound prosperity, but not before Ian impressed upon them the wisdom of keeping the matter silent. For now.

He returned alone to Mountain Laurel, where Naomi took him, dirt and all, under wing.

"There's plenty set aside for you, Master Ian. Come get yourself washed and fed."

He went gladly, but hunger vanished upon finding two unexpected guests awaiting him in the kitchen. While Ian had been climbing the ridge with Spencer, Karl Gottfriedsen and his nephew—a strapping, straw-haired fellow called Jost—had come rattling up the carriage drive in their peddler's wagon and joined in the burial dinner.

Shock over the Camerons' misfortunes had given way to sympathy by the time Ian sat across the table from the pair, while Naomi bustled about, putting together a plate of food.

"It's good to see ye again, Karl. Jost," he added, having met the younger man when he'd escorted Gottfriedsen to Salem the previous autumn.

While Ian ate, they talked of his uncle, of his marriage to Judith, their newborn daughter. He made a point of telling the aging peddler that he wasn't responsible for those items he'd sold the Camerons last autumn turning up again in his wagon. "It was down to the machinations of my aunt and my uncle's overseer, a means to get me away long enough to carry out another scheme, but ye've my apologies in their stead for the way ye were badly used."

An apology the man graciously accepted.

Then Ian found himself speaking of what had been brought out of the fire and his need to see Seona and Lily to Boston before the spring.

Though his back was to the door, he knew when Seona entered the kitchen. Even with her hair covered and a baby in arms, she drew the eye. Motherhood had deepened her, casting over her something of Lily's mystery. He caught the peddlers' trailing looks. Jost's eyes held a frank, if shy, appreciation. There was something else in the older man's eyes: startlement and a quick comprehension.

"I cannot leave Judith for the time it would take me to travel to Boston and back," Ian said after Seona went out again. "Not with only Malcolm and Ally for protection."

Slaves could provide no true protection in any case, not against the possible interference of Judith's kin. He'd given Judith the option of following her mother's exodus, one she'd resolutely refused. Still he feared he'd return to find his wife and daughter whisked off to Chesterfield, willing or no.

"It is a predicament," Karl agreed, staring into the mug of cider cradled in his hands.

"But not impossible." Jost was nodding enthusiastically. "Manfred and Anna. Uncle, you remember—they are to leave Salem for Connecticut. Perhaps . . . ?" He left the statement dangling.

"*Ja*," said Karl, considering. "They have the two sons. One they could spare for driving a wagon for your freedwomen."

"All the way to Boston?" Ian asked, caught between startlement and doubt . . . and sensing an impending loss rushing at him with far more speed than he'd ever thought it could.

Both men were nodding now. "It is not so much farther, *ja*? This could be arranged. But your two must be in Salem with all haste," Karl added, "or the chance will be missed. If you cannot do this, we can see them there. Jost and I will do this for you."

"Karl, I don't know." Ian had thought to have weeks, months even, to prepare himself for the parting. But here was the chance and the means come right to his table barely two days after he'd learned of the need.

Glancing around, he found they were alone. Naomi had left the kitchen unobserved. Seona and Lily would hear of Gottfriedsen's offer before he put a foot out the door. He felt the weight of the inevitable bearing down.

"It's a lot to ask of ye," he managed. "And your kin."

Karl's expression warmed. "I am glad to do this, for reasons you know."

Again Jost nodded. "We are in your debt, Herr Cameron. Manfred and Anna will want to do this."

Though touched by their eagerness to aid him, it took Ian a full minute to make his mouth form the words. "In the morning? Will that be soon enough?"

Karl Gottfriedsen smiled, not without compassion. "*Ja.* In the morning we can start."

She'd feared Ian would decide against going with them even as far as Salem, until Mister Charlie agreed to bunk in an empty cabin and look after everybody for a spell. If Miss Judith minded, she never said so in Seona's hearing. Miss Judith had other things to say to her.

She came to the cabin that night, toting her newborn baby girl. Before Seona could say a word, Lily got up off her cot where she'd been changing Gabriel, took up the dirty clout, and left.

Seona took over the task, taking the time to compose herself. They'd talked since the fire, she and Miss Judith—it could hardly be helped—but this felt different. Seona's hands shook as she bent to pick up Ian's son.

"Would you leave him on the cot?"

She straightened as Miss Judith laid her daughter next to Gabriel. Both babies were awake. Gabriel's eyes were turning the blue of

625

his daddy's. Miss Judith's daughter seemed tiny as a doll beside him, even dressed in a gown nearly twice her length.

"Sit by me?" Miss Judith said, motioning to the other cot. She was looking spent, though she hadn't made the walk up the ridge to the burying plot—not two days after giving birth. She'd never been strong. How would she get along with Naomi her only woman-help?

Naomi. Malcolm. Ally. In the morning she was leaving them all. Seona's eyes blurred with tears.

Miss Judith didn't speak right off. They stared at their babies lying side by side. Mandy, as she'd heard Ian call her, was too new to mind what was going on around her. Gabriel, three months old, set to flailing his legs and arms. A fist closed on the sleeve of his sister's gown.

Seona stiffened, knowing how those little fingers could pinch. But Mandy didn't fuss. He wasn't hurting her, just holding on.

"Like he knows somehow," Miss Judith said, and Seona felt something like a fish bone caught in her throat. She couldn't speak past it. "Please understand," Miss Judith went on, still watching the babies. "I know he loves you."

She didn't mean Gabriel. "Miss Judith—"

"No." Miss Judith turned to her, pain in her tea-brown eyes. "Let me say this. Wrongs have been done. Some to me. More to you. Years and years of wrongs. God says in the Bible He will restore the years the locust has eaten. But I don't see how He can do any such thing unless we're of a mind to let it happen. And look there—our children have shown us the way."

Miss Judith touched Seona's hand, lying on the cot between them. "Will you let me do what I need to do, so this can happen for us?"

Seona understood. Ian's wife had come to pray for her. She turned her hand over and let Judith clasp it in her own.

45

In the clearing off the road, Mister Gottfriedsen and his nephew had turned in for the night, sleeping under their wagon. Their mules were tied to the box, champing at oats. The horses were hobbled and ruckling down their noses to one another. The rest of them weren't talking much. The ache of leaving squeezed Seona's throat until she hadn't the heart to force out any but the few needful words.

Across from her and Lily, on a log rolled up to the fire, Ian sat, Gabriel sleeping on his lap. Now and then Ian's lips moved—speaking to Gabriel or to God. Likely both. She'd kept her distance as they traveled, knowing he was struggling to be faithful, but now she got up, stepped round the fire, and settled beside him, wrapped warm in a new woolen shawl someone had given Miss Judith, who'd given it to her. A parting present.

Ian looked across the fire. "Lily, will ye fetch a thing for me?"

Her mama obliged, coming back with what he'd asked for: a thick, flat leather pouch, bound with tattered ribbon. He smiled his thanks. "Give it to Seona, please."

She took it from Lily, who sat beside her. "What is it?"

"Letters to my da. I've written him every week since I came to Mountain Laurel."

"You never sent them?"

His mouth drew up crooked. "Too much a coward. Would ye take them, see them safe to Boston and into his hands?"

He couldn't seem to hold her gaze. He dropped it to their baby on his lap. Seona put the pouch to her face and breathed. The leather smelled of smoke. Of him.

"I will. But, Ian . . . Is Mountain Laurel going to be all right?" That wasn't exactly what she wanted to ask, and he didn't answer right off. She hoped because he was searching for a truthful answer, not trying to soften a hard one.

Lily sat in silence, watching the fire. Listening.

"Aye, by the Almighty's grace," he said at last. "My uncle's farm will never be what it was, but I don't believe it should be."

Tobacco couldn't be planted like it was all these years past. Not with the field hands run off. But Ian sounded content with that, no matter the uncertainties looming. He didn't sound bitter. Or afraid. She'd hoped he and Thomas had made their peace on the banks of the creek that day he came back to free the ones he could. Now she suspected they had, and it gladdened her.

"But you, Mandy . . . Miss Judith?" she pressed, thinking, *And Naomi, Malcolm, and Ally.* It was a wrench to her heart, all these partings. "Will you get by all right, truly?"

"Girl-baby," her mama said, but Ian smiled.

"We'll grow enough to feed ourselves come spring. That's about as far ahead as I'm looking just now." He brushed the crown of Gabriel's head, silky white blond.

Another boy with moonbeam hair. This one forever hers. Seona stifled the urge to touch those curls too, to let her hand stray near to Ian's.

"It's the past I want to talk to ye about, Seona," he said. "I want to tell ye some of what they say, the letters. I never told ye what came between Da and me. I've spoken of it to no one. I gave my solemn word not to, ye see?"

She didn't. And wasn't sure she wanted to. Past and future—both seemed fraught with pain. She wanted to stay wrapped in the fire's warmth, in the sound of his voice, and never go forward another day. Another moment. How was she to live without him?

She stuffed that grief down deep to wait its time.

"I was a lad," he was saying now, "with no notion of the cost my silence would exact. But I've learned a thing or two about secrets . . . sometimes the keeping of them only compounds the harm that was done in the first place." He glanced at Lily, then at her. "My da deserves to know the truth, for his own comfort. Let God be the judge if I'm wrong to offer it." He laid a fingertip to the leather pouch. "Ye'll hear the lies in Boston, so I mean to give ye the truth as well."

"This is for your ears, girl-baby," her mama whispered, then got up and headed for their bedroll, though Ian hadn't asked her to go. Seona wasn't sure he noticed.

"I was thirteen when I was made apprentice to a master cabinetmaker, Wilburt Pringle, in the town of Cambridge, near Boston. It was a six-year indenture, meant to end in me becoming a journeyman in his shop. The Pringles had no children."

It had been a sadness to Pringle, Ian explained, a man of middle years having no son to carry on his trade. But for his wife the lack of a child had cut deeper. Anne Pringle had been three and twenty, married for five of those years, when Ian came to board in their house in Cambridge. She was an affectionate woman, often ruffling his hair or pressing a kiss to his brow at the close of day. So had she been with her husband's other apprentice, a lad a year younger than Ian—even with Pringle's new journeyman, who'd seemed grown to Ian at the time but was likely no more than eighteen. "I made nothing of it, save for the comfort it lent me. I was young enough to miss my mam."

Sparks went up from the fire into the tree limbs. Leaves came down in golden twists. Seona dreaded what was to come.

"When I was seventeen, the journeyman left us—to become his own master, we assumed, though the manner of his leaving was odd. Sudden. Not a word of farewell. But then we hadn't been close—I was a child in his eyes. I shrugged it off. Our lives settled down with a deal more work fallen to me. I relished the chance to prove myself, to master the craft."

Soon after the journeyman's leaving, Anne Pringle's manner toward him changed. Ian would catch her watching him across the table at meals. Other times. He began to be aware of her, and not as a stand-in mama. He found himself waiting for her to come to the shop with tea, anticipating the brush of their fingers, her smile, her laughter. She made sure there was plenty of brushing, smiling, laughing. "I reasoned away her behavior, never quite believing she wanted what it seemed she did. Her attention flattered me, but deep down I knew what was happening was wrong, no matter how I excused it."

At first he'd gone in dread of his master noticing the flirtation, but Pringle seemed blind to his wife. One evening she came to Ian in the library, where he often sat up late to read. In the course of conversation she placed a book on his lap and, bending over him, kissed him on the mouth.

"The next time Pringle was away—a guild meeting, it was—she called me from the shop."

He leaned over Gabriel, speaking so low Seona strained to hear. "She led me to her bed and begged me to give her a child. She meant to pass it off as her husband's. She told me so, bold as brass, as if it were the most reasonable proposition to be heard."

Anne Pringle hadn't taken the answer he'd given. *No.*

"She burst in on me packing my things to leave. She was hysterical. She had a *knife*. She attacked me with it." He spoke as though he still couldn't believe it had happened. "Before I got the knife away, Pringle was there. Next I knew she was crying *rape*. Pringle didn't say a word, but I saw it in his eyes: the man knew exactly what his wife had done. He took her away weeping, and I sat on my cot and waited, covered in shame so thick I couldn't move."

His apprenticeship had ended eighteen months shy of its term. Pringle gave him the set of tools and clothes promised in the contract and signed him as a journeyman—in return for keeping silent about Anne. *You weren't the first,* Pringle told him, and Ian remembered the journeyman who'd left without a word. "I kept that promise, even when Anne Pringle spread it about that I'd tried to force my affections upon her, and her husband caught me in the act and tossed me out on my ear."

"That's why you went to Canada?" Grief for

the boy he'd been, for the hurt and shame still paining him, softened Seona's voice. "With your uncle Callum."

"Aye. It seemed best at the time. But Callum was right. I was running away, hiding." The fire had settled to embers. Gabriel had slept through his daddy's confession. Ian's hand cupped their baby's head. "I'll not ask d'ye think the less of me. I don't suppose ye could think much worse of me than ye must already."

Seona shook her head, so full of love for him she could hardly speak. "She was Potiphar's wife."

He gave a strangled laugh. "Maybe. But I was no Joseph."

She might have said a lot of things to that, but this was a weight he'd carried too long for any words of hers to lift. If only he'd told his daddy the truth, years ago. What a load of shame and heartache he'd have spared himself. But then he mightn't have ended up at Mountain Laurel. She'd never have loved him, never had Gabriel. Might even be at Chesterfield now, at the mercy of Gideon Pryce.

Malcolm's words of last autumn came back to her. *Your mama carries a mountain of grief along with her love for ye. Naomi wants to see ye spared that.* She'd asked which they'd meant to spare her, the love or the grief. She hadn't forgot Naomi's answer. *The two goes hand in hand for the likes of us. . . . There's no future in you pining after a white man.*

Naomi had been right about the love and the grief. Not about her future. It wasn't the future they'd hoped for, but she had one all the same. He lay sleeping across his daddy's thighs.

In Salem, Ian acquired a small covered wagon, provisions to stock it, a team to pull it, with instructions for his father to sell them to provide a living for Lily, Seona, and Gabriel. Such a sum wouldn't stretch far. More must needs follow. He hitched Uncle Hugh's sorrel, which Lily and Seona had ridden from Mountain Laurel, to the wagon box. The sorrel wasn't young but the youth who'd agreed to drive the wagon was happy to take it as his hire.

He'd gone about in haste, loading the wagon, checking every trace, hitch, and buckle, so the time of parting came upon him with alarming swiftness. While the farewells of Gottfriedsen's kin took place some distance off, he stood with Seona under the fiery shade of a maple at the town's edge, holding Gabriel asleep against his shoulder.

It was late morning, the sun risen behind clouds that promised rain. Seona's hair had grown over the summer. Though she'd pinned it up under a cap, wisps had escaped to curl about her face. "Ye've the letters to my da?"

He knew she did. She knew he knew.

"In the wagon box. With our free papers." Tucked inside the long-promised desk for Catriona.

He cradled Gabriel in one arm, freeing the other hand to reach into a coat pocket for the portraits of Aidan and Miranda Cameron. "I want ye to have these as well."

She tilted her face up to him, creek-water eyes the living reflection of those in the paintings. "They're your kin."

"And yours. Ye're my family, Seona. Ye and Gabriel are as dear to me as my life's blood. I don't want ye to forget that." He stopped himself saying more. So much more. "Please."

"I won't forget." She took the portraits. The green of her eyes seemed impossibly vivid in the gray of morning; they glistened with tears.

"I cannot stop thinking of all the promises I broke," he said.

"I'll mind the ones you kept," she said.

In no way did he deserve such grace. Ian bowed his head and touched his lips to Gabriel's silky hair. The boy slept on, heavy in his arms. He wanted to see his son's eyes a final time, alight with recognition of him.

Maybe it was better this way. Better this boneless weight and the scent of sleeping innocence be the last memory he carried. *For now.*

Time was a tide-pull dragging at his heart. The wagons were secured, the Moravians ready to embark. Lily found them. He encircled her with an arm, Gabriel in the other.

"God keep ye, Lily."

She pulled his head down and boldly kissed his cheek. "And ye also, Ian Cameron."

Then she was gone, and he was bending his face a final time to Gabriel, filling lungs and memory with the scent of him, before he passed him into Seona's keeping. His hand brushed a sleep-flushed cheek, then covered the hand that would cradle his son to Boston and through the years that followed. "They'll open their hearts to ye, my parents. Not just their home. Don't be afraid."

Seona nodded. "God's watching over my lot. What was meant for evil, He'll turn for good."

They were Ian's words, those last, spoken on the creek bank the day of Gabriel's birth. Words he'd feared she couldn't receive from him.

He reached into his pocket again and put into her hand the arrowhead she'd found that day. The words that went with it came hard. "I'm setting ye free."

"I know," she said, uncertainty in her eyes.

"No, Seona. I want ye to have a life—a whole life. I'm setting ye free of *me*."

Her eyes filled with understanding, but she shook her head and gave him back the arrowhead.

"Keep it for me," she said and was gone in a swirl of petticoats and shawl. Gone before another word could leave his lips.

He watched as she was helped onto the wagon bench, clinging to the last sight of Gabriel being handed back to Lily, under the canvas.

Drivers shouted. The wagons lurched forward, starting on their rumbling passage north. Ian pressed the arrowhead against his palm. Seona didn't look back. He thought she didn't mean to, but at the last moment she leaned out and he saw her face a final time, before the road bent through a stand of gold-leafed trees and took her from sight.

Ian stood alone with the threads of his heart spooling out, unraveling after them and stretching thin, until it seemed his breath, his heart, even time, must stop. Or snap in two.

He went on breathing. The pieces of his heart kept beating.

He moved from the spot where time should have halted, relieved when Gottfriedsen, seeming to understand, held back from approaching. He rested a hand on Ruaidh's head, drew comfort from his horse's deep-brown eyes, then swung into the saddle and turned the roan southward.

And on that road grace met him.

He was half a day's ride out of Salem when he spotted them ahead on the road. Two men in a horse-drawn cart, one a Quaker by his dress. Hearing his approach, the one who wasn't a Quaker cast a backward look—a man of Thomas's coloring. Ian kicked Ruaidh to a canter to overtake them, which alarmed the pair into pulling to a halt.

The darker-skinned man appeared to be about Ian's age, well-muscled from work, but he wasn't Thomas. The Quaker was an older man, bearded and grizzled. Not Eden. Ian lifted his hat and smiled, though disappointment twisted in his chest. "Sorry to give ye a fright. From a distance I mistook the pair of ye for acquaintances of mine."

The Quaker spoke, a gravelly voice at odds with his gentle nod. " 'Tis no harm done. Thee made an honest mistake." He glanced at his companion, who, though clearly shaken, whipped off his hat and bobbed his head.

Ian stared at the bared forehead. A scar ran across it, just below the hairline, pale against the man's dark skin. A scar shaped like a fishhook.

Eyeing him quizzically, the Quaker made introduction. "Amos Fisher of Lexington, Kentucky. My friend here once called Carolina home but resides now with me and works in my smithy."

Ian reassessed the younger man, his heartbeat quickening. That scar . . .

"Whereabouts in Carolina was your home?"

"Place called Mountain Laurel, sir. Planter by name of Cameron sold me and my brother off long time back. We fetched up together in Kentucky. I free now, got myself a free wife." At a rumble of throat-clearing from Fisher, the man's eyes widened. "I got papers. . . ."

But Ian was grinning, as he'd thought he never would again.

The young man stared at him, wary, puzzled. "Does I know you, sir?"

It was Sammy had the scar, he could hear Naomi saying in the shadowed kitchen that first morning. "Aye," he said. "Leastwise ye did, Sammy."

Dark eyes widened again, this time in surprise. "How you know me, sir?"

"We were lads together, for a brief while—at Mountain Laurel. D'ye not remember me?"

Ian waited until a spark lit the man's searching eyes. "You that boy come visit with his daddy? Kin to Master Hugh?"

"I'm Ian Cameron. Mountain Laurel's mine now."

Eagerness and fear crowded the face of his uncle's ex-slave, now clutching his hat into a mangled ball. Sammy drew a shaky breath and said, "If you'd be so kind as to tell me, sir, seeing we come all this way . . ." He faltered. Amos Fisher placed a steadying hand on his shoulder. Sammy swallowed. "Might you remember my mama at all? Her name be—"

"Ruby," Ian said, awash in the light that blazed from Sammy's face at the name. "Aye. She's been expecting ye."

Sammy and the Quaker were effusive in their joy after Ian told of finding Ruby, of the neighbors who sheltered her, but when the three finally got underway again, he found himself riding beside the cart in silence, isolated from the two by the grief he carried. What was certain to be an interminable parting was only just begun, whereas Sammy was visibly restraining himself from taking the reins out of the older man's hands and whipping the cart horse into a hurried frenzy. As if his heart threads, like Ian's, spooled out northward, pulled him irresistibly toward his long-lost mother.

Grief cut the deeper, until Ian looked ahead down the road to the joyous reunion Sammy anticipated and remembered there were those awaiting *his* return as well. Not all the threads of his heart were stretched out taut behind him. There was another. There were two. They gave his heart a quieter tug, leading him home.

A Note from the Author

Once upon a time, somewhere in the American colonies, someone chose to aid an escaped slave along the road to freedom. Perhaps he hid the fugitive in his barn. She might have offered food or told of a friend, miles to the north, willing to shelter the runaway for the night. Maybe he just turned a blind eye when the laws of the day dictated otherwise. Whoever was the first to aid a runaway slave, by the mid-1800s an organized network of such people extended from the southern United States into Canada. My research into the grassroots beginning of what would become the Underground Railroad uncovered many compelling characters who played a part in ending slavery, one man, woman, or child at a time. Levi and Vestal Coffin, North Carolina Quakers, established the earliest known system for conveying fugitives north to the free states. Josiah Henson, once a slave in Maryland, became a conductor for other fleeing slaves. Giles Pettibone, justice of the peace and state assemblyman, helped hide a family of slaves for weeks. Isaac Hopper, a tailor's apprentice in Philadelphia, assisted the first of many fugitives to freedom with directions to a sympathetic Quaker's house. They and many others merit further study. Toward that end I recommend Fergus M. Bordewich's *Bound for Canaan: The Epic Story of the Underground Railroad, America's First Civil Rights Movement.*

Narratives such as that of ex-slave Olaudah Equiano, which inspired the character of Thomas Ross to put feet to his convictions, began appearing in print in the mid-eighteenth century and continued to be published throughout the antebellum period, educating white Americans and persuading them of slavery's cruelties and horrors and its immorality as a system. "Argument provokes argument, reason is met by sophistry. But narratives of slaves go right to the hearts of men," wrote a northern reviewer of a slave narrative in 1849. Hearts as well as laws must change in the face of such an entrenched evil as slavery. Individual slave narratives like Equiano's played their part in affecting that change.

The main setting of this story, a range of mountains considered the oldest in North America, ancient, worn, isolated in the central Piedmont—called the Carraways on my mid-1700s map of North Carolina—today encompass the Uwharrie (*yoo-WAH-ree*) National Forest, the Birkhead Mountains Wilderness, and other recreational areas. During my childhood a family acquaintance lived on the edge of this landscape, near the town of Asheboro, North Carolina.

After I set eyes on the collection of arrowheads and knapped stone chips his tractor turned up each spring in the long furrows of his garden, he let me do some digging of my own. I spent an enjoyable few hours in the pursuit, never knowing I was unearthing—in the very soil the plows of Mountain Laurel might have turned—the seeds of a novel I'd one day write.

While I didn't find any gold nuggets, Ally's discovery of the shiny yellow rock he gave to Seona, and which Lucinda Cameron subsequently identified, is not a far-fetched story element. The first documented gold discovery in the United States occurred in 1799 in Cabarrus County, North Carolina, five years after and fifty miles southwest of *Mountain Laurel*'s setting. A boy, Conrad Reed, spied a shiny yellow rock like Ally's in a stream on his family's farm—only Conrad's rock weighed seventeen pounds. The family used it as a doorstop until, in 1802, a Fayetteville jeweler recognized it for gold. It was worth over $3,500. Gold was eventually discovered in the Carraways/Uwharries as well. Along with the remnants of old homesteads, mining sites mark these ridges and hollows today. In the pages of this novel I've imagined how it might have been if gold were discovered there in the 1790s and its existence carefully guarded. Who can say such a thing never happened? History is full of secrets.

A brief note concerning anachronisms—something out of its proper or chronological order. For the sake of verisimilitude, I avoid anachronisms in my stories. My editors help me greatly with this because despite due diligence, they still slip in, usually in the form of language, words that had their verifiable origins later than the story's setting. However, there is an anachronism in *Mountain Laurel* that I included intentionally. One of the songs sung by Mountain Laurel's enslaved people, at the clearing on the ridge, had a date of origin later than the last decade of the eighteenth century. Its first line, "Jesus Christ is made to me all I need," said exactly what I wanted to convey in that moment of Ian Cameron's spiritual journey. This is a work of historical fiction; the choice between Ian's journey and precise historical accuracy was an easy one to make.

Speaking of historical accuracy, it's often impossible to trace a novel's development back to the initial spark that ignited it, but in the case of *Mountain Laurel* that moment remains vivid in my memory. In the late 1990s I read a novel by Diana Gabaldon, set in 1760s North Carolina. In the novel a minor character—an enslaved young man on a plantation who appeared in just a few scenes—left an indelible impression on me. Having grown up living with a family of Scottish immigrants, hearing that manner of speech, he spoke with a Scottish accent too, though his ancestors were African. Having not yet begun my own writing sojourn into the eighteenth century, I asked Diana whether this character was purely her own creation or she'd found evidence of someone like him in her research. (It proved the latter, and I read the source for myself.) Along with a few other factors, that unusual historical tidbit sparked my interest in the eighteenth century *and* my storyteller's imagination and eventually led to my writing *Mountain Laurel*. But before I had crafted more than the faintest outlines of a story, I was diagnosed with Hodgkin's lymphoma and stopped writing altogether. After a six-month battle with cancer and a much longer one with chemo fog, I finally felt ready to write again (not able exactly, just ready). The story that was calling to me was the one sparked into being after reading Diana's book.

To write *Mountain Laurel*, still no more than a group of characters and a vague idea of their conflict and connection, I had to first learn a great deal about a time period I knew very little about. (I couldn't have told you then what years the Revolutionary War spanned, much less what people wore, ate, drank, read, built, drove, or sang during the eighteenth century.) Between giving myself a crash course in this fascinating time period through reading many dozens of books and retraining my chemo-damaged brain to write again, it took four years to finish a first draft of what I'd working-titled *Kindred* (now the title of this two-book series). It took a couple more years to edit it into something marketable. My agent signed me on the strength of the novel, but there proved to be no market for it a decade ago. We went on to sell six other eighteenth-century novels starting with *Burning Sky* in 2013 . . . until last year, when we decided to give the Kindred books, *Mountain Laurel* and its forthcoming sequel, *Shiloh*, one more chance to find a publishing home. Which, of course, they did.

Looking back on this novel's long journey to the book you hold in your hands, I see how the timing for its publication is fitting in a way I could never have planned. While it isn't a sequel to my 2019 release, *The King's Mercy*, readers of that book will recognize *Mountain Laurel*'s main setting, as well as some of its characters. If you read that book, then you've had a glimpse into Hugh Cameron's, Malcolm's, and Naomi's life some forty-five years prior to meeting them in these pages. And then there's *Burning Sky*; over the years I've had requests from readers for more of certain characters' stories. But no character has been the subject of more such requests than Joseph Tames-His-Horse, introduced in *Burning Sky*. Well, dear readers, if you've been wishing to see more of Joseph's story, then you won't want to miss *Shiloh*. While it primarily continues Ian and Seona's story, it could be considered a sequel to *Burning Sky* as well. If you haven't yet read *Burning Sky*, now would be the perfect time to do so.

I suspect my next most frequent request will be for a flowchart to show where and how all my novels are connected in this sprawling eighteenth-century world I've been weaving, book by book. That's not a bad idea. But when it comes to threads that weave through all my novels, the most important to me are the threads of God's unfailing mercy when we stumble, His grace for every challenge and trial, and a love so boundless He paid the ultimate price—dying in our place—to set us free from sin and bring us into fellowship with Him. For this life and for His Kingdom that is coming soon. My prayer for you is that you've drawn closer to Him as you read this first part of Ian and Seona's story.

I hope we'll all meet again in the pages of *Shiloh*.

Lori Benton
loribenton.com

Acknowledgments

Along with my appreciation for author Diana Gabaldon, who has made herself available online at TheLitForum (thelitforum.com) for readers and writers alike to conversate with and learn from for well over twenty years, I have many to acknowledge for their contribution to a novel that has taken nearly a twenty-year journey from conception to publication. Some of them, like Lauri Klobas, are no longer with us. Lauri, also recovering from chemo fog at the time, taught me how to self-edit my work and helped me in the initial stages of trimming down a first draft of *Mountain Laurel* that had clocked in at 300,000 words. I honestly don't believe I'd have ever published at all without her thorough, valiant, and patient red pen. I learned to love the editing process because of Lauri. Thank you also to Beth Shope, Jo Bourne, Janet McConnaughey, Kathleen Eschenburg, Julie Weathers, Amarilis Iscold, Barbara Rogan, Carol Krenz, Marsha Skrypuch, KC Dyer, Elise Skidmore, Linda Allen, Sallie Blumenauer, Claire Greer, Allene Edwards, Bridget Eyolfson Courchene, Wayne Sowry, Ron Wodaski, Rafe Steinberg, and many others from TheLitForum for countless questions answered and guidance given when I was still new at this writing thing—and ever since. If you remember my writing this book, and we talked about it, I'm thanking *you*.

As this book's dedication reads, my agent, Wendy Lawton, never gave up on this manuscript but held these characters in her heart for nearly ten years. Thank you, Wendy, for believing they deserved a second chance. You've helped make so many of my dreams come true. This was a big one.

Jan Stob and Sarah Rische (editors), Libby Dykstra (designer), and everyone at Tyndale, thank you for welcoming me into the fold and for taking Ian and Seona into your hearts and lending your considerable talents and insights into the creating of this book. I've said in the past that I do some of my best writing during the editing stages and this time was no exception. Jan and Sarah made it possible for me to take this story to a deeper level, and their contributions shine. I look forward to doing it again with *Shiloh*.

About the Author

Lori Benton was raised in Maryland, with generations-deep roots in southern Virginia and the Appalachian frontier. Her historical novels transport readers to the eighteenth century, where she expertly brings to life the colonial and early federal periods of American history. Her books have received the Christy Award and the Inspy Award and have been honored as finalists for the ECPA Book of the Year. Lori is most at home surrounded by mountains, currently those of the Pacific Northwest, where, when she isn't writing, she's likely to be found in wild places behind a camera.

Discussion Questions

At its core, *Mountain Laurel* is a story of choice and consequence . . .

1. Ian tells his neighbor John Reynold that he hopes to settle to a life that will atone (for past mistakes and failures, particularly in his father's eyes). In what ways does he try to do that? At what point in the story do his choices begin to lead him down a different path? Do you think he ever could atone? Does he even need to? Why or why not?

2. Seona's and Ian's artistic outlets are an early point of connection. Ian even unwittingly plays a part in Seona's childhood choice to pick up a slate and draw a picture. Is it a kind or a thoughtless impulse when he provides Seona a new outlet for her creativity? How does this choice complicate Seona's life? Does it enrich it as well? How so?

3. Hugh Cameron's choice to suppress the truth of Seona's parentage and "leave things as they be" (in Naomi's words) is typical of eighteenth-century slaveholders in such circumstances. How does this choice shape him as a man? What effect does it have on Lucinda, Rosalyn, and Judith? In what ways

might his choices contribute to his physical and mental decline? Does Hugh make any *good* choices in this story?

4. Judith often finds herself caught in the middle: between her mother and Seona, between Ian and Seona, between Ian and her mother and sister. Does she navigate those relationships well? How does she respond to situations of injustice, to others and to herself? Did you sympathize with her choices? Did she surprise you in any way?

5. Perhaps the most difficult choices in this story are Ian's. First, the choice to remain at Mountain Laurel as his uncle's heir or leave and go back north. Second, the choice between Seona and Judith. What makes these decisions so difficult? Do you believe he makes the right choice each time? Why or why not?

A story of bondage and freedom . . .

6. Thomas Ross risks not only his friendship with Ian but his very life in order to aid slaves to freedom. Is he ever needlessly reckless? How do his choices clash with Ian's? Did you agree with his assessment of the man Ian becomes at Mountain Laurel? At what point might Thomas's perception of Ian have changed for the better?

7. Malcolm's words "Every man makes himself a slave to someone or something" leave a strong impression on Ian. Are they true? How does this idea play out for different characters?

8. An imbalance of power and agency exists between Ian and Seona as an eighteenth-century man and woman, even more so as free and enslaved. Does Ian misuse his greater power and agency, even without meaning to? In what ways? Who helps him understand that Seona's perception of their relationship and his own might very well be different?

A story of family and faith . . .

9. As the story begins, Ian views himself as a prodigal, a misfit, and an outcast—from family and from God. Did you see him in that light? In Ian's search for belonging and redemption, Malcolm, John Reynold, and Lily are examples of steadfast faith in God. What specific truths does each character speak into his life? What truth does Seona speak?

10. As an enslaved person, Seona's choices are limited, but she has the freedom to choose what she thinks and believes. How is her faith in God's sovereignty challenged? Who models trust in God for her? Who sows seeds

of doubt? What is Seona's most difficult choice to make? In what ways does her faith grow because of it?

11. Mountain Laurel's past is still alive in many ways. What reminders do we witness of Hugh's long-dead son, Aidan? How did that death affect various characters? What other characters, either dead or gone, have bearing on Mountain Laurel's present?

12. *Mountain Laurel* and its upcoming sequel are joined under the series title Kindred—a word that can refer to family relationships or to similarity in character and nature. How do you see the themes of kinship and of kindred spirits woven through this story? What do you imagine is ahead for Ian? For Seona? For Mountain Laurel itself?

Center Point Large Print
600 Brooks Road / PO Box 1
Thorndike, ME 04986-0001 USA

(207) 568-3717

US & Canada:
1 800 929-9108
www.centerpointlargeprint.com